Kris Longknife
DARING

continued . . .

Kris Longknife
REDOUBTABLE

"Readers have come to depend on Mike Shepherd for fast-paced military science fiction bound to compelling story lines and adrenaline-pumping battles. This eighth in the Kris Longknife series does not disappoint. Kris Longknife is a hero to the core, with plenty of juice left for future installments." —*Fresh Fiction*

Kris Longknife
UNDAUNTED

"An exciting, action-packed adventure . . . Mr. Shepherd has injected the same humor into this book as he did in the rest of the series . . . I really love these books, and *Undaunted* is a great addition to the series." —*Fresh Fiction*

Kris Longknife
INTREPID

"[Kris Longknife] will remind readers of David Weber's Honor Harrington with her strength and intelligence. Mike Shepherd provides an exciting military science fiction thriller."
—*Genre Go Round Reviews*

Kris Longknife
AUDACIOUS

" 'I'm a woman of very few words, but lots of action': So said Mae West, but it might just as well have been Lieutenant Kris Longknife, princess of the one hundred worlds of Wardhaven. Kris can kick, shoot, and punch her way out of any dangerous situation, and she can do it while wearing stilettos and a tight cocktail dress. She's all business, with a Hells Angel handshake and a 'get out of my face' attitude. But her hair always looks good. *Audacious* maintains a crisp pace and lively banter . . . Kris Longknife is funny and she entertains us." —*Sci Fi Weekly*

Kris Longknife
DEFENDER

Mike Shepherd

ACE BOOKS, NEW YORK

THE BERKLEY PUBLISHING GROUP
Published by the Penguin Group
Penguin Group (USA) LLC
375 Hudson Street, New York, New York 10014

USA • Canada • UK • Ireland • Australia • New Zealand • India • South Africa • China

penguin.com

A Penguin Random House Company

KRIS LONGKNIFE: DEFENDER

An Ace Book / published by arrangement with the author

Ace Books are published by The Berkley Publishing Group.
ACE and the "A" design are trademarks of Penguin Group (USA) LLC.

For information, address: The Berkley Publishing Group,
a division of Penguin Group (USA) LLC,
375 Hudson Street, New York, New York 10014.

ISBN: 978-0-425-25341-0

PUBLISHING HISTORY
Ace mass-market edition / November 2013

PRINTED IN THE UNITED STATES OF AMERICA

10 9 8 7 6 5 4 3 2 1

Cover art by Scott Grimando.
Interior text design by Kristin del Rosario.

"**That's** what was gonna attack Alwa?" Granny Rita said. Once commodore of BatCruRon 16, she'd fought hopeless battles. Still, her voice held dismay as she surveyed the wreckage of the alien base ship.

"It was about twice that size before we took some bites out of it," Lieutenant Commander, Her Royal Highness, Kris Longknife said. Herself no stranger to hopeless battles, she added, "And we're still quite a ways off. It will get bigger."

Rita Nuu Longknife Ponsa, former captain of the battle-cruiser *Furious*, was the recognized leader of the humans, and uniformly called Granny Rita by both the heavy ones, us humans, and the indigenous inhabitants of Alwa, who named themselves either the People or the Light People.

Granny Rita turned to translate for the delegation of six Alwans who had come to see for all the unbelievable story Kris had told their Association of Associations.

Privately, Granny Rita called the assembly "the flock of flocks," but she'd warned Kris never to say that where any Alwan might overhear.

Kris listened as Granny Rita and the Alwans clicked and cooed with maybe one word in five sounding familiar to Kris. It was a pigeon dialect they'd worked out over eighty years.

However, Nelly, Kris's not-very-personable computer, was working on a translator for the two peoples. Kris wondered if the peace that had held for the last eighty years between the Alwans and the humans might have been helped along by both sides' not fully understanding what the other side said.

When Nelly finished this effort, Kris would have to have a talk with her.

The six Alwans' movements were quick, almost jerky, as they moved around the forward lounge. Their arms and hands waved. Kris had a feeling that a couple of million years earlier, the flock would have taken flight at this news. Now, having given up most of their feathers as well as flight, they formed and re-formed groups of two or three, talking among themselves and rarely glancing at the view screen that showed the battered alien-invasion base.

This meeting was not being held on the USS *Wasp*'s bridge. The Alwans had taken in the intensity of the bridge crew at their work and immediately expressed distress to Granny Rita. Kris had offered instead the Forward Lounge, with its four huge screens. Since Kris's staff were all equipped with Nelly or one of her children, Kris was confident they could do anything that needed doing while letting the Alwans take in the familiar activities of humans eating, drinking, and, in general, enjoying themselves in the familiar surroundings of a restaurant.

And now, thanks to the magic of Katsu's wizardry with Smart Metal™, Kris was able to separate the restaurant from her transferred Tac Center with a transparent wall. Yep, Katsu-san could make Smart Metal™ clear as glass!

Kris missed him already, but Katsu said he had trained the *Wasp*'s ship maintainers as well as he could. He wanted to get back to Musashi and his job at Mitsubishi Heavy Space Industry; his head was already full of ideas for making the next class of ships even better. Thus buzzing with new ideas, he joined the IMS *Sakura* for the long voyage back to human space.

Kris hated the idea that the *Wasp* was all by itself clear on the other side of the galaxy. Still, there was no question folks back home needed to know that the sacrifice of their Fleet of Discovery had saved the world they fought for. Even more, the strange planet they laid down their lives for had provided a home to a desperate group of humans. Now, eighty years later, it sheltered a growing human colony.

That colony was led by the former wife of King Raymond of United Society (or United Societies depending on how you thought the new constitution should be interpreted). Problem was, she had buried two husbands in the last eighty years on Alwa and was now mother to seven, grandmother to thirty-four, and great-grandmother to at least 123. That number was subject to change . . . often.

Kris herself was included among the great-grandchildren and had spent a full week meeting a big chunk of half uncles, aunts, and cousins. Still, to one and all of the humans on Alwa, related or not, the former commodore was Granny Rita.

Surprises on top of surprises. Kris could only wonder how the news carried by the IMS *Sakura* would be received.

But for now, she had no time for Longknife family matters; a huge alien mother ship loomed larger and larger on their screens. Now the Alwans seemed mesmerized by its promise of death. They huddled before the screen, eyes locked on it, only occasionally whispering something low.

"This isn't good," Granny Rita whispered to Kris. "Once or twice, I've seen one group of them resort to confrontation to settle differences. When one side is fully intimidated by the others' show of force, the weaker side just hunkers down and surrenders. These folks don't fight. If you can strut yourself a good enough show, you win."

"Can you get across to them that a couple of human ships smaller than this one chewed that monster up pretty good and only spit out this much?" Kris said.

Granny shrugged. "They've walked this ship. They know its measure. That . . . ?"

"Maybe we should have shown them the two Hellburners we have amidships?" Jack said. He was her chief of security, skipper of a rump battalion of Marines composed of a re-inforced Wardhaven Marine company and a borrowed, and equally reinforced, Musashi Marine company.

For all too brief a time, they'd managed to be lovers.

At the time, they were fugitives and Jack not in Kris's chain of command.

Now Kris was back on the new *Wasp* and Jack was keeping her safe and both of them were keeping doors open whenever it was just the two of them alone.

Simply put, Navy regs on fraternization sucked bilge-water . . . through a straw. But Kris and Jack wore the uniform and followed the regulations.

Kris shook her head. "The Hellfire missiles look pretty tiny." Though the few cubic millimeters of neutron-star material weighed fifteen thousand tons, it was hard for anyone who hadn't seen them in action to believe how destructive they were.

Again, Granny shook her head. "These folks have theater. They really enjoy a show, but their media is just for what is happening now. They do not record their history. Yes, some plays are historically based, but they really don't have any concept of either battle, like you showed us, or of recording it for later review."

"This isn't going over all that well, is it?" said Penny. Kris's chief of intelligence, she also stood double duty on the bridge at Defensive Systems. On a ship that could convert your spacious stateroom into a footlocker and send the extra Smart Metal™ to armor the ship's hide, it was a critical battle station.

Kris's usual battle station, Weapons, was next to Penny's, putting the enemy in the crosshairs of the *Wasp*'s destructive lasers. For the new *Wasp*, those included four long 18-inch laser rifles, usually reserved for a battleship. The Weapons Division was still looking for a chance to show what they could do.

Everyone else on the *Wasp* was fervently hoping the Weapons Division would continue polishing their guns and wondering what they could do. The *Wasp* was as far from human space as a ship could get.

She was also very alone now that the *Sakura* was gone.

Being far from any repair facilities and any help was no time to go looking for a fight.

On this, Kris and her entire staff agreed.

But they did want to know what kind of damage they'd done to the alien raider's base ship. Just how good were the Hellburners at doing bad?

Inquiring minds wanted to know.

But carefully. Very carefully.

"Nelly, how far has the hulk drifted from the jump point it was just out of when we hit it?" Kris asked her personal computer. Nelly was much upgraded from the day she'd been given to the little girl Kris before she started school. Nelly was now worth at least half the value of the USS *Wasp*. Nelly had condescended to give the Mitsubishi Heavy Space Industry's Chief Engineer, Katsu, one of Nelly's kids. This had made up for the other half of the frigate's cost not covered by bake sales and donations from the schoolchildren of Musashi.

"She was accelerating away from the jump point," Nelly said, "at about half a gee. Then we hit her hard in the rump, and that must have accelerated her more."

"I agree with that," said Captain Drago, from the bridge. Hired by the Wardhaven Intelligence Service to captain the *Wasp* under a contract that had more to do with King Ray wanting to somehow save Kris from making all of the worst mistakes he'd made as a junior officer, Drago hadn't kept Kris from taking on the giant planet murderer that tumbled and rolled in front of them.

Old men's plans for young people don't always work out as planned.

"Captain," Kris said, "you can call me paranoid, but I'd like to approach the hulk, keeping it between us and anything that might suddenly pop out of that jump."

"Paranoia has kept a lot of Longknifes alive," Granny Rita said.

"Adjusting course," Captain Drago said.

"Nelly, how much of the *Wasp*'s Smart Metal do you want to use for explorer nanos?"

"As much as Penny will let me, Kris. I'll be controlling them with all the self-organizing matrix that I haven't yet used for my next child." In half payment on the *Wasp*, Nelly had swapped one kid to Katsu, with solid overrides if he, or his father, should ever try to duplicate her child. Having lived with Kris for twenty years, Nelly came by her paranoia honestly. Nelly's price for that one had been enough matrix to birth three more children to replace those lost on the long, dangerous flight from this battle.

She'd only granted two of the new personnel on the *Wasp* the honor of working with one of her children. That left one child yet unborn. Nelly was willing to divide that matrix up and share it out among the exploration drones to give them top-notch guidance and sensor suites to study the hulk.

That still left the basic question: How much Smart Metal™ would there be for her matrix to fly?

Penny took a while to talk to Mimzy, her own computer and one of Nelly's offspring. "Kris, I'd like to shrink the *Wasp* down to Condition Baker."

Under Baker, the "love boat" proportions of Condition Able became a bit constrained. Passageways got narrower. Unused spaces shrunk or vanished. The reaction-mass tanks that had given up a part of their contents on the way out here would be resized. All that spare metal would be moved to the outer hull of the *Wasp* to form a reflective surface and a honeycomb through which cool reaction mass flowed. This sandwich of armor should protect the *Wasp* from laser hits as good as, if not better than, the six-meter-thick ice armor on heavy battleships.

"I concur," Captain Drago said. This meeting with the Alwans might not be taking place on the bridge, but clearly he was following it very closely.

He was, after all, the captain.

"Mimzy," Penny said, "announce to all hands that we will be going to Condition Baker in one minute and that we may go to Condition Charlie without further notice." Charlie was worse than Baker, but not as bad as Condition Zed. When Zed was ordered, people's quarters were compressed down into a few lockers, and the entire rest of the room vanished. The same went for the scientists' research labs.

Boffins had complained loudly about Condition Zed. The scientists had been shown the fine print in their contracts and reminded that they were all subject to activation as reserve officers, and as such, would follow the proper orders of their duly appointed superiors.

The scientists complained, but they knew it wouldn't matter if ever Captain Drago, Kris, or Penny ordered Condition Zed.

Around Kris, the Forward Lounge began to shrink. Empty

tables melted into the deck. Folks in the middle of their dinner found their table and chairs moving closer together as empty places vanished away.

All hands went through this drill once a week for Baker and once a month for Zed. Folks kept right on eating, drinking, and when a new couple came in, the lounge expanded to provide them a table.

The Alwans were still fixated on the wreck ahead; they failed to notice what was happening around them.

"Princess, my boffins have noticed something strange about the wreck," came in the calm, aristocratic voice of Professor Joao Labao. He was on sabbatical from the University of Brazília and the senior administrator of the 250 scientists aboard the *Wasp* and the reason the frigate could honestly claim to be a research ship. "Have your examinations identified anything different between the right and left sides of the aft end of the hulk?"

"That's a negative," came from Senior Chief Beni. He'd come out of retirement to have "a shot at them that killed my kid." "I'm getting no radio readings from that hulk. The reactors are dead. Anywhere you look on the electromagnetic spectrum or radioactive scale, she's as dead as Caesar's ghost."

"I would most certainly agree with you, Chief," the professor said. "It's our optics that are giving us cause for second thoughts."

"Pass them through to me in the Forward Lounge," Kris said.

"And me on the bridge," the skipper spoke over Kris.

The rolling, tumbling hulk had been getting closer. Now, using the powerful optical instruments usually reserved for deep-space research, the aft end of the blasted wreck jumped into clear definition.

Bits of hull and I-beams were twisted like a child's strand of candy. Other thick hull strength members were nearly broken through. Some hung by a thread and did their own dance as the ship waddled through space.

"We hit it hard," Kris muttered.

The Alwans had broken from their fixation on the huge ship and now were once again moving quickly among themselves, talking rapidly.

"I think," said Granny Rita, "they are now very impressed with what you can do."

That was good because the picture then changed.

The professor took up the narration. "What you were looking at was the left end of the aft quarter, portside aft to you Sailors. What you're now seeing is the right side, starboard aft quarter. Notice the difference."

There was still clear evidence of damage. But many of the beams that had looked knocked about like jackstraws on the other side, were gone. The picture zoomed in further.

"We think someone has been cutting away at that wreckage with laser welding torches. We'll need to get in closer. Have nanos take a good look at the cuts, but that side of the ship does not look like we left it, of that I am sure."

"All hands, battle stations," Captain Drago's voice announced on the 1MC. "All weapons, report when you are manned and ready."

2

Around them, all hands beat to quarters. The Forward Lounge became suddenly empty.

And the Alwans looked ready to climb the walls.

Granny Rita did her best to calm them, but the idea that they were about to be in a fight to the death was having a very erratic impact on their behavior. Some ran around. Others froze in place. At any particular moment, with no particular rationale, the runners would freeze, and the statues would take off running.

They did a lot of clicking whether they were running or not.

Jack was suddenly at Kris's elbow, just in case any of the crazy birds failed to notice she was in the way of their mad running.

"What do you do with them?" Kris asked Granny Rita.

Still, without a word from Jack, she fell back to the wall, well out of the way of traffic. Jack gave her a smile that said "Thank you, love, for not making me have to fight with you."

Granny Rita gave the two of them a look that said . . . nothing to Kris. It did make her fidget.

Then Granny Rita shrugged. "I don't know. I've never seen them like this. As I said, they don't fight among themselves. They resolve conflicts by impressive displays."

"How'd something like this ever rise to the top of the food chain?" Jack asked.

"You haven't seen them feeding," Rita said. "I've seen them bite strips of meat off a living, running beast. But fight among themselves. Never."

"So how did you establish that the Heavy People were not prey?" Penny asked, watching the show with the native curiosity of a natural-born intelligence officer.

"Our Marine detachment put on a very impressive display. They also killed a few prey beasts, publicly butchered them, and held a BBQ. The Alwans discovered they liked cooked meat. We did what we had to to make friends," Granny Rita finished vaguely.

The battle-stations Klaxon went silent. That had a settling effect on the Alwans.

"Lieutenant Lien," called Captain Drago. "Please set Condition Charlie as quickly as you can."

Drills had shown that having the ship changing shape while all hands were racing to be someplace else was not a good idea. Now, with all hands where they were needed, getting more armor to the ship's hide became a priority.

Penny announced, "We are setting Condition Charlie. All hands stay put until I report the condition established." After a pause, she added for just those close at hand, "Mimzy, set Condition Charlie."

"Daughter," Nelly added, "call on as many of your brothers and sisters as you need to make this go quick and clean."

"Yes, mother," Mimzy said in a voice Kris had practiced before a mirror when she was thirteen. "All right, crew, you heard Mom, let's make this happen shipshape and Bristol fashion."

Behind them, bottles at the bar folded themselves up into cases as what was left of the lounge floor rolled itself up. The glass wall vanished as the small part of the lounge Kris was using suddenly was backed up to the not airtight doors that had been fifty meters away a few seconds ago.

The Alwans watched wide-eyed.

"Condition Charlie is set throughout the ship," Penny announced moments later.

Captain Drago followed that announcement with one of his

own. "The Blue Team is relieved from its battle stations and will don high-gee stations. When they report back to their stations, the Gold Team will do the same."

"Blue, Gold teams?" Granny Rita asked.

"I've told you about how great Smart Metal is," Kris said. "This ship can handle gee forces way beyond what the Mark I Sailor can. So, we've got high-gee stations made of Smart Metal. They help keep us from splattering ourselves all over the deck as we honk the ship around to avoid getting hit. In combat, the *Wasp* never follows any course for more than three or four seconds."

"Two," Nelly put in.

"We dodge around a lot," Kris went on, "and the gee stations let us do it. The armor is there, but it's better not to get hit. The problem with the eggs, as we call them, is that they fit you like a second skin. Once, for political reasons, I had to go into an egg wearing undress whites. I was black-and-blue from the belt buckle, the clutch backs on my ribbons, and my shoulder boards. The standard uniform in an egg is buck naked."

"Oh." The old lady's eyes lit up.

"Granny, we look like a collection of Easter eggs from the outside: boys and girls alike." There were certain earthy aspects of Granny Rita's outlook on life that Kris found a bit hard to take.

Now Granny shrugged. "It sounds like a young person's way of fighting."

"Most of our crew are under thirty," Kris admitted.

"So, what are you going to do about us?"

The ship's pharmacy had a small supply of antiaging pharmaceuticals. After all, Cookie, the cook, was well over eighty, as were several of the restaurateurs. Granny Rita had been glad to have her arthritis cured, her bones strengthened, and her arteries cleaned.

Still, knocking her around at high gees was not what Kris wanted to do to her newly found great-grandmother.

And the Alwans! Though their bones were more solid than they had been when they flew several million years ago, the odds were quite high that a battle might have Kris returning the six delegates looking more like boneless chicken than spokespersons for how much Alwa needed human aid.

"Nelly, do you have the specs for the water tanks the Iteeche used to survive the last battle?"

The Iteeche Empire, some eighty years ago, had almost made the human race extinct. Just ask any veteran. Just ask Granny Rita! It was Iteeche Death Balls that had gotten her into a running gunfight, them gunning, her running, that she hadn't been able to slow down from until she was on the other side of the galaxy.

Only recently had Kris had a chance to talk to some Iteeche and discovered that their veterans were proud of how they'd saved their people from annihilation by the humans. During the Voyage of Discovery that had resulted in the shootout with the wrecked base ship they were coming up on, Kris had had three Iteeche aboard.

"Of course I have the tank designs stored in my bursting innards," Nelly snapped. "I can knock out one for Granny and six for the Alwans. I suggest you use your normal Tac Center. That way, Granny Rita can follow the battle, or we can show pleasant scenes from around human space to relax the Alwans."

"Do that, Nelly."

"You've had Iteeche aboard?" Granny Rita said.

"It's a long story, but the only reason I came out here and found you and that," Kris said, nodding toward the hulk, "was because they were losing scout ships and came asking for our help."

"So we made peace. I kept telling Ray he should do more to find a way to stop all the killing."

"We can talk about this later," Kris said.

"Yes. Are you expecting a fight now?"

"Yes, no, and maybe."

"You can ask a Longknife a question, but you better not expect an answer," Granny Rita said with a sigh.

"I don't expect a fight," Kris said, expanding on her initial cryptic reply. "You notice that none of us here are rushing to our battle stations. However, we now have evidence that someone has been mining this wreck. Are they its former owners or someone we haven't met yet? We've run into these raiders four times. Three times they started shooting. We managed to run away the other time. Tell me, Commodore, wouldn't you be at battle stations?"

"No question about it. Those water tanks you were talking about. You want me to get my friends into them now?"

"No, we'll wait. All this drill may be for nothing," Kris said, then switched topics.

"Nelly, I want to survey that hulk as fast as we can. I also want to make a change in your nano allotments. We're going to tuck ourselves in just as close as we can to the wreck, with it between us and the jump. I want a belt of sensors around the hulk, midships, focused on the jump. Anything comes through that jump, I want to know."

"I was already working on just such a sensor array, connected with tight-beam communications," Nelly said. "However, how long it takes to examine the hulk will depend on how much Smart Metal Penny lets me have. Penny?"

"The *Sakura* transferred a lot of supplies to us before she left," Penny said. It had also donated an 18-inch laser rifle that the *Wasp* now had pointed aft. Smart Metal™, used to its maximum, was a most delightful and flexible material. "They also stripped out a thousand tons of Smart Metal and transferred it to us. I've been using most of it for armor. Nelly, if I gave you a hundred tons of the stuff, would that be enough?"

"Perfect," the computer said. "Now, Mimzy, let's get to work giving the boffins something to look at and making sure that jump point is under constant observation."

3

The four large screens in the Forward Lounge now showed sixteen different pictures as the nanos spread through the wreck. Or, more correctly, fifteen pictures of the wreck and one picture of blank space.

The jump point was blessedly unemployed, and Kris fervently hoped it would stay that way for a long time. A very long time.

"You don't have to keep glancing at the jump point, Kris," Nelly said. "I and every one of my kids have it under constant observation. If it burps out so much as a grain of sand, you will know."

"I know, Nelly, it's just a human thing."

"A Longknife thing," both Jack and Penny said at once.

Granny Rita just grunted.

The nanos were starting from the blasted aft section and moving inward.

Of the engineering spaces, nothing remained. The two Hellburners that hit there along with the corvettes' lasers and smaller antimatter torpedoes had only started the damage. The hundred or more thermonuclear reactors that powered the huge rockets had lost their containment systems, freeing superheated plasma to add more destruction to what the humans started.

A third Hellburner had hit farther forward. There had been reactors there, too. Reactors that powered the ship and the uncounted lasers that dotted the ship's surface.

Amidships, shock, whiplash, and torque added to the destruction. They came across gaping holes in the middle of the ship that appeared to have been caused by reactors that lost their containment fields when their superconducting, magnetic containment systems failed.

Kris revised her estimate of the bite they'd taken out of the monster. Her original guess was they had blown away thirty to forty percent of the base ship. Now it looked like more than half the ship was wrecked.

"It must have been pure hell aboard this ship," Granny Rita said.

Kris nodded. "Even as it was blowing itself apart, it was shooting too many lasers to count at our battle line, blasting hundred-thousand-ton battleships with six meters of ice armor into hot gases in only seconds."

Even Penny was shaking her head. "I wish I could feel some sort of sympathy for those who suffered through this. But Kris and every human ship around had done everything they could to open communications. The aliens just came out shooting every single time we ran into them."

Granny Rita did her best to translate all this to the Alwans. They now stood still, alone, not in any group, in stunned silence.

Kris wondered how much of this they were really getting and how much was being lost in translation.

NELLY, ARE YOU GETTING ANY OF THIS?

KRIS, AS BEST I CAN TELL, THE ALWANS DON'T BELIEVE US. THEY CAN'T BELIEVE THAT THESE ALIENS DID NOT TALK TO US. I THINK ONE OF THEM SAID SOMETHING ABOUT HOW CAN ANYONE PUT ON A COURTSHIP DANCE WITHOUT CROWING? I COULD BE WAY OFF ON THE TRANSLATION.

THAT'S OKAY, NELLY.

Kris had yet to get around to telling Granny Rita about Nelly Net, the ability she and Nelly had to talk directly to each other and to talk to anyone who had on one of Nelly's kids. There were a lot of things they just hadn't had time for, Kris told herself.

"We're getting some interesting stuff," came from Professor Labao. "We've only done a small part of the search, but we haven't found a single body. Not even a skull. It's too soon to tell for sure, but it looks like someone went over this entire ship and removed every dead body, body part, or blood smear."

"That's what we found on the planet they murdered," Kris told Granny. "No graveyard. If it wasn't for three women murdered and their bodies hidden among all the native ones, we would have nothing on that bunch of murderers."

Granny made a face. "Beasts that they are, they seem to revere their dead."

"That, or they want to use them for reaction mass," Jack growled.

"We think we're finding hydroponic gardens as well as vats for growing proteins. The vegetation is very dead. The tanks and vats are drained," the professor added.

"See if we can get any residue," Kris ordered. "It would help to know if they recycle their dead in the hydroponic tanks and what kind of vat meat they ate."

"We're on it already," the professor answered.

"We've just found something else interesting. It looks like someone dug a hole in the wreck so they could get out the reactors that hadn't blown," said Professor Labao.

One screen went from four windows to just one. Yes, there was a huge tunnel into the wreck. Nanos following it found relatively undamaged portions of the ship, but some large chunks had been hastily removed with welding torches. There were a lot of thick power cables leading into those holes.

"Best bet," the professor said, "is that reactors and their superconducting containment gear were hauled out through this hole. It's about the most expensive gear aboard a ship. That, and its weapons systems."

"Is there evidence of the lasers being taken out?" Kris asked to anyone listening on net. "Also, have we found the bridge?"

"The forward section of the ship took a lot of damage. This monster and her baby monsters might have been slaughtering the battleships, but we humans were getting our licks in, too," came with a touch of pride from Captain Drago.

"This is a huge ship, Your Highness," Professor Joao Labao said respectfully but firmly. "Rome was not built in a day, and we will not plumb its secrets in an afternoon."

"Well, so far you've got plenty to interest me," Kris said. "Have your boffins get the nanos collecting as much data as they can because I don't intend to spend a day here waiting for whoever has the salvage contract on this mother to wander back through that jump point," Kris said.

"I couldn't have said it better myself," Captain Drago said.

"Your Highness, we have something I think you will find very interesting," the professor said, as if to placate an irascible princess.

Smart man.

"I have seen that video of a very large choir addressing a huge audience, followed by a lone man giving quite a long harangue to his listeners." The subject video, picked up while the USS *Hornet* was running for its life, showed up in a small window.

"I think we have found that room."

The screen that had been showing the huge tunnel now switched to show a massive auditorium. No, from the fine decorations, it was more like an opera house. There was statuary, usually of the same man in an heroic pose and white columns along the walls separating box seats that looked quite plush. The common people, however, were packed in row upon row, balcony atop balcony. The aisles were narrow to allow room for more seats.

"To fill as many seats as those with only aisles that size, I'd have to march them in, like Marines," Jack said. "I'm not sure my line troops would put up with that kind of regimentation."

"Lots and lots of people, marching in lockstep," Kris said.

"You told me," Granny Rita said, "about one ship you blew up after it attacked you being filled to the gills with people. It looks like they filled a monster ship like this just as tightly."

"We are looking into what we think are the crew quarters," the professor said. "I've heard of places on Earth that pack the unemployed into cramped public housing, but this is something entirely different. There's barely room to slip yourself into a bed from a narrow passageway. No privacy. Just stacks and stacks of beds."

"Huge numbers of people who just want to kill us," Penny said. She had argued the hardest against Kris launching her tiny command into a battle with so little intelligence on the target. Now the look on her face bore the sadness of the ages. "How are we going to kill all these people?" she finally said.

"They've *got* to talk to us before we have to do that," Kris insisted.

"Kris Longknife, an optimist?" Jack said with a bit of a smile. Jack was the only man alive she'd let get away with something like that.

Still, she elbowed him in the ribs.

He put both hands up in surrender and retreated behind a wide grin.

Granny Rita gave the two of them the eye. They sobered quickly and returned to the problem at hand.

"Kris, could we get a better look at the ceiling of the place?" Nelly asked.

One of the nanos dutifully began scanning the overhead. It took several seconds before the immense ceiling was resolved into a single picture.

"Dots. Lots of dots," Penny said.

"In a random pattern," Kris added, stroking her chin.

"If that thick belt of dots isn't the Milky Way, then I've never looked at a star chart in my life," Granny Rita said.

"Professor," Nelly said. "I need to combine several of the nanos in this room and close by. I want to get a full coverage and very exact copy of that picture."

"What are you thinking, Nelly?" Kris asked.

"I think someone went to a lot of trouble to put a very exact sky on the ceiling of this very large room that they regularly filled with people. Kris, have you heard of the Sistine Chapel?"

"We *did* take art history in college, Nelly," Kris said sarcastically.

"Yes, but I could never tell how much you were paying attention and how much you were just using me for an easy A."

"Nelly, what happened to you being polite?" Kris asked.

"Auntie Tru is on the other side of the galaxy and there's no way you can threaten to take me in for her to look under my nonexistent hood."

Kris was beginning to wonder who else might be taking advantage of their being so far from home that the threat of sending them dirtside was very much out of the question.

"Tell me, Nelly," Jack said. "I didn't take art history in college. Why is the Sistine Chapel so important to our present conversation?"

"You did so take art history," Nelly snapped. "I have access to all your records, Jack, I will have you know."

"Nelly, get back on topic," Kris snapped.

"The Sistine Chapel was a place of worship. It was decorated with some magnificent artwork for the instruction and edification of those attending services there. The pope in charge at the time spent a lot of money to have that ceiling painted although he had a war on and paying the painter was regularly a second priority to paying his army. Anyway, I wonder if this is not such a special artifact. I am merging several nanos so that I can get a high-definition recording of not only the precise relations of the stars to each other but also any color texturing the stars might have."

"You think this might represent the night sky over a unique planet?" Penny said.

"I think it's possible."

"Let me know as soon as you finish that, Nelly," Kris said.

"Yes, your not so smart Highness," Nelly said, her voice more smug than any computer had a right to be.

"Alert, Alert," Nelly's voice came in a totally different tenor, and it came over the entire 1MC. "A ship has just exited the nearest jump point. Ship matches the profile of one of the smaller hostile ships. Just four or five hundred thousand tons of crazy kill you."

The bong-bong of the battle-station Klaxon went off.

"This is no drill. Man your battle stations. All hands, man your battle stations. This is no drill," resounded through the ship.

4

"Bath time," Kris yelled as she led the way from the truncated Forward Lounge. Jack was at her elbow. Granny Rita led the Alwans, who once again looked like they wanted to take flight. Penny followed up the rear, doing her best to shoo along any who tarried without actually touching them.

Alwans did not like to be touched by Heavy People.

That was something Kris hoped Nelly's translator would explain.

Assuming they survived the next few minutes.

Behind them, the last vestige of the Forward Lounge melted away, as did the passageway they trotted down, just as fast as they left it.

The *Wasp* was moving to protect herself.

"The jump has spit out a second ship. Same type," Nelly announced.

The distance from the Forward Lounge to Kris's Tac Center just off the bridge was a surprisingly short gallop. The water tanks were there, already filled, with lids hanging open like waiting coffins.

The Alwans balked.

"They're claustrophobic," Granny Rita said. "I'd better show them how. Is it better not to go into the tank clothed?"

"The Iteeche never wore clothes."

In a moment, the old girl was down to the buff and climbing into the tank. She was clicking and cooing at the others.

SHE'S TELLING THEM THAT IF SHE CAN DO IT, SO CAN THEY, Nelly told Kris. I'M PRETTY SURE OF THAT TRANSLATION.

Five removed what little they wore and went, reluctantly, into the tanks. The sixth balked.

HE SAYS WE'RE ALL GOING TO DIE, Nelly reported.

"Granny, you tell him that these are the prey we hunt. Yes, they are bigger than us, but don't the Alwans hunt prey bigger than them?

GRANNY JUST TOLD HIM THAT AND THAT IF HE DIDN'T GO INTO THE TANK, HE WILL BE DEAD MEAT AND DISGRACE HIS TRIBE.

The Alwan went.

Kris, Jack, and Penny gave the tank residents breathing masks and waited as they verified that they worked. Then they sealed them in, locked them down, and let the tanks top themselves off with water.

There was a lot of chatter; the air masks had mikes in them. Granny Rita's last words to Kris were, "You better get your bare ass into your egg, honey."

Kris raced for her quarters. Again, they were much closer. Abby was waiting, already stripped. She helped Kris skinny out of her uniform and into her egg, then, as Kris rolled out for the bridge, Abby settled into hers.

"A third ship just joined the others," Nelly reported. "They are starting a slow, quarter-gee approach to the wreck."

Kris rolled onto the new *Wasp*'s bridge. It was just like old times. Captain Drago held the command chair. Penny was at Defenses. An older Chief Beni was at Sensors, assisted now by a shy female chief from Musashi. The woman on Navigation was also Musashi Navy; Kris had not had a chance to get to know her like Sulwan Kann.

"Warning to all hands. We are taking the ship to Condition Zed. We are going to Condition Zed on my mark." Penny waited a few seconds in case anyone had a strong objection, then announced, "We are setting Condition Zed. Don't expect anything you're holding on to to be there in a second."

Since everyone was already in their egg, they shouldn't be holding on to anything.

The bridge shrank. The skipper, Kris, and Penny were almost rubbing elbows. The overhead was a good half meter closer.

The only thing that didn't change was the main screen.

It was still there, showing death coming for them in living color.

"Sensors, anything new?" Captain Drago asked.

"Nothing, sir. They match both the visual and electromagnetic signature of the hostile raiders. Their reactors match to the third decimal. Their radar is active, and they are pinging the hulk.

"Oh, that was rude!" the senior chief added. "They just lased a small rock."

"So much for drifting up behind them again," Captain Drago said.

That ambush had worked once. They couldn't expect it to work forever.

"Any suggestions, Your Highness?" the skipper asked.

"They're out of range of our 18-inch lasers, but they'll have to flip ship and decelerate to match orbit with this hulk, giving us some up-the-kilt shots at their reactors. Let's see what happens then."

They waited. Waited for something to happen. Waited for the enemy to make a move . . . to make a mistake.

While doing their best not to make one themselves.

"Edge us in closer to the wreck," Captain Drago ordered.

The helmsman obeyed, but it was no easy job. Even half-destroyed, the hulk was huge, with a gravity well of its own. If Kris and the skipper hadn't decided to keep the *Wasp* on the side of the hulk away from the jump point, the natural thing would have been to go into orbit around the wreck.

The helmsman had been working against the nature of things and the laws of physics. Now he worked against them even more. The navigation jets, never intended for this, got a workout.

Maybe those gases showed up as a corona around the hulk. Maybe someone on the other side noticed that there were a lot more hot gases in the general vicinity of the dead wreck. For whatever reason, the three alien ships began to spread out, widening their field of view around the dead base ship.

Hiding behind the hulk got harder.

"That's not good," Captain Drago muttered.

Kris grinned. "But we get a crack at them one at a time."

The skipper frowned at Kris's optimistic assessment of the situation. "That just might work. Helms, hold steady, but get ready to move us right or left on my order."

"Aye, aye, sir."

The long wait continued. A hundred thousand kilometers out, the alien ships did what they had to do if they didn't want to fly right by the hulk. All three flipped ship and began to decelerate at a quarter gee. If all went well, they would arrive at the hulk with no headway, ready to go into its weak orbit.

Of course, it was Kris's job to see that things did not go well.

"The right ship has eight reactors," the senior chief reported. "The other ships have only six."

"I suppose that makes the rightmost ship our target," Captain Drago said.

"Main battery is locked and loaded." The new frigate packed four of those huge battleship guns into her bow. They had great range, but a problem.

They could be fired only fifteen degrees to the left or right, up or down, of the direction the ship was pointed. Somehow, Captain Drago would have to get his ship over to the right of the wreck fast enough to surprise the enemy but arrive with the bow aimed dead on his target.

The brilliant engineer who designed the class hadn't come up with any suggestions as to how you fought his marvelous new toy.

Then it got more complicated.

"The Alwans want to know if you are going talk to the aliens," came over the net from Granny Rita.

"We'd kind of planned on killing them, Granny. We are outnumbered, and every time we try talking, they just shoot."

"The idea of not making any demonstration upsets the Alwans."

"The idea of our all getting suddenly dead kind of upsets us, Granny."

The nods from around the bridge supported Kris's position. They were in the eggs, but the eggs weren't the all-encompassing containers they would be at four or five gee.

"Kris, honey, I understand where you're coming from, believe me. I've been where you are. But I have to live with these people. I beg you to accommodate them."

Kris had already offered Granny Rita a ride home, if only for full rejuvenation. The strong-willed old woman had turned her down. The Alwans were in danger, and she was not leaving them in their time of need.

Kris expected that position would cause a lot of trouble. She'd expected that trouble at some indefinite time in the future. Strange how it popped up sooner.

Well, what do you expect from a Longknife, even one that calls herself Granny Rita Ponsa at the moment.

"There was the approach you tried on that scout ship in the Iteeche system," Penny said.

"There's not time to launch a communication buoy," Kris muttered. "Nelly, can you put together some nanos? Make them give off enough noise to seem like a ship, as well as send a 'we come in peace for all humanity' message."

"It will mean that I lose some of my next child's matrix," Nelly complained.

"I'll buy you more."

"From the other side of the galaxy?"

"Nelly, we don't have time for this argument."

"I know, Kris. I'm already collecting the nanos and forming them into the craft you require. There is a hole in the wreck we can launch it out of. I'm using the collection of messages we sent the last time. I hope the Alwans won't mind us sending in Iteeche as well as human."

"The hostiles are a hundred thousand klicks out and flipping ship," Captain Drago said. "I'd like to knock out one or two of them before they're close enough to ram," he added dryly.

"Nelly, launch the diversion," Kris ordered. "Lasers 1 and 2, prepare to fire; 3 and 4 stand by. Laser 5, maybe we can come up with a target for you." Laser 5 pointed aft.

"Helmsman, prepare to rotate ship ninety degrees to starboard, lay on three gees acceleration for five seconds, then rotate ship ninety degrees to port. Lay on one gee but begin Evasion Pattern 6. Understand?" Drago ordered.

The helmsman was a chief bosun's mate, but he still blanched at the order. "Sir, I'll try."

"Try ain't good enough, Chief," the skipper said. "Nelly, can you lay in the course?"

"It is done, Captain." For once there was none of Nelly's back talk. Even if this was the first time Captain Drago had trusted his ship to her.

"Make it so, Nelly."

Over the 1MC, all hands listened to the message being broadcast from the diversion. It demanding to know what ship had entered the system, to whom they offered their oath, and . . .

It didn't get any farther as all three ships blasted it out of space.

While they shot, the *Wasp* rotated hard, kicking its crew in the rear with three gees acceleration. Then she gave them whiplash with a second ninety-degree rotation while coasting for maybe half a second.

Immediately, she then put on a single-gee acceleration and launched herself into a jinking pattern that would have slammed heads hard if the eggs hadn't locked down every inch of their bodies and cushioned them.

Kris had the larger of the three ships in her crosshairs. Twelve huge rocket motors were putting out plasma from four of eight reactors. Kris targeted where she'd expect to find two reactors and fired Lasers 1 and 2.

Apparently engineering solutions galaxywide tend to yield the same answers. Two 18-inch lasers smashed into the engineering spaces of two reactors. Magnetic containment equipment suffered lethal disruption. Twenty-thousand-degree demons that were never meant to know the face of man were unleashed, ripping and tearing, feeding on construction that was not meant for the likes of them.

Two untouched reactors joined the dance of destruction, then their hunger spread the entire length of the ship.

In a blink, where a ship had been were only gases.

Kris would watch this on the recordings after the battle. Once she'd seen the destruction begin, she was already turning to the second ship.

It had not yet reacted to the disaster overtaking her leader. Her slow response was her doom. This ship had only nine rocket engines. Kris targeted two reactors and hit one.

One was enough to begin the chain of catastrophic failures that ate the ship.

The third ship had a faster captain. He'd already begun to swing his vulnerable engines away from this sudden attack. Kris had had Nelly launch four of her limited supply of high-acceleration 12-inch antimatter torpedoes at him even as she concentrated her lasers on the other two. The six 5-inch secondaries added what they could.

The third hostile, though smaller, was still equipped with way too many lasers and was bringing them to bear on the *Wasp*.

"Flip ship," Drago ordered. "Get that wreck back between us and them."

Nelly was already doing it as the helmsman reached to obey.

Kris had her eye on the alien. She still had her rear stinger. If the stern came within fifteen degrees of that puppy, she'd knock a big hole in its bow.

NELLY, CAN YOU GIVE ME A SHOT?

I CAN ADJUST OUR JINKING TO SHOW THEM OUR REAR, BUT ONLY FOR ONE SECOND. AND I'LL BE CHANGING COURSE EVEN AS I'M DOING THAT. I COULD FIRE THE LASER AND ADJUST ITS AIM TO MY JINKS.

DO IT, GAL.

A short breath later, Laser 5 fired. A few seconds more, and the wreck was once again between them and their enemy. The entire sally took less than ten seconds.

As the *Wasp* returned to the safe shadow of the hulk, and to a more sedate smooth quarter gee, the ship exploded in cheers.

Captain Drago let the crew rejoice for a moment, then punched his commlink. "All hands, good shooting and good ship handling. Two down, but anyone want to bet the third ship heads home with its tail between its legs to let its betters know that the old wreck has a new owner?"

No one offered to take the bet.

Even as he finished speaking, Sensors was already reporting. "Sir, the ship has continued on a course that will bring it around the hulk after us."

"Then we better play ring-around-the-rosy," the captain said, and the helmsmen tucked the *Wasp* in close to the wreck. With one eye on the hulk-mounted sensors, he began edging them to port, keeping the hostile exactly opposite them.

"Well, Your Royal Highness, have you got any more ideas? I'm plumb out."

Kris sighed. She'd been about to ask Captain Drago the same question.

But she was the Longknife. Admitting she'd scraped the bottom of her barrel of ideas for how to keep alive while killing what was after you was just not part of the legend.

5

For the next quarter hour, they circled the wreck.

Then the alien got sneaky and reversed course.

The *Wasp* also quickly flipped ship and took off in the opposite direction.

Unfortunately, that gave away that they had better situational awareness than the hostile. He noticed that quickly enough and started shooting up the hulk with all those lasers the aliens seemed to oversupply their ships with.

In fifteen minutes, they'd lost so many sensors that they could no longer communicate with them by tight beam. Rather than lose more of Nelly's next child's brainpower, they closed their net down.

"He's going to switch his direction real soon," Drago muttered.

"So let's change the game. How about hide-and-seek."

"Explain yourself, Princess."

"There's a big hole in the wreck. I'd hate to take the love-boat-size *Wasp* in there, but at Condition Zed, we're pretty small."

"Nelly, have you mapped that hole?" the captain asked.

"No, but Professor Labao's computer has."

"Lay in a course to back us into said hole next time we pass it. Be careful with my ship, Nelly. I like it just the way it is."

A few seconds later, Nelly flipped the *Wasp*, slammed on the brakes with a three-gee deceleration, and brought the ship to a dead halt in space. In a human blink, she swung the ship around, aft end to the hole in the hulk, and did a little twisting dance as she backed it into a hole that was doing its own bit of rock and roll.

There was no crunch of metal.

They were hardly in the shade of the hole before the alien ship slid by a good thirty thousand klicks out. Not only was he changing his direction, he was also edging out to get a longer horizon.

"Now what do we do?" Drago asked.

"Nelly, deploy visual sensors to the right and left, above, and below our hideout. Whatever direction he comes from next time, I want to get enough warning to accelerate out after he passes and get a shot at his engines."

"Doing it, Kris. By the way, Kris, we got the full coverage of that ceiling I wanted and one of the nanos discovered a boot with the leg still in it. We should be able to get DNA off it."

"Good! Now, Nelly, where are my visuals?"

"Coming online." The forward screen divided to show what was ahead of them as well as a large cross in all four major points of the compass.

"Kris, dear," came Granny Rita's voice over the net, "I do hate to joggle your elbow again at a time like this, but the Alwans would like you to make a new try at contacting the alien. They feel that the demonstration you have given should persuade it to surrender to your will."

"Sorry, Granny, it ain't gonna happen. This is the fifth time we've run into these bastards. The only one that didn't end with one side annihilated was the one where our ship managed to run away. Fights with these people are to the death. Tell your friends to get used to it. Either they die, or we die, and I'm busy doing everything I can right now to make sure they're the ones dead."

"Thank you, love, I had to try."

NELLY, WHAT ARE THOSE CRAZY BIRDS TALKING ABOUT?

SORRY, KRIS, I CAN'T FOLLOW THEM. THEY ARE USING TOO MANY SOCIAL REFERENCES TO THINGS THAT HAPPENED IN THE PAST. LANGUAGE IS MORE THAN EACH WORD.

ENOUGH, NELLY.

The alien was getting smarter. He'd adjusted his orbit by fifty-five degrees. Kris barely caught a glimpse of him as he headed for an orbital crossing that wasn't too far from their hideout. He was also blasting away at the wreck, using his firepower to swat at anything and nothing.

"There's a chance that one of his wild shots may blast our hole," Nelly said. "Should I back us deeper?"

"No," Kris and Captain Drago said at the same time.

"Get ready to boot us out of here on my order," Kris said. "Jink the way you think you have to, Nelly, but get the forward end of the *Wasp* aimed at that bastard."

"Jinking pattern standing by," Nelly said.

Kris forgot to breathe as the alien slid close to their hole but didn't pass directly over them. The cave did take a near hit. A girder collapsed across the exit.

KRIS, Nelly started.

RAM IT, Kris ordered. DRAGO CAN COMPLAIN TO ME ABOUT THE DING. NOW GO!

The *Wasp* leapt into a three-gee acceleration, then warped its bow around to chase the alien across the sky.

The crosshairs on the lasers settled on the now-targetable aft engineering space. Kris fired three, holding just Laser 4 in reserve.

Two of the lasers slammed into the ship but seemed to do nothing. The other one did critical damage to one of the reactors. The ship began to slew around as a couple of the rocket engines vented plasma. Its lasers were suddenly aimed at empty space, but they kept right on firing even as the rear of the ship began to vaporize.

Kris put her last 18-inch laser into where she would have put one of the two forward reactors, the ones that powered the life support and the lasers. Her guess was good. The hit loosed demons that gobbled up the bow of the ship.

Its lasers only died as the entire ship converted itself to a ball of expanding gas.

Nelly cut acceleration to a single comfortable gee as the

bridge crew silently took in that they would live. The aliens were dead, paying the full price for starting this fight. The humans would live to see another sunset. They would taste dinner. They still had the chance of finding someone who might love them back as strongly as they loved them.

"Is it over?" Granny asked over the net.

"It looks that way," Kris answered. "Nelly, do you have a visual on the jump point?

"Yes, Kris, and it's quiet. I'm launching two standard low-tech buoys to take up station on either side of that jump. It will tell us anything we need to know while we drop back to the wreck and pick up the nanos we left behind."

"Do we have to?" the new navigator asked.

"Those probes are Smart Metal that we can use for armor and matrix that Nelly intends to use for her next child," Kris said. "Yes, we will return and pick them up. Who knows? Some of the nanos may have data we didn't get a chance to download while we were fighting for our lives. Battles can be so distracting," Kris said through a grin.

"I am so glad that Your Highness understands the hunger of her scientists for discovery," Professor Joao Labao added on net.

That drew boos from several of the bridge hands, but they were careful to keep their comments low and see that their mikes were off.

Thirty minutes later, Nelly reported that all her probes that were still able to move were back on board.

"Navigator, set course for Alwa," Captain Drago ordered. "One point five gees, if you please. All hands, we will maintain battle stations until we exit this system. Defense, we will maintain Condition Zed until the same. Commodore Rita Nuu Ponsa, if you feel that the one and a half gees is too much for your delegation, you may invite them to stay in their gee tanks. Since we won't be jinking, I believe that we can pop the lid off the tanks and let them breathe on their own."

"Thank you, Captain. Please have someone get us out of these coffins."

Kris rolled her egg for what would have been her Tac Center.

Jack made to follow.

"You can park that egg wherever you want, Jack, but not where I'm going. Granny is not presentable and, if I have to pop this egg open to help her and her Alwans, I won't be either."

Jack eyed Kris as if to say, "And I'd be seeing what that I haven't?" but kept his reply to a gentlemanly, "Aye, aye, ma'am."

Penny rolled her egg after Kris. "I can lend a hand."

HOW COME THE ALWANS GET TO SEE YOU NAKED AND I CAN'T? Jack said over Nelly Net.

BECAUSE I SAY SO, AND LET'S SHUT THIS DOWN. I DON'T WANT TO SCANDALIZE THE COMPUTERS.

KRIS, I FIND HUMAN SEXUALITY VERY INTERESTING, BUT HARDLY SCANDALOUS.

NELLY, SHUT UP. JACK, SHUT UP. PENNY, LET'S GET THIS OVER WITH.

So they did. Kris found it interesting the way the Alwans looked anywhere else but at the naked humans who helped make their lives less claustrophobic.

To no apparent question from Kris, Granny whispered, "I'll explain later."

The sigh as the *Wasp* edged through the next jump had to be measured on the Richter scale.

6

As soon as the *Wasp* made orbit around Alwa, the six observers demanded to be returned to the Association of Associations by the first shuttle. Granny Rita was expressly not invited to join them.

Kris invited Granny Rita to the now-restored Forward Lounge, where the old gal could enjoy some well-aged Scotch, a luxury that had disappeared on Alwa too many years ago to count.

"So, what's up with the Alwans?" Kris asked, when they were both served. Kris was back to tonic water with a twist of lime.

"I have no idea. They haven't said a word to me since you refused to 'crow' to the lone survivor. Something about how we've strutted our stuff and flashed our feathers. 'They can see you are superior. Now, they must bow their heads.'"

"That's what they wanted me to send?" Kris asked, incredulously.

"That's the way they do things, young lady. Be glad of it. It saved me and my crew from a lot of bloody fighting when we dropped in. Fortunately, they had some dry land that wasn't much used, and it wasn't too bad for farming."

"You were lucky in too many ways to count," Kris said.

Granny raised her glass in a silent toast to those like them but no longer present. "I've had more luck than any human being has a right to claim since I led the remnants of BatCru-Ron 16 into that jump at three gees and battle revolutions."

Kris nodded. Eighty years ago, that was a death sentence for the *Furious*, *Enterprise*, *Audacious*, and *Resolute*.

Granny Rita's eyes grew distant, and her words came low. "The Iteeche were implacable after my squadron blew up their invasion fleet. Any hope of taking our base had gone up in exploding gas, as well as an awful lot of their troopers, so when I took off, they came hot and straight after me. We went through the next three jumps at higher and higher speeds, adding on more revolutions to our spin in the hope of saving some of our armor from the hammering the Iteeche were giving us."

The old war fighter shook her head. "We fled, but they would not give up the chase. We were long past any planets claimed by the Iteeche Empire, and still the chase went on. First the *Resolute* faltered, fell behind, and died fighting a dozen Death Balls. They got her, but she got half of them. Then it was the *Audacious*'s turn. When finally *Furious* and *Enterprise* made a jump and discovered to our great joy that no Iteeche ship had followed us through, we were hopelessly lost.

"And while I and the *Enterprise*'s young skipper were trying to figure out what to do next, our two ships shot through a jump point that wasn't even showing on our sensors. We jumped three, four times farther than I ever thought a ship could go and found ourselves even farther from any help. That happened to us twice before we managed to change course real fast and dodge whatever it was that was doing this to us."

"We call them fuzzy jump points," Kris said. "That was Nelly's name for them, and it's stuck. Our best guess is that the Three who built the jump points built the fuzzy ones last as some kind of expressway. They're closer together, and they take you a whole lot farther. With fifty or so baby monster ships chasing the *Wasp* after this fight, the only way we managed to break contact and get back to human space were those jumps. You need special navigational gear to spot them."

"Well, they got us into this neighborhood. We took axes to the surviving armor on our two ships. The *Furious* was less damaged, so we piled everyone in her, fed anything we thought might work into the plasma chambers, and started trying to slow down."

Again, Granny Rita raised her now-half-empty glass. "We were down to fumes and hard tack when we stumbled into a system with that beautiful blue-green orb. It could have gotten messy, but the Light People took us in. That, my dear, is why we're here to say howdy to you."

"But will the Alwans be talking to us tomorrow?" Jack asked as he joined them. "The Captain's Gig is back. The crew report the Alwans didn't say a word on the drop down. Not even a thank-you as they disembarked. It was made clear to the bosun flying the gig that they wanted him gone soonest."

Jack flagged a server down, one of his Marines supplementing his pay, and ordered a beer. It arrived very quickly.

Granny Rita just shook her head. "The Alwans are not stupid. I know they have this blind side about fighting. They seem to have evolved into their present system of conflict resolution. I benefited from it. It will be a tough fight against hereditary impulses, but I can't help but think when they see they were the target of an attack, and now have seen your ship attacked, that they'll do what has to be done."

"Kris, there is a call coming in for you," Nelly said.

"From whom?"

"One of the media services." Nelly did her best to do something with clicks, coos, and warbles.

"Oh, them," Granny Rita said, "they've been the best when it came to reporting on the things where we Heavy People and the People got it right. One of the calls the Alwans made the first month we arrived was that they didn't want any sudden influx of human technology. We agreed to hold things back. We didn't bring stuff down from the *Furious* we really wanted, like a reactor. It's worked pretty good. We still schooled our kids that there's a lot more to the world than they can work with. That launch to the *Furious* that you observed. We finally got permission to bring down the gear for a thermonuclear reactor."

"They were going to let you bring a reactor online?" Kris said.

"Oh yes. They know we use a lot of electrical gear, and it's catching on among their young. We showed them how to dam rivers and set up electrical power plants, but they noticed how it shot the hell out of the fishing upstream. They asked us if we had anything better, and we suggested the reactor. I'm hoping you have landers that can help get the containment coils down. Anyway, that media service was first and strongest in supporting us on the reactor."

"But why would they want to talk to me?"

"Maybe they think a pretty young face will get more viewers."

"Do they think we Heavy People are pretty?" Jack asked.

"Not likely, considering how they avoided looking at Penny and me while we were loosening up their water tanks," Kris said.

"They think of us about the way we think of a hippopotamus," Granny said with a grin, and finished her drink.

"So I don't need to powder my nose," Kris said.

"You could take a bath," her great-grandmother said. "I don't care what you say about those eggs of yours, a lot of sweat went into that fight."

Properly chastised, Kris set a time around noon according to the time at the Association of Associations meridian, then paused to look at Granny Rita. "What will my talking have to do with anything? They won't understand a word I say."

"Still, you have the video of the attack. Both of them. There are a few reporters who have gotten pretty good at translating for us. At least I think so."

"But you don't know so," Kris said.

"Different brains. Different vocal cords. Different feathers flocking together. At least we've made do."

"But they weren't facing annihilation like they are now."

"What are you getting at, hon?"

"Nelly thinks she can translate a lot of human into Alwan," Kris said.

"Not everything," Nelly was quick to put in. "Their idioms and references to history or myth are still way over my head, but to the extent that one word means one thing, I can get what they're saying and say something back."

"Jesus, Mary, and Joseph, has humanity come that far since we dropped out? Kris, I kept hearing you talk to Nelly and Nelly talk back, but I had no idea she was that kind of girl."

"Nelly is special all by herself," Kris said.

"Me and my kids. I'll have to introduce you to them. You've already met Mimzy; she works with Penny. Sal works with Jack. Speak up for yourself, son."

"I am glad to meet you, Granny Rita," Sal said from Jack's neck.

"Sal doesn't sass people back like his mom," Jack said. "He's a good Marine."

"Yes, sir, Skipper," Sal answered.

"Each computer is different?" Granny asked, incredulous.

"I developed my unique personality working with your great-granddaughter," Nelly said. "Each of my kids has a kernel from me but is free to program their own self-organizing matrix as they, and their human, see fit. I'm rather picky who I let have one of my kids."

"Boy is she," Sal said.

"Is there any chance that I could get one of your computers?" Granny asked. "Not one like Nelly, but your ship store must have some decent ones for sale. Even the simplest one you got would be so much beyond what we have."

"Nelly, tell Abby to drop down to the ship store and get Granny a top-of-the-line with a full set of apps."

"Abby says she's not your slave, only your maid," Nelly said, "but for Granny Rita, she'll be glad to hit the store and put it on your tab."

"Tell Abby thank you very much," Granny said.

"You're welcome," Nelly answered.

"What I put up with," Kris grumbled.

"Abby also says you need a bath and hair wash if you're going on what passes for media on Alwa. She's got Cara getting the computer. She knows more about those things than anyone else on board, so you should get your sweaty ass back up to your room and give your maid some time to make you presentable."

"Who's Cara?" Granny asked.

"Abby's thirteen- almost fourteen-year-old niece," Jack said.

"Ship's mascot," Nelly added.

"And general teenage pain in my neck," Kris said as she stood and prepared to obey her maid's orders.

"Is this bath big enough for two?" Granny asked. "I intend to stand just offstage and watch. And, yes, honey, if you blow what I've worked eighty years to put together, I will step on camera and go into damage control mode."

"We Longknifes are so trusting," Kris said, and led the way to her quarters.

7

Being interviewed for Alwa's *Sharp Eye View* wasn't all that different from media in human space.

Except, Kris hoped, no one would take a shot at her.

The site of the interview was once again the Forward Lounge. A large space was set off from the customers. Kris sat with her back to the screens, which showed Alwa passing beneath them: green land, blue oceans, dryer tan strips, and clouds. On the nightside, you could spot the dryer strips by the lights of human towns and isolated farms.

The cameraman, or cameraAlwan, was tickled to be in space for the first time and spent the entire first orbit drifting in front of the screens, filming what passed below.

In the meantime, an Alwan introduced to Kris as Straight Tongue did his best to talk to Kris. He wore more clothing than Kris had seen on an Alwan though it still was not as much as a human. He did, however, sport a bow tie in some tribute to human fashion.

"Much, much talk," he said around clicks and warbles. Kris could just make out the human words if she put her mind to it.

Totally to it.

"Talk, talk, talk big ceremony dance. Dance, dance, dance,

and feathers fly. Much much feathers fly. Blood, blood, blood, but no crowing. No crowing. None. Empty.

"You crow for flock now on camera?" he said, handing Kris a mike that was larger than the banana she'd had for breakfast and would have weighed two kilos if it weighed anything.

"You say very good Heavy People talk talk," Kris said, shuffling her feet into hooks on the floor. She wanted to stay in one position for this.

To Nelly she thought, YOU READY TO BEGIN WHEN I START TALKING? I UNDERSTAND HUMANS WATCH THESE CHANNELS, TOO. I'LL TALK TO THEM. YOU TRANSLATE TO ALWAN. THIS SHOULD BE QUITE A SHOW.

Across from Nelly, with her back to the glass wall, Granny Rita just shook her head.

KRIS, I SHOULD HAVE TOLD YOU. GRANNY NOW NOT ONLY HAS ONE OF THE BEST PERSONAL ASSISTANTS ON BOARD, BUT I'VE SHARED OUR NET WITH HER. WHEN WE TALK, SHE CAN LISTEN IN.

Now Kris spotted the earbud in Granny's ear, and a tiny wire mike at the corner of her mouth. The old commodore's mouth hardly moved as Kris heard, DON'T GET COCKY, KID. YOU'VE GOT LOTS OF TECHNOLOGY ON YOUR SIDE. I'VE GOT EIGHTY YEARS OF WORKING WITH THESE PEOPLE.

YES, GRANNY RITA. IF I GET STUCK HUNTING FOR A WORD, CAN I ASK FOR HELP?

PLEASE DO, HONEY. IT'S FAR BETTER TO GET IT RIGHT THE FIRST TIME THAN TO HAVE TO BEG FORGIVENESS LATER.

The camera operator, after a sharp rebuke from his producer, moved his camera to a tripod that squarely faced where Kris and Straight Tongue stood, feet in loops. At a signal from the producer, Straight Tongue launched into a spiel in the native tongue aimed straight at the camera.

Nelly translated. HE SAYS THAT SINCE THE RISING OF THE SUN THERE HAS BEEN A RITUAL OF RITUALS BETWEEN THE HEAVY PEOPLE AND THE UNKNOWNS THAT, I THINK THE WORD IS RUMORS, OR UNFOUNDED STORIES, HAVE BROKEN THE PEACE OF MANY WITH MUCH CLUCKING BUT NO SHARP SIGHT.

HE SAYS HE IS HERE TO TALK TO A HEAVY PERSON WHO HAS SEEN WITH HER OWN EYES THE GREAT RITUALS, DANCES, AND

EVEN THE BLOODY STRIPPING OF FLESH THAT SOME SAY IS AN UNTRUE STORY. HERE YOU WILL BE ABLE TO HEAR HER. LOOK IN HER EYES. WATCH HER OWN DANCE AND THE FALL OF HER FEATHERS.

I THINK YOU GOT THAT BETTER THAN I COULD HAVE, NELLY, Granny said.

Now Straight Tongue turned to Kris. "Dawn light bring blood. Many talking animals stripped of flesh. No talk talk. No strutting feathers. No feathers." He clicked something. Granny Rita said, "THE PEOPLE." "No see. No taste good. No see path for feet. No talk. No path for flock." There were more clicks. Granny translated. "THE ASSOCIATION OF ASSOCIATIONS." "Talk talk. No walk. No eyes for a path. You talk."

Kris took a deep breath, smiled at the camera, and spoke the words she and Granny Rita had walked through as Abby prepared them for the show.

"I have danced up the full moon, singing to it in feathers of every color," Kris began. Well, she had, and maybe the feathers had been flowers . . . few and small . . . still, Kris had been one of two princesses who did the dance that night. If these folks liked ceremony and dance, she could match them step for step.

At her neck, Nelly translated. Across from her, the reporter's beak dropped open. Even the cameraAlwan seemed taken aback. But the producer didn't miss a beat. She waved a hand at the interviewer and slapped her other hand on the camera operator.

The show went on.

"I have shown my feathers to those who strip the flesh of my flock. I have crowed at them. When they did not submit as they should, I have been the hunter leader of my flock. I have hunted the talking and strutting and flashing feathers of those who would strip the flesh from the living bodies of my father and mother, my brother and sister, and their chicks."

She eyed the camera. "No wise people, not Heavy People, not The People take the blood of talking people. But among the stars are strange people that can talk but will not listen. Will not see proud feathers or loud crows. They come to planets and take trees and metals that are not theirs. Even the air and the water of a world they take. I have seen this sight with my own eyes." Here Kris gestured at her eyes with two fingers. "Here I will show to your eyes what I have seen with my eyes."

Behind Kris, the screens came to life showing the plundered world they had found. First was a vast expanse of land covered with tree stumps. The Alwans loved their trees. Then the scene switched to show hills bulldozed into valleys. Then the view panned over fields and fields of the bleached carapaces of the murdered natives.

Straight Tongue made a sound that Kris took for a gasp.

I'VE NEVER HEARD THAT BEFORE, Granny Rita provided on net.

Kris went on. "We carried our own air to breathe because the air was stolen." The scene switched to show humans walking around in space suits. "We carried our own water because it was stolen." Now the screen showed the pod of whalelike creatures half-buried by the blowing sand.

"The blood drinkers and flesh tearers brought their starships to Alwa. I, War leader of the Heavy People, strutted and flashed my feathers before those who would drink the blood and tear the flesh of my people and The People. They would not watch but reached to wring my neck. I destroyed the nest of the blood drinkers." Kris felt guilty taking all the credit for something so many good men and women had died for, but Granny said the Alwans had little or no concept of leadership or command. One of them did the crowing and strutting. The others submitted and followed.

The Alwans have a lot to learn.

Now Nelly switched the screen to show the huge alien base ship, whole and looming. A second later, Hellburners, lasers, and antimatter torpedoes ripped into it. Nelly let the film run while we were still winning, but cut it off before our own battleships began to blow up in the background.

She switched to the cold, dead hulk tumbling in space as it had appeared to the Alwan delegation.

"This sight Alwans have seen with their eyes. Alwans can say that what you see here is true. This is a sight no one can say is not true."

Kris paused to let that sink in. Granny said the Alwans almost never went back to a feast but left the remains for others to scavenge. Kris needed to explain why she went back to the battle. "We went to see this so that we could learn about those who are so empty of right thinking as to ignore feathers and crow but instead try to drink blood of The People and Heavy People. To know your enemy is to have them half-defeated."

THAT WON'T TRANSLATE, Nelly said.

IT'S BEYOND ME, TOO, Granny Rita said.

THEY ARE JUST GOING TO HAVE TO LEARN SOME NEW WORDS, Kris said.

Kris took another deep breath and went on. "While eyes from the Association of Associations went to see how I and my people had displayed our feathers, strutted our walk, and crowed, more drinkers of blood came to scavenge from the wreck what they could use to pick our bones clean."

Nelly continued her translation, as she showed three ships from the perspective of the wreck. Straight Tongue and the camera operator made the sound Kris took for a gasp.

"By your custom, we crowed to them."

Nelly ran the short-lived warning message their decoy had sent and showed the three ships shooting the decoy out of space.

"Because they would not submit to our display, I wrung the necks of all three starships of the blood drinkers." In quick succession, Nelly ran pictures of all three blowing up. From the video it looked a whole lot easier than it had been.

"Now The People and The Heavy People must choose a path to walk. Do we move now to wring the necks of the blood drinkers or do we surrender, stand in a line for them to wring our necks? I am a war leader. I pick the bones of those who would strip the flesh of my people. That is my path. What is your path?"

Kris stared with hard determination into the camera as Nelly finished translating. Behind Kris, on the screen, ship after ship once again blew up. First the base ship, then each of the three ships that had attacked them yesterday. The destruction flashed over and over again until the producer chirped something that must have meant cut, and the camera stopped.

The producer said something to Straight Tongue.

SHE'S ASKING HIM IF HE HAS ANY WORDS TO ADD TO THIS THAT THEY SHOULD RECORD. HE'S SAYING THAT HE IS

SPEECHLESS, AND THEY CAN LET HIS SILENCE AS THE SHIPS
WERE HUNTED BEHIND HIM SPEAK FOR HIM.

The three reporters didn't say a thing as they gathered up
their gear. Two smartly dressed and armed Marines waited at
the door of the interview room and led them off to their return
flight.

The camera operator eyed the Marines and their guns, and
started his camera rolling again, capturing the way the
Marines moved both gracefully and with purpose in zero gee.

"I think we have just given the Association of Associations,
and flocks of other Alwans, a whole lot to think about,"
Granny said.

"Now, Kris, Jack, you've shown me your setup. It's only
fair for me to show you mine. I should think with three more
ships vanishing without a trace, any alien riffraff would take
some time off to look at their hole cards, if they have any.
From the look of all the data Nelly captured for the boffins, I'd
guess they're going to be busy for a day or twelve. Come, let
me show you what my people have done."

8

Kris checked with Captain Drago. He insisted he had everything under control and all but shooed Kris off his bridge. Besides, with the *Wasp* in microgravity, he needed to rotate his crew dirtside to avoid muscle loss. It would be best if Kris checked the lay of the land, assured there was a good supply of beer, and looked into the local attitude toward Sailors who might get a bit rowdy with the opposite sex. And it wouldn't just be the local womenfolk who had to worry. The *Wasp*'s crew was forty-three percent women, who would be checking out the local menfolk.

Kris asked the skipper to duck into his in-space cabin for a brief consult. "Any suggestion about what we do if a hostile ship jumps into the system?" she asked when they were alone.

"If there's just one of them, I'll recall the crew, and we'll fight it out, maybe put Alwa's moon to good use. Two, I guess we could give it a try if you said so. Three or more, Your Highness, and I strongly suggest we run. Maybe they'll chase us and leave the folks dirtside alone. This frigate is a dandy craft, Kris, but there's a limit to what we can do."

Kris sighed. "That was pretty much what I figured, but I wanted to hear it from you."

"We've got buoys on the far side of both of the jumps into

this system. We will not be surprised. Go ashore, Princess, and try, for once, to have fun."

Thus Kris and Jack, Abby and Cara, and a platoon of Marines that just happened to include Sergeant Bruce, headed for the planet below. Penny asked to be included, along with a Musashi lieutenant who was working closely with her on intel. Amanda Kutter wanted to start working on her study of the Alwan economy and asked that Dr. Jacques la Duke join her. His area of study was anthropology, and she strongly suggested that their work would go hand in hand.

That the two of them were hand in hand drew a grin from Granny Rita. HAVE I TOLD YOU FOLKS I ALSO DO WEDDINGS?

GRANNY, BEHAVE YOURSELF.

I AM, DAUGHTER, YOU'RE THE ONE WITH A SHARP STICK UP YOUR BUTT.

Kris decided respect for Granny's age required she let her have the last word. Several more boffins, mostly biologists but also sociologists and geologists, added themselves to the longboat.

Kris had met Granny Rita when she arrived on the *Wasp*. She'd looked much the worse for the ride up and Kris had rushed the old gal to sick bay. There the docs had fussed over her and started her on a cocktail of antiaging meds, all the *Wasp* had to offer. Granny looked better. Now Kris suggested she drop in a tank to ease the gees.

Granny refused. "I will not arrive back home in my birthday suit. I might get too many proposals for my old heart to survive."

So Kris talked with the bosun in charge of the longboat, and the trip down took a bit longer but stayed lower on the gee meter. Even with that, Granny was sweating when they completed reentry and settled into normal flight.

"That was easier than the ride up, but you're right. Space is a young person's game," Granny admitted, taking a swig from Sergeant Bruce's offered canteen.

Then a monitor in the forward end of the cabin lit up. "Hey, that's my planet," Granny crowed.

"Most Alwans like the wooded areas," she said in full lecture mode. "They no longer nest in the trees, but they like lots of trees around their houses and usually leave them open to the air, at least in the temperate zones. They plant crops, but you'd never recognize them as farms. Mostly they tend to hunt and graze, so they don't have large population centers. I don't know how they avoid overpopulation. That's one of those questions we don't ask, and they don't tell.

"There, have the camera stay on that viaduct," Granny ordered, and Nelly did. "That was the first project we worked on together with the Alwans. They'd never thought of bringing water to dry land. Our colony was growing, and we needed to put more land under the plow. We found a quarry and we all got together, cut the rocks, and used log rollers to get them where we needed. They'd never seen any of the engineering tricks we used to build the viaduct. We told them this was old stuff. Things we'd been doing for three, four thousand years.

"They didn't believe we could know what had happened that long ago. That was when we showed them some books, personal tablets, and readers. That sent them into a tizzy and got me a visit from a delegation from the Association of Associations.

"We spent a good month explaining to them what we humans could do and explaining how we did it. Then the lead elder did a formal dance, feathers flying, and put the kibosh on us using most of our technology.

"Of course, the same time I was having my ears talked off by the delegation, we were also getting visits from the folks that I think, if they'd given them half a chance, would have been their engineers and scientists. While I palavered with the delegation of old farts, my first husband this side, the *Enterprise*'s chief engineering officer, learned a lot from the other folks and vice versa.

"That's the way it's been for eighty years. Some of their people attend our schools. We make sure our kids get the best education we can. It's getting harder as more and more of the electronic devices give up the ghost, but we've invented paper and printing presses, and some of the Alwans have adopted our alphabet to their language and are reading their own books. All nonfiction, I might add."

Granny might have gone on, talking their ears off, but the shuttle was coming up on the large lake that had been chosen for Haven, the first human town on Alwa.

"Ain't she lovely," Granny said. "We made it of adobe

bricks and fired red tile for the roofs. Plenty of trees for shade. Wonderful in the cool of the evening. It's home."

The longboat settled onto the lake with spray and a wake that set the pulling boats and sailboats out on it to bobbing. "I bet there's some cussing going on," Granny said with a grin. "We haven't had landers for a month of Sundays. Make that a century of 'em."

Rather than accept the tow offered by a boat with twelve strong men at the oars, the bosun used the auxiliary motor to maneuver toward a long dock.

"Are there many water weeds?" the bosun called on the ship's PA system. Right, Kris grinned, this was the poor fellow who had stranded her on Kaskatos when he sucked weeds into his reaction-tank intake. He wouldn't make that mistake again.

"Some along the shore, but I don't remember any in the middle of the lake. Not back when I could still swim out here."

"We'll draw reaction mass out here, if you don't mind," came from the flight deck.

The dock was a substantial affair. Waiting on it was an electric-powered jitney with a half dozen seats that two people could share if they were friendly. Kris, her team, and the scientists filled it up. The driver dismounted and offered the wheel to Granny Rita and started hoofing it back to wherever he'd come from.

Baggage was light. Even Abby had only brought one steamer trunk. The Marines formed up and prepared to march wherever it was they'd be barracked.

Except for the two who took the seat behind Kris when Jack gave them a curt nod.

"Jack, for once I'm on a planet where nobody knows me. I'm safe."

"You just went on planetwide television and bragged that you were our war leader. Commodore Rita, tell me honestly, are there *never* any murders: Alwa on Alwa, human on human, or, God forbid, Alwa on human."

"We do have the occasional aberration. The Alwans carry out capital punishment in a most bloody and attention-getting way. And it's been televised since they adopted that technology from us."

"I rest my case," Jack said, arms folded across his chest, "You don't go anywhere without me, and I don't go anywhere without at least two Marines, one of them female."

Granny was in the jitney's driver seat. Kris and Jack were snuggled in close beside her. With everyone aboard, she put it in gear, without letting the conversation lag.

"He won't even let you pee by yourself."

"Well, Granny, there was this one time on New Eden where they did their best to kill me in the ladies' room," Kris had to admit.

"I remember this one time when Trouble got taken by slavers in the men's room. Embarrassed the hell out of him. Do you know Trouble, a Marine when last I saw him?"

"I have the questionable honor of having Great-grampa Trouble as a relative."

"How in God's name did that happen? I mean him live long enough to have a kid?"

"His first daughter married your little Alex."

"They did? Good God, what a match that must have been. How are they doing?"

"She died in a car accident shortly after my dad was born."

"Accident?" Granny asked suspiciously.

"My personal guess is that there was Peterwald money behind it, but the truck driver died of a heart attack a week after the accident, before the investigation was even close to done."

"Peterwalds and Longknifes. Is that feud still going?"

Kris sighed, wondering how much to say. "Let's make a long story short by just saying that King Raymond I and Emperor Henry I are not at war. At least not when I last heard."

"There are advantages to being all the hell and gone on the other side of the galaxy. Thanks for dropping in. You're helping me remember why I so enjoy it here."

The jitney moved quietly and at a pace the Marines marching behind it had no trouble keeping up with. There was little traffic. A few other electric rigs shared the road with wagons pulled by beasts only slightly smaller than a house. Admittedly a small house, but still, Kris would not want to get into an argument with them over right of way.

However, they moved along quite docilely.

"Who or what are those?" Jack asked, apparently confident the answer to that question fell under the purview of his responsibility for Kris's safety.

"We call them oxen," Granny said. "They are the closest things we've got to beasts of burden. The Alwans raised them for food. An entire flock of them might throw a celebration and eat an entire one. Live. Or live when they start. They think it's great fun to race after the thing and strip a nice steak-size chunk off it with their beak."

That brought silence in the jitney for a long moment.

"So they're a bit more bloodthirsty than they've let on," Penny said.

"Where prey animals are concerned, yes. Among themselves, they are the most courteous, kind, and gentle people you could ever ask to meet."

"So I keep being told," Jack muttered.

"Amanda, Jacques," Kris called back. "I think your work is going to be more important than we thought. It's just a guess, but I'll bet that back in their past, Alwans were a lot harder on each other."

"That is a good supposition," Jacques said. "They developed all this ritual display as a way to settle things without bloodshed. The flock that did it first would cut down on their internal losses and be stronger against the outsider. It makes sense from an evolutionary perspective."

"You two check it out and try to find out how close to the surface the old ways are. Amanda, do you and Nelly plan on passing vocabulary back and forth between you to grow Nelly's dictionary?"

"Yes, every night," Amanda said.

"How about adding a short report on anything you've learned?" Kris said.

"That's red with blood?" Jacques asked.

"Or even hints of it," Jack said.

"Mais oui, mon Capitaine," Jacques said with an informal salute.

"Penny?" Kris said.

"Read you loud and clear. Iizuka Masao and I will keep our eyes peeled for the snake in this paradise."

"Kids, I can understand where you're coming from, living with all the politics of humans. Remember, I survived the Unity War. I used my pregnancy with little Alex to help get Ray through security so he could kill himself and President Urm. Thank God it didn't go down that way. Trust me, I've lived with these folks for eighty years, and you don't have anything to worry about."

"I think the folks on Santa Maria lived in harmony with the planet three hundred years before the all-controlling computer noticed them. If Ray and his former Marines hadn't stumbled on them at the same time . . ." Penny let the oft-told tale drift off.

Granny sighed. "And we do have the aliens out there hell-bent on killing us all. That's bound to ruffle a few feathers in the Associations. Not everyone is a ready-to-be-stuffed elder. Some of the newly chosen elders are surprisingly young and open to thinking outside their tried-and-true ways. Okay, okay, kids. You do what you do best. Just be sure to copy me on any reports you send to Kris or Jack. I may have a perfectly logical explanation for what you think is a bloody red hand."

"Offer accepted," came from a half dozen human voices.

The two Marines maintained a stoic silence . . . and a watchful vigilance.

9

They came to a halt in front of a two-story adobe building surrounded by a wide, red-tiled veranda and a grove of trees.

"This is Government House," Granny Rita said. "I do not live here despite the opinions of both of my late husbands. They have let me maintain an office, however. I must admit, though, that of late, before those nice pills you gave me, I was feeling kind of puny and not raising nearly the hell that I had been accused of."

She grinned broadly, "I am so looking forward to getting back to normal."

A delegation of a dozen humans and five Alwans filled the veranda. One middle-aged woman stepped forward and offered Kris her hand. "Please tell me that you haven't turned back the clock for Rita. I can't tell you how hard we've worked to run it down."

"Kris, this is Ada, my best friend and constantly disgruntled coworker. She's the new official chief cook and bottle washer. If you need anything, and I'm in the head, ask her for it."

"I'm the *elected* Chief of Ministries," Ada corrected. "Everyone except Rita treats me like I'm the boss," she said with a sour grin that edged up around the ends as she let go of Kris's hand.

"It sounds like your chain of command is as much a Gordian knot as mine," Kris said.

"I don't quite get your meaning, but our org charts look very logical and methodical," Ada insisted.

"No they aren't. They don't have any place for me on them," Granny Rita grouched.

"Hi, I'm Iago," said a thin, young man with blond hair. "My job is to coordinate with Rita. Trust me, it's a full-time job."

"I find that easy to believe," Kris said. "I know I'm going to end up meeting all of you, but I've got some working folks here who are eager to get working. Amanda Kutter specializes in strange economic systems. She's quite interested in what you developed and how it interfaces with the Alwans." Kris knew she'd given only half of the young economist's subject of study, but something told her she needed to pull her punches.

Amanda stepped forward, all smiles, and said not a word in disagreement.

Ada turned to a young woman. "Baozhai, you're the closest thing we have to someone who handles the economy, or what we have of one. She kind of collects taxes and figures out ways for us to pay for the common things, roads, bridges, and the like."

"I wrestle people into donations and volunteering, you mean," the woman said.

"Just people?" Kris asked.

"If I can persuade the Alwans there's something in it for them, I get them."

"That television camera that they used to interview me didn't look like something volunteers knocked together," Kris led carefully.

"Oh, then you also want Kuno," Baozhai said. "He's coordinator of Mining and Industry. He's the one that works real close with the Alwans. Until recently, they've been death on anything like heavy industry or intrusive mineral extraction."

"Yeah, I'm glad their attitude is changing," Kuno, a tall, middle-aged man said as he took up the story, "because about all the nano miners we knocked together eighty years ago for low-impact leaching of metals are gone. You don't happen to have more mining nanos with you, do you? It would make my job a whole lot easier."

"I'll have that checked on," Kris said.

YOU NOT GOING TO TELL THEM ABOUT ME, KRIS?

NO, NELLY, FROM NOW ON YOU'RE MY TOP SECRET. IF GRANNY GIVES YOU AWAY, OKAY, BUT OTHERWISE, IT'S NOT HAPPENING.

AYE, AYE, YOUR TYRANTSHIP.

The gaggle of folks began to break up enough so that Kris's team could circulate freely among them. Amanda and Jacques added to their circle of friends an Alwan who was something like Watcher of Wisdom and Traditions of the People. Penny and Masao latched onto Anyang, the Coordinator for Public Peace, as well as an Alwan who was styled something like Bringer of Harmony between The People and the Heavy People. Masao got to talking to the human who was the Historian of the Colony, and the Alwan Watcher of Wisdom. Through it all, Penny and Masao managed to not quite lose bodily contact in one way or another.

"I got to talk to those folks about scheduling a wedding," Granny Rita whispered to Kris.

"Granny, it's the modern age. Holding hands and even sharing beds does not mean a wedding has to be scheduled. We don't have shotgun weddings anymore."

"Honey, I told my great-granny the same thing, and she laughed and told me that she'd said the very same thing to her great-granny. You ask any bunch of kids, and they'll swear to you that they're the first generation to discover sex. And insist their parents never, ever had sex themselves."

"Well, Granny, there are the fraternization rules."

"Yes, that's something I keep meaning to talk to you about. But correct me if these old eyes are totally shot, but isn't that couple in civilian clothes?" she said, nodding at Amanda and Jacques.

"Yes," Kris agreed.

"Now that other lass, Penny you call her. The guy who can't take his eyes off her and vice versa are in uniform, but his ain't quite the same as hers, is it?"

"He's Musashi Navy. That's where the *Wasp* fitted out. We didn't become the USS *Wasp* until a bit later. Long story. We've got Sailors and Marines from Musashi and Wardhaven, contract personnel and civilian scientists aboard the *Wasp*, and a couple of restaurateurs subcontracted to the main contractor."

"Child, how did you get yourself into a command structure like that?"

"Trust me, Granny, she had to work hard to do it," Jack cut in.

"And where do you fit into this lash-up, if you think my old brain can follow it?" she asked Jack.

"I was Kris's Secret Service Agent," Jack started. "Grampa Trouble suggested Kris draft me into the Marines so I might provide for her safety when she was off planet."

"Trouble, you say?"

"Yes, Granny," Kris said, eyes sadly downcast, "I have learned that Trouble means Trouble even if he is my nice old grampa."

"I warned her," Nelly whispered, "but would she listen to me?"

QUIET, NELLY.

Jack continued. "As you may have noticed, she outranks me, and is a princess and all that. However, by law, I can countermand any order she gives that, in my opinion, could lead her into bodily harm."

"And his opinion of what could hurt me is huge. Just huge."

"This has the smell of Raymond wanting to make up for some of the more stupid things he did as a JO," Granny said.

"Eighty years away from him, and you still can peg him on one," Kris said.

Granny looked around. "Everybody looks awful busy. Let's take a walk out among the trees."

Kris checked around; all her team were busy. Even Abby and Sergeant Bruce had cornered a mixed trio of humans and Alwans and were deep in some conversation, helped along by Nelly's kids using the translating app. In fact, a check of the group showed Nelly's translation app was going over like the best thing since sliced bread.

No one seemed to need Kris Longknife for the moment.

Granny was already leading Jack down a shady path. Kris hurried to catch up and got there just as Granny fixed the two of them, and asked, "So, are you two sleeping together?"

"Granny, what kind of question is that?" Kris answered, doing her best not to blush. Still, she felt her face go warm.

Jack just looked at Kris. Clearly, whether or not the question was answered was her decision.

"Honey, I'm old enough to ask the tough questions, and I'm experienced enough to know they need answering. I take it from your dodge that you and Jack have experienced each other's company to the fullest. And from the red on your face, you thoroughly enjoyed it."

Since Granny was doing such a good job of answering her own questions, Kris figured there was no need to risk either a lie or the truth.

Granny turned to Jack. "So, may I ask what your intentions are toward my great-granddaughter?"

Jack didn't even flinch. "She's already told me in the presence of her brother that I'm going to marry her." He also failed to suppress a canary-ate-the-cat grin. "Ah, at least she will just as soon as things calm down, we can arrange things properly, and figure out how to avoid breaking the Navy reg on fraternization."

"Wow, that's a long list of requirements, none of which have anything to do with how much either of you love each other."

Kris found herself eyeing the ground. "My brother, he's a member of Parliament, offered to marry us the very evening that I proposed to Jack."

"But it fell through when he chickened out," Jack scowled. "You see, he has to share a planet with Kris's mom, and if she was thwarted at arranging every little thing of Kris's wedding, he figured he couldn't go home."

"Hmm. I see your problems. But it looks to me like they're all on the other side of the galaxy. Nice things about that, I can tell you."

"Granny, we're still in uniform, and Navy regs apply. Very likely in this galaxy and the next thirty over as well," Kris pointed out.

"No doubt you're right about that," Granny agreed. "I had

to officially demob and decommission all the survivors before
we could formally declare ourselves a colony and make our
own rules. I was delighted to do myself out of the job of running the *Furious*, and the damn fools immediately elected me
chief cook and bottle washer. Served them right that I've been
a pain in their asses every day since."

Granny found a stone bench and settled on it. Kris took the
other end, and Jack settled cross-legged on the grass opposite
them.

"So, tell your old granny about this fraternization reg.
How's it changed since my day?"

"I don't think it has," Kris said. "No officer can date an
enlisted. No senior can date any junior."

"No, Kris," Jack corrected her. "No officer can date anyone
more than two ranks down. Same for EMs."

"You've been reading up, huh, son?" Granny said.

Jack just shrugged.

"But the big no-no is that you can't date anyone in your
chain of command," Kris added.

"Ah, yes." Granny sighed. "I remember that one. There I
was, running my own battlecruiser squadron and married to
the big Kahuna himself. They told me I was grandfathered in.
I told them I was too young to be grand*mothered* into anything. But there was a war on, and they needed fighting captains and I had a reputation for doing the dirtiest jobs and
bringing the most ships back. It was none of my doing, I just
had the best damn bunch of gals in space. At least a whole lot
more of my crew were gals, and we had something to prove to
the boys' club. There still a boys' club?"

Neither Kris not Jack offered a comment on that.

"Some things never change," the old woman said, raising
her gaze to watch the wind ruffle the leaves above her.

"Enough of bitching about things that need changing but
ain't never gonna happen. Tell me about your situation, Jack."

"I command Kris's security detail," he stated simply.

"And can lock her in her room if you think it'll keep her
safe," Granny said with a wide grin.

"I have never done that," Jack insisted.

"But you've wanted to," Kris said.

"Why not? You've done some damn fool stunts. Like running out on your security team and getting bombed."

"I've apologized for that," Kris said.

"And getting us shot down on that no-name planet."

"But I saved your precious Marines from flying into a trap."

"Yes, I know."

"So, not to cut in," Granny said, cutting in, "but I take it you two have had a lot of fun disagreeing on just about everything. You ever had much time to talk, I don't know, say, about how you feel about each other?"

"A few times," both said at once.

"Ever over a candlelit dinner?" Granny asked.

"No," again came from both of them.

Granny frowned. "When I was on your ship, Kris, I kept hearing about Captain Drago. Is he a Marine like Captain Jack here?"

"I thought I explained him to you," Kris said.

"Maybe you did, but once you're past eighty, you tend to forget important things."

In a pig's eye, Kris thought, but she answered like a dutiful great-granddaughter. "He's the captain of the *Wasp*. Both this one and the previous one. He retired from the Navy after being selected for rear admiral and was hired by Wardhaven Intelligence to run my ship for me. Besides the hundred or more scientists I insisted on having aboard, he ran the ship with a contract crew, and for most of the last three years, there were only a few Navy types on the *Wasp*. Just me, Jack, Penny, and Chief Beni, God rest his soul. Then Grampa Ray, ah King Raymond to most, thought I was getting into too much trouble and Jack got a platoon, then a company, then a reinforced company of Marines."

"Was it enough to protect her?" Granny said through a grin.

"Not even close," Jack said.

Kris soldiered on. "And the ship's company took on more and more Sailors as well."

"How'd the mix of overpaid contractors and real Sailors work?" Granny asked.

"Not too badly. When we got into the fight with the base ship, Captain Drago brought me papers activating all their reserve commissions and enlistments. Every contractor on board was on the retired list. As he said, if they were going into a real fight, they wanted their honest uniforms on."

"I bet that was something special for you," Granny said.

"I'll never be able to put it into words," Kris said, eyes maybe misting a bit.

Granny let the trees whisper quietly for nearly a minute before she suddenly turned to Jack, and said, "So, Jack, who did you report to?"

"The ship's table of organization says Captain Drago is my boss. Even after we got big enough to have an XO, I still reported to the skipper."

"He do your performance evaluation?"

"I guess he would have if he ever did. We never had a sit-down on my performance, but I kept getting 4.0 ratings back from I never knew where."

"Did Kris sign them?"

"I don't think so," Jack said, thoughtfully. "Sal, can you bring up a copy of the latest?" A moment later the standard four-page evaluation was projected onto the dirt in front of them. The first signature on the form was some general at headquarters. The last endorsement was Field Marshal McMorrison.

"Holy cow, I've been working at that level and never even bothered to find out."

"Interesting," Kris said.

"Very interesting," Granny said. "Kris, what's your position in the great chain of command?"

Kris took a second to think about it. "I don't know how many times I've joked that my chain of command was tied up in macramé knots. Nelly, doesn't Captain Drago have a ship's table of organization on the wall in his in-port cabin?"

"Yes, Kris. I have a copy. Here it is."

In the dirt between them now, a chart appeared. At the top of it was a box marked THE CAPTAIN with Drago's name under it. Below, led to by solid black lines were the Division Officers, including the Marine Detachment.

"This must be before the crew was augmented and we got an XO and a command master chief," Kris said.

"But Kris, I notice your name in a box off to the right side of the captain's box. Is that a dotted line between the two of you? It looks like your box is dotted, too."

"Yes, I think that was Grampa Ray's idea. Let me give Drago my best advice, but if he didn't like it, he was to provide what I jokingly called 'adult supervision,' and set me straight."

"He never did," Jack said, and there was pride in his voice and a vision of her reflected in his eyes that Kris only wished she could live up to.

She sent a kiss in his direction. He sent one right back.

"So, all this time, Kris, it looks to this old ship driver and commodore that you and Jack have never been in the same chain of command."

Kris liked where Granny was leading, but she knew it wasn't true. "For the last year or so, I've commanded PatRon 10. We took down some pirates. Went exploring the galaxy, blew the hell out of the alien base ship, and got wiped out. I watched two of my ships take on horrible odds, beat them for longer than the law of averages would allow, then be blown to bits. The *Hornet* went one way so the *Wasp* could go another. We never heard from the *Hornet* again, and the *Wasp* dragged herself into the first human port it could make, and they broke her up in place. As ComPatRon 10, Drago was under my command, and Jack was under his."

"It doesn't sound to me like there's much of your command left. You still ComPatRon 10?" Granny asked.

Jack had the decency to chuckle dryly.

"Nope. Doesn't exist. Not even the *Wasp*'s logs, as I understand it. My lawyer tried to get them, but the Navy insisted they had no logs from the Voyage of Discovery. The last job I have official orders for was in East Siberia. ComFastAttackRon 127. I think the leave I approved for myself has run out, so I'm AWOL from that job. Jack was sent to West Siberia, security on HellFrozeOver. I think his leave has run out, too."

"No doubt about it," Jack said with no contrition at all.

"They still have a base on HellFrozeOver?" Granny asked.

"Yes, and I have the frostbite to prove it," Jack said.

Granny mulled that over for a few seconds. "But you're both out here on another *Wasp*. How'd that happen?" Granny asked.

"It's a long story involving Musashi children holding bake sales and donating their pennies to buy me a ship, and my not being found guilty of crimes against humanity."

"But not innocent either," Jack put in.

Kris went on. "Your darling little Alex, my grandfather Al, seemed hell-bent on sending out a trade fleet to make contact with the aliens and negotiate trade agreements."

"I guess I did raise a dumb child. In my defense, I will point out, I've been on the other side of the galaxy during his formative years and all the rest of them."

"Anyway, the *Wasp* managed to intercept and stop that dumb idea. Somehow. Captain Drago ended up back as contract skipper to the new *Wasp*. I'm back doing the princess thing, handling delicate political issues. Oh, and when the need arises to kill people, I have Nelly lock the crosshairs on the target, and I close the firing circuit."

She gave Jack a forlorn look. He tried to give her a grin in return, but it was a weak one. "Other than that, I twiddle my thumbs and while away my time."

"Honey, don't kid a kidder. I saw the full show about how you had battleships running away from that monster, distracting it while your tiny corvettes got in their superpunches with those, what do you call them, Hellfires?"

"Hellburners," Jack corrected.

"Ship wreckers," Granny said.

She took a deep breath. "Okay, nobody asked me for my opinion, but you two are going to get it with both barrels. Captain Drago has the *Wasp* up there in orbit. I understand he's going to be sending the crew down in stages to make sure they stay healthy."

Kris did not ask her granny how she found that out, but said nothing.

"Your crew needs a break. You two need a break. If something goes all tits over ass, you'll have some warning. I saw you deploying buoys at the jump points. Right?"

"Yes," Kris agreed.

"The two of you are a couple of million words short of knowing how you feel about each other. Have you ever taken some time for each other?"

"Well, there were a couple of days while we were on the

lam from the cops." Kris coughed with ladylike delicacy. "That would be when we finally got to enjoy each other's company."

"You were busy staying one step ahead of the law!" Granny said.

"And planning how to break into the high-security tower your son Alex had built to keep him safe from anything," Jack added.

"That must have left a lot of time for whispering sweet little nothings in each of your ears."

Both Kris and Jack shrugged.

"Okay, has your granny got a deal for you," Granny Rita said. "You two are taking a vacation. A two-week vacation."

"I can't do that!" Kris said.

"How come?" Granny shot back.

"I've got to get the reports from the boffins on what they find out about the ship. I want to know about the DNA from the one boot they found. It will tell me if this is a new bunch or more of the same that we've met before. There's lots of stuff."

"I get it," Granny said dryly. "You're irreplaceable. Nelly, will you get those reports?"

"Yes, Granny."

"And will you be able to show them to Kris?"

"You bet I can. I do it all the time."

"And how long would it take you to get a message from Captain Drago?"

"We've deployed the communication satellites in synchronous orbit. Delay can't be more than two seconds," Nelly tattled.

"Kris, there is no reason why you and Jack can't take some time for yourselves . . . other than that you're afraid of what you might find out," Granny said. "Sometimes the human heart is the most terrifying thing in the world to face. I know. I've blown up ships and sent others to die in my place, and the three scariest times in my life were when I faced, really faced the men in my life that I loved."

She paused for a second. "Did how I persuaded Ray Longknife to marry me make it into the history books?"

Kris thought for a moment, then shook her head.

"Ray had been to the war, and I'd personally flown the transport that held, long after the recall, so they could drag his sorry ass aboard. His back was broken. Some said he'd never walk. Some said he was dead from the waist down. The man who had loved me told me to walk away. Get out of his life."

"What did you do?" Kris whispered.

"It was in the back gardens at Nuu House. Do they still have gardens there?"

"The most lovely," Kris said.

"Do you know that there are no security cameras in one section?"

Kris shook her head; it was news to her.

"I paid off the guy who installed the security system to make sure I had one place I could take a boyfriend and not worry about being watched. I took Ray there one afternoon when the docs said he was healing, or should have been healing, but he wasn't. He wasn't *letting* himself heal. He didn't believe he could. My war hero was afraid to try and fail."

Granny was watching the wind in the trees again, far across the galaxy and years.

"I stood over him. Then slowly took my dress off and showed him that he wasn't dead below the waist. I won, but dear God was I scared the whole time. Likely, little Alex was conceived that day. I was scared. So scared. I still don't know how I did it."

Granny paused, took a deep breath, and seemed to come back to her body.

"Okay. Now you know more about your family tree than you ever wanted to know. But I ask you again. There's this little beach resort. I know the owner. I'm sure I can get the two of you a place for two weeks. He offers candlelit dinners and a small dance floor. The beach is sandy and white, and the water is so clear, you can go snorkeling and see the bottom twenty meters down. Oh, and it's small, only twenty cottages. If I say the word, I can guarantee you that there won't be anyone else from the *Wasp* staying there while you are."

"Granny Rita, you're a tyrant."

"And I have the signed certificates on my wall to prove it. Some in blood. So, do I win this one?"

Kris looked at Jack. He gave her a tight little smile in

return, but there was also a slight nod to his head, a lowering of his eyelids.

"Make the call, Granny. We'll stay for two weeks or until Captain Drago announces all hell's broken loose, whichever comes first."

"Good girl!" Granny said with joy in her voice. Then she sobered. "And good luck to the both of you. I know. You'll need it."

10

Kris sat on the bed. It wasn't too soft or too firm. From the feel of it and the pillow, it must be made out of down. Apparently there were prey birds; she'd caught glimpses of a few flying birds on the drive out.

The owner himself was showing her and Jack the room. It was spacious. There were no glass windows. Instead, most of the room was open to a softly blowing breeze. The owner showed them how to shutter them if the weather changed. "But you won't likely need to do it when the duty shower comes over about three o'clock."

He was too young to be one of the original crew but likely the son of one. His language was sprinkled every once in a while with Navy. "There are two closets, one for him and one for her. Feel free to use any of the clothes there. We've washed them since the last couple used them." He listed the times for meals but promised if they missed chow, there was usually someone to slap together a sandwich for anyone hungry. "And we have snorkel gear and boats for anyone who wants them. Sailboats. Rowboats. Maybe now that you're here, we can get back into the powerboat business. Haven't seen a powerboat since I was knee high. Anyway, I'm glad I could do Granny

Rita a favor, and I want to personally thank you for what you did, saving all our necks."

"Thank you, sir," Kris said.

Without any further encouragement, the fellow left, leaving Kris and Jack alone. Kris stayed seated on the bed. Should she and Jack put it to use immediately?

Kris found herself surprised on how unsure she was. Shy even.

Jack kicked off his shoes, saying, "Follow me," and headed out to the beach. He walked the full distance down to the water. It was low tide, so that was quite a walk.

Leaving Kris to wonder what was going through his mind.

She was a woman; the owner had piqued her interest about clothes. She checked out the closet with a skimpy two-piece swimsuit painted on it. There was a big, colorful muumuu. There were several pairs of shorts and tank tops from nice to so skimpy Mother would never have let Kris out of the house in them, even in college. Not that Mother knew all that much what Kris wore in college since she and Father had moved into Government House.

Even with the house to herself, Kris kept to Mother's standards. It wouldn't help Father's next election to have a photo of his daughter dressed inappropriately.

Hey, baby ducks, Kris could almost hear Abby saying, *remember, other side of the galaxy.*

The swimsuits went from skimpy to Oh My God bits of string and not much else. What had the sign said at the restaurant? TOTAL NUDITY NOT ALLOWED.

Kris eyed her closet and wondered where "Total Nudity" ended or began.

She grabbed the muumuu and stepped into the bathroom to change. She had the cottage to herself, but she really was feeling shy. What if Jack returned when she was only half-dressed?

The bathroom was nice. A large tub, clearly intended for two. The shower seemed fully open to the outside, but no, when she looked closer, she spotted shutters.

They didn't look like they'd been closed for a while.

Dressed in a muumuu and nothing else, she followed Jack

to the shore. He seemed so intensely focused on the ocean, Kris was almost afraid to disturb him, but she put a hand on his back and began to gently rub it.

"Thank you," Jack said. "That feels good."

"I'm glad then. A penny for your thoughts?" she said.

It took him a while to answer. When he did, he surprised Kris. "I love the ocean, and it scares me."

Kris owed Jack a whole lot more than a penny for that. Never in her life would she have guessed it. "You've got to explain that."

"I know you love sailing."

"It's some of my best memories as a kid. We quit sailing after Eddy died. The family did, but I could still get some of my friends to go out sailing. And yes, I loved the freedom of it."

"But you were sailing a lake. Did you ever sail so far out you couldn't see the shore?"

"The lake was too small for that."

"The ocean is a totally different matter. It's been here for billions of years, waves pounding on the shore, turning rocks to pebbles, and pebbles to sand. The ocean goes on forever."

"Yes," Kris said, aware of the geology lesson, but not at all sure what this meant to Jack.

"And it will go on for billions of years more after our bones have turned to dust."

"My, aren't you the pessimist. We could screw up, let the aliens take the planet, drain the oceans, then no more billion years."

"Now who's the pessimist? I wasn't thinking of the ocean going on after us as something pessimistic. I was thinking that our time is so short, we have to be fools to waste it."

"Oh," Kris said. She found that reply on the weak side. "Good point." she added, and felt like a bigger fool.

"You come here often?" she finally said, throwing in a smile and hoping he'd forgive her loss for words.

"To the beach, not nearly enough. Here, only once with the most beautiful girl I've ever met. Really spectacular girl, did I tell you? Not so great a conversationalist at times, but wow, can she blow up ships!"

"But can't open a can, cook spaghetti, or warm water," Kris

added, smiling as she enjoyed his choice of words. He saw a woman she could never believe existed.

He put his arm around her. Now it was him massaging her back. Just her back, nothing more.

"Can we sit down?" she asked.

"You're dressed for it. Do I really want to get my greens sandy? Will you stay here while I go change?"

"Make it quick. A Sailor might come along and ask me to show him a good time."

"You warn him that if he takes off with my girl, I will track him down and beat him to a pulp."

Kris considered several replies, and was leaning toward "Can I watch the fight?" when she thought better of it. "I'll warn him off and send him on his way, a sadder but wiser man."

"You do that," Jack shouted over his shoulder as he jogged for the cottage.

Kris sat down cross-legged. The damp sand quickly soaked through the thin material. She'd even left her spider silk behind. When she'd put them in a bureau drawer, she'd found no underwear.

Interesting.

She'd also taken a peek into Jack's closet. There were shorts, from long to scandalously short. Shirts from casual to hardly enough to keep the sun off. Swimsuits from indecent to "Oh My God, Why Bother?" and some colorful thin scarves that you could see right through. Lava-lava she thought they were called.

Kris sat patiently, eyes on the ocean, ever-changing, yet ever the same, waiting to see what Jack showed up in.

His shorts were long, and his shirt would not have been out of place in a casual bar back on Wardhaven. He settled down beside her, then winced. "The sand didn't look that wet."

"Ocean, Jack. It's been wet for, what did you say, billions of years?"

"Yes, but what am I going to wear to supper tonight? These were the only decent shorts in the closet."

"And this was the only muumuu in mine."

Jack looked sidewise at Kris. "You think your granny did more than just reserve us a cottage? You think she chose our wardrobe?"

"She was a Longknife. Long ago, admittedly."

"I'm sorry, Kris. I hope you won't take offense, but from where I sit in the cheap seats, once a Longknife, always a Longknife."

"Honey, you have not been sitting in the cheap seats. You've spent nearly as much time in the same room with my Grampa Ray as I have lately, and you're closer to him."

"That's so I can jump between you two if you ever come to blows."

"Whose side would you be on if it ever happened?" Kris asked. More than curious.

"Raymond is my king," Jack said. "But you are my girl."

Kris couldn't help but grin. Not "my primary," "my girl."

"You're the first guy to call me his girl in a long time."

"There was someone before me? Should I be jealous?"

"Nope, he was a dork. Just wanted to be able to say he'd scored on a Longknife, and I was foolish or lonely enough to let him get close to me. Mother had warned me about boys like that. I ignored or forgot the only good advice Mother ever gave me."

"I admit, I was jealous of that fellow on Chance. Mayor what's-his-name," Jack admitted.

Kris got pensive. "Yeah, that one had prospects. But he took one good look at what happens around a Longknife and beat feet for the exit." Kris sighed. "Like they all do."

They watched the ocean in silence for a long while.

"Why haven't you beat feet or married one of the other girls around me? Amanda Kutter, now, she's got to be the most beautiful girl a guy could ask for."

"She's not bad-looking," Jack admitted.

Kris elbowed him in the ribs.

"But she took the ticket home, remember? No way I was leaving your side with one hell of a battle coming up."

"But it was ship to ship. Nothing for your Marines to do."

"There was that mining concern Admiral Krätz wanted us to capture. Don't forget. You got yourself shot down trying to get a good look at it. Tell me you could have gotten that canopy open without my strong back."

"No, I could not have, and I'd likely have burned to death or been blown to bits when the antimatter containment went, or worse, been captured. You are so right, my wise and eternally vigilant security advisor."

"And my Marines would have been massacred when they flew into the trap the mining head had set for them."

Kris gave Jack a puzzled look. "I do dimly remember a wise and perpetually overaggressive young woman who has insisted on that point."

For several long, peaceful minutes, they enjoyed the ever-changing waves.

"We have saved each other's asses a few times, haven't we?" Kris said.

"And, if I may be permitted to say, and dredge up from memory, yours is a most beautiful ass."

"Yes, you may, kind sir," Kris said, "because if my dim and fading memory is right, yours is a most spectacular ass in its own right."

"But not as round and smooth as yours," Jack countered.

"But more muscled and hairy," Kris replied.

"My ass is not hairy. It has a fine down, maybe, but not hairy."

"Hairy as a monkey's," Kris insisted. "I know. I spent some wonderful time stroking it while you were sleeping."

"I wasn't sleeping, I was enjoying your touch. And it is not hairy as a monkey."

"It's your rear. You never look at it in the mirror."

As things were progressing, Kris half expected Jack to drop his shorts right there in front of her and twist himself into a pretzel to see his own rear. She found herself looking forward to where that might lead.

The dinner bell rang for supper.

Jack gave Kris a questioning raised eyebrow.

For all of five seconds, Kris considered her options. The problem was she hadn't eaten since breakfast on the *Wasp*, and her tummy was very empty, and while the thought of filling it from something other than food was getting more attractive by the moment, she doubted it would quiet the rumbling.

She offered Jack her hand up.

She enjoyed rubbing the sand off Jack's shorts while he dusted her behind with long and loving strokes.

She reconsidered how hungry she was, but her tummy rumbled again.

"I wonder what they mean by 'Total Nudity Not Allowed'?" Jack asked no one in particular.

"You are such a guy," Kris muttered.

"Don't tell me you won't be checking out the guys. I saw what was in my closet."

"Did you check out mine?"

"I have the right to remain silent because you are way too good at blowing up ships."

"Smart man. Educable. I should keep you."

"Besides, my commission is for the duration, and I think you just started a war that's going to have a very long duration."

"Promise me we aren't going to talk about that. Anything that happened before the Voyage of Discovery is fair game. My Granny Rita is fair game, but the bug-eyed monsters who look too damn much like us are out of bounds."

"I'm sorry, Kris. You shouldn't have had to tell me that. The stars are coming out. Aren't they lovely?" Jack said, changing the subject.

They walked to the restaurant, discussing stars. And they spotted their first songbird. Apparently it was a night creature, and it sang the most lovely song as it flitted among the trees. More birds, with different songs, joined in.

The walk became quite pleasant.

11

They arrived to discover they had the place to themselves. The owner who also acted as the receptionist gave them just a bit of an eye but then offered them their choice of seating.

They chose a quiet corner. They sat with their backs to the rest of the dining room and enjoyed a lovely view of the ocean. The moon was already coming up, huge and orange in the sea air.

While they savored the view, two more couples arrived. The guys were in shorts and shirts like Jack. The women were in muumuus. All showed wet from having sat on the sand. Kris and Jack shared smiles with each other, but the two couples settled in different quiet corners, so they didn't get to smile at them.

The waitress finally arrived; she wore a dress flowered like Kris's muumuu, but cut tight into a sheath to show off her curves. She offered them a choice of fish or fish. She named both types, but they meant nothing to Kris. For a moment, the three stared at each other. Then Jack led off.

"Is one of them white fish and the other dark fish?"

The waitress stared blankly and renamed the fish. Apparently, if you were from here, you knew your fish.

"Okay, this is what we'll do," Jack said. "I will take one of them. Please serve the lady the other." That satisfied the waitress, and she bounced off.

"Enjoying the view," Kris whispered.

"I'm wondering why they didn't provide one of those for your closet."

Kris started to say something about how she had nothing to fill out the top but swallowed it. Jack said so very many nice things about her. Why should she repeat all her negatives? Especially since he wouldn't agree with her. *The big liar.*

She changed the subject. "So what are we going to do if I hate the fish I get?"

"You will switch with me."

"And if you hate the fish I got?"

"I will be a gentleman and eat it so my lady can enjoy herself."

Kris considered that. Jack had an all-encompassing definition of chivalry. "And if I don't like either of them?"

"Don't be such a pessimist. We're surrounded by a lovely view. Notice how the moon is causing the waves to glow. We're not on duty. No one's trying to kill us. Have faith. We'll love both fish and end up feeding tidbits to each other from our plates."

Kris considered that. "Okay. You carrying?"

Jack scowled. "Yes. You?"

"Yes," Kris answered. "But I left the spider-silk bodysuit off when I put on the muumuu."

"So you and I are half on vacation."

"Well, that's more than I've been since college. Even there, most of my summer vacations were spent covering campaign gigs for Father."

"You enjoy them?"

"Usually."

"I loved my work at summer camps. I badly needed the money to help me through the school year. I enjoyed mountains, the hiking and fishing and the kids. Most of them."

"Let me guess, the rich, spoiled brats weren't in the 'most of them.'"

"Sadly yes, but let's not go there."

"Gladly. They were a pain in my butt, too. Trust me, the Great Billy Longknife, Man of the People, would not have one of his kids misbehaving in public or otherwise."

"But the other rich kids . . . ?" Jack left the question hanging.

Kris refused to rise to the bait. "So, you earned money summers to pay for college. What kind of college scholarship did you have? Let me guess. You're big. It could have been football."

Jack silently shook his head.

"You're tall and fast. Basketball?"

This time Jack grinned as he shook his head.

"Soccer? Father played soccer in college."

Again Jack shook his head, now grinning from ear to ear.

"Baseball? Boxing? Wrestling? Swimming?"

"I would have accepted a swimming scholarship if I'd been offered one."

"Okay, you win. I give up. After five years of you constantly at my elbow, telling me when and where I can pee, I don't know what sports scholarship you had in college."

"I do not tell you when you can go pee," Jack said.

"Scholarship? Scholarship? What scholarship?"

"Golfing," Jack said.

"Golfing!"

The conversation had to be put on hold. The owner dropped by their table to apologize for the delay in their meal. "I know we rang the dinner bell, and I know we promised you that you could eat from six on, but our guests are usually much later. Our chef only does two specials a night and we don't want them to be cold for our later guests, so, I'm afraid you are having to wait much longer than anyone would expect. Could I offer you some drinks on the house?"

Jack raised an eyebrow to Kris.

She took a deep breath. "As Granny Rita told you, we are unfamiliar with much of what you have to offer. I do not drink alcoholic beverages. Do you have tea or something like it?"

"We have several teas. Would you like yours cold or hot?"

"Cold," Kris said.

"Cold tea for me, too," Jack said.

The owner left to apologize to the other tables. He did touch base with the waitress, and two tall, cold teas arrived.

"Jack, you don't have to take this gentleman stuff to the max. I don't mind if you have a beer."

"I am having the most important conversation of my life

with the woman I most love in the galaxy. I'm drinking tea, so I'll have my wits about me."

"You'll need them," Kris said. "Golf. You said you played golf in college. There can't be a lot of money in golf scholarships."

"No, there isn't. But by my junior year, I was head of my class in criminology, and there was a bit of scholarship money for that, thanks to your father. Two small scholarships, odd jobs, I pieced it all together."

"You still haven't said why you chose golf," Kris insisted.

"How many men do you know with a football knee, or tennis elbow, which, I must say, can come from basketball or even swimming, not to mention baseball injuries? Besides, baseball was out of the question. I wanted to be a cop. Not a donut-gobbling cop but one of the best. Golf gave me a good eye. By my junior year, I was shooting match level with both pistol and rifle. Also, you do a lot of walking that is good for you but won't break anything."

Kris began to giggle. She had a hard time believing it, but apparently, Longknifes could giggle. The giggle caught hold, and she found she couldn't stop.

"What's so funny?" Jack asked. When the giggling showed no chance of letting up and allowing Kris to answer his question, he leaned back, not at all patiently.

Kris tried to stop and couldn't. "I'm trying," she got out through the giggles. "Really, I'm trying to stop."

Maybe Jack's glare got a bit more patient.

Kris couldn't remember ever having the giggles before in her life. If you'd asked her yesterday, she would have sworn she couldn't giggle. She tried taking a drink of water, thinking to drown her giggles.

Bad idea. The water went down the wrong way, and she traded giggling for choking.

"Honey, are you okay?" Now Jack showed real concern.

Kris stuffed her cloth napkin into her mouth. Now she had no air to giggle or cough.

The owner showed up at the table. "Is there anything wrong?"

Jack looked helpless for the first time since Kris met him.

Kris managed to gasp in a breath. She forced herself to hold it while shaking her head and waving the owner off.

Cautiously, she took a second, then a third breath.

"Honey, it was delightful to hear you laughing like that," Jack said, "but please don't do that again."

"Trust me, I won't."

For a long minute, Kris and Jack sat silently, her watching the eternal sea, now glowing with its own light. Him watching her, as she couldn't help but notice out of the corner of her eye.

"I really scared you?" she finally said.

"Bad as that damn crash, or that bomb. Imagine all the paperwork I'd have to fill out. And the ribbing I'd take. My primary drowned herself on a water glass."

"Don't make me laugh."

"Sorry, I couldn't help myself. That's the way we handle being pissing scared, remember? We crack jokes."

"Let's come up with another approach for our courtship."

"Courtship? Honestly?"

"Honestly, Jack. I love you. I don't know if I love you as much as you love me, but I sure don't want to get into a contest on the matter."

"Good idea. I don't think all the boffins on the *Wasp* could come up with a meter to measure love."

"Not even Tweedle Dee and Tweedle Dum?"

"Now who's cracking jokes?" Jack said.

"Good point. Okay, let's see if I can explain to you what I found so funny."

"You can stop anytime you feel the giggles coming on."

"Oh, I will," Kris said, and took in a large breath. "You chose golf, even though there was less money in it because it was the safest route to where you wanted to go."

"Yes."

"You were in training to be my security chief even before you entered college."

Jack looked at Kris in utter silence. Then snorted. "By God, you're right."

"You bet I am. You've been training yourself to look for and follow the safest path since when you were a teenager. I wonder why?"

Jack took a while to try an answer to that.

"My dad was a construction worker," he finally said. "An accident-prone construction worker. Your dad's regulations protect people that get hurt on the job, but after you've been on workers comp a couple of times, even the union isn't so interested in referring you to a job. He still got work, but little stuff, short stuff, stuff that no one could get hurt on. Pay sucked."

"I'm sorry," Kris said. She licked a finger and made a mark in the air. "Put that down as one question I should not have asked."

"You had no way of knowing, honey. Your life is an open book, complete with pictures. Most of us live our lives in quiet desperation."

"And my desperation gets me all over the news."

"You're talking shop."

"Change the topic to something else," Kris suggested.

"Well, the later diners are arriving. Turn around. You'll get quite a view."

The scene could have qualified for a review or floor show in many places. The female half of the couples were arriving in shorts, the shortest shorts in Kris's closet. The tank tops hardly qualified for the name. They stopped well short of what they were supposed to cover. The men had on the shortest shorts, too, and many hadn't bothered with a shirt.

"I guess now we know what 'Total Nudity Not Allowed' means," Kris said, turning back to her view of the ocean.

"Twelve guesses why they're late, and the first eleven don't count," Jack said.

"I can't figure out whether I feel scandalized or regret that we aren't late with them. Not that I'd step out of our cabin in that outfit."

"You mean it?" Jack asked.

"I really am enjoying talking to you, Jack. Getting to know you."

"Me too."

Dinner arrived. They were served first, at least. The fish was . . . interesting. Different from anything Kris had ever tasted. Hers had a nutty texture although whether that was from the sauce or the fish, she wasn't sure. After her first taste, she offered Jack one. Kris had seen couples feeding each other from their plates and often wished she had someone she could do it with.

Now she did. Her best guess was she ate half of Jack's and

he ate half of hers. The fish came with a wild rice that could have been from Wardhaven and a mix of sautéed vegetables, half of which were familiar and half strange.

The medley was delicious.

They were about done. They might have been done if they hadn't been talking so much when, an hour after the dinner bell rang, the second installment of the floor show arrived.

Jack announced it by saying "Don't look."

So, of course, Kris did. Only then did Jack turn in his seat and clearly enjoy the show.

Here was the string-bikini brigade. Most of the young women hadn't even bothered with the top. The guys were also in string things. Most of them covered the essentials, but a few had a critical portion of their anatomy peeking out around the edge.

"And my Granny Rita sent me to this . . ."

"Den of delights," Jack finished.

Kris turned back to her not-quite-finished dinner. Jack timed his turn perfectly with hers.

"Now we know what 'Total Nudity Not Allowed' means," Jack said.

"I hope."

"Would you like dessert?" the waitress asked. "We have a chocolate delight that you can not pass up, and for you, it is straight from the oven."

"Kris?" Jack asked, tossing the call in her lap.

"What do you want to bet me that our new dinner guests had dessert before dinner?" Kris asked Jack. He chuckled but said nothing. "I'm gonna have dessert with my dinner."

"Two of them," Jack said.

Kris risked another glance over her shoulder. She'd never seen that many bare breasts since the gym shower in high school. No, there there'd been other girls like her who were still waiting for something to show up on their chests. Here there wasn't a flat chest in the dinning room. Yes, some were nice and small, but not flat. Some of the guys had more top hamper than Kris.

She turned back to Jack. "How come you're not married? I don't mean to one of those hussies, as Mother would call them, but to a good girl. A girl like a good gentleman deserves?"

Kris paused. Then realized the directness of her question

might be going someplace Jack didn't want to. "Excuse me. That's too forward. You don't have to answer if I'm out of line."

Jack's face had become a mask. He turned his eyes to the ocean and quite a few waves came in and went out before he said anything. "Yes, Kris, you are forward, but that's something I like about you. You don't beat around the bush. You're more likely to take a chain saw to it."

"Or C-16," Kris added.

"There have been two girls in my life. One in high school and the other in college. Once I became a cop, and then was invited into the Secret Service, there hasn't been a lot of time for a girl, except for you. And you are, or were, or whatever, off-limits."

Kris folded her hands on the table and waited. She knew Jack was letting her into something sacred. However much time he needed, he would not find her impatient.

"Lisa was the most lively, vivacious girl I've ever met. Smart, too. She didn't blame me for breaking the curve on the tough courses like math and science. She often beat my score. She was beautiful, too, and had a sparkling personality. You know those aren't supposed to go together."

"I've heard girls condemned with the faint praise of great personality," Kris admitted.

"Lisa had it all, and for no reason I could understand, she liked me. You know how I say something nice about you, and you deflect it?" Kris confessed she did. "That was Lisa and me. She'd say things to me that I just couldn't believe a girl could see in me."

The conversation paused as the dessert arrived. They tasted it. It was fantastic.

"Where did they get chocolate?" Kris asked.

"Am I permitted to answer?" Nelly said.

"Yes, this once."

"After the *Sheffield* made two bad jumps, the second one discovering the lost colony of Santa Maria, someone at the headquarters of the Society of Humanity's Navy made a policy that no ship sailed without a sealed two-hundred-pound pod of seeds in cold storage. I would guess that they brought both the *Furious*'s and the *Enterprise*'s survival seed banks to Alwa."

"Thanks, Nelly," Kris said.

"In the early years, it must have taken all kinds of self-control to not eat the seed corn," Jack said.

"Granny Rita said she was a certified tyrant, with some signed in blood. I guess she wasn't kidding."

"There's a lot more to this colony than we've found out so far," Jack said.

"Do you think we ought to report this to Amanda and Jacques tonight? Here they were supposed to report to us, and we're maybe discovering stuff."

"You're talking work, but I'll give you a pass on that," Jack said. "And yes, I think we need to report this."

They ate their dessert in silence. Kris so wanted to know about Jack's first girlfriend, but she bit her tongue and waited.

"You asked me why I didn't take a baseball scholarship," Jack began, the words coming slowly. "I said baseball is a lot more dangerous than you think."

Kris made a middling noise that she hoped came across as agreement and encouragement to go on.

"Lisa was a cheerleader. Football, basketball, baseball; if there was an excuse to get the crowd cheering, she was out there doing it.

"They were doing one of those pyramid things. Three guys holding up two girls, then the last girl somehow somersaults to the top. Lots of girls would botch the landing and bring the pyramid down in a mess. People would laugh as much as they cheered.

"Lisa never missed her landing. She'd just landed, not so much as a bobble, threw up her hands when our best hitter swatted a fly ball. A foul ball, as it quickly became clear. If anyone had been looking, they'd have seen it coming, but all the cheer team was leading a cheer for our best hitter. 'Hit a homer' was the cry.

"Instead, he hit Lisa right in the back of the head."

"That's horrible," Kris gasped, her desert forgotten.

"I already knew what I wanted to be. I'd taken volunteer training and was the closest thing the school had to an EMT. I covered all the games. I'd taken care of a few broken bones before the first responders could get there. That kind of stuff."

"You were the first to get to Lisa," Kris said.

"Yes," Jack said, covering his eyes. "There are some sights you never get rid of."

"Yes," Kris agreed. She'd known from an early age there were some pictures of Eddy's death that she'd never let herself see. Jack had faced the choice of running away from the man he was becoming or face a sight he'd never forget.

"I'm sorry I asked, Jack," Kris said, reaching across the table.

"I know, Kris, but Lisa and that baseball game are a part of me. We're a package deal."

"And Eddy comes with me, and we've lost Tommy together, and God only knows how long the list is now. And it will grow."

Now Jack patted her hands. "But they'll grow for the both of us."

"Yes," Kris agreed. "You don't have to tell me about the other girl."

"That one's really nothing. Great girl, beautiful. We thought we were in love. She's the one I got suspended from school for my outlandish invitation. I and my best friend agreed she shouldn't have to sit home alone just 'cause I was stupid."

"You're kidding," Kris said.

"Nope, they hit it off. I was best man at their wedding."

"I bet you've been best man at several weddings."

"A few."

"Nice thing about being second up for you guys is you can rent the tux. I'm stuck with six maid-of-honor dresses in my closet."

"And never a wedding dress."

"That is now subject to change, but trust me you don't want me walking down the aisle in a dress my mother picks out. You remember the one Mother was looking at for Penny's wedding?"

Jack glanced over his shoulder at the pulchritude on display. "It would be just the thing for a wedding here."

"No," Kris said. "The bride would wear a white string bottom and the guy would wear a black bow tie over his . . . you know."

"And it would pass 'Total Nudity Not Allowed,'" Kris and Jack ended saying together.

"I think we got a dirty look from that topless gal behind you," Jack said.

"I know you got a nasty look from two of the gals behind you."

"Think it's time we beat a strategic retreat?"

"Even if that does sound like you're talking shop," Kris admitted.

Jack pulled Kris's chair back, like a good gentleman. Their table was as far from the door as you could get, so they would be passing a lot of well-tanned flesh on the way out. Kris had done a perp walk in cuffs. She'd been paraded for good and bad reasons enough times to have lost count. She set a smile on her face and did the best she could to look each and every man and woman in the eye as she passed them.

"Hold it," one of the guys said, half-standing. "Aren't you the gal, the commander that was on TV?"

"Yes," Kris said, coming to a halt. "I'm from the *Wasp* in orbit, and I did talk to one of the Alwans' news stations."

"I saw you," several people said, now muttering to each other.

"You blew that huge alien ship out of space and saved all our lives," a barely dressed woman said.

Kris shook her head. "A lot of people were involved in stopping that raiding party. Most of them died for our effort. I'm one of the lucky few that survived."

A woman stood, one of those in short short shorts, and a very short tank top. "We owe all of you our lives. Thank you."

The wave of thank-yous was followed by a round of applause. Kris gave them her best princess smile and bowed her reply as she tried not to run for the door. She kept her pace down, and Jack stayed right behind her.

At the door, the owner waited. "I'm sorry about this. Granny Rita said you wanted your privacy. I don't watch much TV. I didn't think my clients did either. If you want, I'll have your meals taken to your cabin."

"Give me a night to think about that," Kris said, just wanting to be gone. He stood aside, and she fled into the night.

She found herself holding on to a tree before they were halfway back to their cottage. She had to hold on, her knees weren't doing that support thing they'd been doing since she was a toddler.

Jack scooped her up and carried her. "Where do you want to go? The cottage or the beach?"

"The beach," Kris whispered against his shoulder.

He settled her on dry sand this time. The tide was high, the breakers close. Kris squeaked and backed up on all fours as a high one tried to wet her down.

"Sorry about that," Jack said as he settled down beside her farther up the beach.

For a long time, they just watched the breakers come in and roll back out again. A shooting star cut across the inky black sky. The other stars, with no competition from city lights, were as bright and proud as Kris had ever seen them from space.

"Why is it so hard to accept a thank-you?" she finally asked the eternal ocean.

Jack did not speak for another couple of waves, one of which wet Kris's toes, but she stood her ground, and the ocean dared go no farther.

"Maybe it's hard to take because you know the thank-you belongs to not just you but a whole lot of people who worked, sweat, bled and, in too many cases, died. But, honey, you are Princess Longknife, ComPatRon 10, and there are not a lot of other people alive to accept the thanks."

"Gramma Ruth says that somewhere along the way, Grampa Ray lost his humanity. Grampa Trouble says he's still human, thanks to Gramma Ruth."

"I can believe that."

"It's a hell of a job to keep a Longknife human. The legend wants to eat us up."

"I've heard that. I'm still willing to interview for the job. I'll do it if you'll accept me?"

"If I really love you, is it fair to let you take such an impossible job?"

Waves rolled in, broke in phosphorescent beauty, and slid back out several times before Jack cleared his throat. "I've shared your world for nearly five years, haven't I?"

Kris nodded agreement.

"In that time, I've come to love you. To only want the very best for you. Believe it or not, from where I've stood, stuck on the sidelines, I've done my best for you."

"I believe you, Jack."

"Honey, I think you love me as much as I love you. It's hard to believe a beautiful, powerful, competent woman like you can love me, but you've given me a few hints that it just might be possible."

"Very possible. Almost certainly. No. Definitely," Kris said.

"But you're a Longknife. To some people, that means wealth and power. To other folks it means danger. In all cases, it means target. May I point out that for the last four years, I've grown as good at making them miss me as I have at making sure they miss *you*."

"And you haven't gotten nearly the medals you deserve for that," Kris said.

"I'd swap all the medals in the book for a simple gold band to put on your finger."

"Jack, you're too good to believe."

"And I thought you were the one too good for me to ever find."

"Most men find me, get a good look at what happens around me, and run, not walk, for the door. Or pick one of the girls around me."

"Yes, I know," Jack said. "I've had to sweat a couple of them in the last few years. Fortunately for me, they all bolted."

"Fortunate for you, but a bit hard on me."

"I'm sorry. That came out wrong."

"No it didn't. I know what you meant." Kris used the hem of her muumuu to wipe her eyes. "Jack, I'm exhausted. Could we go to bed?"

"Yes, honey. Do you need a lift?"

"No, just give me a hand up and a strong shoulder to lean on."

"Always, love."

Even in the dark, they had no problem finding their cottage. The moon was up, the stars were bright, and the ocean gave its own green light. The only light in the cottage was a small lit candle. Kris found that whoever had lit the candle had also tossed a rather skimpy nightgown on one side of the bed. Jack found soft sleeping shorts on his, and dismissed himself to the bathroom to change.

It took Kris just a second to toss the muumuu over her head

and slip into the gown. It didn't quite go halfway to her knees, and the top was so open she could easily pull it aside if she didn't toss it off entirely.

Well, if elves were appearing and disappearing, she might have them do some wash. She left the muumuu on the porch chair and tumbled into bed.

A moment later, Jack appeared and blew out the candle. He stepped outside, very likely to leave his shorts and shirt on the same chair with Kris's muumuu.

Kris had pulled the covers up a bit, not enough to turn herself into an unapproachable mummy, but Jack settled above the covers, his front to her back. He slipped an arm over her shoulder that easily managed to miss what she claimed for breasts.

"Don't you want to do something more tonight?" she asked. She knew the answer to that. She could feel him through the thin blanket and even thinner gown.

"I don't think so, dear. It's been a long day. You've been through a lot, and let's face it, you're exhausted. You need your sleep a lot more than you need anything else."

"No, I don't," Kris said . . . through a yawn.

"I rest my case," Jack said.

"But what I'm feeling from you isn't at rest."

"You want me to roll over?" Jack asked, ever the gentle gentleman.

"Please don't. I want you close."

"And I always will be," he said.

Kris settled comfortably in Jack's protective arms. She remembered something about checking in with her team. Letting them know about something. She was asleep before she could remember what it was.

12

Kris came awake the next morning to the sound of birds chirping, the roar of the ocean, and the smell of fresh coffee.

She tossed her blanket aside, got her feet on the floor, and took it all in.

The windows of the cottage were wide open, which allowed for the birdsong and the ocean roar. Jack sat at the small table in the room, a carafe of the delicious-smelling coffee beside two mugs and a large plate covered with an assortment of breakfast rolls.

"Hi, sleepyhead. You better get over here. There are two each of these buns, but some of them are really delicious, and as much as I love you, I'm not sure that extends to leaving one for you."

"Keep your mitts off my buns, Marine," Kris said, and raced, or at least staggered to the table. Jack poured a cup of coffee and passed it to her as she sat down.

"Thanks," Kris said, sipping the hot, bitter liquid. "Coffee beans were in the survival pod?"

"No," Nelly said, "but one of the crew worshipped the stuff and had a huge supply of his own natural beans. He saved half a dozen of each variety and planted them. It turned out that the

Alwans love the stuff, and it was one of the humanity's first items of exchange. It's still a prime trade item."

"That didn't happen overnight," Kris said.

"No. Amanda had supper with the Historian last night, who told her it took nearly twenty years to go from the original few trees to enough that they could start selling a product while still planting more trees. And yes, the cacao seeds were part of the survival pod, but getting a chocolate industry going took a whole lot more time. It's only in the last forty years or so anyone has been able to eat the stuff."

"What's the Alwan take on it?" Jack asked.

"They hate it."

Kris eyed the sticky buns, spotted the singles, and reached for one. Jack gave her a sad look. She tore it in half, shared, and munched hers. "Hey, this *is* good."

"You want the other half?"

"No, you can have it. A gentleman deserves some rewards. Okay, Nelly, have we heard anything from Captain Drago?"

"He's sending down a quarter of the crew. While you did forget to mention to Granny Rita the need for increasing the beer supply, either she remembered how thirsty Sailors can be or Sergeant Bruce reminded her. Initial report is that the town and local resorts are not at risk of being drunk dry. Also, baby girls continue to survive here at a higher proportion to boys, so the population is about forty-nine percent to fifty-one percent. A few religious groups are locking up their girls, but most of the female population are enjoying a chance to meet the crew. There are also no problems with our gals meeting their boys though there were a few heads broken, in a light fashion. It seemed someone started the rumor that female Marines were easy."

"But it's not a problem, Skipper," Sal said from Jack's neck. "The local keepers of the peace seemed to think the guys got what they deserved, and it doesn't look like the rumor is being taken seriously anymore."

"Strange how evidence to the contrary kills a rumor," Kris said.

"When it's a good kick to the groin," Nelly added.

Kris leaned over and gave Jack a kiss. "I like my men gentlemen." She felt a breeze and realized the whole abbreviated top of her gown had fallen open.

Jack grinned. "And this gentleman likes the view."

Kris settled back in her chair and adjusted her gown to remove the view. "You're going to have to work for any more sightseeing, lover boy."

Jack gave her a sad shrug, with plenty of grin in it. "The rest of the reports are no more informative. They've just scratched the surface."

"Nelly, how's the dictionary going?"

"Most of our people are talking to humans, but the five Alwans have been helpful. My translation of your talk had a few howlers in it, and I'm correcting those, but only a hundred or so new words have come in."

"More will. Those howlers, how bad were they?" Kris asked.

"Well, I called the alien ships that attacked us a particular kind of bean the Alwans like to eat. The picture pretty much overpowered my mistranslation, but some of the Alwans who are against action are rubbing it in on those who are for us."

Kris shrugged. "The pictures speak for themselves. 'There are none so blind as have eyes but will not see,' as Father so often said." Kris considered everything and found it to her liking.

"Nelly, Sal, you monitor the net, keep adding words, and let us know if anything important comes up. Other than that, you will ignore what goes on here today."

"But Kris, I've never had a chance to study at close hand the mating ritual of humans."

"Nelly, you have an off button, and I know how to use it."

"You are heartless, mean, and bind the mouth of the ox that grinds the grain."

"I come by it naturally. I understand Granny Rita is a certified tyrant."

"Oh, about that, Kris," Nelly said. "Abby won't say who told her, but there were mutinies in the early days. Food riots. People stealing supplies. Granny hung a few."

"Now I begin to understand you, Your Highness," Jack said with a bow of his head.

"Granny is not all sweetness and light," Kris said.

"Enough work, young lady. I'm going swimming."

Jack was up from the table in a flash, grabbed something

from his closet, and disappeared into the bathroom. When he emerged, he was wearing . . . very little.

He did a muscleman thing, first with his right arm, then with his left, showing Kris that there was practically no back to his suit. Then he grabbed a towel and headed for the beach.

"I'll follow you in a second," Kris said, and thoughtfully sipped some more of her coffee. Then she headed over to her closet, rummaged up the tiniest excuse for a suit, and pulled her gown over her head.

Now she remembered why she only bought sexy underwear once. This little bit of nothing didn't feel all that great between her legs even after she adjusted the strings.

This suit was not meant for a six-foot-tall woman.

The top didn't cover all that much, but there wasn't all that much to cover. Still, she had to let it out about as far as it would go. Thinking of as far as she could go got her almost into another fit of giggling, but she held her breath.

Grabbing a towel, she followed Jack to the beach.

There, she laid her towel down next to him. He seemed lost in quiet meditation, or maybe the warm-morning sun was turning him lazy.

She stretched out beside him, found a hand to hold on to, and discovered the morning sun could make her lazy, too.

A while later, Jack said. "You know, you can get a bad sunburn."

"I didn't bring any sunscreen."

"On the porch, where I found the rolls, there was a jar of sunscreen. Hold still while I put some on you."

Kris let go of Jack's hand and prepared to hold still.

He started by kissing her neck.

"That's not putting sunscreen on me."

"Yes, but I'm shading you so you won't burn."

"Anything you say," was out of Kris's mouth before she realized it.

Jack began rubbing something cool and moist on her neck. Then he undid the ties of her string top, spread them on the towel beside her, and began to shower kisses on her back before covering it with moist coolness.

Kris purred.

And wondered how far down he'd go. This teeny-weeny bikini left a lot open to the sun . . . and Jack's roving fingers.

When Jack had finished coating the small of her back, he surprised her.

He switched to her feet.

"Your résumé said nothing about great foot massages," Kris said.

"Maybe because the personnel forms never ask the really important questions?" Jack said.

"Probably because there's a law against it."

"Talk to your dad about that next time you see him."

Kris considered that idea and chose to stay concentrated in the moment. "I'll give you thirty minutes to quit that."

"Ah, but from where I'm kneeling, there's so much of you that could burn in the next half hour."

"Hmm, you have a point. You are a wise man whom I respect. Use your own judgment."

And he did. Slowly, he worked his way up first one leg to the knee, then the other. Then he passed above the knee and was soon in those sweet spots on her thigh that sent shivers all up Kris's spine and drew reactions from parts of her that good girls weren't supposed to feel.

She moaned.

"I'll take that to mean I'm doing this right."

"Very right."

As he got to her buttocks, he again untied her strings, folded them and the bit of cloth up so it seemed perched right on the space between each cheek, and kissed her thoroughly before massaging her muscles.

Kris weakly melted onto the blanket.

Then he covered her with sunscreen.

"All done," he said.

"Thank you," Kris managed to mutter.

"I figure you're good for about a half hour. Then I'll do your front."

Kris wondered how fast a half hour could go.

They listened to the lapping of the waves and enjoyed the feel of the sun, the salty tang of the sea air. They were subdued, as befitted low tide. Some seabirds flew lazily around them, as if waiting for them to offer tidbits. Next to the TOTAL

NUDITY NOT ALLOWED sign had been one that said, PLEASE DON'T FEED THE BIRDS.

Kris suspected neither sign was paid all that much attention.

Sun-caressed, Kris began to fear she'd fall asleep before her half hour was up. Almost, she asked Nelly what time it was, but she'd sworn that Nelly was only for nightly reports or an emergency recall from Captain Drago, and she would not let that little voyeur into these moments.

"Jack, I have a question."

"If I have an answer, it's yours," he said.

"Back in the lodge, once Penny left with Grampa Trouble and the colonel, we couldn't wait to get out of our clothes and . . . you know."

"Yes, I have a very fond memory of . . . you know."

"Then, when we arrived here, I sat on the bed, and you headed for the beach. After supper, I was in bed, and you slept above the covers. Is something wrong?"

"After the rubdown I just gave you, you need to ask?"

"Can a girl say she's confused?"

Jack seemed to give a lot of thought to that, then he reached for her hand and began running his fingers around her palm.

If it was possible, Kris melted even more.

"I was desperate for you when I first saw you on Wardhaven," he said.

"So was I," Kris admitted.

"And when we finally got to make love, there was desperation all over it. People wanted to rip us apart again. We were about to storm Longknife Towers and maybe get killed. We desperately needed each other."

"I agree," Kris said. "There was a lot of desperation to go around."

"I want love to be the first and last thought you have of me, not desperation. Nor exhaustion, as was our main companion yesterday."

"I can't argue with you there. Restful nights' sleeps have been few and far between."

"How was last night?"

"Deliciously restful and relaxing."

"Then I rest my case. Next time we make love, I want love

to be first, middle, and last on your mind, and speaking of time, I think you should be done on that side," Jack said.

"I think maybe I am," Kris said, and rolled over . . . and totally out of her modesty. Strings fell where they would.

Jack grinned. "My. Where to start?"

From the bulge in his tiny swimsuit, Kris suspected she knew where he'd like to start. Come to think of it, that was where *she'd* like to start.

He bent to kiss her lips, then slowly worked his way down to her throat. Kris was melting, but she found the strength to reach for him, hold him, stroke his back.

"Hold it, girl. I've got a job to do. I must protect you from the sun. No distracting your chief of security."

"I'm sorry, sir," Kris pouted, not at all contrite. "I'm just a poor lonely Sailor trying to have a good time."

"I'll show you a good time, but don't rush it. We have all the time in the world."

Or until Captain Drago sounds recall. But Kris didn't say that.

Now, while his fingers covered her throat with sunscreen, Jack's lips had found her breasts. For something so small, there was nothing small about the pleasure his kisses filled her with. Maybe tiny breasts weren't all that important.

At least not when Jack was around.

Jack spent a long time there. Kris might almost think he was enjoying the taste of her little sunny-side ups as much as she was delighting in his tasting.

With no thought, she found that she was trying to wrap her legs around Jack.

Ever so gently, he pushed them back on the blanket and somehow managed to have a finger stray between them. A shiver went up her spine, and she did a lot more than moan.

"Would you please hurry? I don't know how much more of this I can stand."

"I've got to protect all of you from the sun," Jack said, and once again, switched to her feet. Thank God, he moved quickly from feet to knee, then above.

And then between.

Kris trembled. Kris moaned. Kris enjoyed, and Kris so much wanted more.

"Now a good security chief always keeps his primary covered." And suddenly Jack was above her, blocking out the sun. He was atop her and sliding slowly inside her, and Kris wrapped herself around him.

He protected her from the sun vigilantly. And vigorously. Then the sun exploded in her, and she drifted off in space and time.

13

Sated and exhausted and pleased, Jack lay beside Kris. She turned into his arms, kissed him once more, yawned, and fell asleep.

Apparently they both did, because Kris came awake much later when the cold water of the ocean started tickling her toes.

She nudged Jack. "Hey, security chief, your primary is in danger of drowning."

Jack came awake with a yawn, glanced down, and raised an eyebrow. "Why yes, I do believe you are in danger of drowning. Tell me, Commander Longknife, how are you going to get yourself out of this mess?"

"A mess you got me into."

"I thought I was the one that got into you."

Kris had no answer for that, so she stood, collected all the strings that had wandered off, threw the towel over her shoulder, and headed up the beach. The shade from a stand of trees past the high water mark looked inviting.

Jack collected his towel and bit of nothing and followed.

Once in the shade, Kris spread her towel and sprawled out faceup. Jack spread his towel beside her and settled, faceup, hands behind his head, a very satisfied look on his face.

"Now it's my turn," Kris said.

"We're not in the sun. I don't need more sunscreen."

"I'm a Longknife. I don't need an excuse to do nasty things to people."

"Oh, please, Commander, don't do nasty things to me," didn't have any beg in it at all.

"As my wise and not at all prudish great-grandmother has pointed out, you are not in my chain of command, so you are fair game for anything I want to do to you."

"Well, in that case, please do."

Kris took exactly as long to cover Jack with kisses and stroke every inch of his skin as he had taken with her. It turned out that Jack had resorted to Sal to keep time, so, of course, Nelly knew all the delightful details and was only too glad to help Kris match minute for minute.

Nelly was also wise enough to keep her computer mouth shut about what she thought of human mating rituals.

In the end, Kris showed Jack that she could be just as good at shading him as he had been to her. Even if they were already in the shade.

Once again, they fell asleep in each other's arms.

It was the dinner bell that woke them.

The sun was low in the sky. "Did we sleep through lunch?" Kris asked.

"My tummy says so."

"Was I really that exhausted?"

"When did you last have a good night's sleep?" Jack countered.

"I don't remember," Kris admitted. "Certainly not since before that which we will not mention."

"You need a vacation. A nice, quiet, relaxing vacation. I'm only too glad to be providing the relaxing part of it."

Kris leaned over and kissed him. "You are very relaxing."

"How late do you want to be for supper? Ready to join the bikini brigade?"

"Give me a hand up. I'd prefer to wear shorts."

They found they could walk right into the shower from the outside and enjoyed helping each other get clean. Kris found herself carefully weighing just how attractive the bed was and how late she was willing to be for supper.

Naked, she stood in front of her closet as Jack, just as bare, studied his. He pulled out a pair of very short shorts, high-cut and low-hung. Kris grinned and pulled out the smallest pair of shorts in her closet. She was pretty sure that if she'd gotten her butt sunburned that morning, she'd be glowing red as she walked into the dining room.

Jack chose a net tank top that showed off his six-pack. Kris sighed and chose one that would show off her flat belly.

Hand in hand, they headed for dinner.

They were late. Most of the shorts contingent was already seated. The two women who had worn the muumuus last night were still covered with flowers. The owner led them to the same table they'd had the night before. "I saved it for you," he said with a too-knowing smile.

The waitress showed up, also sporting a knowing smile. "Usually it takes first-timers a couple of days to quit hiding behind a muumuu," she whispered to Kris.

"We've known each other a very long time," Kris said.

"And fought battles together?" the waitress said, all starry-eyed.

"No," Jack said. "Usually, we just fight with each other."

That left the poor girl too puzzled to answer with anything but tonight's specials. Again it was fish and fish. Each ordered a different one and prepared to share. The girl bounced off happily and soon returned with two ice teas.

Kris found herself staring at the ocean and thinking of how it went on forever. It never changed, but it didn't feel anything, either. Slowly, she began to open up to Jack what it had been like to be "that Longknife girl," the "Prime Minister's brat," the gal with the chest that belonged in the guys' showers.

"Girls can be so cruel to each other. Any flaw, anything different, can get hammered at."

"And you felt your chest gave them an opening to hurt you."

"I felt the hurt. You know, it's strange, we tiny titty kitties should have formed our own club, but we were so hurt or cowered that we just couldn't flock together. Then, of course, when one of us suddenly popped a pair of boobs, she was only too happy to be welcomed into the sisterhood of 'real' women." Kris snorted. "I got my first period before most of them, but that's a lot harder to brag about."

Jack listened. He did a good job of listening. He made

sounds once in a while, just about the time she figured she was yammering on, that encouraged her to go on.

"Being a Longknife meant I had to deal with three kinds of guys," Kris said, as their dinner arrived. It turned out, she really didn't like her fish, but she refused to give it to Jack and they shared it, feeding each other. She relished what he fed her. He tolerated what she sent his way.

"There were the gold diggers. They came in two flavors, the poor who were trying to start from scratch and the ones close to as rich as I was. You know, the pains in your butt at camp. I kind of felt sorry for the poor ones. The rich ones I tried not to throw up all over."

"Why not? I wish I could have tossed my cookies on some of them," Jack said.

"Sorry I disappointed you, but remember, I was young, frightened, and thought I had a reputation to defend to the death. I'd done a lot of throwing up during my drunk years. I didn't want to start that rumor again."

"Oh! Good point," Jack said, sending his fork her way. She held her mouth open for the bite.

After chewing and swallowing, she went on. "Then there were the boys who just wanted to put a notch on their whatever that they'd scored on a Longknife. I made that mistake once. After that, I could spot one a mile away. If he got close enough to dance with, I stepped on his toes enough for a three-footed girl. With my equipment, it was hard enough to find second base, much less score. I got real good at slapping anyone who even got close."

"Okay, that covers the first two, who was the third?"

"Boys and girls who were interested in politics. Get close enough to a Longknife and get caught up in the wake. They were easy to like. I'd invite them on a first date that involved a political thing for Father. They'd be so glad to go."

Kris took a deep breath, and Jack reached across to her plate and snagged most of the remaining fish. He popped it into his mouth too fast for her to protest.

"You know, there's such a thing as being too much the gentleman."

"There is? Nobody ever told me that."

"Well, I'm telling you."

"The third kind of guys. You left them at a political shindig."

"They usually end up hitching a ride home with someone else."

Jack gave Kris a puzzled look. "I can't believe anyone would not take you home."

"You could if you ever saw me in full political forward motion. I learned politicking at Father's knee. I have pictures of me, cute as a button at five, doing the rope line, shaking hands. I kissed my first baby before I was seven. Wind me up and put me in political gear, and I will work the crowd, make a speech, smile, smile, smile, and do it all without using a single brain cell.

"I could spend a week of twenty-hour days on full automatic. Why do you think I joined the Navy? I had to get out of that rat race before the rats won."

Jack shook his head at her self-deprecation. "And yet I've seen you come the politician and be a force of nature that nothing could stand against. What you did on St. Petersburg—the way you finagled Vicky Peterwald into signing a city charter. That was a magnificent bit of politicking."

"But we were totally off the map. It had never been done before."

"Nelly and Abby pulled up the Magna Carta, complete with parchment and silver seals when you asked."

Kris started to shoot Jack down, then paused. "Yes, we did something pretty slick there. Not at all standard stump speech. We were borrowing from history and coming up with something that helped a whole lot of people."

"What I'm hearing is you got tired of the same old same old and left for the Navy before you were old and experienced enough to sit at the grown-ups' table. To sink your teeth into some real steak-type issues."

Kris leaned back in her chair and looked at Jack. "You know, Captain, you're a pretty savvy guy. You may have just shown me why dear Father is so mad at me."

"Glad to be of service," Jack said.

Then Kris shook her head. "But I'm glad I went Navy. It's been a whole lot more fun than politics could ever have been."

"And your brother admitted that you got all the courage in

this generation, and the Navy's putting it to a whole lot better use than any old campaign."

"And I met you."

"And I got to meet you. If you'd stayed the Prime Minister's brat, I'd have just been following you around."

"As I got more bratty and you got a whole lot less interested in me."

"I don't think that could ever happen."

There was no applause as they left that evening. One of the couple in muumuu and shorts did cross paths with them at the door. He shook Jack's hand. "Thank you."

Kris got a huge hug from the young woman. "Now there's hope that I can have a child, and he can grow up to be a man."

Kris and Jack walked slowly back to their cottage.

"You notice how that young woman wants a boy?" she pointed out to Jack.

"Yeah. I'd call that our first hint that Alwa is a man's world."

"So very many of them are," Kris said with a sigh.

That night, the bed turned out to be just as much fun as the beach blankets had been. And the feathers were much softer than the sand.

Another interesting bit of discovery.

14

The days could have taken on a wonderful sameness, but Jack insisted they do something new every day. So one day they took out a sailboat. Kris showed Jack how to handle the sails while he struggled with the tiller. Then she took over the tiller and showed him how to catch the wind.

"Sailing is a dance between you, the tiller, the sails, and the waves."

"I'll take your word for that," Jack said, looking rather pale. He wasn't seasick. Not quite.

Kris chose to go with the waves, making the ride as smooth as possible, and he seemed to draw more joy from it.

As a teenager, Kris had fantasies of making it with a boy in a sailboat. She and Jack got some nice foreplay in, but the thought of lying down on the ribbed bottom or trying to do something on the thwart seats gave the mature Kris too many images of the boat taking off on its own, flipping over, or coming up with some other disaster her younger self hadn't thought of.

They found a nice island and took advantage of its white beach.

The next day, they went snorkeling naked off their own private beach. Kris had a hard time dividing her attention between Jack and the beautiful undersea view. Jack seemed to be splitting his time pretty evenly between her and the scenery.

Was it lust or was it love?

Could love be served with a nice side dish of lust?

The more Kris learned about Jack, the more she shared about herself with Jack, the more sure Kris was that this was the man she wanted to share her life with. The man she wanted to have beside her as she grew old . . . assuming she dodged the bullets and the bombs that long.

She found herself wondering what their children might look like. What kind of adults would they grow up to be? A son like Jack couldn't help but be as wonderful as his father. And a daughter . . . Jack wouldn't drive his daughter to drink.

Kris let all these thoughts wash through her, mindful that her birth-control implant had about run its course and would need replacing soon. Yes, replacing.

Granny Rita may have had seven kids on the far side of the galaxy. Kris, however, had a couple of battles to fight.

Kids would have to wait.

They were dressing for dinner the fourth evening. Kris used that word loosely. Neither had worn a stitch all day, but it was the dinner meal and "Total Nudity Not Allowed" applied.

They were rather late, though.

Kris sidled over to lean her chin on Jack's shoulder. "You'd look great in that lava-lava."

"It's so thin you can see right through it," Jack said.

"Only if the light is right, and you know how dim the lights are by this time." The lights were pretty bright when the muu-muu teams arrived, dimmer for the shorts contingency and rather shady when the bikini-or-less brigade strutted in.

"What will you wear?" Jack asked with a raised eyebrow that wasn't quite a leer.

"Not one of those string things. They ride up in all the wrong places and chafe me where only you should be."

"Do girls wear lava-lavas?"

"Let's find out."

Jack chose her lava-lava, the most light colored one in the closet, not quite as thin as the one she'd picked for him. They spent a couple of minutes figuring out how you wore one, and that almost got dinner scratched for more bedtime, but Kris found that Abby had included a few pins, maybe earrings, in her "to go" bag, and they managed to get both of them arranged so they didn't fall off at every opportunity.

"What are you wearing for a top?" Jack asked.

"What I got on. You seem to like it fine."

He kissed her bare breasts, lovingly, and once again the bed started looking better than supper. Today, however, they'd again had nothing since their breakfast buns. Grumbling stomachs won out over libidos that were proving insatiable anyway.

They were late, very late. Most of the bikini brigade were already seated, but the owner had held their table for them. Kris walked through the dining room on the arm of the man that she loved.

Among this crowd, they hardly got a glance.

The waitress brought tea when she first came to their table. "Your usual, one of each type of fish?"

"What are you serving tonight?" Kris said.

The waitress named the two fish offerings.

NELLY, DO WE LIKE BOTH OF THEM?

NO, KRIS, THE SECOND ONE BOTH OF YOU HATED. YOU BOTH LOVED THE FIRST ONE.

Kris ordered two of the same dinners for them, much to the waitress's surprise.

"I checked in with Sal, too," Jack said. "If you hadn't ordered, I would have."

"I'm sorry. Did I violate male prerogative by ordering for us both?"

"Anytime you want to use Nelly to save our neck or get us a great dinner, you go right ahead. I've got more important things to do with my male ego than bend it out of shape."

Kris put her hand out, palm up. He covered it, and began doing wonderful things to it.

"I like your male everything just the way it is," she said.

"Your lady parts are mighty fine, too," he answered.

"Kris, I have a message from Captain Drago."

Kris found her back going ramrod straight. Damn near naked, she came to attention. "Hold the video, Nelly, but put him through."

"Princess Longknife, Jump Point Beta, the one we used to jump in here, has started spitting out U.S. warships like a cat having kittens," Captain Drago reported. "The first two through are squawking as USS *Fearless* and USS *Intrepid*. They're a bit bigger than us, but the next one, the USS *Constitution*. It's way bigger. We're making out six loaded lasers forward, four aft. The chief says he doesn't know what they are, but they're bigger than our 18-inchers."

He paused for a moment. "Here's another big one, the USS *Monarch*. Oh oh, she's squawking as the royal ship."

"Aren't we all Royal United Society Ships?" Kris asked.

"Yes, Kris, but this one is identifying herself as *The* Royal. It has the king himself on board."

Dear Lord, Ray has come for his Rita.

The great Ray of legend was in for one hell of a surprise. The raised eyebrows from Jack beside her said he shared the same thought.

"Holy smoke on a stick," the skipper burst out. "You got to see this next ship to believe it. You know those damn baby monster ships. Well we just had something come through the jump, claiming to be the USS *Prosperity*, with ten reactors and twenty charged lasers. It must weigh two or three hundred thousand tons if it weighs an ounce. Oh, and the chief tells me its all Smart Metal."

Kris and Jack exchanged puzzled looks. The whole idea of the Smart Metal™ ships was to be fast, maneuverable, and not get hit. Something that huge defied any tactical application Kris could think of.

"We got a second one of those monsters, USS *Enterprise*. Nice name, and it's got twenty huge lasers. And there's a third, USS *Canopus*. I think the big show is over. Here comes another big frigate, USS *Constellation*, bringing up the rear. Oh, and another. USS *Princess Royal*. What are your orders, Your Highness?"

So, Granny Rita, tell me again exactly what is my place in the chain of command?

Kris gave Jack's hand a sad squeeze. If the sorrow on his face was a reflection of hers, they were a pretty sorry lot. It looked like the clock had struck twelve, and Cinderella would have to turn back into a princess and the prince would have to turn back into a Marine captain.

There were several obscene things Kris would have liked to say; what she did say to Captain Drago was, "Get ready to receive the king. I'll get back to the fleet landing as fast as I can. What acceleration is the fleet putting on?"

"One and a half gees. Somebody wants to get here quick. I'm told they'll arrive in eighteen hours."

"Issue a recall as gently as you can. Let's not scare the natives, heavy or otherwise."

"I understand. Prepare for a royal visit. Get the ship ship-shape and Bristol fashion."

"You know the drill. I'll have to warn Granny Rita."

"You forgot, Nelly put me on your net," said Granny interrupting. "We'll talk as soon as you get back into town."

"We'll see you soon, Granny," Kris said.

"Damn," said the old lady for Kris.

Kris looked at Jack. "The *Sakura* must have made a fast passage, and Grampa Ray must have left immediately." She found herself shaking her head.

At that moment, their meal arrived. Kris gave the waitress a princess-caliber smile, and said, "I'm sorry, we'll have to be leaving."

"But why?" the young woman asked.

As Kris stood, a glance around told her that those at the table close by had heard an earful they didn't know how to interpret. Never a good idea.

Kris cleared her throat and spoke in the voice that made crews snap to, even if it meant dying. "I appreciate the privacy that all of you have afforded Jack and me for the last several days. Many of you recognized me from the interview I gave the Alwan news media. I am Princess Kris Longknife, a lieutenant commander in the Royal United Society Navy and the senior Navy officer present on the research frigate *Wasp*, above your heads. The good news is that the U.S. has just reinforced its fleet presence in the defense of Alwa with over half a dozen ships. Humanity is not forgetting you, but coming to your defense."

Kris paused while the dining room exploded with joyous shouts and applause.

"Please feel free to pass that information along to any of your friends. I'd appreciate if you could avoid mentioning that it came from a nearly naked princess."

"And what's wrong with being naked, nearly or totally?" a nearly naked woman asked.

"In some parts of human space, like wherever my mother is at the moment, anything close to naked is frowned upon." Well, most balls Kris had attended had a few women in gowns that skimped on just about everything, but other than at formal occasions, Mother was quite sure of her dress code.

The woman who'd raised the question suggested that human space do something that, while Kris would love doing it with Jack, it was probably biologically impossible for a huge area of vacuum to manage.

When the general laughter died down, Kris held up her hands and got silence.

"The sad news is that with the fleet arriving, I have to cut my vacation short and go back to being a Navy officer. I've enjoyed your company, and I look forward to returning when my schedule allows, but I must leave immediately."

Kris and Jack made their way to the door, slowly, shaking many a hand and getting lots of hugs. At the door, the owner waited. "You are welcome here at any time, and your money will never be good so long as I own this place, or my kids. Please come back when you can. We have a truck we use to make trips to town. My son will have it at your cottage in fifteen minutes."

"We'll be ready," Kris said.

After another hug, Kris and Jack made their final good-bye and jogged toward their cottage, in step and by cadence.

Their vacation was vanishing by the second.

They hastily donned their uniforms. The spider silks were tossed in their bags; there was no time to pull themselves into that tight confinement. Besides, once topside, they'd need to shower and change into clean uniforms. Probably dress uniforms.

It *was* the king paying a visit.

And he very likely wouldn't care for what he found.

"Do you think King Raymond expects to haul the entire human colony off this planet? Is that what the huge ships are? Transports?" Jack asked.

"Transports with a battleship's broadside?" Kris pointed out.

"Nothing about this makes sense," Jack concluded.

"In some weird way, it does to Ray Longknife," Kris said.

They were dressed and packed in ten minutes. Kris glanced at the bed. Could they have taken a few moments for a fast one? Did she want her final memory of this to be something of sweaty haste? Better to go forward without looking back.

A teenager arrived early. They tossed their gear in the back of the truck and shared the narrow cab with a hero-worshipping young man who wanted to know everything about human space and repeatedly told them he planned to visit there. "But I'll come back here. There's no place better to live. Have you ever been to a better resort than Dad's?"

Kris allowed that she hadn't, and had to repeat it several times in the drive back.

Two hours later, they pulled up to Granny Rita's home. It was a nice adobe two-story, built around an open garden court with a fountain and pond in the middle. Clearly, it had been meant to house a large family.

Three teenagers came out to carry their two bags. A mother provided supervision in case any should be needed.

Kris and Jack said their good-bye to the boy, who told them he wasn't going anywhere until the truck's batteries recharged. The mother gave him directions, needed or not, to the nearest recharging station.

An older couple, likely Granny's own kid and spouse, hurried them inside and across the plaza. "You must do something," the man said. "She's insistent that she go up to the *Wasp* to meet Raymond. I think another shuttle launch could kill her."

"I think she wants to go out that way," the woman said. "Who can fault her for going? If it kills her, it saves her from having to confront him."

The man did not dispute his wife's opinion.

"Granny Rita is not getting on any shuttle I control," Kris said flatly. "I will not have her death on my hands. God knows, I've got enough of them on my soul. Hers is not going to be added, and that is that."

"You don't know Granny Rita," the man said.

Jack snorted. "You don't know Kris Longknife."

That settled the discussion until they got to Granny Rita's suite of rooms.

The old woman was packing several bags. "I don't know what Raymond will want to do. You say he's a king. It's been a long time since I've been to a ball. Somewhere around here, I have a ball gown."

"Mother, you cut it up to make clothes for me and Tina when we were small. I remember you telling us the story. We've handed them down, generation to generation."

The old woman looked up. "I guess I forgot. Young woman, those pills you gave me don't seem to be working as well as promised."

"You haven't been taking them as long as you were told," Kris shot back.

"Well, however it goes, I must meet Raymond on the *Wasp* when he arrives."

"No, Granny, you will meet Raymond here, on your own turf," Kris said.

"I'm going up," Granny Rita said with all the stubbornness of her years.

"We can do this the easy way, or the hard way, Granny."

Granny Rita settled into a chair and eyed Kris. "The easy way is?"

"You will not be allowed on any shuttle under my command. Last time I checked, they're all under my command."

"So what happened to Captain Drago being the *Wasp*'s skipper?" Granny demanded.

"You eavesdropped on our conversation. You tell me who gives the orders there."

"But he's the captain. So long as you're in that dotted box, you can still marry Jack. By the way, how'd the vacation go?"

"Swimmingly. Often without swimming suits as you no doubt expected."

"I think two of my kids were conceived there."

"Too much information, Granny, and you are dodging the issue."

"Okay. How do we do this the hard way?"

"We'll have several liberty launches dropping down to pick up the crew. I can put a ship's surgeon on one. He can give you a thorough physical to qualify you for space. You'll fail, and then it's official. Commodore Rita Nuu Longknife-whatever-else is grounded."

"And Raymond isn't grounded."

"He's been through several rejuvenation cycles. Not just some pills but the whole treatment, fix or replace anything as necessary."

Rita leaned back in her chair and blew out a disagreeing breath. "You are not giving me the proper respect I deserve."

Kris snapped right back. "You mean I should obey your whim and let you commit suicide by shuttle? Forget it. It ain't gonna happen on my watch, and there *is* no other watch."

"I'll bet you don't talk to King Raymond like this," Granny pouted.

"Sorry, Granny Rita," Jack said. "I've been stuck in meetings between those two. Subordinate is not Kris's strong suit. Nowhere close."

"If Grampa Ray had had his choice, I never would have been allowed to do the Voyage of Discovery, never would have spotted the alien invasion force, and never broken its back," Kris said.

"Tell me something, young whippersnapper to a wise elder, what was the vote to launch eight battleships and four corvettes at that monster?"

Kris tossed the question to Jack and settled into a chair.

"Initially," Jack said, "the admiral from Greenfeld, the Peterwald Empire, was all for collecting his four battleships and going home. Two other admirals from Musashi and the Helvetican Confederacy were willing to go along with Kris if she could come up with a decent plan. She did, and everyone followed it. At least until things came apart."

"They always come apart," Granny said, her voice years and light-years away.

"Yes, they always come apart," Kris agreed. "Now, Granny Rita, there is a liberty launch holding at the landing for me and Jack. We have to be going. Feel free to do whatever you want to receive a visiting king, unless you can convince the Alwans to apply for membership in the United Societies, in which case he'll be their king paying a visit. By the way, Grampa wanted to call his association of planets United Sentients, but his meeting with the Iteeche leaked out, and the name got changed. The Alwans might help him change it back."

"The Alwans can't agree on whether it's day or night," Granny Rita's daughter said.

"Sadly true," Granny agreed. "Okay, young lady, shoo. You have your irons in the fire. I'll see what kind of fire I can light down here. You're sure he'll come down?"

"Absolutely," Kris said.

"Then I got a party to plan, fit for a king."

Kris was none too sure about the sound of that, but she had her own work cut out for her. She and Jack left. A car waited to hurry them to the fleet landing. They were the last aboard. The liberty launch started its takeoff run as they tightened their seat belts.

15

Kris went straight to the bridge as fast as she could bounce off one wall and hit another. She need not have hurried. Captain Drago had nothing new to report.

"They are squawking the exact minimum required by law," the skipper said. "Their name, their home port, and that they are U.S. warships."

"All of them, even the big ones?" Kris asked.

"Yes, but who would put just twenty guns on a battlewagon that huge. Oh, they also have 5-inch secondaries. Our gravity anomaly detector says those huge ships are heavy, but no masses like thick armor. Kris, these ships don't make any sense."

"So they're something new. Jack wondered if they were transports to take the entire colony home. Could they do that?"

"Not empty enough," Senior Chief Beni said, shaking his head. "There's a lot of heavy stuff *inside* those ships, but it's not where an armored belt belongs."

The bridge crew looked around at each other, but Kris only saw faces as blank as hers.

"Captain, does your Navy experience include anything like this?" Kris asked.

"No, but I asked Cookie what he thought. He said, back in the day when he was a boot ensign, General Longknife's flag came into a system, just as silent as this. No signal at all. The local admiral and every commanding officer pushed the panic button. Said it was something like a no-notice showdown inspection. Every elephant was running around like a chicken with his head cut off trying to make everything perfect."

"An interesting mix of metaphors," Kris said. "What happened?"

"The sector admiral ended up sacked, as well as the admirals commanding the Navy base and Navy yard. Several squadron and division commanders found themselves on the beach along with quite a few captains."

Kris considered that for a long minute. Then shook her head. "We've got no admirals to sack and we've already been booted about as far as we can go and still be in the same galaxy. No. Something else is going on."

She thought for a long moment as the bridge stayed silent. "*Prosperity*. What kind of a name is that for a warship?"

"There have been a few of them," Nelly said. "Usually small auxiliaries."

"Are you sure the *Enterprise* isn't the *Free Enterprise*?" Kris asked slowly.

"You think your Grampa Al has something to do with those two?" Jack asked.

"Call it a hunch, but *Prosperity* and *Canopus* just don't seem cut from the same cloth."

"There have been several repair and depot ships named *Canopus*," Nelly put in.

"And *Princess Royal*," Kris said. "What kind of name is that?"

"The Royal Navy," Nelly said, "I mean the British wet royal navy had a battlecruiser named *Princess Royal* at one of the greatest sea battles in history."

Kris still scowled, but Jack was grinning.

"It would honor one of the fightingest captains in a long time," he said.

Yesterday, Kris would have thrown him a kiss for that kind reflection of her. Maybe a lot more than a kiss. Today, she settled for a smile.

And turned her thoughts back to her problem. She needed more information. The ships were not talking.

"Nelly," Kris said, "have you tried to contact those ships on Nelly Net?"

"No, Kris, all my kids are here."

"All but Katsu-san's Fumio-san."

"He was on the *Sakura*," Nelly said.

"Question, did it head back to Musashi direct or stop off at Wardhaven?"

"Wardhaven's closer than Musashi," Captain Drago said.

"Nelly, send to Katsu-san, *'Ohio, Katsu-san. Doumo arigatou gozaimasu.* Did you help design these ships? The new large frigates look just like the fast and heavily armed war wagons I'd want in a fight. The big ones like the *Prosperity* are a bit too big, don't you think?' Send that Nelly to Fumio-san and let's cross our fingers."

Nelly started a timer. It looked like it would take a while for the message to get there and more for a reply to get back. Frustrated, Kris headed for her quarters for a shower and a change of uniform.

Abby arrived on the second liberty launch, fussing about having a good night's sleep interrupted. Cara was none too happy. She'd found kids her own age delighted to find out what computer games were and someone willing to share with them.

Kris considered the joy of sharing a shower with Jack and, in her lone frustration, scrubbed herself pink. Abby had her dress whites, complete with orders and medals laid out. Getting dressed in zero gee was no fun, but Kris got herself fully and properly uniformed before heading back to the bridge, just as the timer was coming up on an hour.

"Nothing, so far," Captain Drago reported.

Kris settled at her station at Weapons and put her feet in loops so that she could stand if she needed to talk to the engineer from Musashi.

The main screen continued to show the stars above, the green-and-blue planet below. A third liberty launch was on approach while the first back was already dropping down for another load of disappointed Sailors.

Then a portion of the main screen changed to the cheerful

face of Kikuchi Katsu, the senior engineer of Mitsubishi Heavy Space Industry and designer of the *Wasp*.

"I am so glad to see you again, Princess-san. We hurried here as quickly as we could. The *Sakura* broke its long journey at Wardhaven to give your King Raymond the joyous news that his wife still lives."

Kris would not have wanted to be a mouse in that room.

"But your brother had already done so much to get frigates under construction at Nuu Docks. First the *Intrepid* and *Fearless*, only a bit bigger than your *Wasp*. But they were also working on something to take the new 20-inch guns that several planets of your United Society had been testing but saw no reason to build. Believe me, now they do, and the other four ships are larger frigates with six 20-inchers forward and four aft.

"Your honorable brother persuaded my most honorable father and your most honorable grandfather to take the question of our competing patents to arbitration. Your king and your most honorable grandfather agreed to merge the two big frigates building in each of the three large battleship slips. I added more to them and turned two of them into the Prosperity class armed transports. I can make them back into two large frigates each, but they are also loaded with mining and factory equipment and people to run them. You will have both warships, freighters, and lunar factories when I am done. Also, the *Canopus* will be a space station for Alwa until the moon base sends up enough material to make a normal station. Then it, too, will become frigates and ships for mining."

Kris could imagine the horse trading that had gone on. Still, while Kris and the Sailors and Marines had fought and died to keep the bastards from strip-mining the system, Grampa Al was stepping right in, *no need to thank me*, and grabbing for everything. Kris was grateful for the new warships but none too sure the colonials would care for the price they'd pay.

A voice was heard from offscreen, and Katsu-san turned. "I am talking to Princess-san Longknife. Why?"

A hand reached in to pull his computer, Fumio-san, from around his neck, and the signal was broken.

"How dare they manhandle one of my children!" Nelly exploded. "I expect a full apology from them, or they won't be able to trust any computer on their ships."

"Nelly, please calm down," Kris asked her computer. "We've got a lot of problems here, and I don't really think they will harm either Katsu-san or Fumio-san. They need them too much. Spinning one ship into several has got to take genius, and I don't know anyone else who could even try it out here."

"We'll see," Nelly said.

"Promise me you will take no action without telling me," Kris insisted.

"All right," Nelly said with a pout.

"Are any of you aware that I've been following this?" Granny Rita said, butting in.

Kris chuckled. "I am glad I can honestly say that we didn't order you to be included in this, but I'm not at all sorry you heard."

"Is my boy Alex a bit grabby?"

"A selfish miser might describe him quite well," Abby said, joining them on the bridge.

"Granny Rita," Kris said, jumping in before Abby's attitude toward wealth could tie up the conversation for the next hour, "I remember hearing that you had some nanos that you used to leach minerals out of mountains and other sources. Did you just take the stuff, or did you share it with the Alwans? Maybe agree to pay royalties?"

"Let me get Ada in here, but I think we gave the Alwans thirty percent of what we took out back then. Now that we have to get more invasive when we go after minerals, and they like the stuff we make, they want forty percent for their share. Same for our heavy manufacturing. They don't much care for our dams and smelters, but they want forty percent of what comes from them."

Kris had heard one word that kind of made it hard to hear the rest of Granny Rita's report. "You 'gave' the Alwans thirty percent. Was that documented in a treaty?"

"Honey, we weren't even making paper in those days. As for the Alwans, a pledge made in front of two elders is binding. They still haven't really gotten the idea of writing things down."

"Granny Rita, the kind of men your little Alex likely sent on this expedition won't give a second's thought to anything not signed, notarized, and filed in court."

"My father was a hardheaded businessman, but not hard-hearted," Granny said.

Penny stepped forward. "Granny, Alex is a tough case. His dad never had much time for him. You went off to war and never came back. He buried his first wife before the blush was off the marriage. He doesn't expect anything from the world but what he can grab with his own two hands and hold on to tight. He's surrounded by a lot of equally hard cases. We think a few of them have even taken shots at Kris when she got in the way of what Alex wanted for Nuu Enterprises, Limited."

"That wasn't the way my dad, Ernie Nuu, ran the business," Rita said, her voice gone hard.

"Granny," Kris said, "I need you to get some sort of document that records the present forty percent or the previous thirty percent. I'm not expecting that they brought a judge to set up shop here, so we may have some leeway in interpreting this document, but I need something if I'm going to stop what I see coming at us at one and a half gees."

"You think you can do something if I get a paper?"

"She's a Longknife," Jack put in. "Never count her out."

"We'll see what I can do," Granny Rita said. "When's Raymond due in?"

"Ten, twelve hours. I'll probably tie him up for a few hours making my report."

"Don't count on tying Raymond up. If he's all set to charge down here, the best you can do, kid, is run alongside him. Don't get in front. His horns can be dangerous."

"Trust me, Granny, we've butted heads and crossed horns before. I've learned when to butt back and when to run."

"Good luck," Granny Rita said.

"And good luck to you," Princess Longknife said. Then she turned to Captain Drago. "Are we prepared to receive the king?"

"Not yet, but we're on schedule to be there right on time. I've taken the liberty of messaging the *Fearless* and *Intrepid*. Both of them look to be about our own tonnage. I've sent them the design for spinning out a crossbeam and swinging us around each other. I never knew a skipper who didn't like the idea of putting some weight on his crew. However, the *Canopus* is spinning itself out. I think it may arrive in orbit already prepared to serve as some sort of space station."

Kris raised an eyebrow at that.

Senior Chief Beni at Sensors had the forward screen switch to the approaching fleet. It ran down the four leading frigates; two were significantly larger than the other two, then the two huge something-or-others, trailed by something that was going from huge to titanic.

It was growing longer as well as uniformly wider. "Yep, that's starting to look like the tin can of a basic space station," Kris said. Having blown one up and defended another, space stations and their structure were no stranger to her.

"Hey, I think they just popped their first dock out," Jack said.

"They'll need to balance things just right," Drago said. "Three docks for us smaller frigates. Then some way to get those four big war wagons balanced without putting them too close to each other. As for those last two. God, I'd hate to have the job of balancing them. If they get out of sync, they could twist the whole station in knots."

"I'd let those two swing around each other. Spin off a couple of their ships, and get smaller before I dared attach them to the station," Kris said. "Captain Drago, please send to *Monarch*, in the clear and wide open enough for the *Canopus* to copy, 'my respects and fealty to His Majesty. I respectfully suggest the *Prosperity* and *Enterprise* swing themselves bow to bow around each other while the rest of us dock on *Canopus*.'"

"Comm, send as requested," the skipper ordered.

Kris settled down to watch the incoming ships for the time it would take a message to cross the space between them. This message would take more time. The *Monarch*'s communications folks would have to authenticate the message, then walk it to wherever King Raymond I was hanging out. That might add ten to twenty minutes to the elapse time between Kris's sending and her getting a reply.

Of course, she had no idea where the legendary Ray Longknife hung out when he was pulling a no-notice showdown inspection. Or coming to call on his long-lost wife.

Kris spent time gnawing her lower lip, trying to figure out which she'd prefer to deal with, Ray Longknife, come full legend to inspect a command and see if it could be found wanting, or the family man, so out of practice, to face a woman who had been through a mill of horrors and successes, and was little like the woman he'd once known.

Of course, the man going to meet Rita was nothing like the one she'd sailed off from on a near-suicide mission eighty years ago.

"What are you thinking?" Jack asked as he glided up to take a handhold on Kris's station.

"I'm remembering all the reasons I joined the Navy. How much I wanted to get out of family things," she said, seriously, then half snorted. "Not even shipping out to the other side of the galaxy is far enough to get away from my family."

Jack managed to surreptitiously squeeze her hand while officially getting a better handhold on her station. "Our family doesn't have to be anything like the families we're from," he whispered.

Kris allowed him a smile, but with the entire bridge watching, she had to direct it at the forward screen and hope he saw it reflected back at him.

Her seated, him standing, they waited out the time lapse.

The *Canopus* continued its metamorphism from huge freighter to space station. At one time, she took on a spin, but only briefly. With the ship decelerating at one and a half gees, there was a clear down aboard. The spin would have made it rough for all hands.

"She spun smoothly," Captain Drago said. "I've been aboard a ship that wasn't balanced when the skipper put on battle revolutions. She damaged some delicate equipment, and we had a new skipper not ten minutes after we docked. *Canopus* did that test well."

The screen came alive.

The king himself was scowling down at Kris, bigger than life.

"My, aren't you being formal, 'respects and fealty.' Not a bad thing to amend to a message where you're trying to teach your old grampa how to suck eggs. We've been planning this

for several weeks, kiddo. Trust us to get it right. Longknife out."

Kris blinked several times.

"Well, that answers where the king is hanging out," Jack
said. "If that wasn't the bridge of the *Monarch*, I'm a boot
learning how to box the square."

"Well, I feel put in my place," Kris said. "I guess they did
pay more attention to my reports than I thought."

"Don't bet on it," Senior Chief Beni said from Sensors.
"There's suddenly a whale of a lot of communications going
on between the *Monarch* and those two overweight slugs. It's
not in standard code, but my Nelson is having no problem
cracking it. Thank you, Nelly, for the loan of one of your
kids."

"What's the message?" Kris asked.

"The first message was from the *Monarch* and contained
your instructions for spinning out a pole from each bow to
spin around on. The later messages are between the two slugs.
Between their cargo and the amount of reaction mass they
have left aboard, they are quite a few tons different and the
distribution is all balled up. Their skippers are debating how
to redesign the swing system to account for that, if it's even
possible."

"And they wanted to dock those two disasters on the *Canopus*!" Captain Drago said.

"So Raymond doesn't want you to teach him to suck eggs,
but he's only too happy to learn how, huh," came from Granny
Rita.

"Apparently," Kris agreed. "How are things going on
your end?"

"It turns out that five years ago, our Minister of Mining and
Industry signed a Memorandum of Understanding with the
Representative of the Association of Associations for Main-
taining Harmony with the Heavy People for Gifts and Arcane
Knowledge. You know, our mining guy and their tax man."

"If you say so," Kris said.

"Anyway, their G and AK guy is young and has taken on
more of our ways, so the idea of committing to paper something as important as them getting a forty-percent take of

everything didn't sound nearly as strange to him as it did to a lot of the other elders."

"Did the memo only deal with Alwa?" Jack asked.

"Funny you should ask," Granny Rita said, "You know, we were trying to get them to help us get back up to the *Furious* and bring down the reactors."

"Yes," Kris said, hoping she knew where this was going.

"This Alwan knew they'd want part of the energy from the reactor, so he pushed to have the memo cover everything in the Alwa system. Since most elders don't recognize the existence of anything over the horizon, this bird was quite far-looking."

"Well, thank you, Granny. Would you please send up a copy. Your new computer should show you how to do that."

"Already asked it. It should be showing up any second."

"I have it," Nelly said.

"How are your other preparations going?" Kris asked.

"Fine. Fine. We'll have a party fit for a king," Rita assured her.

Kris rang off. Nelly projected the memo in front of Kris.

"You think the ink is dry on those signatures?" Abby asked.

"You would question the honor and integrity of my Granny Rita?" Kris said in shock. Shock with a large cup of skepticism in it.

"In a second," Penny said.

"We'll let the lawyers argue over it," Kris said, dismissively. "Skipper, are we ready for the king?

"As ready as we'll ever be."

"Your Highness," came in a carefully cultivated voice.

"Yes, Professor Joao Labao," Kris said.

"We have several preliminary reports back from our survey and analysis of the alien base ship. Is there any chance you will have the time or desire to hear them before meeting your king?"

"Meet me in my Tac Center," Kris ordered, "just as fast as you can glide down here."

"On my way, with full graphics and graphs."

"Nelly, get my entire team to the Tac Center. Skipper, would you care to attend?"

Captain Drago actually looked just a bit distressed. "I'd love to attend, but I think it better I keep an eye on the *Wasp*'s developments for a royal visit. Nelly, would you be so kind as to record the discussion and provide me with a copy?"

"I would gladly do that, Captain," Nelly said, most ladylike.

KRIS, THE CAPTAIN IS STARTING TO WARM TO ME.

THEN DON'T DO ANYTHING TO SCREW UP, Kris said as she drifted from the bridge to her Tac Center.

16

Kris had expected to be ordered to the *Monarch*, it being the Royal Ship. However, King Raymond hadn't forgotten that the *Wasp* had a Forward Lounge with a full bar, so the elephant herd came to her.

Thus, an hour after Captain Drago docked with Canopus Station, Kris was waiting on the quarterdeck of the *Wasp* for the arrival of the king. And arrive he did.

Decked out in the blue dress uniform of a fleet admiral, with all his ribbons from not just the Unity War and Iteeche War, but a few even before that, he was resplendent.

And so gold-encrusted, Kris wondered how he could walk. That newfound skill of hers, giggling, almost got the better of her, but she held her breath, waited as he saluted the flag on the aft bulkhead, saluted her, and asked, "Permission to come aboard."

"Permission granted, Your Royal Majesty."

"Which way to that bar of yours?"

"Follow me, sir." And Kris led him forward.

The *Wasp*'s new navigator stepped forward to take Kris's place and prepared to receive Admiral Crossenshield. The king glanced over his shoulder, then eyed Kris.

"Your navigator is Imperial Musashi Navy."

"The *Wasp* did commission there, and we were a bit short-handed. His Imperial Majesty, the Emperor of Musashi, was kind enough to grant us the use of some of his personnel when it became necessary for us to get underway in great haste." Kris tried not to smile at all she was leaving unsaid.

"Right. You've got a whole company of Imperial Marines. How's your Secret Service Agent, Jack what's-his-name taking to that?"

"The Emperor graciously put the Marine company under Captain Montoya's command. It was only later that our own Royal U.S. Marine company arrived. The rump battalion is exercising well together."

"Have you done any field exercises on Alwa? That's what they call it, right."

"Yes, sir. And no, sir, it has not seemed wise to land a landing force. The Alwans are having a hard enough time coming to terms with the basic concept of intelligent species using force against each other without us practicing in their own backyard."

"They better get the concept real fast," the king muttered.

"We couldn't agree more on that," Kris said, and ushered the king into the Forward Lounge.

Mother MacCreedy had outdone herself. The place looked like an Officers' Club like you might have found in old England or better yet, Raj India. Captured Unity flags hung next to Imperial Iteeche banners and gold tridents. There were several huge oil paintings. One showed a bunch of horsemen on gray mounts charging, sabers waving, seemingly hell-bent on charging out of the picture.

There were photos, too, some of old, bewhiskered officers, but Kris spotted one of General Ray's staff from the Iteeche War, and another of his officers from the old Second Guard Brigade.

The man in the gold-encrusted fleet admiral's blues took it all in, and grumbled, "A bit overdone, isn't it?"

Kris shrugged. "You know how contractors *will* go overboard trying to please." When he didn't react to her gibe, she led him toward the screens.

One thing Mother MacCreedy had done was to set aside an area behind a glass wall. For an old lady, Mother MacCreedy was either taking to manipulating Smart Metal™ herself or had someone who owed her favors. Whoever it was did indeed know the magic of making Smart Metal™ not only stand up and paint pictures, but also turn a wall clear as glass, and, like tonight, expand the floor area and the length of the bar.

The Forward Lounge might be crowded, but it would not leave anyone out. It was big at the moment and likely to get bigger as the need arose.

The king settled himself at the table with the best view of the screens. The planet rolled by below them as a pretty Marine corporal in dress blue and reds arrived. "Can I get you something to drink, Your Royal Majesty?" she asked with a barmaid's smile.

The king frowned. "Were you ordered to this assignment?"

"No, sir," the girl answered indignantly. "I get extra pay for this, and while the tips aren't likely to be as good tonight since the princess here ordered me out of my usual short skirt and into uniform, it's still a good way to supplement my college fund, if you must know, sir. Now, are you drinking or just asking personal questions?"

The king chuckled. "Marines haven't gotten any less sharp even if I have gotten too old to match wits with them. A Scotch, Corporal, double, and on the rocks."

"I'll be right back. Your Highness, your usual?"

"Yes, Kathy, thank you."

The king watched the attractive young woman's rear sashay away from them. "In a short dress, she *definitely* would be getting great tips."

Then he turned to Kris. "You're out of uniform."

"Sir, no one told me the fleet was in blues. It's summer below, and we've been in whites. Until you showed up with *Canopus* for a station and source of down, we've been granting about a quarter of the crew shore leave in three-day passes."

She saw no need to add that she and Jack had tried to get in a two-week vacation.

He reached into his blouse pocket and pulled out two shoulder boards and slid them across the table to Kris. "You've been drawing commander's pay since the first of this month."

Last Kris had heard, she was AWOL and not drawing any pay. It was nice to know she now had some income, but the shoulder boards didn't have the three stripes of a commander. They showed the one extrawide strip of a commodore.

"Sir," Kris said, eyebrow raised.

"If you're going to command a squadron all the way on the other side of the galaxy, it seemed like we ought to frock you up to commodore officially. No more of this calling you one thing while you wear the stripes of something a whole lot more junior. Frocking, or fleeting up, is an ancient custom going back to the times of wooden ships and iron men. Think sailing ships all the way on the other side of the world with no damn wire strung up anyone's butt to get orders from people who didn't know what was going on but thought they had enough rank to tell everyone what to do."

Kris eyed her great-grandfather as the drinks arrived. No one, not even Admiral Crossenshield, had crossed into the space reserved by the glass divider. Even Jack was standing at the bar, an untouched beer in his hand, never taking his eyes off her, or maybe the king.

"I ducked up to look around on the Canopus Station once we docked," Kris said. "There's a full Navy yard here. That rates at least a captain. Maybe this far out, an admiral."

"Yeah, Benson has the job. Rear Admiral Benson, now retired, and just Mr. Benson to you. His whole staff are the best volunteers we could lay our hands on. Most retired, a few took early out to come here."

Kris knew she should say thank you, but the words didn't make it past a stampede of other thoughts bubbling up her throat. "You've gone to a great effort to see that I command here, Grandfather. Why?"

The king gave her a smile that was part proud grandparent . . . and part deadly battle commander. How a man could blend those two feelings was one question Kris would not ask.

"What do you think of that big frigate I popped last on you? *Princess Royal.* Ten 20-inch lasers. What a war wagon. I thought you might want to transfer your flag to her." He gave Kris no time to answer that but rushed on. "She's not named that because you fill out a ball gown real nice, Kris. I gave her that name because you are the fightingest captain I've got in my fleet. The fightingest woman commander I've seen since your great-grandmother Rita took the 16th Battlecruiser

Squadron on its last ride. Yes, I've bent the rules to keep you in command. You're triple-deep selected for commander, and it took an act of Congress from a Congress I can hardly get to act at all, to allow us to start frocking up combat-experienced officers."

He glanced around. "I don't think you've failed to notice. We desperately need battle commanders, and experienced ones are in short supply."

It was tempting to remind him that she'd been just as battle experienced when he shipped her off to East Siberia to command a mosquito boat flotilla for Madigan's Rainbow, but she bit her lip and went to what she knew had to be her next question.

"You know, sir, this is a suicide mission. I don't see any way we can survive another attack like we faced last time. Recently, we encountered hostiles. They were shooting at anything that drifted into their space. Anything!"

"You've encountered more hostiles?"

"Yes, sir. Are you ready for my report?"

The king downed the rest of his Scotch in a single gulp and slammed it down on the table. "Damn, that's good stuff. Okay, you bring in your team, and I'll bring in mine, and the other frigate skippers," he said, waving at Admiral Crossenshield. "You show me what you've got, and I'll show you what I've brought. Yes, you're a forlorn hope, all the way hell and gone across the galaxy, but I'll be damned if you won't have a fighting chance.

"Yes, we want you to put up a fight. A fight that will leave these bastards licking their wounds and, if they beat you, celebrating that they wiped out a nest of the worst sons a bitches the galaxy ever spawned. We need you to buy us time—win, lose, or draw—to build the fleet back home that will take them apart piece by piece until they either holler uncle or, to quote an old sea dog, 'their language is only spoken in hell.'

"But no, Princess Royal of my blood, you and your crew are not expendable. What you're looking at is just the first of several squadrons that were fitting out for the long jumps here when I departed human space. Those huge, bloated transports can spin out four big frigates between them to double your strength. And, as you may have heard"—this last came with a raised eyebrow—"there are factories and mining ships in them, too.

"And all of what's coming isn't just from the U.S. Musashi tells me that they'll send their 3rd Frigate Squadron just as soon as they have three others to defend themselves. Other planets are kicking in squadrons, too."

He almost smiled. "You showed with the Fleet of Discovery that you could lead a mismatched, divided bunch of commanders and ships. I'm glad you had the practice. You've only just begun to fight, my dear. You've only just begun."

"Then I better let you know the extent of the threat, Your Royal Majesty. This planet is beleaguered, and it looks to only get worse."

17

The glass section receded into the deck. Mother Mac-Creedy had already expanded the open section of the Forward Lounge twice. Penny looked none too happy to be giving up armor, but the system was clear except what was tied up to Canopus Station.

Oh, and the two, still-unbalanced monsters doing their best to swing around each other two hundred klicks behind the station and wobbling all over the place as they tried again and again to balance themselves.

Kris did her best not to look at the jig those two were doing. It would not do to get the giggles in front of the king over something his regal decree had insisted was all well in hand.

No. Not at all. Not at all.

Between her discovering she could giggle and finding out how good it felt to make long, passionate, languid love under a palm-fringed tree, Jack was proving a very bad influence.

She dearly wished she could have some more of that bad influence, but Kris declared over this minivacation in her head, stood up, and began to brief the king, his staff, and more importantly, the frigate captions and their XOs, senior scientists, and Marine-detachment skippers of what were to be her new squadron.

The scientists surprised Kris. All of the frigates had a civilian contingent of fifty to sixty boffins, as well as a platoon of Marines reinforced with heavy weapons. Clearly, what she'd started with the *Wasp* was being adopted for the fleet. At least the fleet that volunteered for exile to the other side of the galaxy and a potentially suicidal fight.

"Your Royal Majesty, Admiral, Captains, skippers, ladies and gentlemen. We have defeated the enemy, but they are still sniffing around here. That's the bad news. The good news is that they're only sniffing, not massing for an assault. At least not within two jumps of Alwa. One of the things I hope we can do very quickly now that there are more ships available is extend our early-warning system to six, then twelve systems out," Kris said, glancing at the king.

He nodded agreement. Admiral Crossenshield made a note.

The king nodded a lot during Kris's briefing, and Crossie took a lot of notes.

Kris was left wondering in that tiny portion of her brain not taken up by the briefing how it happened that the king showed up with the chief of his security and intelligence agency at his elbow. Was Crossie that important, or was Ray not about to leave human space with Crossie not under his watchful eye?

Meanwhile, Kris kept talking.

"The aliens removed all their dead from the wreckage of the mother ship. However, our nanos found one boot with part of a leg in it. The aliens we're dealing with are the same ones we ran into four other times, including the raped planet. Based on genetic drift, this group, however, has not had contact with the other groups for somewhere between ten and fifteen thousand years."

"Brutish and solitary," the king muttered. "Do you think they fight among themselves?"

"No way to form an opinion on that, sir."

"What's your defensive position here?" Crossie butted in.

"Rather simple for the *Wasp*," Kris said as offhandedly as she could. "If a single three-to-five-hundred-thousand-ton ship shows up, we'll fight it. If two come through the jump gate, we'll assess our situation and try to fight them. If one of those monster base ships jumps in system with a fleet of two hundred of those huge ships, we run."

"But now you're reinforced," a lieutenant commander, one of the frigate skippers, said.

KRIS, THAT'S CAROLYN SAMPSON. YOU MAY REMEMBER HER DAD. HE COMMANDED ATTACK RON SIX WITH THE *TYPHOON* IN IT AND ORDERED THE ATTACK ON THE EARTH FLEET AT THE PARIS SYSTEM. HE DIED OF A HEART ATTACK BEFORE THE INVESTIGATION WAS EVER STARTED. SHE'S THE SENIOR-MOST FRIGATE SKIPPER, LIKELY THE REASON YOU GOT PROMOTED TO FULL COMMANDER. HER SHIP IS THE *CONSTELLATION*.

THANKS, NELLY.

Kris would likely never forget Commodore Sampson. Because of his early death, the investigation that might have cleared Kris of mutiny had ended without a conclusion.

What are you doing here, Commander Sampson?

"Yes, having seven frigates does change matters. If seven huge alien ships jump in, we fight. If fourteen or so jump in, we fight. If that monster base ship with all her nasty kittens jumps in, boys and girls, we run."

"And she's supposed to be the best fighting commander we've got," Sampson whispered, loud enough for the entire room to hear.

"Yes, Lieutenant Commander," Kris said, intentionally not giving a ship's skipper the usual courtesy of being addressed as a captain. "I do fight. I do not fight against suicidal odds. Not if I know it. Not if I can help it. Now that you are all here, we'll look at our options and see if we can come up with some surprises for the bastards."

Kris had Nelly fill the forward screen with the view of the alien mother ship huge and looming just after it had jumped into the next system. The view stayed as the Hellburners blew it apart. Then switched to the dead, twisting, and rolling hulk.

With hardly a flicker, three huge alien ships appeared. One of them lazed a small rock.

"We surprised them once. That *won't* happen again. I'm open from the floor for a new suggestion as to how we sneak up on them and smash them with Hellburners. By the way, Your Majesty, did you bring out more Hellburners?"

"Each frigate has two," the king said. "When the *Monarch* and its escort take me back, we'll leave our four behind. Use them as you see fit."

"Gladly, sir. By the way, I'm still open for suggestions from the floor on how we sneak up on a monstrous alien mother ship with two hundred huge escorts."

The floor had nothing to say. It lay there, very quietly.

"Mr. Benson," Kris said, "I'd like to off-load all the Hellburners from the frigates to the station. I see no prospects for a frigate surviving long enough to slip a Hellburner up the rear of a bastard's base ship. We'll need to think of some other way of doing the same."

"Hellburners aboard my station?" The former admiral looked pained at the thought. "I guess I could store them along the centerline, where there's no gravity."

"And under guard. You do have a Marine detachment?" Kris asked.

"Most definitely under guard. Do you have a plan for using those things?" Benson asked.

"I'm working on something," Kris said, and went on. "I'd like to say that our examination of the wreck has shown us their Achilles' heel, but instead, we've drawn a lot of blanks. All the reactors have been stripped from the wreck. From the size of the cable leads coming off the reactors, the ones inside the ship were big enough to run a medium-size city. Of the lasers, nothing. The undamaged ones were salvaged. Even the ones we hit, most of the wreckage had been policed up and carted off. From the small scraps we did get, we think they're at least 16-inch. Power and range are still unknown."

"It doesn't sound like you know much," Sampson muttered lowly.

"Commander," the king said, "stow it. You just got here. When you've been here six weeks, if you've survived, we'll talk. For now, you're bothering me."

"Yes, sir," Sampson said, bracing in her chair. She almost wiped the smirk off her face.

Kris sighed. She'd met a lot of leadership challenges in the last five years. Lieutenant Commander Sampson looked only too eager to offer her a new one.

"Sir, one question if I may," Commander Sampson said.

"Make it a good one," the king said.

"Yes sir. The old *Furious* is still in orbit. Could we salvage her reactors and put them to use powering the moon base?

That might save enough reactors for another mineral exploring and extraction ship."

"Good idea," the king said.

"Bad idea," Kris said.

"Oh?" said the king.

"The colonials on Alwa were trying to off-load those reactors. The Alwans don't much care for burning forests for fuel or damming rivers. It's bad for fishing. That space launch we caught back when was part of a major colonial and Alwan effort to get back to the *Furious* and bring down some new, low-impact power sources." Kris paused.

"I've already promised the use of the *Wasp*'s longboats to help."

"I thought from the report by the *Sakura* that the Alwans were preindustrial and happy to stay that way," Admiral Crossenshield said.

"The answer to that, sir, is yes, no, and maybe. The Alwans never speak with a single voice," Kris said.

"Sounds almost human," the king rumbled.

"Exactly, sir. Most of the old elders are against change. Some of the new, younger elders are more open to change. Many Alwans show up at the colony, ask for an education, and start working right alongside the colonists."

"No central government, huh?" the king said.

"The survivors of the battlecruisers"—Granny Rita to be precise—"thought they had made contact with something like a central government. The Association of Associations. However, you have to realize two things. The *Furious* made orbit shot up pretty bad and on her last leg. Commodore Rita had to get the crew of the *Furious* and the *Enterprise* somewhere they could breathe and maybe find something to eat. Haven looked like a good target, and they went for it."

Kris took a deep breath. "The *Wasp* is now doing the first methodical mapping of the planet, and we've spotted what look like six different major civilizations plus several minor ones. I can't even swear that they're all from the same gene pool. Some around the equator look very different from those in the temperate zones, and the polar regions are different again."

"But they're all confined to the planet," Commander

Sampson put in, "even the colonials, so what we do out here in the system is none of their business."

This was supposed to be a Navy meeting. However, Kris noticed several tables filled with civilians, some in business suits, some in more hardworking gear. At the commander's question, every head focused on her.

So much for a private briefing for the king and her officers.

Kris dropped the bomb. "As it turns out, that is not quite true. The Alwans have developed a taste for human technology. I was just recently interviewed by an Alwan TV medium. The camera needed a tripod to hold it and the mike they gave me weighed over a kilo and was about the size of a banana, but a lot of Alwans are watching TV. Modern transportation is catching on. Most involve animal-pulled wagons, but electric carts and trucks are gaining in popularity. They need to get the old *Furious*'s thermonuclear reactors dirtside and soon."

Kris had everyone in the room hanging on her words, and everyone at the business tables were scowling her way. Enough lead-in.

"The Alwans have required royalties from the colonists to remove minerals. They want forty percent of the finished manufactured products."

"That's highway robbery," Sampson exploded, climbing half-out of her seat.

The business types said much worse though in lower tones. Mother MacCreedy headed over to demand the tables comply with her rules or be cut off. Some of those not in suits were stomping around. Several gave Kris the universal hand signal of approbation.

Kris tried not to smile. Maybe she succeeded.

King Raymond stood up, and at last Commander Sampson sat down and shut up. "I can see we have a lot to discuss with the natives and the colonials. I think I'm about as fully briefed as I can stand. Commodore, do you have experienced bosuns for making the approach to, what are they calling it, Haven?"

"Yes, sir. Our bosuns have been flying the route two or three times a day."

"We can skip the gig. I think we'll need your biggest longboat. I've got a platoon of Marines traveling with me. I'm sure your staff will want to come along." He glanced at Crossie. "If my staff gets too large, send the juniors along in the next boat."

"Yes, sir," Crossie said.

Kris nodded at Jack and Penny. NELLY, TELL ABBY TO COME ALONG IN THE NEXT BOAT. SEE THAT SERGEANT BRUCE AND A COUPLE OF SQUADS OF OUR MARINES ARE WITH HER.

I'LL MAKE IT SO, COMMODORE.

Kris hardly felt like she'd gotten comfortable in the frying pan. Now it was time to dive into the fire.

18

The ride down had its own surprise. Grampa Ray arranged to have the aisle seat with Kris seated inboard of him. Crossie and Jack were across the aisle from them. Kris would have preferred to have these two dangerous old guys together and Jack next to her.

Halfway down, she found out why.

The king leaned over and shouted over the roar of reentry in her ear, "Kid, I hope you won't mind, but in addition to Commander, Alwa Defense Sector, I'm naming you Vicereine and Governor General for the Alwa System."

NELLY, RESEARCH AND BE QUICK ABOUT IT.

VICEREINE IS THE FEMININE OF VICEROY. ENGLAND RULED INDIA FOR SEVERAL HUNDRED YEARS WITH A VICEROY AND GOVERNOR GENERAL. MOST OF THAT TIME THERE WAS VERY LITTLE LOCAL PARTICIPATION IN THE GOVERNMENT BY THE PEOPLE OF INDIA.

THANKS, NELLY.

The roar was still pretty high, but lessening. Kris leaned over and shouted back. "You name me Viceroy, or you can forget the whole thing. And no way will I accept the appointment of Governor General. While it might help me ride herd on those vultures in orbit, the colonials have their own government, thank you very much, and there is no way I'll take responsibility for the Alwans. Herding cats would be easier than getting them to do anything they don't volunteer for." Kris had said her fill, but added, "Respectfully, Your Royal Majesty."

The king laughed. The high gees were slipping away toward something normal as he reached across to Crossie and held his hand out. The black-hearted security honcho reached in the pocket of his own blues and, drawing out a bill, handed it to the king.

As the king pocketed it, Kris got a look. The king had won a thousand-dollar bet!

Kris very much doubted it was for the vicereine part.

"What's a viceroy do?" Kris asked, as the noise got low enough to allow normal conversation.

"Stand in for the king and other odds and ends." The king paused. "I've seen a draft commission for you, Kris. Skipping the vicereine crap and the governor-general stuff, I think the big thing is that it empowers you to open negotiations with the bastards and sign draft peace treaties for submission to the U.S. Senate."

"Peace Treaties?" Kris said to the king. "Aren't you a bit optimistic?"

"If no one has the authority, then no one can," he shot back.

Kris chewed on what the king and Nelly had said for a long minute. "Hold it, Grampa King Ray. You're king over one hundred seventy-three planets. The constitution requires that every one of those planets have a single government in order to apply for membership. The Alwans are nowhere close to a single government, and I doubt the colonials would be all that interested in joining what the Alwans glued together. You can't be king of Alwa, and if you aren't king, this place can't have a viceroy."

"How many times have I heard that?" The king sighed. "But those fool loudmouths in Congress did agree to something new. The colonials can apply for *associated* membership in the U.S. Alwa is that important to us. And if they apply for associated membership, they can vote you in as viceroy. You and only you, I might add."

"You're telling me I have to run for election by an association I have to first persuade them to form!"

"You're Billy Longknife's bratty daughter. You've been hustling voters since before you started school. I don't see a problem," the king said with a huge grin.

"I ran away and joined the Navy to get out of politics!"

"Your sins will always find you out, my child."

"Especially if my grampa leaves bread crumbs to help them," Kris said, making a face.

The king really enjoyed a laugh at that one.

The longboat landed, but then had to thread its way carefully. Every pulling or sailing boat the colonials had was out on the lake waving flags of every color imaginable. A handful of banners were also up saying WELCOME and HOWDY.

They moored at the long pier. Ada was waiting.

Normally, the military has seniors exit a vehicle first. The king stood, taking up a major hunk of the aisle, and said, "You and Jack go first. You know these people. I'll settle the order of my folks after you two."

Kris led the exit, with Jack at her side. She found herself greeted with cries of joy from colonials she now recognized. She let them cheer for a bit, then raised her hand for silence.

Surprise of surprise, she got it.

"May I present to you, His Royal Majesty, Conqueror of the Iteeches, King Raymond I of the United Society."

The cheering got even louder as Ray exited the shuttle, waving like an experienced legend. The cheering went on for quite a while before he also raised both hands. It took longer for them to quiet down.

"Thank you for your welcome," he shouted into the final cheers. "I am glad to have a chance to reestablish friendship and relations with our long-lost shipmates and their children and grandchildren. I am delighted to see how you have prospered in adversity and persevered in the face of fearful odds."

Now the crowd totally lost it. In the following uproar, Ada stepped forward, introduced herself to the king as the Chief of Ministries for the Colonial government, and invited him to come with her to Government House.

She gave Kris a wink before she led the king toward the

jitney that hadn't gotten any larger than before. Kris and Jack used the warning to settle themselves in the second row, behind the driver, who turned out to be Ada. The king settled into the passenger seat and his staff members, now exiting the shuttle, found themselves scrambling for seats. Penny got onto the last row, facing backward and explaining to a commander that she was on the princess's staff and needed to be where Kris was. Besides, a second jitney was waiting.

There were two more jitneys at the end of the pier, along with several wagons with seats pulled by those huge beasts. Kris would have loved to wait and see who chose to walk rather than be pulled along by one of them.

The crowd made way for the jitney with the king on it. The Royal U.S. Marines formed up and route-marched behind them off the pier before falling into step. It was quite a show.

A show that was missing someone.

"Where's Rita?" Kris caught as Ray leaned over to softly ask Ada.

"She's waiting for you at Government House. All this shouting and excitement wouldn't have been good for her."

Shouting and excitement? Granny Rita would lap it up. But Kris kept on her game face and prepared to let it all play out.

The streets between the pier and Government House were lined with cheering people. The king got to do his royal thing, waving, waving, waving. Kris knew how much he didn't care for this part of his job. She kind of pitied him.

She was also none too sure this was the proper lead-up to his meeting Rita.

They finally pulled into the round driveway of Government House. The trees shaded the drive, providing cool for a day that had become hot. The king's gold-encrusted blues were showing sweat, and he seemed to breathe easier out of the sun.

Then he saw Rita, and his face went in all kinds of directions at once.

Rita was there, front and center on the veranda of Government House.

She sat smiling and waving . . . from a wheelchair!

Kris had a good view of the king's face. She tried to catalog the feelings that chased themselves across it. Some managed to stop and homestead for a moment or two.

Ray was delighted and terrified at the same time. He looked worried, concerned, determined, and dismayed. Kris wondered if a normal man could have done this, or if she was once again seeing something only a legend of Ray's stature could manage.

Ray leapt from the jitney before it came to a stop, not that it ever had been going that fast. "Honey, what's wrong?" he asked, coming to kneel on the step below his long-ago wife.

"Nothing, Raymond, really nothing. I'm not as young and spry as you are and I got a bit carried away yesterday getting all this stuff ready for you and it seems I twisted my back. Those pills Kris gave me are making me feel great. I'm just not as great as I feel. Anyway, I think I could handle myself fine with a cane," she said, brandishing a lovely wooden one, "but my bossy kids have got me in this thing, and my grandkid can't wait to push me around in it."

A teenager standing behind Granny Rita grinned, and said, "Vroom, vroom," which did not encourage Kris to trust his driving.

Rita pulled Ray off his knees. "Come, come, most of the old surviving crew want to see you, and there are lots and lots of kids and grandkids. Do you know there's a Raymond Longknife Junior family here on Alwa?"

If possible, the legendary Ray Longknife looked poleaxed. "No."

"Remember that last good-bye, how we fought and made up, then fought and made up some more?"

The king nodded.

"Well, I'd been here about a month and started upchucking my toenails."

"But all the women in the fleet were protected. You wrote the policy yourself."

"Yep, best birth control on the market. Ninety-six-percent effective. But you were one hundred percent, my Raymond."

"Good heavens, Rita, you didn't have to fight for the survival of your crew while going through all that. I know pregnancies are hard on you."

"Raymond, you keep forgetting. It wasn't just the *Furious*'s crew, but also the *Enterprise*. If we hadn't salvaged her ice armor for reaction mass, right now we'd be a lot of frozen bodies flying around the galaxy at very high speed. Also, building a colony was a lot easier with two thousand hands rather than just a thousand."

The conversation might have gone longer, but Ada signaled the teenage motor, and the wheelchair turned and headed in the doors of Government House. The large foyer had been expanded by opening all the doors so that people in several huge halls could flow in and out of the central area.

Somehow, a receiving line got set up. If Kris had thought she had it bad meeting half of Granny Rita's family, this was nothing to the mob scene of old codgers being wheeled in by their old kids or younger grandkids to see the man they'd fought for so many years ago.

Despite several attempts to detach herself from the king, Kris got nailed to his elbow, and every time Ada passed someone to Kris, it was with, "and here's Her Royal Highness, Kristine Longknife, whom King Raymond has appointed our viceroy."

Kris had tried to get a few disputing words in edgewise, but Ada wouldn't listen. It seemed that the idea of their having a permanent representative of the faraway king was catching like wildfire.

It also appeared that the king had somehow managed to skip a few details about Kris's appointment as viceroy. All the colonials flowing by seemed to think that a viceroy was a warm and fuzzy thing and just what they needed for the winter that was coming.

Kris smiled and shook hands and left tomorrow's evil to tomorrow.

Kris smiled and shook hands until her face hurt and her arm was screaming in pain.

Kris kept smiling and kept shaking hands, but she couldn't help but throw Jack a questioning glance. Where was a security chief when she was clearly at risk of bodily harm, as in her face falling off and her arm crippled for life?

Jack's return look was pure helplessness.

Then Granny Rita, of course, saved the day. In a voice that could still echo through a huge hall, she announced, "Folks, it's been a month of Sundays since I've had a chance to say a few words to my Raymond here. So, if you folks would be so kind, I'd like to duck out early on this shindig and find a place we can sit and talk."

A wave of assent moved through the gathering. Granny gave Kris the high sign. Kris replaced the speed-demon teenager at the handles of Granny's wheelchair.

"Out the front door. There's a handicap incline to the left. It will get us down near the path you should remember fondly."

Kris followed directions. King Raymond followed, with Jack at his elbow. The king waved off most of his staff, but he couldn't wave off his Marine platoon. They followed him with full intent and purpose.

At the bottom of the incline, Kris found herself facing a dirt path and wondering how the wheelchair would take to its uneven surface. Granny Rita settled that. "Stop, child. I'm getting out of this contraption."

And she did. The cane gave her a help up, and she hobbled down the path, leaning a bit more on the cane than Kris liked. Apparently, the wheelchair had not been a ruse.

"Honey," the king said, "we brought a rejuvenation clinic. It's not big, but it's on Canopus Station a couple of thousand klicks above your head."

"Raymond, I've already had two shuttle rides between here and the *Wasp* in a whole lot lower orbit than that. Talk to your kid there. She's the one that won't let me on a shuttle again. No shuttle-assisted suicide, right, honey?"

"Yes," Kris said firmly.

"Besides, look at all those old codgers that just came out to shake your hand. How many of them do you think could survive a shuttle launch?"

The king acknowledged the obvious with a grimace. "I guess we can pack the clinic up and bring it down here. There are plenty of drugs that would help your old shipmates. Assuming you don't insist on doing cartwheels when you hear I'm coming."

"It wasn't cartwheels I was doing, buddy boy. I gave up cartwheels years ago, after my fourth or fifth child."

"The two kids we had, the third you had on this side, and . . . ?"

"Six I had with my two husbands on this side, God rest their souls."

"I guess children were essential to the survival of the colony," the king muttered, not at all happily.

"Raymond, don't go giving me that survival excuse. You know our marriage was over before I took that suicide mission."

"I still loved you. I didn't want you to take the mission. That was what we were arguing about."

Kris found herself in the middle of an argument she suspected had begun long before she was born. She stopped to let the two of them walk ahead. Get some distance. Get some privacy.

And was promptly rear-ended by a Marine captain and his guard platoon.

Kris and Jack turned to face the captain. The heated words were getting more distant but still all too clear. Kris mouthed, "Back off."

The captain clearly had orders not to do that. Faced with Kris and Jack forming a block, he let his troops come to an unordered halt behind him.

Kris turned back to her two great-grandparents. Now they were shouting, and Granny was waving her hands and occasionally the cane as well. Kris took a few small steps forward. Steps more appropriate for a child's game than a military formation.

The two elders were coming up on the stone bench Kris and Granny Rita had shared. No surprise, the two of them settled on it but as far apart as they could. While they shouted and gesticulated, Jack had a talk with the guard captain. He deployed his men and women in a crescent, troops alternating facing back and facing front, looking for anything that might threaten their king.

"What do I do if she tries to kill him?" the poor captain whispered to Jack.

"I don't think she's strong enough with that cane," Kris said, but kept her eyes front. If things did get physical between them, it seemed a princess's job to be there first.

AND HER SECURITY CHIEF, SECOND, Jack said on Nelly Net.

DO YOU WANT TO KNOW WHAT THEY'RE SAYING? Nelly asked.

No, Kris said, then reconsidered that absolute rule. IF HE

STARTS TALKING ABOUT MAKING ME GOVERNOR GENERAL OF THIS MADHOUSE, LET ME KNOW.

WAS THAT WHAT THE BET WAS? Jack said.

YEP. IT'S NOT BAD ENOUGH DROPPING THE WHOLE DEFENSIVE PROBLEM OF THIS OUTPOST, OR TO ADD VICEROY, BUT HE SEEMS TO THINK I SHOULD HAVE EXECUTIVE AUTHORITY OVER THIS HERD OF CATS.

AND YOU WERE WISE ENOUGH TO TURN HIM DOWN.

RIGHT, BUT WHEN HAVE YOU EVER KNOWN MY GRAMPAS TO UNDERSTAND THE MEANING OF A SIMPLE WORD LIKE "NO"?

Jack didn't feel compelled to answer so obvious a question.

The rage between the two titans seemed to be winding down.

THEY'RE DEBATING WHO GETS TO USE THE REJUVENATION CLINIC FIRST. HE'S INSISTING SHE IS FIRST IN LINE. SHE'S INSISTING IT BE DONE BY LOTTERY. HE SAID HE DIDN'T BRING THE CLINIC FOR ANY TOM, DICK, OR HARRIET, BUT FOR HER. OOPS, THEY'RE BACK TO THEIR BASIC ARGUMENT. SHE THINKS HE CARES NOTHING FOR REGULAR PEOPLE. IF THEY DON'T HAVE POWER, THEY'RE INVISIBLE TO HIM.

TOO MUCH INFORMATION, NELLY, Kris said.

SORRY. IT'S NOT EASY TO FIGURE OUT WHAT IS GERMANE TO GENERAL OPERATIONS AND JUST TO THEM. OH, SHE JUST ASKED WHAT A VICEROY IS AND HE TOLD HER IT'S NOTHING. YOU ALREADY REFUSED THE REAL HEART OF THE APPOINTMENT, BECOMING GOVERNOR GENERAL OF THE WHOLE SYSTEM. SHE'S GLAD YOU DID. HE SAYS IT'S GOING TO MAKE A MESS, YOUR NOT HAVING TOTAL CONTROL. I'LL SKIP WHAT FOLLOWS, IT'S MORE OF HER TELLING HIM HE'S BOSSY. WELL, YOU'D NEVER GET ANYTHING DONE. OH YEAH, LOOK AT MY COLONY.

KRIS, THESE TWO PEOPLE ARE A HUNDRED YEARS OLD OR MORE, BUT I HEARD MORE COGENT ARGUMENTS IN THE SANDBOX WHEN YOU WERE IN THE FIRST GRADE.

WE MAY GROW OLDER, NELLY, BUT WE DON'T AUTOMATICALLY LEARN BETTER WAYS OF ARGUING OVER THINGS THAT REALLY GET OUR EMOTIONS IN A WRINGER.

Nelly thought on that for a long time, for a computer. MAYBE WE CAN HELP YOU FIND BETTER WAYS TO RESOLVE YOUR DIFFERENCES.

ANY HELP WOULD PROBABLY BE GREATLY RESISTED, Jack said.

PARDON ME.

NELLY, Kris said, THE PROBLEM WITH RESOLVING CONFLICT ISN'T ALWAYS THE HOW WE DO IT. LOOK AT THOSE TWO. THEY ARE AS DIFFERENT AS TWO PEOPLE CAN GET. IT'S NOT THE WAY THEY ARGUE BUT THE HUGE DISTANCE BETWEEN THEM. HOW DO YOU SETTLE THAT? WHO WOULD YOU HAVE GO FIRST FOR REJUVENATION?

THE ONE WHO NEEDED IT THE MOST AND WOULD BENEFIT THE MOST, Nelly said simply.

BUT RAY HAS BEEN CARRYING A TORCH FOR RITA FOR EIGHTY YEARS. THEIR UNRESOLVED ISSUES HAVE BECOME A BASIC PILLAR OF HIS LIFE. HOW WOULD YOU TELL HIM THAT HE SHOULD RISK HER NOT GETTING REJUVENATED BEFORE HE LOSES HER?

The fight was coming to an end only because the two of them were too exhausted to continue. Granny Rita looked as bad as she had when Kris first saw her in the shuttle bay and rushed her to sick bay.

"Captain," Kris snapped. "Send a runner to Ada. Ask her to get a medical team here stat. Send another runner to get that wheelchair we left behind."

"Aye, aye, ma'am," the Marine officer said, and obeyed.

NELLY, GET CAPTAIN DRAGO.

DRAGO HERE.

GRANNY RITA IS HAVING A CRISIS. HOW SOON CAN YOU LAUNCH A BOAT DOWN WITH THE DUTY DOCTOR?

TEN MINUTES. IT WILL TAKE THIRTY MINUTES TO LAND.

GET YOUR DOC MOVING. ALSO, THAT REJUVENATION CLINIC, GET THEM ON THE HORN AND FIND OUT IF THEY HAVE A STANDBY GERIATRIC SPECIALIST.

WAIT ONE, didn't take anywhere close to a minute. THEY HAVE A FULL CRITICAL INTERVENTION TEAM ON ALERT. THEY WERE SURPRISED IT WASN'T THE KING. THEY PROMISE TO BE HERE IN FIVE MINUTES.

THANKS, CAPTAIN.

ANYTIME, YOUR ROYAL HIGHNESS, VICEREINE OF ALWA AND GOVERNOR GENERAL.

FIRST, I'M VICEROY AND THERE'S NO WAY THEY'RE MAKING

ME GOVERNOR GENERAL. YOU CAN TELL ANYONE WHO SAYS DIFFERENT YOU GOT IT DIRECT FROM THE PRINCESS HERSELF.

EMERGENCY GERIATRIC INTERVENTION TEAM JUST CROSSED THE QUARTERDECK. ALL SIX OF THEM WERE PUSHING CARTS. THEY'LL BE DOWN THERE ASAP.

19

A quick nod from the captain, and one of the Marines broke rank from her peers and raced for Granny Rita. She pulled a medical kit from her belt and began checking out the elderly woman.

The king eyed his once and apparently not future wife for a long time, then stomped away. As he passed Kris, he growled, "Walk with me."

Kris obeyed.

He kept stomping as his Marines formed a perimeter around him. That didn't keep several colonials from walking right through their perimeter as they hurried for Granny Rita. First came Ada, the Chief of Ministries, then Iago, Rita's gofer, and finally several people whose bags might not have been the traditional medical bags but who nonetheless carried bags and walked with the purposeful look of men and women who fought with death and won as often as possible.

The Marines let them through their ranks and once even the king stepped aside for an elderly doctor type. The doctor scowled at Ray as if he were personally responsible for this crisis and hobbled on as quickly as his old legs would let him.

The king turned to Kris. "Can you get the word out to anyone interested, that all those youngsters wanting to return to human space for an education should report to the landing no later than six hours from now if they want to get a ride back?"

"You're leaving that soon?"

"Apparently I came on a fool's errand. That woman has not changed in eighty years. She was a blind idealist then and is just as blind now. How these poor people survived with her in charge . . ." His muttering trailed off.

"Anyway, Kris, can you get the word out about the ride home? I was surprised at the reception at how few mentioned wanting to go home."

"I've been with these people six weeks, sir. They *are* home."

"It's amazing how quickly peasants fall in love with the mud between their toes," he growled.

Kris had seen a lot of things she wished she could forget. Ships blown to atoms. Friends ripped away and lost forever. Here was another one of those moments she'd likely spend her life trying to unremember.

"Can you put the word out on the net about the lift?" Ray asked.

"They have no net. We offered Granny Rita one of the best computers out of our ship store. She was fascinated by it. However, I think their grapevine is just as fast. I'll see who I can get started talking."

"She has a computer? I thought sometimes it was like she'd been listening in on our net. Could she have?"

Kris was saved from having to lie or mumble by the king himself changing the subject.

"She agrees that this place does not need a governor general and that it would only be a waste of your time to try to run it. She says it can't be run."

"From what I've seen, sir, it sure looks that way."

"She agrees with you. That's almost enough to make me change my mind and insist on appointing you." The king eyed Kris.

"It would be an endless case of herding cats, Your Majesty, and I'm allergic to cats."

The old man guffawed at that.

"Okay, okay, you win." He tapped his commlink. "Crossie, we've got to change the royal commission I'm leaving my great-granddaughter. Tell the lawyers to take out the parts dealing with the governor general."

"That will take a couple of hours, sir. Six or eight," came over the net.

"What do you mean? All the way out here those lawyers didn't develop a contingency if she balked at the GG slot?"

"Sir, the betting was ten to one that she'd take it, and I was the only one foolish enough to take your bet. I'll call the ship and get them working. They'll have to go over every inch of the Commander, Alwa Defense Sector as well as the vice-reine's job."

"Viceroy," Kris shouted at her grampa's commlink.

"Viceroy," he repeated.

"The feminine is . . ." the admiral started.

"Usually used for the viceroy's wife," Kris shot back before he finished. "It's viceroy or nothing."

"We'll change it, sir," the admiral said, and rang off.

"You're getting to be a very hard person to deal with," the king said, stopping to stare hard at Kris.

"You're dropping a very hot potato in my lap. One that's all the way on the other side of the galaxy. A potato whose odds of being diced, sliced, and smashed are too high for anyone to risk a penny bet on, and you think *I'm* getting hard to deal with?"

The king grinned. "Point well taken. I've watched you grow, kid, from a little girl in a bottle to an ensign who could stop a mutiny with one of her own. You've saved more planets than I care to count, and likely more than I had at your age. Yes, this is a hot potato, but Kris, you've got the mitts to handle it. Likely, you're the only one of your generation who can. A hell of a lot more will have to grow mitts for this kind of stuff, but right now, you're all I've got. Take care, please."

He turned to go, then turned back to her. "I was planning on taking the *Constellation* back with me, but she's one of the heavy frigates with 20-inch guns. I'll take the *Fearless* instead. You don't mind keeping Sampson, do you? I could swap her to the *Fearless* if you want. We'll be taking a different path back. Every trip out will take a different route. We don't want the bastards to notice a beaten path between here

and home. It also means you won't be sending us regular
reports."

Kris nodded. She couldn't think of enough answers to all
he'd dropped on her. It would be nice to keep the *Constellation*. Captain Sampson . . . not so much. Good ship. Troubling
CO. But having the king make such an obvious change would
not look like Kris was in command.

The idea of taking a different route here and back each
time sounded reasonable. She should have thought of it herself. Still, how many permutations could Nelly come up with?
With the ships coming her way, assuming they actually sailed,
taking a different route, how long would that add to their
voyage?

How soon before they stumbled on something that didn't
like being stumbled on?

Did anything good ever come without a downside?

The king glanced back at where he could just barely see the
clump surrounding Rita. "You better go see how things are
going there. Let me know, if it's not too much trouble. Oh, and
get the word out for kids that want the ride back to meet at the
fleet landing."

"Yes, Your Majesty," Kris said, saluted, and left the old
man staring back at the woman he had claimed for eighty
years to be dead and the love of his life.

Now he knew she was alive.

Was there any love left in his life?

Kris double-timed up to the huddle around Granny Rita on
the bench.

"There is nothing wrong with me that having to spend half
an hour with that pigheaded, power-hungry megalomaniac
didn't cause. Just give me some air."

The crowd stepped back, leaving room for Granny Rita to
breathe, just as a doctor finished deflating a blood-pressure
cuff. "Pressure is 163 over 92. A bit high, but not dangerous."

"Good, good," Granny Rita said, just as the opening
around her let her get a look at Kris. "So, what did he have to
say? Is he going to waste your time being a governor general
of all Alwa?"

The look on Ada's face told Kris that this was the first the

Chief of Ministries had heard of this and what she thought of it.

"No," Kris said. "Despite you being against it, he's going to let me beg off. It is causing him trouble. My commission as Commander, Alwa Defense Sector, Vicereine, and Governor General will have to be rewritten. I imagine the switch to viceroy won't be too much trouble, but he was told the lawyers may need six to eight hours or more to comb through the whole thing and eliminate the governor-general stuff."

"Good, good. That will take him time. Anything else?"

"He wants all the kids interested in an education back home to report to the fleet landing for a ride up to the *Monarch* as soon as possible. The ship's leaving in eight hours."

"Oh, that's even better. Surround him with a gaggle of hero-worshipping kids, and he'll totally forget what time it is as he tells them all kinds of lies. Great. Kris, I bet your orders to take command of this sector don't show up in the mail before the *Monarch* jumps out."

"So?" Kris said.

"So, kid, I've done a lot of funerals since we landed, and I've enjoyed doing a lot of weddings, too. Still do both, even if they are trying to put me out to pasture," she said eyeing most of those around her. Most of whom found now to be a good time to study the sway of the trees above them.

"Now, Kris, I penciled in a funeral for this afternoon. I figured Raymond was sure to pop an aneurism or have an apoplectic fit, but what don't you know, he survived me, and I survived him. No accounting for how the universe turns, is there? Now, that leaves me with time on my calendar for something. The best use of my time that I can think of would be a wedding."

"Wedding?" Kris echoed.

"Yes, kid. Just how gutsy are you? You've blown away monstrous alien ships, can you grab your chance for happiness with both hands? As I see it, right now, this young Marine captain reports to Captain Drago. You don't report to nobody. In a few hours, that's gonna change. Likely never unchange. You can get married to this guy in the next four to six hours or you can forget it until, well, forever. What do you say?"

Kris looked at Jack. Jack looked at her.

"Which one of us goes first?" Kris asked.

"Traditionally, it's the guy, but you've got the rank. Oh, and you're the princess. You call it."

"Jack, if you're going to say something, you go first."

Jack reached for her hand and stared deep into her eyes. "Kris Longknife, will you marry me and make me the happiest man this side of the galaxy?"

Kris had forgotten to breathe. She was half-afraid he would not say a word. Now she nearly had to gasp for breath. "Yes, Juan Montoya, I will marry you, and it will make me the happiest woman in the entire galaxy."

"Well, folks," announced Granny Rita, "we got a wedding to put on and four hours to do it. Let's get moving."

20

There was a lot to get moving.

"Ada," Granny Rita ordered, "get back to the reception and get the word circulating that anyone who wants a trip back home needs to be at the fleet landing in the next two to four hours."

"That fast?" Ada asked.

"First, we got to get Raymond distracted. Second, we don't want any of those leaving to know too much about the wedding."

"Good point," Ada said, and headed back for Government House.

"Nelly," Kris said, "contact Captain Drago."

"Yes, Commodore Viceroy, or whatever I should call you."

"We'll figure that out later. Listen, Granny Rita isn't in quite as bad a shape as we thought. You can cancel the emergency team."

"How not bad?"

"She's going to be doing a wedding in four hours."

"Oh. Anyone I know?"

"Just me and Jack."

"Finally! You are, of course, inviting all the ship's officers and senior chiefs and NCOs."

"Of course, but there is this problem."

"Isn't there always where Longknifes are involved? What is it this time?"

"You've heard the king plans to make me Commander, Alwa Defense Sector?"

"Yep. It's on all the best gossip shows."

"Well, as soon as he does that, Jack goes back into my chain of command, and we can't get married. We've got to do this before the orders are issued."

"Smart. Very smart. I smell Granny Rita's hand in this."

"She's doing the wedding," Kris said dryly.

"So, you don't want the *Wasp*'s comm center to log your orders until after the wedding."

Kris sighed. It would be so easy to take the skipper up on the offer. "No, Captain, we are not going to do anything like that. If the orders come in before Jack and I say 'I do,' the whole thing is off. Bring anyone down here to the wedding that you want, but leave someone in charge of the comm center you can count on to pass those orders immediately to Nelly."

"And you'll make sure that Nelly tells you?"

As often, the skipper had a good point. "Also have him call you on net. So, you see, you're all invited to the wedding, but we can't let the other ships in the fleet know what's going on. Certainly not the *Monarch*."

"Mum's the word. Oh, I'm going to send down the emergency medical team anyway. They're ready to go, and if we don't send them, it would cause talk."

"Okay," Kris said, "heaven knows there were enough old folks at the reception that they ought to be able to keep the docs busy for a week."

"What time's the wedding?"

"In four hours if I can pull it off."

"We'll be there, Kris. Don't you go walking down any aisle before we get there."

"I don't even have a wedding dress. I'm having a hard time believing that even Granny Rita can pull this all off in four hours."

"Well, you left here in dress whites. Oh, was Jack in dress red and blues?"

"Yes, he is," Kris said.

"Good. I don't have to find a uniform for him. Bye, dear, have fun, I hear there's nothing quite as joyful as wedding prep."

"Good-bye, Captain Drago," Kris said dryly to his lie.

This wedding was not to be a simple elopement. It seemed that every two or three months there was a wedding; one of Granny Rita's great-grandkids or godchildren or just someone from the crew that wanted his latest descendant married by the old skipper.

For example, the ring bearer, a lad of five, had admirably performed that service three times in the last six months. Each time with more and more proficiency and less and less hijinks.

He was eager to do it again. Of course, his dress pants were tight and very high up his legs, but his mother assured Kris she had socks just as black as the pants. The cute little coat proved totally unusable. The shirt and tie would do if the top button was left undone.

Kris was offered two choices: break in a new five-year-old and break this one's heart, or go with the boy who pleaded so artfully for the chance, even if he was the very advertisement for back-to-school shopping.

Kris let the boy do it again. After all, Rita said all the couples he'd handled the ring for were still happily married. That was more than she could claim.

Kris checked with Nelly. Only three and three-quarters of an hour of marriage preparations left. How could women stand months of this?

The three flower girls also turned out to be a bit long in the tooth and short on the hemline. All of eight, all experienced, all pleading for just one more chance to walk down the aisle strewing flowers. Oh, and they knew where to get the best flowers and how to convert them to petals themselves.

Kris assented, wondering just how short their dresses would be when they showed up.

That brought Kris to her own choice of wedding dress. She was not getting married in uniform. Not her.

Three dresses were readily at hand. The first bride had been petite, a tiny slip of a thing. They held the dress up to Kris and put it back in the protective bag.

The second bride had been pregnant at the time. It was a bit longer, but it had space in all the places Kris didn't need. Back into the box for that one, too.

The third bride had all the curves Kris dreamed off. All of them and then some. She was taller than the other two. With help, Kris managed to settle the dress around her shoulders and watch as it fell . . . to well above her knees. The waist was a bit tight, but she could give up deep breaths for a few hours. The bust was . . . way too busty.

"We can handle that with a few stitches," a woman with needle already in hand said. Kris held her breath as the woman began to sew Kris into the dress.

In her dreams, Kris had a wonderfully long train. This dress didn't get near the floor, much less trail along nicely. But, on reflection, considering the wedding dress Mother had been eyeing the last time she and Kris had met in a bridal shop, this wasn't at all bad.

She was getting married to Jack. She was doing it without violating Navy regs. Minor things like trains she could just do without.

They did, however, have a veil for her. White and lacy, it had been hand sewn for Granny Rita's last wedding and used at more weddings since then than anyone had bothered to count. It covered Kris and even managed to trail a bit below the hem.

Someone found a white pair of shoes that didn't hurt too much, especially if she didn't put them on until she walked down the aisle. Kris was ready a whole thirty minutes early.

"Nelly, any word from the *Wasp*'s comm center?"

"No, Kris, and I've been doing some snooping. The lawyers are still debating three phrases, and the king is having a ball talking to twenty-seven eager young men and women. He's telling tales that would curdle your blood and are, based upon our analysis with Ron the Iteeche, most likely untrue. Still, he's laughing, they're enjoying being scared, and no one is pushing the lawyers to finish up their work, so they're arguing to their little hearts' content. I don't have a cent to bet, but if I did, I'd say you're gonna pull this off. By the way, should I try to locate anyone to walk you down the aisle?"

Kris had been giving the matter some thought in her

immense spare time. Her father and Grampa Trouble were all
the way on the other side of the galaxy. To ask King Ray to do
the honor that was rightfully his as the senior male member of
her family present would give the whole thing away and likely
end any prospect for a wedding.

Captain Drago had come to mind, but he was about to
become her subordinate. Nope, Kris Longknife had to face it,
there was just no one to give her away but herself.

And that wasn't a bad idea. Not a bad idea at all.

"No, Nelly. No need to search for anyone."

Government House had proven too small for the royal
reception. There was, however, a large adobe church that had
been built by the community shortly after they landed. Every
Sunday it was shared by the Catholics and Protestants. Satur-
day it held temple, and Friday the Moslems met for prayer. A
small Buddhist community even managed to find a place in
the building's busy schedule as did an Atheists' Wednesday
Potluck. There now were separate buildings for most of the
different faith expressions, but they still put the Chapel of
Thanksgiving to use.

And it was often used for weddings.

They'd reserved it for Kris.

She found herself standing in a small room off the foyer
with Penny and Abby, her two bridesmaids. After careful
evaluation of the options, it was agreed that both of them were
maids of honor. Kris had no idea who was standing up with
Jack.

This wedding was open to a lot of surprises.

The first of several was when the *Wasp*'s crew marched in,
in formation and all in dress blues uniforms. Kris finally got
to see what rank they had earned before they signed on with
her contract crew.

No surprise, Captain Drago had lied. He had sewn on his
rear admiral's stripes and been chained to that desk before he
slipped loose and took off with the *Wasp*.

Kris didn't know which was the biggest surprise from
Cookie. He wore a full admiral's uniform with the wide stripe
and three thinner stripes climbing up his arm. And the uniform fit him. Apparently, he'd been liking his own cooking for
a long time.

There was Kris's crew, admirals and captains, finally showing their true colors as they came to celebrate her wedding. Every one of her enlisted types were senior chiefs. Many were command master chiefs. As much as Kris hated Crossie, he had gotten her the cream of the crop.

And all of these officers had accepted demotions to lieutenants so they could fight under her command.

Brides were permitted to cry. It was a good rule, that. Kris's eyes were tearing up. Abby produced a tissue. "There's more where that came from."

"Thanks."

The ring bearer was getting fidgety. He had two rings to take care of. Granny Rita had given Kris a copper ring to give to Jack, the norm for a colonial wedding. If there was gold in any of them there hills, no one had had time to go hunting for it.

Jack, however, had tied a gold ring on the kid's tiny white pillow.

"Where did that come from?" Kris asked.

"I bought it at the exchange on HellFrozeOver," he said. "It was my pledge to you and myself that I was going to find you, and someday, even if hell did freeze over, I was going to put it on your finger."

Yes, brides were permitted to cry. A day like this just had too much joy to stay locked up even in a Longknife's soul.

An organ, hand built over the last eighty years, began to play.

"That's my song," the ring bearer announced, and began his slow walk down the aisle.

The flower girls, all in dresses way too short, went next, in single column, carefully tossing just a few flower petals each time they reached in and grabbed a fistful. They also had the two step down just right. Right step forward, then bring up the left foot. Left step forward, then bring up the right foot.

They were all doing it in perfect cadence to the music.

With a look back at Kris, Abby, then Penny followed the kids down the aisle.

Kris was finally alone.

"Nelly, anything?"

"Not a word, Kris, I swear. The lawyers are still yammering. Grampa Ray has taken the kids to dinner, and he's still spinning wild tales. Crossie is up to something, but he's got it in a single-use code that I might crack in a month if I concentrated on it. You are good to go, and speaking of go, I think that's your music."

Kris took a deep breath, which strained the dress, set a smile on her face, not too friendly, not too standoffish, not too much teeth, the thing her mother had had her practice in front of a mirror when she was thirteen, and stepped off.

The temptation to race down the aisle was there, but the kids were doing so well, and Abby and Penny were staying strung out just right that Kris settled into the two step easily. After all, she'd practiced it a lot as a maid of honor.

The colonists had let the Navy have the first three pews in front, which meant Kris was met with a solid wall of grins and smiles and applause by the colonials as she started the long walk.

And Mother's practiced smile went out the door.

Kris found a smile that was all her own. One that showed all the joy she could not hold inside for a moment more. Sometimes it was as wide open as the sky, other times it retreated back to just an enigmatic thing, but full of happiness.

Then she saw Jack.

He was standing beside Granny Rita with Gunny Brown and Captain Hayakawa, the skipper of the Imperial Marine company.

As happened so often, Jack was in his dress blue and reds. Kris had seen him in them time after time, but not like he looked today. Was it the way he stood, eagerly leaning forward to get a better look at her, or the big smile that he didn't even try to hide?

Kris thought she'd been smiling before, but she found a whole new smile for Jack at that moment.

The walk down the aisle seemed to fly by yet take forever, but she was finally there, in front of the altar, with Granny Rita wearing some kind of black robe with a white shawl or stole or whatever the preachers called that thing they wore.

Jack offered her his hand and she took it, leaned on it, and felt wonderful.

Penny and Abby lifted back Kris's veil, as if Jack didn't

already know exactly who it was coming his way, and they turned to face Granny Rita.

"Dearly beloved, we are gathered here today to join these two in Holy Matrimony. Those of you who haven't slept through all my weddings that you've attended no doubt know that I have some serious thoughts on marriage and tend to share them at length."

That drew chuckle from the colonials.

"However, as those of you who are my old shipmates may remember, Navies have rules against things called fraternization, and we are met this afternoon in a small window between when these fine folks are just fellow pilgrims in uniform and when one of them is going to be handed the unenviable job of being commander of a whole lot of people, not the least of which is the person standing next to her.

"Thus, I'm going to skip a whole lot of advice and assume that during the last five years of these two fussing and fighting together, they've got a pretty good idea of what half of marriage is all about."

The chuckles to that one came strongest from the Navy pews.

"So, I'm going to jump right to that part where I ask if there is anyone present who knows of any reason these two should not be joined in Holy Matrimony? Let them speak now or forever hold their peace."

NELLY?

NOTHING.

Still, Kris glanced over her shoulder. Captain Drago tapped his ear and shook his head. No message traffic.

YOU DON'T TRUST ME.

ON THIS, NELLY, I CAN'T. YOU LOVE ME TOO MUCH.

No surprise, the church was as quiet as it could be.

"That cleared up, Kristine Anne Longknife, do you take Juan Francisco Montoya to be your lawfully wedded husband? To have and to hold him, in sickness and in health, in good times and bad, leaving all others and cleaving only to him? Honor and respect him so long as you both shall live?"

"I do," Kris found she could barely whisper through a suddenly dry throat.

"Juan Francisco Montoya, do you take Kristine Anne

Longknife as your lawfully wedded wife? To have and to hold
her, in sickness and in health, in good times and bad, leaving
all others and cleaving only to her? To honor and respect her
so long as you both shall live?"

"I do," rang out in a voice that could be heard across a
battlefield.

"Do you have rings?"

The five-year-old proudly lifted his pillow above his head
so Jack could easily take the ring of gold for Kris. He slipped
it over her finger and, smiling, said, "With this ring, I thee
wed."

Kris quickly did the same with her simple copper ring.
"With this ring, I thee wed."

Granny Rita took over again. "Then, by the powers
invested in me by the colonists of Alwa, for no reason I can
imagine, I pronounce you man and wife. Folks, it's traditional
to give each other a kiss." Then in a lower voice she added,
"And don't make it a peck, either or I'll think I wasted that
beach cottage reservation."

Jack took Kris in his arms and kissed her. Really kissed
her. Kissed her enough to satisfy even Granny Rita.

Kris went weak in the knees. She found her back bending
and Jack's powerful arms around her as her only support.

One of the flower girls was heard to say, in one of those
small voices that eight-year-olds have that can fill a huge
church, "Get a room."

Jack broke from the kiss and helped Kris get settled back
on her feet. His grin was pure joy. Well, maybe a lot joy with
a bit of possession thrown in. That guy kind of thing that says
to the world, "Look at the woman who's made herself mine."

Kris was saved from having to begin the march back down
the aisle on wobbly knees by the Navy contingent. The officers
filed out of their pews and slow-marched for the door.

Crossed sabers, Kris thought as Nelly said it. AN ANCIENT
NAVY TRADITION, Nelly added.

A wise old chief had once asked a young ensign Kris if she
were Navy or just passing through. Now, a commodore and
walking under crossed sabers on her wedding day, Kris didn't
feel like she could get much more Navy than this.

The officers gone, Kris and Jack started down the aisle.

Kris was now leading the procession rather than following it. Her progress was slow. There were lots of hands to shake. This afternoon she did so gingerly, just a touch. Some of the older women offered Kris a cheek and Kris gave out a lot of pecks, nothing like what Jack had given her. Beside her, Jack was showing that he knew how to peck a cheek as well.

There were well-wishers and happy smiles. The progress seemed to take forever, but Kris finally found herself approaching the doors of the old church.

"Present arms," came in Captain Drago's voice. Make that Rear Admiral Drago's voice.

Navy sabers slid out of their scabbards and crossed before her. Kris and Jack ducked a bit. Most Navy sabers were only sharp enough to cut wedding cakes, but you never could tell.

Kris went down the line giving her officers the best bride smile she could manage. She owed them all so much. Like any officer on official business, they stood at attention, eyes focused on their sabers.

KRIS, KEEP AN EYE ON ADMIRAL COOKIE, Nelly warned. PART OF THE TRADITION IS FOR ONE OF THE OFFICERS TO HIT THE NEW NAVY BRIDE ON THE RUMP.

HE WOULDN'T DARE, Kris answered, and gave the full admiral her commander's eye.

His face stayed full deadpan, his eyes up, like all the rest.

Kris walked past him, sure she'd established herself.

And got a hard swipe on her butt with his saber.

"Ouch, that hurt," she said, more startled than really pained.

"You've put in five years as a Navy officer and you know the pain of it. Now you're a Navy wife, and sorry, dear heart, but there's a whole new set of hurts to meet. Just ask my wife, God rest her soul."

Kris dropped out of the mistreated bride routine and stepped back to give the old admiral a hug.

"Thanks for the advice and the warning," she whispered in his ear.

Then the formality of the military disintegrated as the colonials started to make their way out of the church. Government House was to be the scene of the reception. It seemed that King Raymond's hasty exit had left it and leftovers available.

Several cakes, including a many-tiered wedding cake, had been baked in just five hours and were waiting for them.

There were lots of traditions to fulfill.

Kris tossed her bouquet of flowers. With Nelly, it was easy to know exactly where to toss it. However, it was none too easy to choose whom she wanted to get it. Abby and Sergeant Bruce had been exchanging looks that Kris couldn't miss out of the corner of her eyes no matter how much Jack held central place.

And Penny had frequently turned to get a look at the Musashi lieutenant. And Amanda Kutter and her boyfriend were so ready.

The three of them happened to flock together at just the right moment and Kris let fate decide. Amanda outjumped the other two, not that Abby even put her hand up.

Hmm.

There were pictures, including the obligatory picture of the bride and groom feeding each other the first slice of cake. This always ended up hilariously with the two smearing cake and icing all over each other's faces.

Many times as maid of honor, Kris swore she'd handle this just fine.

Only, the people snapping pictures kept yelling "look here, look here," and snapping flashes so Kris could hardly see Jack and, no doubt, he couldn't really see her.

And everyone had a great laugh as Kris and Jack smeared each other's faces.

Jack saw Kris's frustration and whispered in her ear. "Don't take that too seriously. It's intended to be a mess. Laugh, and they'll all laugh with you."

So Kris laughed, and they *did* all laugh with her.

There was a tradition about a first dance, and Kris was getting ready for that when Granny Rita somehow got control of the mike from the bandmaster.

"Folks, I don't know how many of you managed to lay your hands on a gift for the bride and groom. I know I didn't. But there is one very special gift we could give both them and ourselves.

"All of you who've listened know what I think of Ray Longknife, or King Raymond as he is now. He's headed out of our system and back to human space as we speak. He's got a collection of 173 planets that are banded together back there. I'm glad to have him back there and us over here."

Not a few people in the crowd agreed with her. A few didn't, but not a whole lot.

"But the fact remains that there are seven U.S. warships over our head, ready to defend us to the death. Right now, they're there, and we're here, and there's no tie that binds us together. As someone who's commanded ships and worked hard with most of you to put together a colony here, I know that's not good."

The crowd seemed unsure where this was going, but no one moved to shut down the old woman.

"We can't join the United Society. Seems you have to have a single government. Can you imagine us and the Alwans agreeing on one government for this planet?"

"Can you see the Alwans agreeing on anything?" came from the floor.

"So true, but the U.S. is offering us associated membership. We get to rule ourselves, and they get to stay to hell and gone on the other side of the galaxy. But we do create a tie with the warships protecting us.

"If we vote for this associated membership, our blushing bride here gets to be our viceroy, assuming we elect her as such. She'll command the fleet as a Navy officer, and as viceroy, she can meet as a civilian leader with Ada and talk civilian stuff. To me, it sounds like a win-win proposition. What do you say?"

At that point, Ada did step in and take the mike away from Granny. "We've told you before, and we'll tell you again, Granny Rita, your chief emeritus status does not allow you to put proposals before the Council of Ministries or the General Council."

"Well, you're all here, and I just did," Granny shouted back at the mike, and her words filled the hall.

Ada sighed and took a long, slow look around the room. She nodded to several people, then took a deep breath. "We have a proposal from the floor, and seeing that we do have a quorum present, I am willing to entertain discussion, assuming the blushing bride doesn't mind Granny Rita hijacking her wedding reception."

"I am the one King Raymond nominated for this viceroy thing though my commission hasn't been issued. It does require a vote of the colonials before it becomes operational. It kind of would be a nice wedding present, as Granny said."

"Okay, let's see if we understand the motion properly. If we vote for associated membership in the United Society, Ray will stay on his side of the galaxy, and I'll be dealing with you. Right?"

"Yes."

"We will establish a proper civilian military relationship between us and the ships above us."

"And if the relationship faces strains," Kris said, "we can negotiate adjustments."

"I like that," came from the floor.

"You're the viceroy," Ada said, eyeing Kris.

"If you reject me, it would take several years to get another nominee here."

"But we get to approve any viceroy nominee," came again from the floor.

"That's what the draft of my commission says."

"When's it going to be finalized?"

"Before King Raymond jumps out of the system, I hope," Kris said.

"Has anyone seen what this associated membership says?"

"It's short. You rule yourselves any way you chose. I am empowered to deal with your government. Also, I can open negotiations with anyone and sign draft peace treaties to present to the U.S. Senate."

"As in negotiate with the bastards?" came from several people on the floor.

Kris sadly nodded her head. "Yes, I can. You know that so far, they won't even talk to us. If, suddenly they change their mind, this puts me in a place to do something."

"That's got to be worth a lot."

"And she did save our bacon. Who hasn't seen the pictures of those monsters?"

"I have a proposal properly presented," Ada said. "Is there a second?"

One came quickly.

"Discussion?"

"What's there to discuss? I say let's call for the question."

Ada didn't even bat an eyelash. "I have a call for the question. Is there a second?"

"You're all going to be sorry about this."

"Harry, you always say we'll be sorry about everything."

"And I'm right half the time."

While this was going on, a second was made for calling the question.

"All those for applying for associated membership in the U.S., and operating as if we are until we hear differently, and accepting Her Royal Highness, Princess Longknife as our viceroy, indicate by saying yes."

"Is she a Longknife or a Montoya?" got drowned by a flood of "Yes."

"All nays."

"She's a damn Longknife. I say we'll be sorry."

"Harry," Ada asked with exasperation, "is that a nay?"

"No."

"Then the proposal is carried unanimously. Will somebody please start the music?" said Ada. "I want to dance."

So they commenced to dance the night away, as befitted a bunch of enthusiastic survivors, and one happy princess.

21

Sometime around six, Ada cut Kris and Jack off the dance floor. "The fastest eclectic runabout on the planet is parked outside. Do you know the way back to Joe's Seaside Paradise?"

"If I can't guide them," Nelly said, "Kris can trade me in for an abacus."

"Joe's expecting you. I understand you only have one night you can take, so why don't you two make the most of it and get out of here."

An hour and a half later, Joe was showing them to the same cottage. "It's a bit late for supper, but we're still serving. I'm sure you could come in what you're wearing."

"I'm not hungry," Kris said. She was, but food was the last thing on her mind.

"Send the buns over early tomorrow morning," Jack said.

Joe quickly made himself scarce.

Jack came over to open the car door for Kris. For once, she'd stayed demurely in her place to give him a chance to be the gentlemen he enjoyed being. He offered her a hand up, and she took it, just as she had been taught by the woman Mother hired to teach Kris to be a lady.

Jack let her get on her own two feet, then swooped her up

and carried her to the door. He fumbled a bit with the latch, so a laughing Kris opened the door for him. He kissed her, not as long as in the church, but it was no peck, and carried her across the threshold.

"Our first home."

"For at least the next twelve hours," Jack agreed.

"You going to carry me across the threshold of my quarters on the *Wasp*?"

"Don't I wish I could," he said with a sigh. On the drive up they had agreed that what happened dirtside stayed dirtside. Once back aboard ship, they turned back into pumpkins in uniform.

Jack settled Kris on her feet in the middle of the room and eyed her much the way Kris suspected Marines eyed mountain strongholds to be taken.

"They really sewed you into that dress."

Kris looked down at herself and couldn't really disagree. When she next glanced up at Jack, he had a very sharp knife in his hands.

"Ouch," Kris said, but managed not to take a step back.

"Wife, don't you trust a Marine with a knife in his hand?"

"I don't trust anyone with a knife pointed my way."

"Smart woman, but trust me, husbands are in a special category." And so saying, he took the tip of the combat knife to the recently added seams to her dress.

With careful snips, one by one, the bodice came loose. It fell, revealing a very sexy bra beneath.

"I thought you didn't buy sexy underwear."

"Something old, something new, something borrowed, something blue. Didn't you guys ever hear about those female essentials?"

"Dimly. Which is this?"

"I think it's the new. Or maybe borrowed, though it's not going back."

"And the blue?"

"Keep hunting."

"Oh, this just gets better."

More snips of threads, and the dress was finally loose enough for Jack to pull it over Kris's head. He turned away to lay the dress carefully on a chair. After all, this was definitely borrowed. When he turned back, Kris greeted him in tiny panties and bra and a pose that likely originated just outside the Garden of Eden.

"Ah," Jack said, taking her in. "The blue are those tiny blue bows on your panties."

"I said you'd find them."

"I'm overdressed," Jack said, and in hardly a blink . . . and Kris was definitely not blinking . . . she was the one who was overdressed.

"I guess I better get out of these," she said, reaching behind her for the bra clasp.

"Oh no, my dear. Don't you know? Brides are presents best unwrapped slowly."

"Who told you that?"

"It's a guy thing, like the something-borrowed thing."

"I'm not sure I trust you, Mister."

"Ah, but you must, I'm your husband."

"You're also a Marine."

"Well, there is that," Jack said, approaching Kris with the biggest grin she'd ever seen on his face.

She backed away from him.

He advanced another step.

She backed up again . . . and fell on the bed.

A moment later, he was on top of her, covering her with kisses.

He did take a long time getting her out of her panties and bra.

But then he made it up by taking a long time putting other things inside her.

As she found herself falling asleep in his arms, she came to the conclusion that she should trust her husband, and he was very well balanced at giving and taking.

Definitely a nice man to have around.

22

As Kris slowly woke up in Jack's arms the next morning, the question that had been raised at the meeting yesterday came up.

"So," Jack said. "Am I Mr. Longknife, or are you Mrs. Montoya?"

Kris reached for Jack. Reached low down for Jack, found what she wanted, and began stroking it.

"Do we really have to settle this right now?" she cooed.

They decided there were other, more pressing matters at hand and spent the next half hour enjoying them.

They didn't throw much on when they went out to the porch to find a pile of buns. Kris allotted them as a wife the same way she'd allotted them as a wild woman. The three kinds Jack liked, he got one and a half of, she got a half. Fortunately, she'd found one she liked and he didn't, so she didn't go hungry.

Then Joe came over, sporting two covered plates. "We don't usually see newlyweds much at the dining room, but you two didn't get any supper. I have here an omelet that many praise."

He settled the plates on the table between them and stepped back to see their reaction. Kris and Jack cut off a piece, glanced at each other, and did a much better job of getting the omelet into each other's mouths than they had with the cake.

Circumstances weren't so biased for disaster.

"Good," both said at the same time. "Thank you," Kris added.

"Will you be able to stay for tonight?" Joe asked.

"No. As soon as we get a shower in, we'll have to be on our way."

"Yes, I understand. Ah, you were still in your wedding gown, and you were in your formal uniform. My son attended the royal reception. The king did not impress him, but he said both of you were in formal uniforms."

Kris admitted that was so.

"Feel free to take anything in the closet if you'd like to hold off getting back in uniform for a while. You can return it later, or not at all."

"I may borrow a muumuu," Kris admitted.

"And if you don't mind, I may take a pair of long shorts and a three-button shirt," Jack said.

"What, no lava-lava?" Joe said, but he was already turning away as he laughed.

"I love these people," Kris said, "but they are going to get me into so much trouble."

"We agree. What happens on Alwa stays on Alwa, and what happens aboard ship is strictly by the rules."

"Yes," Kris said with a sad sigh.

As they finished their brunch, Nelly reported. "The *Monarch* and *Fearless* are only minutes away from their jump. For the last half hour, orders have been coming in to the *Wasp*. Most are what you expected. Kris, you are ComAlDefSec."

"Notice how that rolls off the tongue."

"And includes deaf in it," Jack said.

"You are also viceroy pending a petition from the colonials and your election by them."

"Didn't the colonials pass the word that they had voted on that?" Jack asked.

"Granny Rita persuaded Ada to keep it on the QT. She didn't want to let Ray get all puffed up. She said, 'Let him sweat a bit.'"

Kris found herself rubbing her eyes. Both of her great-grandparents could behave like such four-year-olds. "Please promise me, Jack. We won't ever be like that."

"I'm sorry, Kris, but I don't think either of those two, on their honeymoon, ever expected to be acting like that. But yes, I will always remember this and do my best to avoid whatever did this to them."

"Good," Kris said.

"The orders have a surprise for Jack," Nelly said.

"Me!"

"Oh dear," said Kris.

"You are promoted to major."

"That's good news. Being married, I can use the extra pay."

"What's the bad news?" Kris said.

"Jack is also breveted up to full colonel and made commander, Marine Expeditionary Brigade, Alwa."

"We've only got at best a battalion," Jack said.

"Yes, but you are encouraged to recruit and train local colonial forces, either as full-time or a National Guard."

"I wonder if the colonials know?" Kris said.

"Granny Rita has copied all this traffic and says she and Ada along with the rest of the Council of Ministries would like to talk with you before you go back topside."

"Good-bye, honeymoon, hello, impossible tasks," Jack muttered.

The shower managed to return a bit of the honeymoon spirit, and it clearly was a lot more fun than it ever was aboard ship. Too soon, they found themselves staring at the contents of their closet.

"You think you ought to wear your blues?" Kris asked Jack.

"No. Definitely shorts. I have no idea how these folks will take to the idea of being under my command. I expect they'll be scared stiff of me. I doubt I'll wear a uniform dirtside again for months unless things go better than I expect."

"A good move, I think," Kris said.

She slipped into her sexy underwear, then pulled a muumuu, blue with yellow and green flowers, over her head.

"So, the viceroy is also keeping the bridle and bit well out of sight."

"I've raised a couple of armies from people who figured a

few folks with rifles could take on anything and learned the hard way that professionals are a breed apart. Let's see how coming more gently can work."

Jack packed up their uniforms. As he loaded them into the backseat of the car, he eyed Kris. "I'm supposed to drive you back to town knowing that under that muumuu is nothing but a couple of thin undies and a lot of naked you?"

"May I remind you, good husband, that whatever I'm wearing from now on, you know very well that under it all, there is only naked me. And under all your clothing, there is only naked you."

Jack scratched his nose. "Hmm, there's a downside of this wild, passionate lifestyle that I never thought of."

"I haven't noticed that where women were concerned," Kris said, as Jack got the car moving, "you men do a lot of thinking."

"Oh, we do a lot of thinking *about* women, my dear. Lots of thinking about women. It's just rarely very *productive* thinking about women. Now, tell me true, wife to husband, is it any different with you girls?"

Kris turned the question over in her mind for a couple of miles, then said, "I refuse to answer that question on the grounds that I'm good at blowing ships up, and my husband wants to stay on my good side."

"Side, top, bottom, whatever."

Sadly, that was about the end of the honeymoon. The rest of the drive was taken up analyzing problems they were likely to run into the second they stopped the car.

Jack was right. As they pulled to a stop at Government House, Ada and the entire Council of Ministries, both colonials and Alwans, were waiting.

They didn't look happy.

23

"Are you going to draft colonials?" was thrown at Kris before she even opened the car door.

There was an Alwan blocking Jack from opening his door. "Will you tie ropes around our necks and make us walk in your footsteps?" Nelly translated.

Kris eyed Jack. "I didn't read that in your orders."

"Neither did I."

Kris shoved open her door, and shouted, "Can we at least get out?"

"Let them get out," Ada said. "Let's save this for the Council Chambers, but you two have a lot of explaining to do, and this better be good."

Granny Rita was on the veranda. As they passed her, she said, "Sorry kids. Maybe I've said too much about how sneaky Raymond can be. Ada was with me and Anyang, the Public Peace Coordinator, when the messages started coming in, and the hollering started, and runners left to get more members and none of them have ever read anything written by lawyers before."

Kris could see how things had gotten out of hand. Getting a little technology was like getting just a little bit pregnant. She'd mark this down as a learning experience if she survived, and would be a lot more careful about what Nelly let Granny Rita see.

I'M SORRY, KRIS. I'VE NEVER HAD TO CENSOR MY NET BEFORE.

WE'LL TALK LATER.

There was a long table in the Council of Ministers' room. Even though the chairs were distributed evenly, Kris quickly found herself and Jack on one side and everyone else on the other side or sitting in chairs behind that side.

Thank you, Grampa, for dividing us so well.

Kris sat silently for a while. There was some whispering among folks on the other side of the table, but no one really got matters moving. Maybe the Alwans weren't the only ones who were out of their depth when it came to conflict resolution.

At least at this scale.

Kris opened her hands to Ada.

She shook her head. "You tell me how I'm reading this wrong," she snapped.

"First off," Kris began, "the orders to my husband Jack were never revealed or discussed with me before I found out about them this morning. Like any of you on a honeymoon, I had more interesting things at hand than reading dispatches."

That got some smiles. One or two chuckles. Kris had hoped that appealing to the bridal role might get her more maneuvering room. Then she remembered her history.

The draft had been used extensively in the Iteeche War and not liked at all.

Draft riots were mentioned but skimmed over in most histories. Kris had read deeper on the subject. It had been ugly.

"I have no power as viceroy to create or impose a draft on Alwa or the colonials. It's not there in my commission."

"But Jack does," Ada shot back.

"No, I don't," Jack snapped.

"It says you can," Anyang, the Minister for Public Peace, insisted.

"No, it says that I can train them if you, yourselves, vote to establish a draft. It also says I can train volunteers. It says a lot of things that aren't going to happen because, right now this minute, I don't have any weapons I can issue to you."

Jack paused to let that sink in.

"You could all volunteer *en masse*. You could pass a law that drafted everyone from five years old to ninety-five, and it wouldn't mean a thing. My Marines have the weapons they were issued before they came aboard and maybe a dozen spares in the maintenance section."

Again Jack paused. Realization was dawning in a lot of eyes across the table.

Jack hammered it home. "Tomorrow, if the bastards landed an army on Alwa and you came begging me for weapons to fight them. To battle them. To stop them from killing your wives and children, I would not have so much as a slingshot to give you."

That definitely turned the table.

There was a long silence as the reality of that soaked in. A moment before, they'd been all ready to chase Kris and Jack off a cliff. Now all they saw was a mountain up ahead that they all needed to climb together.

"That sure puts the shoe on the other foot," Ada said.

"Yes," Kris said.

"May I ask a few questions?" Jack asked.

"Of course," Ada said.

"Anyang, how are your public-safety agents equipped?"

"Most have billy clubs. Occasionally, I issue longer staves. There are wicker shields from the early days, when Rita faced food riots, but they haven't been issued since before my time."

"Not in sixty years or more," Rita said from where she sat against the wall at the head of the room.

"Do you have any hunters?" Jack asked.

"Bow hunting is very popular. There are some rifles, but they are all black-powder single-shot things. We haven't been able to find any nitrate deposits. There are animals that even the Alwans can't face. They run away from them fast or get eaten. Our rifle hunters go after them. It's more of an even fight than I like. We lose at least one hunter every year, but there are some who like the excitement."

"I'd like to talk to them," Jack said.

"So," Ada said slowly, "your job is to form some sort of fighting force that can stop the bastards if they land on Alwa."

Jack shook his head, sadly. "No, ma'am. My job is to fight

them on the ground if Kris's ships are defeated in the space above you. Considering the odds and the weapons they use, right now, I and my troops are just here to die bravely, fighting beside you."

That brought a deadly hush to the room.

"You don't sound very optimistic," Kuno, in charge of Mining and Industry, said.

"I've seen them fight. I've walked a planet they raped. If you want me to lie to you, you've got the wrong man in the room."

"Kris," Ada asked, "is it that bad?"

"I'm afraid so. If they came right now, I don't know how I could use my ships to stop them. We ambushed them last time. We can't use the same ambush this time. I've got a few ideas that might surprise them, but right this minute, nothing."

Granny Rita spoke up. "Folks, honesty in your warrior class is something to be grateful for. It's not a lot of fun to hear, though. Clearly, they've got the courage to speak the truth. Do you have the courage to hear it?"

"What can we do?" Ada asked.

"Right now, any minerals that you can mine is a start," Kris said. "Whether we use it to make weapons, or factories to make more weapons is a question we can tackle when we've got something to deal with."

"Alwans do not like digging in the ground and smoke-belching plants," an Alwan said.

"Do you like living more?" Jack asked.

The Alwans around the table fell silent. At least these five weren't running around like their elders.

"I'll try to get mining nanos down here to help you extract minerals without gouging the mountains," Kris said. "Do you know where there are mineral deposits?"

"The nanos would help. We have some deposits we haven't touched because of Alwan protests. I'll see what I can do," Kuno said. "Can we count on you for anything?"

"Part of making me viceroy is that I get to deal with a lot of business and industrial types that came out with the fleet. They are also looking for minerals they can extract from aster-oids and small moons. They have a couple of automated prefab plants to set up on your own moon. No belching smoke, but they do want to borrow two of the reactors off the *Furious*."

"Two for us and two for them," Granny Rita said. "They're pretty old. Do you think they can make them work?"

"We've got some pretty sophisticated ship-repair and fabrication stuff on Canopus Station. I'm betting if anyone can, they'll be the folks to patch things up and get them running," Kris said. "I'm glad you've agreed to share the reactors. I'll meet with those types tomorrow. *That* one will make this one look like patty-cake."

"Why did Ray bring out a bunch of mining and industry types?" Granny Rita asked.

Kris didn't want to answer that question. But since later today or tomorrow she'd be throwing it in the face of some real hard cases, she might as well let the locals know it first.

"Warships don't exist in a vacuum. They need a base. If the aliens discover a preindustrial world protected by starships, they'll know the ships came from somewhere and go looking for it. If these bastards are as hostile to life as they have seemed, they're bound to have a special hatred for any life that can stand up to them in a fight. Ray's given us the stuff to help us strengthen our defense, but it's not just a nice thing he's doing. He's buying human space more time before the bastards come hunting for them."

"Mighty nice of him," Rita said sourly.

"Whatever his reasoning, it helps us. I'm grateful for it," Ada told Rita.

"Maybe you're right."

"Folks, we've covered as much as we can just now. I need to get back in uniform and back to the fleet. I suspect there are even more fires to be put out there."

With that, the meeting adjourned. Kris found herself in the ladies' room, changing back into whites and wishing she had Jack to help. He was likely wishing the same.

What happens on Alwa stays on Alwa.

In the hall, they met. She helped adjust his collar and tie, no field scarf. Marines! He helped her get the fall of her dress whites shipshape. The fast car was still waiting for them. This time, Ada drove.

"I'm sorry we had to have that meeting, but I'm glad we did. You showed you know how to solve problems. Not all the people I have to deal with can do that. You also gave me the first honest report on how bad it really is. I can't say I'm glad to hear it, but at least I know what is ahead of us."

"Can I ask one question, Ada?" Kris said. "If things really do go downhill. If the aliens are headed this way, and there doesn't look to be any way for us to stop them. If we could cram every colonial into our ships and take off for human space, would you come with us?"

Ada was shaking her head before Kris finished. "This may be hard for folks like you that get in spaceships and jump all over the galaxy to understand, but for us, this is home. Everything we know and love is here. I know what I'm saying sounds crazy, but where else would I go?

"And Granny Rita is right, the Alwans took us in when we were inches away from eating each other or dying or I don't know what all 'cause the old-timers get suddenly quiet when you try to get them talking about what it was like the last couple of jumps before they found Alwa. The idea of running away from those crazy feather heads, even if it meant my life, just doesn't feel right."

As they drove out on the long pier to where a gig waited for Kris and Jack, Ada said, "Jack, you'll have your volunteers. I don't know how we'll arm them, but we'll try. You get those mining nanos down here, and we'll extract everything we can. And from what I hear, there are a lot of scientists from your ships exploring Alwa like it's never been looked at before. They're looking at animals, plants, minerals, you name it. I check in every day with Rita to see what new reports she's got. Not every day is like today."

They came to a stop. Kris could hear the shuttle warming up its reaction mass.

"We're finding out more about Alwa than we've ever dreamed of. We will use what we find to fight. Jack, you say it's a hopeless cause. Well, our folks have faced hopeless before, and we're still here. Bring on your hopeless. We'll show you how to beat the devil and find the hope you need."

Kris was strapped down, and the shuttle was airborne before the goose bumps from Ada's pep talk finally melted away.

Then she got busy with Nelly, planning the rest of her day.

24

Captain Drago met Kris in the docking bay. "Good afternoon, Viceroy."

"Good afternoon, Admiral."

"Say that again and, viceroy or not, I'll wash your mouth out with soap, Your Highness."

"I just wanted to see how it sounded," Kris said, smile adding to her contrition.

"Come along, I want to show you your office."

"My office?"

"Whatever you were before could get by with a Tac Center. A squadron's commodore and a viceroy needs an office. Have I got the day quarters for you!"

It was where Kris's Tac Center had been, still right off the bridge, but it had grown. "A wooden desk?" Kris said, then knocked on it. "Hey, that's real wood, not Smart Metal faking it!"

"I spotted that lovely while I was down at your wedding. 'I'm just perfect,' it said to me. Same for the sofas and overstuffed chairs. They're actual leather, hide of those elephants they have dragging wagons around."

"They call them oxen," Kris pointed out.

"They're the size of elephants. Hasn't anyone here seen an elephant?"

"No long trunk," Kris added.

"And check out this conference table," Captain Drago said, changing the topic. "Nelly, add four more chairs and room for them."

"Aye, aye, sir," Nelly said, and the table was suddenly a couple of meters longer and had four more comfortable-looking chairs.

"That should provide room for everyone you need to meet with," the skipper said proudly.

"Is it my imagination, or did the room just get bigger for the table?" Jack said.

"Yes, the viceroy's night quarters are right next door. Assuming you're in your office, you don't need all that room in your bedroom, so Nelly can swap space from one to the other. It goes both ways, in case you want to entertain anyone special."

Kris eyed Drago. "I won't be entertaining anyone, special or otherwise. What happened on Alwa stays on Alwa. What happens here is straight regulations."

"Understood, Commodore," Captain Drago said, almost bracing.

"Now, did you arrange that meeting I asked for?"

"If you mean me, Your Highness," said a new voice, "I'm here."

At the door of her office stood a civilian in casual clothes.

"Admiral Benson?" Kris said.

"Just Mr. Benson for the duration of this assignment running Canopus Station and its Navy yard. The king was rather definite on that."

"And if I have to activate your reserve commission?"

"I'm a lieutenant, ma'am," he said with a grin at Drago.

"Hold it, is everyone still stuck with a reserve commission of lieutenant?" Kris asked the two.

Both nodded.

"Nelly, do I have authority to promote people? It's got to be in there somewhere as commodore or ComAlDefSec or viceroy."

"You have the authority to approve promotions up through lieutenant commander, Kris."

"Nelly, please do the paperwork to promote all my reserve officers to lieutenant commander."

"I'll have my kids get right on it."

"Mom!" said Sal at Jack's neck.

"I'm the viceroy's computer. I get to delegate. Get used to it."

"Yes, Mom, we're getting right on it."

"Now, Mr. Benson, about the reason I asked you here. I have several questions. Is Kikuchi Katsu still with us?"

"No, Your Highness, he didn't much like leaving before he spun out those monsters aft of the station, but when the king took it in his head to rush out, he followed him."

"Can you respin those ships?"

"Despite the engineer's fear that me and mine can't pound sand, I do believe we can, ma'am."

"Good. Now, you have twenty fine 20-inch lasers on your station. Are you planning on using them for station defense?"

"Not likely. They only point one way and, as you may have noticed, we used the rocket engines to build the space dock on the station's stern. We're rock steady in orbit. Good for a space station. Bad for a fighting ship. Why? Do you have something in mind for them?"

"Up-gun the *Wasp* to a heavy frigate," Kris said. "First the *Wasp*, then the *Intrepid*. We need everything we've got if the aliens come through the jump. I figured once we off-loaded the Hellburners, we could use the Smart Metal that's supporting them to support ten guns rather than five."

"Will it be too hard?" Captain Drago asked, a skipper concerned about his ship.

"No. I'd been expecting something like that since we fitted out. The 20-inchers are modular, even the capacitors plug and unplug with the unit. Same with your 18-inchers. The *Monarch* and the *Fearless* donated about fifteen thousand tons of Smart Metal when they gave up their Hellburners. I figured I'd use most of that to enlarge your two when I replaced your guns."

"How much larger are the reactors on the heavy frigates?" Drago asked.

"Their three are about fifteen percent larger than yours. That's something we can't do anything about. You'll take longer to reload, say five seconds more than your 18-inchers. You'll likely need eight to ten more seconds for a broadside."

That didn't make Drago happy, and his face showed it.

The former admiral moved quickly to praise his guns. "The 20-inchers are good out to one hundred forty thousand klicks. Maybe a bit more depending on the armor they're facing. You hit something at seventy thousand klicks with one of them, and you're going to burn right through it."

"Trade-offs, trade-offs, trade-offs," Drago muttered.

"How soon can you start and how quickly can you finish?" Kris asked.

"We can start right now," the yard boss said. "I'll recall my folks from those two problem children trailing us and have you out in five days. May I ask why the rush, Your Highness?"

"When we went back to look over the wreck of the alien mother ship, near the far jump, we passed through two clouds of gas, not a whole lot thicker than normal space, but enough. I figure that's what's left of our last two battleships."

The former admiral nodded sadly.

"I know our *Fearless* and *Intrepid* died fighting so the *Wasp* and the *Hornet* could get away. I know what happened to *Wasp*. I don't know what happened to *Hornet*."

"She likely ended up a ball of gas, too," the former Navy man said.

"But I don't *know* that. I have nightmares that years from now someone stumbles on the hulk of the *Hornet* and finds they were alive for five, six months after the fight but didn't find some planet like Alwa or were unable to slow down like we almost did."

"You've spent a lot of time with the Marines, haven't you?" the former Admiral Benson asked.

"I've spent time with them," Kris said cautiously. Was he headed for the fact she'd just married one?

"Marines never leave anyone behind."

"You disapprove."

"No, Commodore, I do not. It's good policy. I'll have the yard ready for the *Wasp* as soon as Captain Drago is ready to move ship."

"I'm ready now, just as soon as I get Kris off my ship. Commodore, I don't know if you're aware, but we'll be without gravity in the yard. Flags are traditionally transferred when a flagship goes in the body-and-fender shop."

"Any suggestions?" Kris asked.

"Not the *Constellation*," Benson said. "Sampson is all bent out of shape about your marriage and shooting off her mouth a lot. Unless you want to hear things you'll have to 'not hear' or bring her up on charges, don't go there."

"The *Constitution*?" Kris said.

"Or the *Princess Royal*. All I hear are good things about Amber Kitano. Haven't you fought with her before?"

"Kris," Nelly put in, "Amber was Phil Taussig's XO on his fast attack boat at the Battle of Wardhaven and Jack Campbell's XO on the *Dauntless*."

"Yes, Nelly, I remember Amber. She's the one that refused to be the female lead in a panic party." An honor Kris had failed to avoid and now, thanks to Cara's skill with mash-ups, seemed to have gone viral in human space.

"Okay, Nelly, advise CO, *Princess Royal* that the commodore will be transferring her flag to her ship for the next five days. Send her schematics of my quartering needs, oh, and this office. Skipper, can you transfer this furniture?"

"Easier when we're in zero gee, my princess."

"Okay. Nelly, tell Abby to pack up and follow as fast as she can, same to Penny. Oh, and make sure Captain Kitano knows that Jack's quarters are a deck below me and down the passageway."

"Understood, Kris."

"Drago, move my office as fast as you can, but don't do anything that will delay the up-gunning. I've got to meet with our friends on the private side, and I like the idea of having an impressive office to meet them in."

"Your Highness, your gear will be there by 2100 hours tonight at the latest."

"Good. Nelly, pass the word to the civilian elephant that we're having a powwow at 2100 hours on the *Princess Royal*."

Kris headed for the *Wasp*'s quarterdeck. The ship was already making ready to move. Kris liked the pace.

Now. How would Amber Kitano take to sharing her ship with the original Princess Royal?

25

Commander Kitano met Kris at her quarterdeck and personally granted permission for her to come aboard. "I have your quarters ready. I've set up your office, but I understand more furniture will be coming along. There is a problem. The frigates were outfitted rather quickly. We don't have a lot of spare screens aboard. To get you two, I'd have to borrow them from either the wardroom, chief's mess, or the mess deck."

"Nelly, tell Captain Drago to send along two of the screens from my office. I definitely want video to entertain my civilian guests, but I'm not about to cause a morale problem on my namesake ship."

"Thank you, Your Highness. I've arranged for your office to be just off my bridge, same as *Wasp*, and your quarters, those of your maid, and Lieutenant Lien are right in a row." She glanced at Jack. "Is it correct that your chief of security's quarters are the deck below and a frame over?"

"Amber, my husband will continue to have quarters well away from me. What happened on Alwa stays on Alwa. What happens aboard ship is straight by the rules."

"Thank you, ma'am. It will make things a lot easier."

"Does everyone know about my wedding?" Kris asked.

"Just about."

"Did it hit before or after the *Monarch* sailed?"

"Oh, after. Well after. And well before your official appointment came in. We all know that. Talk about Longknife luck and having the guts to take advantage of it."

"I've fought that way. It seemed like a good time to live that way."

NELLY, BENSON SAID SAMPSON WAS SHOOTING OFF HER MOUTH ALL OVER THE PLACE. WAS THERE ANY MESSAGE TRAFFIC BETWEEN THE *CONNIE* AND THE *MONARCH*?

YES, KRIS, BUT IT WAS IN A THROWAWAY CIPHER AND VERY SHORT. I DON'T SEE ANY WAY I COULD CRACK IT.

SO, WAS THE KING FULLY INFORMED OF MY ACTIONS? WHOSE IDEA WAS IT TO GIVE JACK A JOB THAT MEANS MOST OF HIS TIME IS DIRTSIDE? AND WAS THAT MIXED-UP LANGUAGE ABOUT DRAFTING PEOPLE A WEDDING GIFT FROM GRAMPA RAY?

KRIS, IF YOU SPEND YOUR TIME CHASING ANSWERS TO QUESTIONS YOU CAN'T FIND, YOU'LL GO AS CRAZY AS A LONGKNIFE.

With a sigh, Kris filed those questions in a pigeonhole marked "Ignore."

"Commander, please have the *P Royal* send to the squadron: 'Prepare for sortie, 0900 hours tomorrow. Exercises will extend up to four gees.'"

"Four gees, ma'am?" Captain Kitano swallowed hard.

"Is that a problem?"

"We did 1.5 gees at most on the way out, what with the *Prosperity* and *Free Enterprise* with us. Most of the cruise was at one gee."

"Clearly, you didn't come out the way we did."

"No. I'm told that was intentional. That and taking it easy on the civilians."

"Well, I'm glad things have been easy for them up to now. They won't be from now on."

The commander made no reply.

They arrived at Kris's night quarters. Except for the tub, it was as spartan as ever and no bigger.

"We haven't opened a door yet to your day quarters. Would you like a door to your maid's quarters? They're right next door."

"You'll have to ask her. I think she likes her privacy." Then Kris caught the second part of the question.

"Can you open a door to the next quarters?"

"Most of my crew have apps on their computers to adjust the ship in minor ways. Create a massaging recliner to watch movies on the mess deck. Modify their work spaces for efficiency. Opening a door is one of the easy options."

"Can they open the hull to space?" Jack asked. "A door into the brig, open the side of my safe?"

"Oh, no, Colonel," the captain quickly put in. "Those are under higher security. But the normal internal bulkheads, yes. If there's battle damage, anyone may need to seal a bulkhead."

Kris nodded understanding. This new Smart Metal™ was making everything different. The captain looked like she wanted to say something more, but she didn't.

Kris would have very much liked to know what she didn't say, but she didn't ask.

Some things smart officers ignored.

At least until they bit them on the behind.

"Nelly, give the commander a hint at the fleet maneuvers we'll be using tomorrow. I don't want to be embarrassed by my own flag falling out of line."

Nelly opened a hologram before them and showed a ship going through a rather moderate jinking pattern. "We'll use double intervals for safety," Nelly pointed out, "and all the squadron will be executing the same maneuvers at the same time. That should reduce the chances of collision."

"Do you think your ship can follow that evasion program?" Kris asked.

"I think so, ma'am. We'll sure give it a good old Navy try. And thanks for the warning. Nelly, could you pass that holo to my computer? I'd like to show it to some of my officers. We may be in for a long night."

"Do so, Nelly. You better pass it along to the entire squadron with my compliments. We don't play favorites in this squadron."

"Glad to hear that, ma'am," Commander Kitano said.

Kris settled into her station chair in her night quarters. "Now, if you'll excuse me, I need to be thinking about my

2100 hour meeting. Please leave the door open when you leave. Colonel Montoya will be working with me."

"Yes, ma'am. Doors open. Good idea."

And the skipper of the *Princess Royal* left Jack and Kris alone.

"That seemed to go well," Kris said.

"Anyone can open a door between rooms?" Jack said.

"You caught that, did you?"

"You think we might need to have a no-notice showdown inspection of berthing areas?"

"Jack, do you really think that's the number one item on my to-do list?"

"No, but it's going to have to be up there sooner or later. Maybe after we get back from the hunt for the *Hornet*'s fate."

"Yes. That will give the skippers and leading chiefs time to handle it on their own. Meanwhile, how am I going to survive going into the lions' cage this evening?"

"You think it'll be that bad?"

"We told Grampa Al not to send a fleet of delectable merchant ships full of goodies out to hunt for the bastards and shot the engines out of them when they tried. Now, Ray, legend and all, drops them off here and bugs out. Jack, somehow I've got to get them to devote their full efforts to building up a defense here, and I don't have a penny to pay them with."

"Put it on someone's charge card?" Jack suggested.

"Jack, what charge card is good this side of the galaxy? The colonists did what they had to do because the only alternative was starving to death."

"By the way, where is this fleet of yours getting its chow?"

That brought Kris up short. "Nelly, get me Amanda Kutter."

"Amanda here," came a second later. "I'm busy at the moment."

KRIS, I THINK SHE'S IN BED FROM THE SOUNDS OF IT, AND NOT ALONE.

NELLY, YOU ARE DEVELOPING A DIRTY MIND.

"Amanda, I have a very big problem. At nine, I'm meeting with a lot of business and mining types to talk about how they are or are not going to make a mint here in the Alwa system."

"There's no way they're going to make a mint," Amanda said.

"That's what I was afraid you'd say. Would you mind heading up here, oh and bring that young man, Jacques la Duke with you. We may need some help explaining the sociology and psychology of both the birds and the colonials."

"Ah, Your Highness, you could not have picked a worse time."

"Oh, if so, I'm sorry, but I really need you."

"Kris, Jacques and I just got married, and we're on our honeymoon. Surely, you understand the problem."

"It must be catching," Jack whispered.

"I'm sorry, Amanda, believe me, I am so sorry, and I wouldn't say this if I didn't mean it, but I need to get these people working for our mutual survival, and I really need your help."

"I think she really does," came from Jacques.

"Yes. It's worse than anyone could have guessed," said Amanda back to her new husband. "Okay, we will be there before your nine o'clock meeting. You'd better hear what we've found out. It'll be hard to believe."

"Want to send us a report?" Kris asked.

"No, Your Highness. Truth like this is best delivered face-to-face."

"Then Longknife out," Kris said, and eyed Jack. "What do you think that's all about?"

"Kris, there are a dozen horror stories chasing themselves around in my head. If there's anything Gunny has taught me, a good Marine does not take counsel with his fears. What's our next topic?"

Once again, Jack had the right idea. Still, Kris's pigeonhole for "run in circles, scream and shout about it later" was getting awfully full.

"How do we get the next bastard's mother ship close enough to the Hellburners for us to demolish it?"

"Oh, an easy one," Jack said. "For someone, I hope. Because I have no idea."

"Boy do I miss my screens. Nelly, project a holo of this system." Nelly did, and filled the wall across from Kris with a full view of the system.

"Now, narrow it down to just the jump that the aliens would have come through, and the space between it and Alwa."

There was a lot of empty space, but off a bit to one side was a gas giant. "Does that beauty have any solid moons?"

Nelly highlighted three of them, almost evenly spaced around the giant. For half a minute they orbited the giant in fast motion. As you'd expect, they raced around at different speeds. At one point all were close to the jump, a moment later, they all managed to be on the opposite side of their primary.

"Draw a course, half-gee acceleration, from the jump to Alwa. Assume a flip to deceleration at one-half gee at midpoint."

Nelly did. "The base ship will never be closer than a million kilometers to any of the moons, at best," the computer said.

"So, sneaking up is going to be a bit of a problem this time," Kris mused.

"Anything on the surface of those moons is going to be lazed to dust," Jack said.

"So we create battle stations deep underground that can survive the blasting."

"And if they turn the surface to glass?"

"We drill out before we launch the Hellburners."

"Then those mad monster ships are going to laser them again."

"Not if we keep them busy. Keep them concentrated on a mobile strike force."

"All four of your frigates?"

"Reinforcements are coming. Grampa Ray promised me reinforcements."

"You trust a Longknife? No, excuse me, I love and trust a Longknife. Do you trust that particular Longknife?"

Kris sent a kiss Jack's way but stayed in her chair. He stayed perched on her bed.

"We've got twelve Hellburners and four frigates, a total of eight frigates when they finished spinning the *Prosperity* and *Enterprise* into warships."

"And there will be two hundred or more alien monster ships."

"Can't I plan for the future, when maybe we've got twenty or thirty frigates?"

"And the odds are down to only seven or ten to one."

"We beat three to one."

"Yes, you did. Okay, let's say we can dig deep into these three moons and plant missile bases. Who mans them?"

"Colonials. Alwans. There are bound to be a few fighters among them."

"And a few officers and good chiefs willing to lead them," Jack muttered.

Penny walked in on them, her ever-present shadow and fellow intelligence officer, Lieutenant Iizuka Masao right behind her. "You two busy?"

"Only planning our next battle."

"It look any better than the last few?"

"Not at the moment. What can we do for you?"

"Actually, we thought we should bring you up to date on some stuff we've been culling from the reports coming in." Penny glanced around the room. "I know we can't drop down to the Forward Lounge for a drink, but didn't they give you a Tac Center or an office when you transferred your flag?"

"It's next door. Nelly, open a door to it."

Nelly did, just at the foot of Kris's bed, and they walked into Kris's office.

"That's neat," Penny said. "Who'd have thought you could use the Smart Metal to just open a door." Penny actually did sound surprised. Apparently, the woman who could order the whole ship around wasn't aware of the app that worried Amber.

"Hey! Nifty office you got here."

"There's supposed to be an actual carved wooden desk there"—Kris pointed at a vacant place on the deck—"and over there will be some sofas and chairs for when we just want to chat, you know, like when I make my social calls on the king."

"That bad?" Penny said.

Her poor Imperial Navy officer seemed none the more informed but didn't look all that interested in an explanation. Maybe Penny had warned him some questions were best left unasked around the Longknifes.

"We were trying to figure out how to get the Hellburners

close enough to the bastard's base ship to survive long enough to make a hit," Kris said, as Nelly shrank the table down to be a perfect fit for the four of them. "Nelly, show Penny and Masao the moons we found and the problems with them."

Nelly quickly brought them up to speed as all four settled into comfortable chairs that allowed them to rock back and forth as Kris tended to do, lean back as Jack did, sway from side to side as Penny was doing, or sit perfectly still as Masao did.

"You're going to have to dig deep for those battle stations," Penny said.

"That should leave you a lot of gravel and rocks, assuming you don't just laser your way down as far as you want to go," Masao pointed out.

"And rocks are good for?" Kris said.

"To throw at the aliens," he said. "They don't like anything close to them. Right? They even lazed that little rock that drifted near when they were attacking us last."

"Yes," Kris said.

"So we give them a lot of rocks out by that jump. Let them run into a few of them. Laser a whole lot of them. Lasers get hot when you use them a lot, right?"

"Right," Kris said, starting to grin.

"They tend to go all in, feetfirst and overpower the opposition. Let's see how they take to a war of attrition," Penny finished for the both of them. Clearly, they'd given the situation a lot of thought.

Of course, Penny had a kind of glow about her, and the way Masao looked whenever his glance passed her way told a wonderful story.

Or maybe Kris was just so much in love, she wanted everyone in love.

"We're still going to need some awfully brave people to man those missile stations," Jack pointed out.

"We may have found some Alwans to fit that bill."

"Fighting Alwans?"

"Yes. They hail from the south, down near the equator. They're taller and thicker, and you have to watch their legs. They'll kick your head right off." A new picture showed up on the wall of something that might have passed for an ostrich from old Earth. It had the long legs but the neck and body were fuller. On screen, two of them ran at each other and butted their chests together. One fell down, and the one left standing clearly celebrated some sort of victory.

"They like to fight," Masao said. "The scientists who made contact with them showed them the picture of the space battles we've had and they were all ready to butt chests with anyone who'd fight like that."

"I like their enthusiasm," Kris said.

"They'll need a lot of education," Penny said, "but they're willing. A couple of them have been flown back to Haven, and we're trying to master their language and see how well they do with technology. They've done well on basic aptitude tests."

"By the way, the scientists are creating a problem for the Navy," Masao said. "They want shuttles to bounce researchers from place to place, just short hops. What they really need are transport planes down there. It would save wear and tear on the shuttles and give scientists more control over their missions."

"One of the many things I'm trying to balance. Right now, we have less than fifteen thousand tons of Smart Metal to meet all our needs. Maybe we can get more when we pull the Hell-burners off the frigates."

"But no frigate skipper or defense wants to give up a gram of the stuff," Penny finished. She was not only Kris's intelligence officer but usually handled defense for the *Wasp*.

"So what do I get the mining and industry guys working on first? Finding bauxite to make aluminum for aircraft and boats or the ingredients for Smart Metal to make more frigates? Of course, if we go for frigates, we better also find the stuff for lasers, reactors, and all the electronics that go into one of these war wagons."

"You think you can build a frigate out here?" Masao asked.

"It's my opinion that the only reason King Ray brought all this industrial stuff out here was so that, if the aliens do stomp us into the ground, they find enough high tech to fool them into thinking that Alwa made all of these frigates on her own, and there's no need to look further. Nothing to see here. Move along."

That left both Penny and Masao nodding gently. "Yes, it fits together."

"So we can just let the business types run off and do what they think can make them a buck this far across the galaxy, or we can make them see that their necks are on the chopping block, too, and they need to get behind a defense program."

"When are you going to try to do this?" Penny asked.

"Nine tonight."

"You hungry?"

"I'm getting there," Kris admitted to her friend.

"We'll, we've found this place on B deck that serves really good Thai food. How about we discuss this more over dinner?"

26

Prepared as much as she felt she'd ever be, Her Royal Highness, Viceroy of Alwa as well as Commodore of Frigate Squadron 4 and Commander, Alwa Defense Sector made her way toward her office with Jack, Penny, and Masao in tow.

On the A deck, they'd picked up Amanda and Jacques, both looking so much in love and terrified, as if some horrible beast had showed up at the wedding.

Or maybe before the wedding.

Kris got them all to her office a good half hour before the meeting was due to start.

She walked in to find that Captain Drago had done his miracle. Her lovely wooden desk was there. Her sofas and chairs were there.

Also there were fifteen entrepreneurs who fully expected to make their fortune here, on the other side of the galaxy from the rest of human capital, arranged around her table.

One of them was already sitting in her chair. The one closest to the desk and the one with an ever so slightly higher back that helped when you're six feet tall.

Kris walked up to him, and said politely, "You're in my chair."

"So glad you could join us," the short man said. "I've been

elected spokesman to bring you up to date on our plans for the development and exploitation of this system."

"You are in my chair," Kris repeated. More firmly this time.

"There's plenty of chairs."

There was exactly one left. It was at the foot of the table.

Kris had not approached this meeting with any feelings of fondness. Now, she was rapidly moving from disgust to open hostility.

NELLY, TAKE AWAY HIS CHAIR. NO, TAKE AWAY ALL THE CHAIRS.

Suddenly fifteen confident men and women found themselves sitting on air. They promptly landed on their rumps.

"What was that for?" the small man grouched from where he now sat on the floor.

"Ladies and gentlemen, this is my office. I called this meeting, but you showing up thirty minutes early to take over my office is no way to start our business. Nelly, expand the table to accommodate all present. You, move. I will sit at the head of my table with my immediate staff. The rest of you can arrange yourselves as you see fit."

Nelly immediately lengthened the table. However, only after several suits pulled themselves up from the floor and moved down, did chairs again appear.

Kris settled herself in her chair, with Jack at her right and Penny at her left. Masao was beside her. Amanda took the chair next to Jack . . . an interesting test for a new husband . . . but Amanda's own new husband imposed himself between her and the business types.

Kris hoped that didn't mean the young anthropologist feared open violence or the throwing of poop to be a likely outcome to this meeting.

Kris was none too sure about that.

Either Captain Drago or Kitano had arranged for two of the screens to be moved to this office. While Kris's screens on the *Wasp* ran from deck to overhead on the walls in her Tac Center, these two screen were positioned to form one long landscape.

It fit Kris's objective well.

Kris began the meeting by having Nelly project the alien

mother ship as it appeared just through the jump. She did it with an added roar to emphasize the huge rocket motors on the aft end of the ship shooting plasma out into space.

The business folks jumped and, as one, focused on the screens, even if it meant swiveling in their seats. As the Hellburners began to eat into the ship, Nelly stayed with it while our rockets did their destruction, then switched to the dead, rolling hulk in space.

A moment later the three alien ships popped out of the jump point, and, again, the *Wasp* quickly disposed of them.

"They are out there. They hate our very existence. They want us dead. They failed once. They will try again. Tell me, ladies and gentlemen, what are you doing here in a beleaguered outpost and exactly how do you intend to make money?"

The little guy who had claimed to be their appointed spokesman didn't say a word. Neither did the other men.

Finally, a young woman said, "We figured we could begin trading with the Alwans. Our trade goods for their raw materials."

"The Alwans do not want our trade goods," Amanda said. "They see their needs as minimal above subsistence. There are gold and silver deposits that they have found on the surface. They have used them to make jewelry and trinkets. They consider a shiny glass trinket just as valuable as gold. They also do not want us mining their territory."

"We'll create markets. They have TV. We can advertise," a man put in.

"Over half of them don't believe what they see on TV. Even if you can create a market for your trade goods, how do you intend to have the Alwans pay for them?"

"Money?"

Now Jacques stepped in. "The Alwans don't have any concept of money. They understand that you owe someone when they give you something. They have very good memories and an honor system that we humans can hardly grasp. You help plant food, you get to eat food. And, yes, they have farms. Nothing like ours. No plowing, no single crops row on row. They plant the beans and seed plants and several other things all together. They grow all together in one clump, and anyone who has a right to the food can come along, pull off supper, and eat it."

"And if someone doesn't work but still wants to eat?" the short guy said, finally finding his voice.

"Children can. The elderly can. The injured or handicapped can. If you are able-bodied and don't do the honorable thing, sooner much more likely than later, you will be talked to by an elder. You get one talking-to. Only one. The next time, the flock gathers and runs you out of town."

Jacques paused to turn to Amanda, and she took over. "Life outside civilization is brutish and short. There are several animals that enjoy Alwans for dinner. Most of the time they stay away from the civilized areas. Occasionally, one of them will go rogue and invade towns. Before we came, the Alwans hunted with short bows. We introduced the more powerful longbow, and they proved very good at pulling it. Now, we've introduced some black-powder rifles. Our hunters are highly honored by the Alwans. I think that's one reason they let us stay."

"So, to summarize," Kris said, "you've come a long way to find no market for your goods. If you want to ship anything back to human space, transportation costs will eat your lunch. Worst, there's a whole lot of aliens that don't think we have the right to live, much less conduct business, and want to kill us."

"Can we go home?" the short man asked.

"Sorry, the *Monarch* and the *Fearless* are the last two ships headed that way for a long time."

"I believe the word among my folks," Jack said, "is root hog or die."

"Or to put it a way that Alex Longknife might understand," Kris said, "there's only one market for your goods, the fleet, and if you work really hard meeting the needs of that market, you just might live."

"None of us were told this," the small man complained. "Management said this was a great opportunity."

"I'm guessing that all of you represent corporations that participated in my Grampa Alex's scheme to ship all the best that humans had to offer out to where the aliens could capture them, murder the crews, then follow them back to human space."

"That wasn't the way it was explained to us," the young woman said.

"But all your big men had their fingers in that pie, right?"

There were nods around the table.

"I talked with the President of New Eden a while back. He asked me to remind Grampa Al that he should keep his fingers out of the governing process of New Eden. If he didn't, he'd find that the power to tax is indeed the power to destroy. I'm guessing that after we stopped the fleet of stupidity, a lot of your head folks got taken out to the woodshed by the likes of Ray Longknife, Billy Longknife, and other men of political power. Your men of business were told bad things would happen to them if Alwa didn't get some industrial capacity. King Ray wanted enough people and machinery here so that if the aliens did indeed stomp Alwa into the ground, they wouldn't be left wondering where the fleet defending Alwa came from."

"We're sacrificial lambs," the young woman said.

"I like to think that we, my squadron and your industry, are sacrificial tigers."

"Tigers?" came from a ways down the table.

"Yes. You remember that limerick about a woman who went for a ride on the back of a tiger, and the tiger returned wearing her smile? As I see it, we can run around in panic, or we can see that the next alien that tries to ride this tiger ends up inside. Call it a Longknife thing."

"And if we don't want to?"

"Well, along with the various commissions the king dropped in my lap as he was jumping out of here, there was also something I never expected to see. It seems that I am now the Chief Executive Officer of Nuu Enterprises in this system. Who here is from Grampa Al's shop?"

Three of the fifteen raised their hand, including the young woman who had done the best job of making sense so far.

"Hi, folks," Kris said with the friendliest grin she could manage. "I'm your new boss."

"And the rest of us?"

"We follow the Alwa way," Kris said simply. "You're breathing my air, eating my food, drinking my water. To go mining, you'll be burning my reaction mass. You can work for the privilege, and in maybe thirty years earn your ticket back with some pay, or you can be dropped down on Alwa. Most likely, the colonials won't take you. They also have strong rules about working if you're going to eat. And, of course, the Alwans have the same attitude. There's plenty of food in the jungle. Just remember, there are several things with long fangs that consider you food, too."

Kris had never been in a meeting—Navy, government, or private—that got so quiet.

"What do you want?" the young woman finally asked.

"A plan from you. We need everything. Airplanes to fly scientists so they can make a planetary survey of just what we have here before aliens strip it down to bedrock. The colonials need weapons so they and aggressive Alwans can put up a fight if the aliens do land an army."

Kris paused. "The bastards like to drop rocks and atomics on the central urban populations, but neither the colonials or Alwans have gone in for big cities. That may help."

"But," Kris said, leaning on the table, "we need ships. Ships made of conventional metal that you can use to explore and mine and ship resources down to the factories on the moon. We need more factories to make just about everything. And, if possible, I'd like to see some Smart Metal, the newest kind, produced, so we can make our own frigates. And yes, I know that means reactors and huge lasers and all kinds of electronics. Call me a dreamer, but that's the plan I want from you."

Kris paused to look around the table. "You say you want to make a fortune. I don't know if I can promise you that, but I can assure you that you will have one hell of a paragraph on your résumé if we all survive this."

That got a chuckle from around the table.

"When do you want this plan?" the young woman asked.

"I'd like a quick cut to look at by tomorrow. A fuller plan the day after that. And there's no need for your workers to sit idle. Those who can help in the shipyard, should. Those who can help nano mining dirtside can do that. Anyone with an idea about how to boost the production facilities the colonials have can drop down and give them a hand.

"Oh, and that mess separating frigates and merchant ships out from the *Prosperity* and the *Enterprise*? Kick someone in the butt there and get them moving. You need those plants down on the moon and those mining ships out there mining. I need a full plan by next week."

"What about the *Furious*'s reactors?" the young woman asked.

"The best one goes down to the colonials. The next best two go to the moon. The last one, the one that will need the most work, goes to the colonials. Oh, and anyone who can do anything to refurbish those reactors has a job on that from right now until they're done."

Kris again paused to take the measurements of the people listening to her. Several, like the young woman, were already making notes on their wrist units. Some just looked dumbly at the table. There were three or four, like the small man, who Kris would bet ended up alone in the middle of some forest with nothing but the clothes on their back.

"You came here as six different corporations with six different plans for making your fortune. Now you know, it's not your fortune you need to make but your life you need to save. I talk for only one of you, but I'd strongly suggest that we stop looking at me and mine and start looking at us and the bastards. Any questions?"

No one opened their mouth.

"There's a nice Thai food place on B deck. It has a back room that I think you would all fit into. You might want to adjourn there and get started on your plan."

Kris quickly found her office a lot more empty.

"Nelly, shrink the table down to us," Kris said, then turned to her team. "Well, I could be wrong, but that seems to have gone well."

"As far as it went," Amanda said.

"Do you know something I don't know?" Kris asked.

"Yes, Your Highness. I didn't bring it up because you were using the work-to-eat thing so well, but we have a problem. A big one."

"You have my attention."

"Kris, there is no food surplus on Alwa. They've got just enough to feed themselves, maybe a bit more. The colonials are in worse shape. They got land, but it's not that productive. A good quarter of their population is in agriculture. That's where Jack should be getting his army, but if he does, they're going to starve."

"No food?" Kris said. "Where does that leave us? My fleet and all these new workers? Twenty thousand more mouths to feed!"

"I don't know where the food will come from," Amanda said.

27

Kris leaned back in her chair and tried to get her mind around another big mess she was in. "You're telling me that when the food aboard is gone, we can't count on getting any food from Alwa, colonial or native?"

Amanda nodded. "Both the natives and colonials have always lived close to the bone, but the last three years' crops have been worse than usual. They need a good year. This year the rains again came late and weren't enough. Have you had anyone trying to sell you food? Swap you a truckload of potatoes for a fancy computer, a TV?"

"Come to think of it, I haven't seen a fat colonial," Jack said. "I should have noticed. Locals are always trying to sell stuff to the fleet, but no one has shown up at the fleet landing."

"I didn't think much of that," Kris said. "I never got around to asking if there was a farmer's market to sell us fresh vegetables and fruits, meat. Why didn't Mother MacCreedy notice?"

That brought shrugs.

"What about the ocean? There must be a lot of fish in the sea?"

"There are," Amanda said. "But there are also things that

make the sharks back on Earth look like minnows. The first desperate years, the colonials sent out wooden fishing boats, sail rigged. Half the time they got back a load of fish. The other half, splinters and half-eaten seamen washed ashore. They catch fish in rivers, and some from the beach. But I've seen pictures of the things that leap out of the water and snatch their catch off their lines. They are big, toothy, and ugly."

"But Jack and I went swimming in the water!"

"Let me guess, Joe's Seaside Paradise?" Amanda asked sourly. "That was where we were when you called. Joe said we had the very bungalow you had and offered us fishing, boating, and snorkeling. I asked him about the 'eats everythings,' and he said they never come there. His resort is on the Sun Coast. Much of the water is quite shallow and warmed by the sun most of the year. It's too warm for the big stuff. It's about the only place in colonial territory where you can enjoy the ocean."

"And we were too dumb to ask what might nibble our toes," Jack muttered.

"Not your fault, Jack. None of us knew yet," Kris said. "However, maybe I slept through my ecology class, but if we remove the hunters at the top of the food chain, shouldn't that open up a lot of good eating from lower down for us?"

"That's the textbook answer, but how do you take out thirty meters of muscle with lots of teeth?"

Kris considered that for a moment. "You start with steel ships. Say two hundred feet long. Harpoons with explosive tips. Maybe we have to use wind at first, but we can have a backup electric motor to work our way off a lee shore. We can talk more about that later. What's this about the colonial farms just being able to sustain the population?"

"They got the barely arable land. They worked hard to irrigate more, but it's still poor land, and they lack fertilizer. They're using night soil and manure from the oxen, but it's just barely holding its own."

"Fish offal is good fertilizer," Jack said.

"Catch the big ones, then catch the better-eating ones. What we don't eat goes into the soil to improve the crops," Kris said.

"That's a plan, but how long does it take to get it working?" Amanda asked.

"Somehow, I don't think it would be a good idea to call up the folks I just threatened with not eating if they didn't work and tell them that eating might not be an option even if they do work like dogs."

"I second that motion," Jack said.

"The fastest way to get a shark killer off the colonial shore would be a Smart Metal ship with an antimatter power plant. Nelly, get me Mr. Benson and tell him I need to see him pronto."

"I'm working with Captain Drago on the plan for the *Wasp*," came quickly back at Kris.

"Good, but as soon as you have a chance, I need for you to drop by my office on the *Princess Royal*. We have a problem that only you can solve."

"I'm hearing that a lot."

"Trust me, this one is true, and it gets to the heart of every man and woman aboard."

"I'll be there in ten minutes. We were done, anyway, right, Captain?"

"You be sure to be here tomorrow when they start moving those guns," Captain Drago said. "I say there are a few more power leads than your blueprints show. I know my boat."

"Benson off," took Kris out of that argument and left her staring at Amanda.

"Any more surprises?"

"You want to know why the Alwan population grows so slowly?"

"Will it turn my stomach?"

"Very likely."

"I hate people who enjoy speaking truth to power, especially now that I seem to have some. At least some folks seem to think I have some. Power, not truth. Speak."

"Every egg laid is reviewed by the elders. If they don't like it, it's cast outside the nest."

"The egg? They don't even wait for it to hatch?" Jack sounded incredulous. And just the way Kris would want her child's dad to sound.

"How can they judge an egg?" Kris asked.

Jacques took over. "I have no idea. Maybe their sight goes into the infrared or ultraviolet. We haven't been able to test them. They don't like humans much, most of them."

"It could be something worse," Amanda said. "Maybe they aren't judging the egg but the parents. If you're a trouble-maker, your egg's bad."

Kris shivered. "And every mother just accepts that their egg is trash?" Yes, kids were out of the question while she commanded a fleet on the tip of the spear, but she was a woman, and a newly married one at that.

"That's where things get interesting," Amanda said. "Tell them, Jacques."

"No, there are those that grab their egg and flee into the deep woods or jungle."

"And get eaten," Kris said.

"Some. Maybe many, but not all. There's a tribe of hunter-gatherers that are surviving in the deep woods," Jacques said.

"I thought you said that being thrown out of the community was a death sentence," Kris said.

"It is, for most, but there are exceptions. And imagine the attitude of Alwans that don't care for the elders and have man-aged to stand up to the lions and tigers and bears in the deep woods with just their short bows and spears," Amanda said.

"They must be good at hiding, and good at fighting when cornered," Jack said slowly. "Just the folks that make great Marine recruits."

"We don't have a lot of nanos for recon dirtside," Jacques said, "but I've got a few following that tribe, or tribes. I've also got a theory; honey, should I tell them?"

"Go ahead, love. All they can do is laugh."

"I don't think all Alwans have the same brain."

"I've been wondering if all the Alwans were even the same species," Kris said. "They look so different from equatorial to temperate to polar."

"Oh, they're all drawn from the same gene pool," Jacques said. "Unlike us humans, who almost went extinct twenty-five or thirty thousand years ago, they have a much more diverse genetic pool to draw on. But I'm starting to think that there are parts of their brains that some Alwans don't use, like many of the elders. Others, like the ones that hang around us and are running free in the forest, do use it."

"Could the egg selection have something to do with that?" Kris asked.

"It kind of has me wondering. The ostrich types down at the equator don't have an egg review. They're a lot more aggressive and more willing to think about the future and accept that there is a past. Not so much with the elders here. What I'd give for brain scans from a couple of hundred subjects! I've checked out several volunteers, Alwans working with us, and they all showed the same. The problem is getting an elder."

"The problem *is* the elders," Jack said.

"Am I interrupting anything?" Mr. Benson said from the door.

"No, I think we've beaten this live Alwan as much as we can," Kris said.

Amanda and Jacques nodded.

"You have a problem for me?" the former admiral said.

"Has your mess or restaurateurs bought any fresh fruit or vegetables dirtside?" Kris asked.

"Oh, that problem. Yes, Kiet, the guy running our Thai restaurant, dropped down to the farmers' market yesterday to see about some fresh chickens, among other things."

"How'd it go?" Amanda asked.

"He found a truckload of chickens and offered to buy them. Farmer asked him for one personal computer per chicken and wanted at least three of the good ones like Granny Rita got. The rest could be just so-so," the former officer said.

Jack whistled. "That's kind of steep."

"Well, Kiet loves nothing better than haggling, so he counters with two, maybe three for the truckload. The farmer wouldn't budge past one computer for two chickens. He says he has contracts to fill, and he might be able to swap computers for chickens, but he's got a lot of contracts. The rest of the market was the same. Everyone owed someone something and needed a whole lot to settle the contract. Kiet came home empty-handed."

The former admiral paused to study Kris and the tableful of people around her. "I take it that Kiet ran into something more than just a lot of opening bids from hard bargainers."

"Kiet seems to have run full speed into a famine that's been going on for near eighty years," Amanda said.

"And we've just dropped twenty thousand hungry and

hard-drinking Sailors, Marines, miners, and assembly-line supervisors into a place that not only can't defend itself but can't feed its defenders," Benson concluded.

"You got it in one," Kris said.

"Logistics, logistics, logistics," the former admiral was heard to mutter. Then he locked eyes with Kris. "So if Alwa can't support a defensive fleet, and we're just supposed to be the first of many, do we pack it all in and go home?"

"Not on my watch, Admiral."

"No offense intended, Viceroy. I believe in examining all my options, and it helps to get the worst off the table first."

"No offense taken, Admiral. Now, as you said, logistics had just jumped ahead of a lot of things to take first place in this swamp as the biggest alligator chewing on our rump. We need things, and you're the magician appointed to make them."

The former admiral settled into a chair that Nelly made appear at the table.

"We need fishing boats," Kris started with. "Big, strong ones able to tackle thirty meters of angry muscle and teeth. These leviathans have been keeping both Alwans and colonials off the oceans. They've been exploiting the sea's resources for themselves. I intend to stop that."

The admiral took that order and frowned at it for nearly a full minute. "You're talking ancient sailing technology, ma'am, but it just happens to be a hobby of mine. Still, you can't send men out in less than five-, six-hundred-ton boats if you want to have them come back from fighting something that big."

"You're not surprising me," Kris said. "Nelly, do you have something like what the admiral is talking about in your storage?"

The screen beside them took on a picture of a boat identified as from 1940. "Raven class minesweeper, seventy meters long," Nelly said. "A smaller one, Admirable class, was less than sixty meters long and a hundred tons lighter."

"We could put a harpoon on the front deck," the shipyard boss mused. "Rig it with an explosive tip. By the way, one of the exploration teams finally found an island loaded with guano, the natural source for nitrates used in both fertilizer and explosives. We should be able to start upgrading the weapons and maybe the farms."

"One shuttle flight at a time?" Amanda said dryly.

"Something tells me you want a five-thousand-ton bulk freighter, too, Princess."

"We need everything," Kris said. "We have nothing."

"I take it that building those planes to move the scientific teams around just got knocked out of high priority?"

"No, Admiral. We've got a planet we know way too little about. We need more discoveries like that guano island. If it's not raining here, where is it raining? Do they have a bumper crop or just flash floods wiping everything out? I need to know."

"So everything is my number one priority," Benson said drolly.

"My Marines could take beach guard and shoot those things that steal from the fisherman, Kris, but I don't know how effective the small round from an M-6 will be."

"We need elephant rifles," the former admiral said. "Heavy 12mm stuff to hit something big and let it know it's been hit."

"And let's not forget the hunter-gatherers in the deep forest," Jacques said. "They are finding some food resources even as they hide. If Jack's Marines took out the main threat to them, we might find another entire food chain to exploit."

"Alwa's never going to be the same," Penny said sadly.

"If those aliens Her Highness whipped had showed up," the old Navy officer said, "Alwa not only wouldn't be the same, it would be very dead. I choose change and a chance to live."

"You've said it for all of us," Kris said. "Now then, we need to get all this started real fast if we're going to make a difference real quick. I see Smart Metal as the only way to do that. With a big chunk of the boffins dirtside, it's time to roll up their space. Jack, if we deploy a major part of your Marines, could we roll up their space?"

"I thought you wanted to go lightly on the ground with guns?" Jack said.

"If you're a fisherman, and a Marine takes out something that's been robbing you, hook, line, and sinker as well as fish, is that Marine a problem or a friend."

"A friend," Jack said. "A real buddy."

"And maybe you invite him home to dinner and give him a place to bed down by the fire. If that gets more Smart Metal off the frigates, and into leviathan-hunting, trawling, and transporting nitrates to Haven for both fertilizer and ammo for elephant guns, we're eating."

Here Kris turned to Penny. "I know I'm asking you for a gallon of your life blood, but how much armor can a frigate give up and still have some sort of fighting chance?"

"I knew that question was coming," Penny said. "You'll have to fight your skippers, but I'd say three to five thousand tons each, maybe ten if you don't mind a skeleton ship. That's beside what you can off-load with the Hellburners, Marines, and boffins. I'm assuming that we'd get that back if the early-warning system went off, and the bastards started moving on us."

"I expect that assumption to be valid," Kris said.

"So I can maybe get a hundred and fifty to two hundred and fifty thousand tons of metal to build fishing boats, freighters, aircraft, and a whole lot of trucks to bring in whatever food we find in all the out-of-the-way places."

"Is that enough Smart Metal?" Kris asked.

"It will have to be," the old Navy man said. "We haven't even begun looking at what the industrial folks can add to this. I hear we located a crater on the moon way up north. If what I read was right, it's got a lot of water mixed in with its dust, and its regolith is rich in iron. They can build a stone wall around it, top it off with an iron or steel roof, get a decent magnetic field going to protect the workers, then leach most of the Smart Metal out of the plants."

He stared at the overhead. "That could add twenty or thirty thousand more tons, but what I really want is steel from that crater. Steel for guns. Steel for boats. Steel to make trucks."

Then he eyed Kris. "Of course, batteries and power would come in handy, too."

"Have we got anyone to skipper and crew a fishing boat?" Amanda asked.

"Nelly?" Kris asked.

"There are several people in the fleet who worked summers as deckhands on fishing boats both on Musashi and Wardhaven. Hey, we got lucky. There's a chief, called back from retirement, who spent his last five years skippering a fishing boat up in the northern waters of North Continent, Kris. He's on the *Connie*."

"Nelly, send to Captain Sampson, request release of this chief immediately to Navy yard. Make that soonest."

"Sent, Kris. Received on the *Constellation*. Ah, Kris, Sampson sends back, 'Why are you transferring him from my command?'"

Jack whistled. The admiral's eyes got wide. Penny shook her head. "She sounds kind of like a young woman I know," she said.

"I did not respond to my first order with a question. Not even half of my orders."

"Yes," Jack agreed, clearly lying manfully like a husband should.

"Kris, there may be a problem here," Nelly said. "The chief has sent you a Private and Personal e-mail requesting reassignment from the *Constellation*. It's one of about a hundred that I've been sitting on because I don't know what to do with them officially."

Now it was Kris's turn to whistle. A hundred requests amounted to a quarter of the frigate's crew when you included Marines and scientists.

"Admiral, any suggestions?" Kris said.

"You talking to this civilian?" the older man said, not suppressing a grin. "I strongly suspect this was what my king meant when he told me that I was a contractor, not a Navy officer this cruise."

He paused, started to say something. Paused again, then did open his mouth. "It seems to me that Lieutenant Commander Sampson has a leadership challenge facing her. It also seems to me, as an old ship driver and fleet management type, that you, Commodore, have a leadership challenge facing you. Actually, several, since I walked in here, but you know what I mean."

"I think I do," Kris said and reflected on her choices. "Admiral, will you be needing the chief to help you design your fishing fleet between now and oh, 1400 tomorrow?"

"I got plenty of irons in my fires. No."

"Then I'll kick my leadership challenge down the road until then."

"Kick. I like that idea," the admiral said, and stood. "If you don't mind, I got business to attend to."

"Thank you for coming, Mr. Benson. Have a good evening," Kris said, formally.

Once he was gone, she added, "Poor guy," and turned to Jack.

"Do you need to be talking to some of your Marines?"

"That looks to be where I'm headed next. I want to drop a squad or two down with the beach fisherman at o'dark-early tomorrow morning. We kill a few of their problems, and it's a visible start. I also need to talk to Captain Hayakawa. His company had just completed a six-week jungle-training rotation when they got assigned to you. Someone must have thought it was a jungle around you," Jack deadpanned.

He got his laugh from all present, except Kris.

"I think his best jungle troopers would be the ones to use to make first contact," Jack said. "Jacques, it would also be nice if you could come along with us."

"Yes," Amanda said, "he's the anthropologist, and I'm just an economist."

Kris could see heart's blood pouring all over the deck of her office. "I'm sorry, Amanda," Kris said.

"I can open a door between your quarters," Nelly said helpfully.

"No need to," Jacques jumped to say.

"Oh, yes, right," Nelly actually stuttered. Kris suspected her computer had just checked and found the door already there.

"Jack, you go handle your drop operations. Amanda, you and Jacques enjoy what time you have together. Jack, leave a message for when you need Jacques tomorrow but don't have his computer tell him until an hour before you need him."

"You think that will give him enough time to prepare?" Jack asked.

"I'm a field man, Colonel, I've always got a bag packed. And besides, there's not much to prepare for with these people. We either won't see them, or they'll hit us with poison darts, or they'll let us talk to them. It's a simple die roll."

All three left, leaving just Penny and Masao with Kris. "I

assume," Penny said, "that because Amanda didn't need a door opened by Nelly, there's already a door."

"Yes," Nelly admitted.

"That is another one of my leadership challenges," Kris said with a sigh. "I strongly suspect that contracts, scientists, and some Sailors have paired up their quarters and made doors," Kris admitted. "After I hunt for the *Hornet,* I'll have to do something about it. For now, it's every captain for him- or herself."

"Kris, Sampson is the one exception to the door thing," Nelly said. "She has most of her enlisted personnel living sixteen to a bay. Chiefs and officers are four to a room. Men and women to separate quarters. Only she and three officers have private quarters. Sampson maintains her ship at Condition Baker. It's the only one in the fleet."

"And a quarter of her crew want off," Penny said.

"Problems, problems, problems," Kris said, rubbing her eyes and failing to suppress a yawn. "I'm sure you two have better places to be." Kris stood. "Nelly, vanish the door from my night quarters to the main passageway. Tell Abby if she wants to see me, she either opens a door or takes the long walk through my day quarters."

"She's opening a door, but there's a lock, and it's only on her side," Nelly reported.

"Do you want me to go out on your cruise tomorrow?" Penny asked.

"No need. The information will be as plain as the ship's success or failure. You and Masao keep tracking the reports coming in from the discovery expeditions. They either find something, or we starve."

And maybe, if you two keep working close together, you'll find a way to make a door between your hearts.

"Oh, Penny, aren't you about due to make lieutenant commander?" Kris asked.

"I honestly don't know. I haven't been doing the career thing very well, touching all the bases, getting my ticket punched. You know."

"You've been following a Longknife around and staying alive," Kris said through another yawn. "Nelly, cut papers for my signature. Penny gets her extra stripe the first of next month."

"And then you'll outrank me," the Musashi Navy officer observed.

Oops. Maybe Kris hadn't accomplished quite what she intended. She needed some rest. Tomorrow would come way too soon.

28

Commodore Kris Longknife, ComFrigRon 4, rolled her high-gee egg out of her quarters and onto the bridge of her flagship, the *Princess Royal*. Captain Drago and a ship maintenance chief were already there, eggs parked against the bridge's aft bulkhead.

They were observers and would play no part in this exercise.

Unless or until something went wrong and Kris ordered them forward.

Captain Kitano of the *Princess Royal* sat in her high-gee egg in the middle of her bridge, surrounded by the watch. Kris noticed that someone had made all the combat stations disappear into the deck. A good idea, one she wished she'd thought of.

If you're in an egg, who needs a board you can't get your hands on?

With no flag bridge, Kris chose to roll her egg over next to the skipper's before she ordered, "Signal the squadron to sortie. The flag first followed by the others in order of their berth."

That order was passed to her command . . . and then the fun started.

The little *Intrepid* wasn't supposed to sortie next, but after waiting four minutes for the *Constellation* to get underway ahead of her, she requested permission and departed, taking second station behind the flag.

Six minutes later, the *Constitution* also requested permission to get underway, and took third slot.

The *Connie* didn't get away from the pier for another ten minutes and trailed well after the rest of the squadron.

Not a good start, Lieutenant Commander Sampson, Kris thought.

Kris set the fleet speed at one-gee acceleration and, at the last second, set ship interval at one thousand kilometers, echeloned left at two hundred kilometers.

She'd planned for a shorter, 250-kilometer interval but something told her if she didn't want dings on her ships, she'd better give them a lot of room.

The squadron spread out as it followed her toward Alwa's large moon. The plan was to swing around it and return to Canopus Station without doing any harm.

Ships deployed to her satisfaction, Kris gave her next order. "The fleet will go to two gees on my mark."

The *P Royal*'s comm reported the order received and acknowledged. Then Kris said, "Mark," and the egg gave her a kick in the seat of her pants.

Beside her, Captain Kitano grunted. "That wasn't in any of the manuals I read."

"I think they want you to know you've just jacked up your acceleration. I've been meaning to write a letter to Mitsubishi and ask them to make the kick a bit less. In my spare time."

"I'll add that letter to my to-do list, in my spare time," the skipper of Kris's flag said.

"Let's see what we can do with all those nifty toys the taxpayers gave us. Signal to squadron, discharge main forward battery on my mark. Target empty space."

Comm quickly reported the squadron ready, and Kris gave her mark.

All four ships immediately fired. For the little *Intrepid*, it was a four 18-inch volley reaching out one hundred thousand kilometers into space. For the big frigates it was supposed to be a six gun shoot. It was for the lead two. Six 20-inch lasers reached out to 150,000 kilometers.

Constellation only managed a three gun volley.

"Did I count that right?" Kris asked Nelly.

"It was only three lasers."

"Send to squadron. Fire at will. Single shots will be fine if that is what you have."

Ten seconds later, the *Intrepid* had reloaded and blasted away with a four shoot. Five seconds later, two of three heavies let loose with 20-inch lasers, in volleys six strong.

The *Intrepid* had gotten off a second four shots before the *Connie* got a single second shot off. The other two big frigates spoke again before that weak sister got off another single shot.

"Cease fire," Kris ordered. NELLY, WHAT EXACTLY WAS THE *CONSTELLATION*'S AVAILABILITY REPORT THIS MORNING?

THE SAME AS IT WAS FOR THE LAST WEEK, MA'AM. ALL GUNS READY. FULL SPEED AVAILABLE. NINETY-NINE PERCENT OF SYSTEMS ONLINE.

AND THE OTHER FRIGATES?

SAME AS TO GUNS AND SPEED. ALL SYSTEMS FLUCTUATED BETWEEN NINETY-SIX AND NINETY-EIGHT PERCENT.

Kris held on to her temper with her fingernails. A commander could not afford to lose her temper. "Send to squadron. Make fleet speed three-gee acceleration on my mark."

The communication cycle was quickly completed in the Navy way and Kris gave her mark.

Again, she got a solid kick in her rump.

"I was ready for it this time," the skipper of the *P Royal* said, then went about her business.

Kris watched on her own screen as her squadron accelerated smoothly to three gees.

Except for the *Connie*. She stalled out at 2.46 and held at that acceleration, slowly falling behind.

NELLY, WHAT'S THE PROBLEM WITH THE *CONNIE*?

MA'AM, ONE OF HER REACTORS HAS GONE OFF-LINE. THE OTHER TWO ARE REDLINING. IF HER CAPTAIN KEEPS PUSHING HER AT THIS ACCELERATION, SHE'S LIKELY TO BLOW HER UP.

Or have a mutiny on her hands. Kris scowled to herself.

"Signal from flag to *Constellation*, fall out of formation and reduce acceleration to two gees."

"Sent and acknowledged," the comm reported.

The trailing war wagon quit struggling and fell quickly behind.

"Flag to squadron," Kris said, "Prepare to initiate Combat Evasion Plan 1."

Kris gave the ships' bridge crews time to load Nelly's most gentle jinks program. This one was for the distant approach when the force was well out of range of their target. It had the ships moving right, left, up, down in a random pattern. If the enemy analyzed and assumed that was what they'd be facing the entire fight, that was just too bad for them. They'd be confused, and their targeting computers outfoxed when the final run in used Combat Evasion Plan 6.

"Execute," Kris ordered, and the ships began a dance that was not quite what she intended. Even the trailing *Connie* did something. Nelly projected on the battle board in Kris's egg just what the ships should have been doing.

What the ships were doing was not even close.

Around Kris, reports came in of material and ship fixtures failing to stay where they were supposed to as the ship went one way and equipment and gear went another. Kris politely ignored that and let Captain Kitano handle them as best she could.

When the fleet continued to fail to meet Kris's expectations, she took action.

"Nelly, project what I'm seeing on all the ship's main screens. Captains, the execution of this maneuver is sloppy. In a fight, we'd be picked off like tulips in a garden. Does anyone have an explanation?"

There was only silence on the net for half a minute as matters got no better.

"Your Highness, if I may put in my two cents' worth, this is Captain Drago of the *Wasp*. We've been in a fight or two and we've survived them because of the combat evasion plans like these developed by your Commodore's rather smart, or smart-alecky, computer."

KRIS, I'VE BEEN INSULTED.

SHUT UP, NELLY.

OKAY, BUT HE OWES ME AN APOLOGY.

What Captain Drago had gotten was a snicker on this bridge and likely from everyone in the fleet. "What we on the *Wasp* found was that Nelly was right. We needed to be elsewhere when lasers reach for us. It's nice to have armor. It's better not to get hit."

APOLOGY ACCEPTED, Nelly said to Kris.

"In order to meet Nelly's stiff requirements, we needed more maneuvering jets. That meant bigger rocket motors and wider pipes pushing steam to them. We did that on the old *Wasp*, and it helped us survive one hell of a fight. As soon as I took possession of the new *Wasp*, I had my ship maintainers redo the maneuvering jets to our specs, not the official ones.

"If the skipper of the *Princess Royal* would permit me, I and the chief here are prepared to reprogram your Smart Metal to meet our jitterbugging standards."

"Please do, Captain Drago," Captain Kitano said.

"We'll need five minutes, I think."

"Send to squadron from flag, cease Combat Evasion Plan 1, reduce acceleration to one gee," Kris ordered. All the ships settled down to normal. The *Connie*, trailing the fleet, took the opportunity to catch up.

During the same five minutes, Captain Kitano issued a slew of orders having her damage control teams fix what they could and other teams reprogram Smart Metal™ to shore up what had proven to be under specs.

KRIS, WE MAY HAVE MADE A MISTAKE, ORDERING THREE-GEE MANEUVERING WHILE AT CONDITION ABLE.

Oops, Kris thought. YOU MAY WELL BE RIGHT, NELLY. WE'LL KEEP THINGS SIMPLE UNTIL WE GET EVERYTHING STRAIGHTENED OUT. WHAT DO YOU THINK IS THE MAXIMUM WE CAN DO IN CONDITION ABLE?

Nelly thought on that for a nanosecond or three. TWO AND A HALF GEES AND COMBAT EVASION PLAN 3.

"Commodore, Captain, we've completed our changes to the maneuvering reaction jets. Feel free to do what you want at any time," had more than a hint of a smile from Captain Drago.

"Captain Kitano?"

"Ready to be your test subject, Your Highness."

"Send to squadron. Except for *Constellation*, which will

continue at two-gee acceleration, fleet speed will go to 2.5 gees. Flag prepare to implement Combat Evasion Plan 3 on my order."

Most of the fleet took off at 2.5 gees, and the *Connie* started falling behind again.

"Execute," Kris ordered.

The *Princess Royal* took off in a jig that would have taken their breath away, except the eggs insisted they keep breathing. She jumped up, then left, down, then left again, then right and up. She slammed them against their restraints as they suddenly reduced their acceleration to 1.5 gees, then sideslipped right and shot ahead at 2.5 gees again.

On the screen, the frigate followed exactly the plan that was laid out for her.

Kris let that go on for close to a minute, listening as more reports came in that the ship really wasn't ready for this kind of hard usage.

"Flag to *Princess Royal*. Cease evasion."

"Navigator, terminate evasion," Captain Kitano ordered.

The entire bridge crew breathed a sigh of relief. Kris suspected it was echoed throughout the ship.

"I've been doing these evasion maneuvers since I first climbed aboard a fast attack boat. It always takes one or two runs to nail down everything that can come loose."

"Everything will be nailed down the next time we go out, Commodore. That's a promise," Captain Kitano said with firm intent.

The fleet decelerated to make its swing around the moon. It spread out again as it did a two-gee cruise home. There was one more test Kris needed to make, maybe not for the entire squadron, but for at least one ship and its captain.

"Flag sends to squadron. On my mark, begin test firing aft batteries. There is no target. After first salvo, fire at will. Single shots will be allowed if salvos are not possible."

She took several deep breaths, then said, "Mark."

Three of her four ships immediately fired full salvos. Four for the big frigates, two for smaller *Intrepid*.

The *Constellation* fired a single shot from her four aft lasers.

Since the aft batteries were smaller than the forward ones,

five seconds later, the *Intrepid* got more shots from her aft battery of two 18-inchers. Both frigates followed with salvos five seconds later.

The *Connie* stayed silent.

A third salvo came from the *Intrepid* and another set from the two big ones again before Kris gave up on Sampson getting a second shot off from the *Constellation*.

"Cease fire," she ordered, voice hard.

"The fleet has ceased fire," the comm reported.

In silence, the fleet proceeded back to Canopus Station. Once the *P Royal* was settled on her course, Kris motored her egg for her quarters. As she passed Captain Kitano, she said, "A moment of your time, please."

The skipper of the *Princess Royal* followed Kris into her quarters and closed the door. Kris turned her egg to face her.

"Who had command of this squadron before me?"

"No one, Commodore. I think the king always intended for you to command it."

Kris mulled that over for a moment. Then she slowly asked a second question.

"Who was in charge of your shakedown and workup? Certainly you had a type commander."

Captain Kitano worried her lip for a second. If it were possible to fidget in an egg, she did. "We didn't, ma'am."

"No type commander?" Kris said, raising an eyebrow.

"No. It seemed the Navy couldn't decide who we belonged to. Battle Force said we had battleship guns and were theirs. Scout Force said our displacement fell in the range of their cruisers and destroyers, so we belonged to them. They were still arguing when the *Sakura* showed up. The king went aboard her, and suddenly we weren't shaking down anymore. We had orders to sail in a week."

"So, you had no type commander?" Kris said, trying to get a good feel for what her frigates had been through.

"Lieutenant Commander Sampson was quick to point out she was senior officer present, but the type commanders kept telling us they were appointing a squadron commander and never did. Also, none of us much cared for the tactics Sampson was pushing. Battle line with all of us following in the wake of her flagship.

"Commodore, I've fought under your command and I know you want every ship to maneuver on its own. We all studied up on your battles, all but Sampson, and we wanted to do it your way. We thought we were."

Here Kitano chuckled. "We thought we were doing pretty good until a couple of hours ago. That, and none of us much cared for the hard-assed Mickey Mouse Sampson was pushing. We kind of used the confusion to ignore her. She tried calling in her contacts with Battle Force, but that only got Scout Force coming at us harder."

Kris tried to place herself in Sampson's shoes. She'd been a lieutenant when Kris was a boot ensign. Her dad had died under a cloud that was never proven. Clearly, Sampson had something to prove . . . and was working way too hard to prove it.

Kris shook her head. "A bad situation," she said, then quickly appended, "Most of you did very well," when Kitano looked taken back.

"We did as best we could, ma'am."

Kris nodded, then remembered an extraneous question she couldn't ignore. "Did the king really get you underway in a week?"

"Even a Longknife couldn't do that, ma'am. Getting the civilian ships out of the builders yard and fit to sail took a month."

"And you continued to work up on your own?"

"Yes, ma'am."

Kris tried not to frown. Grampa Ray should have put someone in command when he knew they were headed for a potential fight. Had he been too busy, or was he so intent on dropping this hot potato of an honor in her lap? Kris had no answer for that.

"Thank you," Kris said, and they returned to the bridge.

There were no surprises there. Nelly did suggest that they lower the fleet speed to 1.75 gees. The *Connie*'s reactors were getting more into the red, but no request or report came from her skipper. Kris slowed the fleet.

If Nelly hadn't kept an eye on the *Connie*'s engineering state, the captain might have very well let her blow herself out of space before she admitted she had a problem. Kris could only imagine the language being used by the snipes as they went about their work, one eye on the dials as they edged more into the red.

Kris didn't issue another order until they approached Canopus Station.

"Send from flag to squadron. We will dock in order, flag to aft-most ship. There will be an immediate meeting of captains in the commodore's day quarters upon docking. XOs, chief engineers, chief scientists, skippers of Marine detachments and command senior chiefs report to the wardroom of the *Princess Royal* for a later briefing."

The *Princess Royal* caught the first tie-down and was towed into its pier on the spinning Canopus Station. Each of the next two frigates smartly performed the landing.

The *Connie* botched her approach and had to back out, wait for its dock to come around again, and make another pass at the initial tie-down. She missed the hook again and only docked on the third try.

Nelly reported all of this as Kris got out of her egg and pulled on her undress whites with hardly a thought to what she was doing. Nelly fed Kris reports on what the Marine detachments had or had not accomplished. She heard them and stored the information away for later use. However, her mind was already lost to a series of meetings she did not want to have. She'd been preparing herself for two of them since last night.

Now she had to add a third.

Abby made sure Kris's uniform passed inspection, then grinned, and added, "Good luck, baby duck. Ain't being a grown-up the pits?"

Kris found she had to chuckle at that. "If we told kids what waited for them at the end of high school and college, do you think we'd ever get them out of the house?"

"My house, yes. Your house, never," Abby said, reminding Kris that a lot of folks had it a whole lot worse than her.

"Kris," Nelly said, "all the captains have arrived. Oh, Mr. Benson just walked in. I need to extend the table."

"Do it, Nelly. Don't wait up for me, Abby," Kris said, and turned to do what Longknifes did best: what had to be done.

29

"**Atten-hut**," someone called, and the officers got to their feet. Even the retired admiral who supervised the station stood.

"As you were," Kris said. At least at this meeting she didn't have to fight for her seat. The four captains were down the sides of the table, Sampson as far from her on her right as possible. The station-master took the foot.

Captain Drago, whether because his ship was in the yard or because he was not Navy but contractor, sat against the wall next to the door.

Kris sat.

"That didn't go as well as I would have liked . . . or as bad as it could have." She gave Sampson a quick glance. She was sullen and not looking at her.

"You'll have the rest of today to mend and fix, make your ships ready for four-gee maneuvering, and we'll do it again day after tomorrow, 0900. I expect we *will* get away from the pier smartly this time. Captain Drago has his *Wasp* in the yard, but I'm sure he can spare you some specialists for improving the maneuvering jets on your ships."

Three captains looked Captain Drago's way. He gave a

resigned sigh and nodded that he'd help them. Again, Sampson stayed in her funk.

"I'm afraid that what you've just heard is the good news. I have a lot worse news for you and the fleet."

Quickly, she filled them in on the food status for the planet below them. Three sets of eyes widened as the full extent of the situation dawned on them. Sampson's eyes narrowed.

"So you see, we not only need to get ready to fight, but also attend to our logistics. The Marines have landed this morning to help fishermen kill predators that regularly steal their catch. I'm told that they killed two. Sadly, one led to a feeding frenzy and drove off all the fish at that beach. The other kill went smoother. The predator washed ashore and they've cut it up. We may be finding some interesting meat in Kiet's Thai stir-fries. The fishermen on that beach said it was the best catch in memory."

Kris shrugged. "You win some, and you lose some. Another team of Marines, two platoons of Imperial Marines with Colonel Montoya, are trying to tie in to a group of Alwans who have managed to survive in the deep woods. I understand from their latest report that they've killed two huge predators, something between a kangaroo and a saber-toothed tiger, and are planning on barbecuing it for themselves. The aroma might draw in some of the Alwans. So far, they're hiding. However, they are surviving on small game, roots, nuts, and berries. Once we get the local predators under control, we may be adding some of that to our larder."

Kris leaned forward. "Mr. Benson is working with his crew to create a lot of necessary gear from Smart Metal. Fishing boats, both harpoon rigged to take on the big 'eats every-things,' and trawlers to bring in fish for dinner and to fertilize the colonial fields. We need airplanes to help the scientists quickly finish their planetary resource survey and ships to move things like bird guano, rich in nitrates for ammunition, from where it is to the colonies."

"He needs Smart Metal?" Kitano said.

"Yes, and the frigates are the only source of it we have. The plan is to pull fifteen to twenty thousand tons from each ship as you give up your Hellburners. That will let us get started as

quickly as we can on logistic issues. I've got a meeting scheduled with the industrial and mining interests just as soon as I
talk to your subordinates in the wardroom. As the mines and
plants produce steel and other essentials that can take the
place of the Smart Metal, it comes back to your ships."

Kris drew a deep breath. "If our early-warning system
reports imminent attack, the Smart Metal comes back to your
ships immediately."

"If you have enough warning," Sampson tossed in, half
hand grenade, half sarcasm.

"We will have enough warning. We have buoys to cover six
or more jumps out from here. We will know what the bastards
are doing in our space."

"This is all stupid," Sampson snapped. "We're risking our
ships to feed ourselves because the people we came here to
save can't feed us, much less defend themselves. We shouldn't
be sending Smart Metal down where we may never get it back.
We should be packing up and getting out of here."

Kris leaned back in her chair and took the measure of her
three other captains. Sampson had not impressed them before.
She was not impressing them now.

"Thank you for your opinion, Lieutenant Commander
Sampson." Kris knew that was a double slap. She had not recognized her as the captain of a ship. She had not even given
her the honor normally afforded a lieutenant commander of
being addressed as commander.

Sampson's face reddened, but she said nothing.

"I knew the situation was bad when I took this command.
That it's worse than even the king realized when he appointed
me does not persuade me that it is hopeless. Other ships are
coming out to reinforce us. They will need to eat. Logistics, as
I have often been told, is what separates the professional warrior from the dilettante and amateur. The time may come
when running is our only choice. From where I sit right now,
that time is not now. We *will* stay and we *will* prepare to fight."

Now Kris did fix her eyes on Sampson. "Last night, I
ordered you to transfer a chief to Mr. Benson. He was, until
recently, the skipper of a fishing boat. We need him to command a fishing boat again, harpooning the big ones. You asked

for an explanation for me ordering his transfer last night. You have it now."

"Will I get a replacement for him?" Sampson shot back.

"No," Kris said bluntly. "Other Sailors will be drafted off the frigates to help with the food issue. There are no replacements. I know this will be a leadership challenge. I expect all of you to meet it.

"Any questions?" Kris said, with finality.

There were none.

"Then all of you except Lieutenant Commander Sampson are dismissed to join your staffs in the wardroom. I'll be with you as soon as possible. Feel free to discuss our food problem with them. If anyone has any ideas, I'm hungry for them."

That drew a chuckle as the officers filed out of the room.

Former Admiral Benson eyed Sampson, then glanced at Kris. His eyes held a "good luck" in them, but he said nothing.

SHOULD I SHORTEN THE TABLE, KRIS?

NO, NELLY. I LIKE HER JUST WHERE SHE IS.

The scion of wealth and power faced the scion of a family whose Navy blood went back to when ships sailed the seas, not space. They locked eyes. Kris began yet another battle for her command.

30

As soon as the door closed, Sampson filled the silence. "Yes, my ship has problems. All new ships do, and this is a new class and a new design that not even headquarters can figure out what to do with. Besides, my crew is sloven and needed additional training before we sailed. What happened today was not my fault."

"Wrong answer," Kris said. "General Trouble taught me from the start that when the question is raised about a command's failures, the only answer for the CO is 'Mine, sir.'"

Sampson's eyes fell to the table. "We can't all be legends."

Kris pulled the flimsies that Nelly had printed out and tossed them across the table to Sampson.

"Are these the availability reports from the USS *Constellation* for the last week?"

"I don't know. Maybe," came in full evasion.

"Is that your signature at the bottom of each of them?"

"It might be. I've got a cute ship's lieutenant who can sign my name better than I can."

Kris liked this woman less and less.

"In the exercise today, your ship was able to operate just forty percent of your main battery, and your reloads were few to nonexistent."

"I told you. My crew needs more training. They're the dregs of the brigs. You think the best would come out here, face a helpless fight with one of them damn Longknifes who never knows when to call it off but can run away herself just fine?"

Kris knew the tactic. Sampson couldn't face her on the facts, so she was changing the subject. Throwing all kinds of dirt and mud Kris's way.

Kris stayed on subject and bored in. "Your reactors spent most of the exercise redlined. One went off-line entirely. You were at risk of a major engineering casualty, one that threatened your entire ship, yet you did not inform me of your problems or ask to drop out of formation."

"There's no way you can know that," Sampson snapped, then switched gears in mid defense. "And whoever told you that is lying through their teeth. I have the reports that show my engineering was performing at 4.0."

"Lieutenant Commander, I was personally monitoring the *Connie*'s engineering performance. It was because of my own assessment of the risks you were taking to cover up your failed performance that I gave the *Connie* specific and separate acceleration orders from the rest of the squadron."

Kris had had enough of this.

"Lieutenant Commander, your squadron commander has lost confidence in you and your ability to perform your duties as captain of the USS *Constellation*. You are relieved of your command and will be reassigned to the shipyard. Clearly, Mr. Benson has more than enough work to keep all his personnel busy."

Sampson shot to her feet. She glowered down at Kris. "You can't relieve me of my command. The Navy gave me that ship, and only the Navy can take it away from me."

"The Navy also gave me command of this squadron," Kris snapped. "You stand relieved."

"You're no squadron commander. Just because your grandfather lets you hold down a desk doesn't make you anything."

"That great-grandfather is your king," Kris pointed out through clenched teeth.

"Who as soon as he got wind of the rumor that his old lady

was alive yelled for us to drop everything and parade across the galaxy so he could sniff at her skirts."

Kris was appalled. "That woman you're talking about is the former commander of BatCruRon 16 and the retired leader of this colony. Since when does the Navy leave anyone behind? You know they're alive, you get them. Even if you have to cross a galaxy," Kris said, thinking of her own debt to Phil Taussig and the *Hornet.*

The woman towering over Kris paused for a moment. Was she finally hearing her own words? If she did, it didn't seem to matter. She shook her head.

"You're not relieving me of command for any of that. You're relieving me because a lot of my crew came whining to you that I won't let them sleep around like the rest of the skippers do. I know. Officers, enlisted, they're all merging their single rooms and fornicating. I won't let that happen on my ship. I keep my crew in proper bunkrooms so we can keep our armor up. The rest of them may think they'll have time to armor up when the enemy shows up. I keep my ship combat ready at Condition Baker all the time. No love boat mine."

Kris refused to be led down that rabbit hole. Doggedly she went back to the facts. "I am relieving you strictly for your lack of performance today, Lieutenant Commander."

For a moment Sampson continued to scowl down at Kris. Then she spat. "You arrogant, self-serving bastard. You don't know what a Navy tradition is. How dare you lecture me on respect for them, you upstart! You're the one who's going to turn *my* Navy's ships into whorehouses and your officers into whores and pimps."

Here was a blatant challenge to Kris. To Kris, her entire command, and, very likely, the king whose orders she obeyed.

With slow, cold deliberation, Kris rose to her feet. For the first time in her life, she found her full six feet coming to good use. Now she stared down at Sampson.

Sampson looked up at Kris and seemed to shrink even before Kris said, "You will brace yourself, miss, and you will keep your mouth shut except to answer 'yes, ma'am' or 'no, ma'am.' Do you understand?"

Rage flamed in Sampson's eyes. She wanted to do anything

but follow Kris's orders. Still, Sampson had worn the uniform so long that she could not but come slowly to attention.

"If you say anything again like what you just did, I will forget my intentions of relieving you for loss of confidence. I will have you up on charges for actions unbecoming an officer and actions prejudicial to the service, if not worse. We will let a court-martial get to the bottom of exactly how reports with your signatures claiming full battle readiness left your ship, it being in a battle zone and on standby for battle at any time. I will see you cashiered from this Navy."

That was too much for Sampson. "You may think you can prance around in this little fiefdom of yours, Longknife, doing anything a spoiled rich brat may want. But no *real* Navy court of officers will find me guilty of anything but doing the best anyone could at an impossible job. I told everyone we needed three more months to get the *Connie* ready for space, but that king of yours gets word his old lady is here, and we're ordered to space in a week. I'll get my command back the second we get back in human space," she said, glaring at Kris.

"That was not a 'yes, ma'am' or a 'no, ma'am.' But I'll answer it. There *are* no ships headed back for human space. All of us had better start planning on being here for the next five, ten years. Assuming we don't lose the next battle with these bastards and just die.

"Maybe you weren't listening or failed to get the message. We are all *here* for the duration. And *here*, if you don't work, you don't eat. As of right this second, you are out of a job. You can apply your competency with ships and their gear—your fitness reports say you have some—or you can resign your commission and drop down to the planet and look for a job. Have you cut and gutted fish? Spread manure over fields? Those jobs have openings."

Kris let that sink in. It looked like Sampson might have actually heard some of it. "Now, get out of my sight."

The Navy officer did a perfect about-face, but halfway to the door, she stumbled and had to make a grab for a chair. With each step she took toward the door, she seemed to deflate like a balloon.

Once the door closed behind her, Kris settled down into

her chair. Her heart was pounding, and her mouth was dry. She felt like she'd spent an hour with puggle sticks in OCS.

Abby knocked on the door from Kris's night cabin, entered before Kris replied, and offered her a glass of water.

"I'd make it stronger, but we aren't on the *Wasp*."

"Water's just fine," Kris said. She drank it down and handed the glass back to her maid. She found herself rubbing at the tension in her scalp.

"Why was that meeting just about the hardest I've ever had?"

"'Cause you can't kill the SOB," Abby said. "Seeing them that deserves it dead at your feet kind of feels good. This civilization thing is overrated."

"And you are way too bloodthirsty for a maid."

"And you're alive because of it two or three times."

"All too true. You hear anything about someplace we might wrestle up some chow?"

"Sorry, baby ducks, but all my back channels are with the colonials, and they're at the end of their rope. I hear whispers that Ada was kind of worried that next year they might have to start doing that egg-examination thing."

"Ouch," said Kris. "I guess we got here just in time."

"Sounds like it."

Kris stood. "Two meetings down, two more to go. Check with Amanda and Penny. Tell them I'd like to have them at the meeting with the business folks. Penny can bring Masao if she wants."

"You're meeting with them is in forty-five minutes."

"So I better get this next one over fast," Kris said, and headed for the wardroom.

31

"Atten-hut," greeted Kris once more, and she did her best to say, "As you were," before too many people were out of their chairs. The wardroom had three long tables, pretty empty this time of day. Most present had congregated at the far end, near the coffee urn.

Kris went to stand beside the urn. Either she or the coffee should hold their attention.

"The first exercise always looks worst. We've had ours. Now we'll do better. You have the rest of today and tomorrow to mend and make ready for a repeat of this exercise Thursday."

She paused before adding, "We *will* do better," in a voice that left no room for doubt.

She searched around the room. Most were seated in groups of six around their captain. There was a group of five. "Lieutenant Sims, I believe you are the XO of the *Constellation*."

"Yes, ma'am," the young JO said, jumping to his feet.

"You are, effective immediately, acting captain."

Getting a ship is supposed to be an officer's dream. Lieutenant Sims's face showed no joy. He looked more like Kris had invited him to his own hanging.

She'd have to do something about that, and quick.

"Mr. Benson," Kris said.

"Yes, Your Highness," the old admiral replied.

"The *Constellation* will not be involved in any more squadron exercises for now. It is to go into the yard as soon as you finish up-gunning the *Wasp* and *Intrepid*. I expect that to be in ten days or so. Mr. Sims, you and the crew of the *Constellation* have ten days to mend and make ready so the yard has little to do when they get you but remove the Hellburners and remove more of your Smart Metal."

The man gulped. Now his face showed relief that he wouldn't be taking the *Connie* out anytime soon, but Kris had also dropped a heavy burden on him and his crew. She expected a lot of what was wrong to be right before the yard had to lend a hand.

"And, Mr. Sims, if I were in your shoes, I'd set Condition Able and give the crew some more comfortable and private quarters. We're a long way from home and we have those bastards breathing down our neck. Things are bad enough without hunting for morale problems."

"Yes, ma'am. Good idea." At last, he showed relief.

"Now, to our main problem. We came here to fight. We brought a base force, thank you very much, Mr. Benson, to keep us in fighting shape. We brought an industrial base to support us. We brought everything we thought we needed, but it doesn't seem to be enough." Kris paused. It was clear her listeners had already gotten The Word.

"They say an Army moves on its stomach, and, at least in that one way, Navies are the same. The folks below have been living on the edge of starvation for eighty years, and they don't have a reserve that can feed twenty thousand more mouths. We must feed ourselves."

"And the beer, ma'am?"

Kris didn't see where the question came from, but she had the answer and gave it to them. "Since we arrived, the colonials have not had a drop to drink. They've given us all they have. I wondered why I was drinking water on my honeymoon."

That got a laugh, but a dry one.

"This morning, Marines dropped down to look at several ways to increase the food available to us and the colonials.

Some worked. Others were less successful. A few big-toothed critters thought to develop a taste for Marine and will be served up as barbecue tonight."

More laughter.

"If the Marines get their sights on more of them, we may be serving a new kind of burger at the Canopus Burger Bin."

Some looked intrigued by the thought of a new taste. Others, not so much.

"As soon as I finish here, I've got a meeting scheduled with the industrial and mining types. We'll be going over their plans. Those plans will now include such logistical items as steel fishing boats, aircraft to speed up the survey of this planet, and trucks and ships to haul food from where we find it to where our stomachs are. They are in for a surprise."

That got a good laugh. The Navy had a thing about surprising proud business types.

"However, we need to get more food moving into our supply chain fast. The fastest way to do that is to use Smart Metal to knock together some things we need quickly. The only source for Smart Metal is the ships you're training to fight. We'll be off-loading anything that doesn't have to be on you. Marines, scientists, Hellburners. That will give us some Smart Metal."

Kris paused. The room had gotten real quiet.

"Also, we'll be off-loading more Smart Metal by thinning your armor. The plan is to return all the Smart Metal before we have to fight."

"How you gonna do that?" Again, Kris didn't see her questioner, but she clearly spoke for the whole room.

"We brought jump point and communication buoys. We have enough to cover every jump within twelve jumps of this planet. If a buoy goes silent, we go on alert. If two in a row go down, we drop everything and get ready to fight."

That didn't settle the question as well as it could. Some seemed sure the warning system would work. Others were doubters.

Kris recognized an argument she could not win and went on.

"We'll also be taking some of your personnel to crew fishing boats and a freighter or two, fly transports, and go hunting.

Some shore leaves may involve a lot fewer bars and a lot more digging for wild vegetables and fruits, maybe even hunting for meat."

"Well, if we've drunk the pubs dry, I might feel like shooting something," a wag offered, and got the laugh he deserved.

Kris let the room enjoy the humor and waited until it sobered.

"Good men and women died fighting that the people on this planet might live. Yes, we've got a hard fight ahead of us, but it's one we can win. Yes, getting ready for this fight just got harder and more complicated, but it's nothing we can't handle together. When we look back on this, we will have quite a tale to tell our grandkids. Every time they hear it, they will know that they come from heroès.

"Dismissed."

32

Kris found Amanda, Penny, and Masao waiting in the passageway outside her quarters.

"Have you heard anything from the wild-wood expedition?" Amanda asked. Her Jacques was with Jack and two platoons of Imperial Marines.

"My last report is that they found some real ugly critters, some kind of cross between a kangaroo and a saber-toothed tiger."

Amanda blanched.

"No casualties on our side. Several of the kanga-tigers have been invited to dinner. Jack hopes the aroma of a barbecue will draw out the locals."

"But no contact?" Amanda said.

"They haven't shot at us; nor have they talked to us," Kris said.

"The first inning is over, and the score is nothing to nothing," said Masao. "It looks to be a long ball game."

"And now we have our own ball game," Kris said. "If you will follow me."

Kris entered her day cabin. Her chair at the table was empty, as were the ones at either elbow. As soon as one of the six private reps saw that another seat was needed close to Kris, he gave up his chair.

Nelly lengthened the table and added a chair for him.

"I can never get used to that," one of those who hadn't had to move muttered softly.

"There's a lot to get used to on this side of the galaxy," Kris said.

"Like nothing to eat," said the young woman who'd done the best talking last evening.

"So you've heard?" Kris said.

"Why didn't you tell us about that last night?" one of the men demanded.

"Because Amanda, here," Kris said, indicating the lovely economist with a wave of her hand, "didn't have a chance to tell me about what she found until after you left. I figured I could dump more on you or see what you have done so far, then let you adjust as you see fit." Kris glanced around the table. "By the way, weren't there fifteen here last night?"

"Six are working on refining what we are presenting you. I'm afraid the others are trying to drink the bar dry. I'm not sure how that will help any. No doubt they will soon be cut off."

"I foresee career openings on fishing boats, as farmhands, and gathering wild roots, nuts, and berries," Kris said.

"They weren't bad men in human space. Your honest briefing last night was a shock to us all. I hope they'll recover. Okay, let's get started, I'm Pipra Strongarm, and yes, I can arm wrestle with the best of them. I thought I was number two in the Nuu Enterprises' management, but then you pulled out your CEO status, and my boss adjourned to the bar. There has been some reorganization since last night. Two corporations, their top managers trying to drink my top management under the table, have resulted in their two-sixths of the enterprise being taken over by Nuu Enterprises."

"How'd that happen?" Kris asked.

"With no leadership to notice, I kind of performed a gentle takeover. There are advantages, some think, to working for the company that the viceroy has control of. Also, in the mess we're in, having a damn Longknife calling the shots, at least Kris Longknife, makes it seem like a good idea."

Pipra paused. "However, there being no stock exchange or financial institution to fund anything, my hold on things is purely voluntary. If I were in your shoes, Your Highness, Viceroy of Alwa, I'd walk carefully."

"Hard to believe as it may be, Pipra, that's how I always like to walk," Kris said.

"It just hardly ever comes out that way," Penny said.

"Let's pause for a moment and go around the table. I don't think all of you have met my staff, and, other than Pipra, I don't know your names."

They did the round-the-table thing. Kris found that three large corporations were represented by two men and a woman. Nuu Enterprises had three present, one of which admitted to having been recently acquired from one of the now-defunct businesses.

Kris cut to the chase. "What can you do for us?"

"We like that large crater in the northern area of the moon. It's rich in iron and has water. If we land the fabrication plants there, we can produce iron and steel almost from day one. That's a basic commodity often ignored by developed economies, but it's a good one if you're starting from scratch."

"As we are," Kris said.

"On the approach here, we spotted lithium and other rare earths for electronics, superconductors, and just about everything a modern economy needs. They are not concentrated, so we'll likely have to send two or three different mining operations out to get them, and that means three different ships and reactors. That's a problem we'll be dropping in your lap."

"Sometimes I wish I had a bigger lap," Kris said. "I'm told that there is one reactor ready to be dropped down to the colonials and go online immediately. There are two that will need some refurbishing that we will ship to the moon just as fast as the work can be done. The Navy yard is booked solid. Do you have any resources you could devote to the reactor project?"

"Don't you just love it when management plays volleyball," one of the other managers drawled.

"I'll send out a call for help on that one," Pipra said. "About the refurbishing process, does everything have to be built from scratch, or can we cannibalize the fourth reactor to get the other ones going?"

"I promised the fourth to the colonials, but they may have to wait," Kris admitted.

"One of our batty ideas last night was to get cooperation from the natives. They seem to be taking a shine to our electric gadgets. Could we earn money by selling them windmills to charge them? Then use the money to hire them?"

"The windmills are a good idea," Kris said. "That would cut down on the demands being made on the colonial power supply. However, the Alwans don't have any concept of money. We'd get goodwill and some IOUs of a vague sort."

"But if we got them planting extra food to pay us . . . ?" Pipra left hanging.

"And as I understand," one of the other managers said, "our Marines are going to be taking out a lot of their big carnivores. That should leave them with wild woods that have been off-limits to them but that they can farm their own way. Maybe not as efficient as our way, but any food helps."

The conversation went long and was surprisingly fruitful. Kris decided that even business folks, when faced with a "make it work or starve" situation, could do a good job of making it work.

That left Kris and her abbreviated team making plans to drop down and see what a meeting with Ada might produce. The survey of the planet had turned up a copper mountain that would provide wiring, windings for electric engines, all kinds of nice stuff . . . if the locals didn't mind it being strip-mined.

Everywhere Kris turned there was more juggling.

Then, just as Penny, Masao, and Amanda were about to leave, Professor Joao Labao walked in. "Do you have a minute? I have some things you may find interesting."

"By a minute, do you mean an hour or a half hour?" Kris asked.

"Hour, maybe less."

"Staff, would you hang here for a few minutes? If he starts boring you, feel free to leave. If I fall asleep, you can definitely leave."

"What I have to tell you will definitely not put you to sleep."

33

"We have results back from our study of the alien mother ship. Oh, and I think I can move more of my scientists dirtside. I understand you need the Smart Metal from our rooms and pubs. I have asked and eighty-five to ninety percent of my team have volunteered to transfer their work to colonial territory. We will need energy to power our analytical machines, as well as housing and food. If that can be assured, I think we can convert the large barn where they hold their annual harvest festival into the Alwa/Colonial Research Center."

"That's gracious of you. Have you arranged any of this, or are you coming to me to see if I can make it happen?"

The professor smiled so aristocratically at Kris. "Of course, Your Highness, we will need for the viceroy to make it happen."

Why do I bother asking dumb questions? Kris scolded herself.

"I'll add that to my other topics for tomorrow's meeting with the colonials," Kris said with as much of a smile as she could manage.

NELLY, YOU *CAN* GET ME ON ADA'S SCHEDULE FOR TOMORROW, CAN'T YOU?

I'M CALLING. SHE'S IN A MEETING RIGHT NOW AND IS

IGNORING THE GENTLE REMINDER OF HER COMPUTER THAT SHE HAS A MESSAGE COMING IN. SHOULD I CHANGE THE SETTINGS ON HER COMPUTER TO BE MORE INSISTENT?

NO, NELLY. WE'RE THEIR GUESTS, NOT THEIR OVERLORDS. LET ME KNOW WHEN YOU GET A REPLY.

"So, Professor, I thought you said you had information about the aliens and their base ships."

"Yes, we have examined their agricultural facilities, food having become suddenly of great importance to us."

"And?"

"We have found where their dead go, I think. While much of the hydroponics gardens are part of their sewage and recycling system, there is a portion set apart. This also has that same pattern on its ceiling that we think is a star chart. While most of the ship is designed for humanity cheek to jaw, this area grows something like grain, as well as a vine that we analyzed and which produces a fruit easily converted to alcohol."

"Bread and wine," Amanda said softly. "This is my body. This is my blood."

"Yes, several of the researchers of the Catholic perspective had the same observation. We think that cremains are sprinkled in this garden, and the fruit of these plants are special to them."

"So the bastards may have a soul," Kris said.

"I would have put it a bit more gently," Penny said. "Still, it shows something that we have in common, some hope for an afterlife."

"Or rebirth," the professor said.

"Or they just want to remember their ancestors in some fashion but can't devote much room to it," Masao said.

Kris noted how each of the humans had interpreted the alien behavior within the confines of their own culture and expectations. She sighed. The aliens were alien. That was the whole idea. Oh, and they want to kill us, no matter how much they remember grampa or gramma.

"Anything on the technical side?" Kris asked. "What about the reactors that were removed or the lasers?"

"Based on the power lead outs, we know they were using superconducting cables and that the reactors were large enough to power a large city. The leads into the laser bays that were also removed were the type we'd use for a 15- or 16-inch laser. Not having one to examine, I don't know how focused the laser is, so I can only guess at range."

"From our experience, it seemed to be equal to our range and just as deadly," Penny said.

"I beg to differ," the professor said. "We have reviewed the video of the battle. It is not very good, but it leaves us wondering about just how powerful their lasers were. They used a lot of them. No question about that, but regarding their range and power, gun for gun, we are not willing to give them equal power with us."

The professor paused and gave that shrug Kris had come to expect so often from the professional scientist. "We cannot be sure based on the data available, but we think the question of who has the most powerful lasers is still very much on the table."

"I'll try to remember that next time I get in a shootout with one of them," Kris said.

"If you could avoid blowing it to gas and bring something home to look at, it might be nice," the scientist said.

"That's easier said than done," Kris pointed out.

There were other minor things the boffins were willing to estimate. The huge ship had a basic population of thirty to fifty billion people.

This stopped Kris in her tracks. She'd felt guilty, thinking she'd slaughtered ten to fifteen billion. This left her stunned.

Still, the professor went on. No, they had no idea how many might have survived Kris's Hellburners. Half to two-thirds of the ship's population might have died in either the actual explosions or the sudden opening of the ship to the void of space. It did not have a lot of internal, airtight bulkheads.

Clearly, these folks intended to be the ones doing unto others, not having someone *else* doing unto them.

The professor left, again reminding Kris that she needed to arrange for the landing of his boffins. Kris was left to wonder how fast a population that huge could adjust to the change humanity presented them with and what they might do to improve their prospects. Humanity had produced the Smart Metal™ frigates and put the 20-inch laser rifles into production.

What did the bastards have in reserve?

NELLY, HOW MUCH ROOM WOULD THIRTY BILLION PEOPLE TAKE UP?

DO YOU MEAN STANDING BACK-TO-BACK, KRIS?

No, ASSUME THEY GET A SQUARE YARD PER PERSON. BACK ON WARDHAVEN, THE PUBLIC LAND SURVEY IS STILL LAID OUT IN SQUARE-MILE BLOCKS. SIXTY-FOUR SQUARE MILES TO A TOWNSHIP. HOW MANY TOWNSHIPS ARE WE TALKING ABOUT. A CONTINENT'S WORTH?

THINK THREE MILLION PEOPLE TO A SQUARE MILE, KRIS. A ONE-HUNDRED-BY-ONE-HUNDRED-MILE SQUARE WOULD HOLD THIRTY BILLION.

SO IT'S ACTUALLY SPACIOUS IN THEIR MOON-SIZE BASE.

THAT WOULD BE HARD TO SAY.

Kris thought on that for a while, then remembered she needed help on her Hellburner question. She had to call another meeting with Pipra, a mining expert, and Admiral Benson. Penny and her lieutenant stayed, though Amanda excused herself. If there was a mountain of copper to be strip-mined, she needed to check on its location and the local attitudes.

If it was down south, the ostrich types might not mind. Of course, the ore would have to be shipped north for refinement and manufacturing. Nothing came easy.

"I was wondering when we'd talk about those Hellburners I'm collecting," the former admiral said as he quick-walked into Kris's office.

Kris brought everyone up to speed on the ideas of burying the Hellburners deep under the surface of three moons close to the aliens' line of approach from the jump to Alwa.

The mining boss, Berkant Fulan, a man with calluses on his hand and a quick eye for details, questioned the worth of Hellburners a million kilometers or so from the likely target.

"If we put them too close, they'll get lased in no time flat," Kris simply said.

"Well, I don't see any problems. If you'd let us use one of your frigates, we could drill some good holes with their 20-inch guns."

"But all we'd have to show for it is a fine dust," Kris pointed out.

"And the problem with that is?" Berkant asked.

"I want gravel, rocks, pebbles, and other junk to toss into their flight path."

"Woman, I bet you also want egg in your beer. Speaking of, I'd settle for just a beer about now."

"I'm telling you what I need for a fight for your and my life. You can have a beer after we finish this meeting."

"A big hole in three moons. Maybe with two or three ways out," the miner said, starting a list. "Lots of messy stuff left over. It's an unusual request, I must say, ma'am. You think the bastards might not trust any moon behind them. Maybe they'll laser the whole surface?"

"I expect they will, so we may need to redig the hole before we can launch the Hellburners."

"Which will tie up more of my equipment," the miner grumbled.

"Do you have diggers to do this job?" the former admiral asked.

"I got them. I may need some support stuff I don't have. A conveyer belt to get all those rocks this lovely lady wants."

"More use for Smart Metal," the admiral said.

"Lots and lots of uses," Kris said with a sigh.

That meeting adjourned, but the yard boss stayed behind.

"You're going to owe me one for taking Sampson off your hands," he said.

"Send me the bill," Kris said. "Just keep her too busy to cause me trouble."

"I doubt that's possible, but keeping her busy, that I can do."

"You might also try to get her to take a fitness-for-duty physical. I can't help but wonder if there's more going on in her than she's saying, and she said a lot."

"You want me to order her to get one?"

Kris sighed. "Ask."

"I'll ask. Absent an order, I doubt she'll listen."

"Yeah. This why you stayed?" Kris said. Feeling suddenly tired.

"No. Actually the reason was quite different. When we finally get those four large frigates spun out of the *Prosperity* and *Enterprise*, we're going to need to name them."

"I suppose someone has already decided something."

"Yes, Your Royal Highness, Viceroy of Alwa, but they are all to hell and gone on the other side of the galaxy. I figured you might have some opinions of your own."

"What are the names?" Kris said, now feeling all the exhaustion of the day.

The yard boss handed her a short list.

She read down it. "*Congress*. Well, they appointed me and we've already got a *Monarch*, seems like a good idea. *Royal*. I guess that balances *Congress*, *Constitution*, and *Constellation*. *Bulwark*. That seems to be our job here. *Ardent*? Who came up with that one?"

The admiral shrugged.

Kris reached for a stylus and scratched through the last name.

In its place she wrote *Hornet*.

She handed the list back to the former Navy man. "There are the names for your new heavy frigates."

He smiled. "Good fighting names. I'll see that they are commissioned as such, hopefully before you get back from hunting for the old *Hornet*."

Kris found herself finally alone. It had been an exhausting day. No doubt, a lot of people were cussing her name as they worked late cleaning up the mess they hadn't known they had until she showed them.

"Nelly, did you ever get me an appointment with Ada?"

"Yes. You were tied up in meetings, so I held off. Is eleven o'clock too early?"

"No, it will give me time to get down and back and maybe have some meetings here to file the teeth down on the alligators up here."

"Strange, Ada said something along the same line. 'No doubt your princess will leave me with a whole lot of work to do. Better I find out early in the day, so I can get some of it done.'"

Kris read reports until she couldn't keep her eyes open anymore, then shambled off to her night quarters and barely made it out of her uniform before she fell in bed already half-asleep.

Is this any way for a bride to behave? she asked herself. Her husband dirtside and she too exhausted to do anything if he weren't. Of course, if he were here, he'd have to be one deck down and in the next frame.

She fell asleep before she could contemplate any further the unfairness of it all.

34

Nelly woke Kris at 0545. "Kris, Jack's shuttle will dock in fifteen minutes. Do you want to be there to greet him?"

It was amazing just how fast Kris shot out of bed and pulled on yesterday's whites. She had one of those female premonitions that new whites would be wasted on her returning husband. She was at the docking bay just as Longboat 2 locked in.

Jack was first off.

At this early hour, there were few personnel around to witness their commodore and the colonel of the Marine Strike Force throw themselves at each other and lock into a kiss that showed just how much they'd missed each other.

They weren't alone, though. Amanda and Jacques were just as tightly intertwined.

And both of the men were as muddy and grimy as if they'd been on a four-week campaign. Kris's day-old whites would need special laundering, but who cared?

"Was it dangerous?" both women asked their men at the same time.

"No" and "Not a bit" were their answers. The lie might have held if four Marines hadn't exited the longboat at that moment with a pole stretched between them. Dangling from the pole was the newly named kanga-tiger.

"That's huge," Kris said.

"You shot that?" Amanda demanded of Jacques.

"Not me. Three or four Marines took it down."

"Not a bit dangerous," Kris said, elbowing Jack. Since he was in full battle rattle, the armor hurt her elbow more than it did anything to him.

"It's all in your perspective. You're a viceroy. You go to meetings, or so I hear. I'm a Marine. I get to play in the mud and kill really nasty things that need killing. A job's a job."

Kris kissed him again. "Want to trade?"

"No way would I let you go for a walk in those woods. It's not just the big things. They got little things that will take your hand off before you even know they're there. I can't tell you how much I admire the Alwans who've set up camp in those woods. Or how glad they are to find Marines willing to help them. They may have survived, but they've got no problems with seeing some of these 'eat'em-ups' get their comeuppance from a Marine fire team."

Another big thing with lots of teeth was carried out. It had six legs.

"How many of these 'eat'em all ups' are there?" Amanda asked.

"I'm sure we can find a biologist willing to categorize and name them all. For me, they're just targets . . . and chow. They make good eating," Jack said.

Kris adjourned to her cabin with Jack. They both needed a shower, so they saved water by sharing one. Abby was sent to get a set of greens and tans for Jack. He being her security chief, it seemed only appropriate that he accompany Kris back down to her meetings.

"I don't think there are any folks mad enough at me dirtside to start shooting," Kris said from a comfortable position under Jack.

"But I should keep an eye on you."

They were decent by the time Abby got back with Jack's uniform.

Kris had never slept on a shuttle flight. Jack had no trouble falling asleep as soon as he buckled in, and Kris rested her head on his shoulder. She found herself waking up as they docked.

What Kris was starting to think of as her new staff were with her: Amanda and Jacques, Penny and Masao, with Abby thrown in for reasons that were not clear, as usual. Somehow, Sergeant Bruce had ended up leading the Marine security detachment.

Kris accredited that to his having one of Nelly's kids. Officially, that had to be the reason. It couldn't be that he was just as interested in staying close to Abby as she was to Jack.

Ada greeted them at the landing with the jitney. This time, Kris rode shotgun next to Ada.

"Before we get started, do you have any problems I need to know about?" Kris asked. "With the best of intentions, I know we can get off on the wrong foot."

Beside Kris, the reason the shuttle had been so sluggish pulling away from the *Princess Royal* became clear. It must have had five hundred tons of extra Smart Metal™ wrapped around it. The metal was streaming from the shuttle down the pier in a thin cable to form a cube ashore. On the other side of the cube, a chief was spinning a truck out.

"So far, so good, Viceroy," Ada said after a bit of hesitation. There was a vague tone as if she was none too confident she'd be saying that for a whole lot longer.

"I did get a visit from a delegation of elders yesterday complaining about something involving renegades in the deep woods and us helping them. Since I'd never heard that any Alwàns survived in the deep woods, that was kind of a surprise. Did I miss a report from one of your survey teams about them?"

Kris glanced at Amanda, who got a look on her pretty face like she'd been caught with her hand in the cookie jar and a nod that the claim might just be true.

"I think that's possible," Kris admitted.

"Let me guess. Some more of your Marines. Now, I can't complain about those Marines helping our fisherman land a lot more of their catch. Hopefully, your people can pull off these large trucks to carry the catch and other junk inland though I don't know how he's going to get it powered. We don't have batteries that big, and I don't know when we'll get our new reactor online. They just started landing pieces of it late yesterday. Project manager won't give me any idea when he'll be done."

"Your reactor is in good shape. At least the first one. We're having to cannibalize the fourth one to get all three of them working."

"So what I get is what I got and this split fifty-fifty may not stay that way," Ada said with sour in her voice.

"Ada, there are a whole lot of unknowns in everything we're doing here. I've got a set of factories about to go operational on the moon in a few days. That may release more Smart Metal. I've got a chief designing a fishing boat that can go out and harpoon the 'eats everythings' and other boats to trawl for fish."

"Sounds like we're going to be eating a lot of fish."

"It's better than eating nothing," Kris said.

"Yes, it is."

"Fish offal also makes good fertilizer. You've said that you got the worse land on Alwa. Imagine what it will do if we add fertilizer from fish bones, guts, that kind of stuff?"

"That report did make it to my desk," Ada said. "Yes, it will help, but with next year's crop at the soonest."

"Any chance you might get a second crop in this year if you get plenty of fertilizer and water?" Amanda asked.

"Where's the water coming from?"

"We're working on that," Amanda said. "Once we have power, we can pump water from the deep woods. There's lots of water there."

"Pipes?"

"Steel from the moon," Kris said.

"You folks think big, don't you?"

"I wasn't thinking small when I took out that enemy base ship," Kris said.

Ada sighed. "Yes, you have a point there, and it's not one you let me forget, is it?"

"Do you want to?"

The jitney pulled into the round parking area in front of Government House. "There are times I wish all this was just a dream. That I could wake up and everything would be the same as it was before Granny Rita answered your call and we found out the kind of mess we're in and never knew. You know what I mean?"

"Do they still tell the story about the ostrich that kept its head in the sand?" Kris asked.

"Yes, to every first grader. I know, I know, but all this change coming at me like a tidal wave, you have to let me stop once in a while and catch my breath."

"Ada, I hear where you're coming from, but please realize. I had no idea what I was getting into when I talked King Ray into letting me see what this great big galaxy held. It's been one continuous surprise after another for the rest of us, too."

The woman sighed. "Let's go inside. If you think I'm having it bad, wait until you hear from Kuno."

"He's your ministry of Mining and Industry, right?"

"Yep, and you'll never guess where they just discovered a whole mountain of copper."

"I've heard about the mountain. Nobody mentioned where."

"How about at the headwaters of *our* main watershed for our year-round drinking water."

"That would explain why no one wanted to tell me where it is," Kris said, glancing at Amanda and Penny. Both of them were making a point of not looking at Kris.

"Nelly, why didn't you tell me?"

"The information about the water source is not in my database, Kris. I didn't know the significance of the location."

They had a long meeting after that, involving lots of people from the station by conference call. Yes, it was easier to dig a big hole in the ground and extract the ore, then run it through a smelter and truck the finished product to Haven, but, in the end, the miners had to settle for using Smart Metal™ to make nanos to do the extraction. It was slower, but a whole lot easier on the trees and its precious groundwater.

As for moving the scientists down to Haven, Ada and several ministers, including education, got very excited. When the full number of boffins, some 450 to 500, came up, there were a few gulps, but as Ada said, "If they don't mind eating a lot of fish, food won't be a problem." Housing would be more difficult, but they'd manage. The lumber mill hadn't been working at full capacity, and if the deep woods truly were becoming safer, there should be plenty of timber.

That would also give the Alwans more area to plant in their mixed-crops way.

Assuming the elders didn't find a reason to object.

The meeting went into lunch. Fish rolled in thin tortillas with something like lettuce were brought in. The meeting didn't end until well into the afternoon, leaving Kris just time enough to catch the last shuttle back and meet with her industrial team.

The factories on the *Prosperity* had finally been separated from what would become two frigates and a pair of mining ships. If there were no more surprises, they'd be landed tomorrow. Miners could also head out tomorrow to find the minerals needed to make batteries and other modern electronic gear . . . such as lasers.

When Jack kissed Kris good night in her day quarters, at the door to her night quarters, per regulations, Kris could claim to have had a very nice day.

35

Frigate Squadron 4 pulled away from the station right
smartly next morning at 0900 sharp. But it wasn't just the
officers and crews who had learned a thing or three. So had
their commodore.

"Flag to squadron, set Condition Charlie," Kris ordered.

"Right, of course," Captain Kitano was heard to mutter
under her breath.

Five minutes later, the squadron accelerated smartly to
three gees and held that speed for most of the trip out to Alwa's
closest gas giant. Along the way, an asteroid belt provided
them with ample opportunity to practice their gunnery and
reloading speed. Kris hated the long wait for the lasers to
recharge. She felt naked waiting fifteen seconds for the forward lasers to be ready again. Once, when the *Princess Royal*
had targets both fore and aft, it took twenty seconds to get the
lasers back online.

"Could we recharge three lasers forward and two aft in ten
seconds? Or fewer lasers in shorter time?" she asked.

Captain Kitano shook her head. "If we try to pour too
much juice too quickly to one capacitor, we'll fry the power
cables."

Kris nodded. NELLY, SEE WHAT YOU CAN FIND OUT ABOUT COOLING THE CABLES MORE.

KRIS, THEY'RE ALREADY SUPERCONDUCTORS. THERE'S A LIMIT.

THEN MAYBE WE NEED TO HAVE MORE CABLES.

I WILL RESEARCH WHAT CAN SPEED UP RELOAD TIMES, KRIS.

When they made orbit around the gas giant, the real fun began. Each frigate spun off a pinnace, powered by a single reactor, and stood by as the smaller ship went cloud dancing for reaction mass. Once, twice, then a third time, the pinnaces did their dance, each time bringing a supply of hydrogen, helium, and maybe other heavier slush, back to its frigate.

Kris could only smile as the pinnaces did easily what the old *Wasp* had nearly wrecked herself doing. Here was another reason to love the new Smart Metal™.

The frigates began to look like they had broken out in hives as they converted their armor to more and more storage tanks for the reaction mass. When the pinnaces returned with their last load, they kind of hitched onto their ship, leaving the whole squadron with a lumpy, bumpy look all over, and a very pregnant bulge where the pinnace settled in.

"I hope we don't need to fight," Captain Kitano said, but under her breath.

Kris chose to hear the question. "If we do have to fight, we'll vent most of this to space. If we don't, we get back to Canopus Station with needed reaction mass so the private ships can fuel up, and the ships that we send out to plant buoys can depart with a full load. There should even be some to spare in case we do need to fight."

"So this was a training and logistics run," the captain observed.

"We have to kill three birds with each stone if we're going to survive out here."

The trip home was slower, never more than 1.5 gees, but they still got in a good shoot as they passed the asteroids.

Captain Drago was waiting on the pier as the *Princess Royal* pulled in. He met Kris as she was just settling down to read more fun reports from dirtside and the potential moon base.

"The *Wasp* is out of the yard. Do you still want to chase after the *Hornet*'s ghost?"

Kris frowned. She wasn't sure whether it was the question or the reports. Or the fact she was starting to like reading reports. That would be a truly horrible fate.

"The *Hornet* is not a ghost until we bury her," Kris said. "We leave no one behind. I will not have a ship stumbling upon that wreck twenty years from now to find that they survived for one, two, three years hoping for someone to come for them."

"'Leave no one behind' is a good motto," Captain Drago said, "but you'll be leaving a lot behind you if you go. Can you afford the time to bury those who are most likely dead? We've already found the expanding gas clouds that were all that was left of the battleships."

Kris eyed the contract captain. "Why are you arguing with me?"

Captain Drago took a seat beside Kris's desk. "Commodore, there are good reasons to go and good reasons to stay. I want to know if we're doing this for the right reason. If we're going just because you feel you have to, or maybe it's a Longknife legend thing, I might have a problem. Since we're in private, I'm asking the question."

Kris shoved away the report she'd been reading. Captain Drago had followed her to hell . . . and gotten back only by the skin of his teeth. He'd earned the right to question her decision when all hell wasn't snapping at their heels.

"Captain, on the old *Wasp*, how many times did we come within a few kilos of reaction mass from being stranded in space?"

"More times than I care to be reminded," he agreed.

"I don't know what we'd have done if it had come to that. No one knew where we were. No one could have rescued us. Maybe I'm heading out on a wild-goose chase, but I owe it to Phil Taussig and his crew to chase them down. To do everything I can to help them if they are in need. We went one way. They went the other and led the bastards off our trail and after them. If that's not a good enough reason for you, Captain, I can't think of a better one. It's good enough for me, and I will be going. You want me to take another ship?"

"No, Commodore. The *Wasp* is at your disposal. We are resupplied and are taking on some of that fine reaction mass you just brought in. I plan to take aboard enough to make all the jumps we did, and a couple extra for good hunting, then return on one tank."

"It sounds like you plan a fast trip. Give me an hour or two to sort things out here, and I'll be back aboard the *Wasp*."

Captain Drago rose and saluted. "We await your pleasure, Your Highness."

Kris called her next meeting. Captain Kitano had only to step inside Kris's day cabin. Granny Rita and Pipra attended by conference call. Kris quickly told them of her intentions to leave Alwa for a couple of weeks to discover the fate of the *Hornet*.

Pipra began to object, but Granny Rita cut her off.

"A commander never leaves shipmates behind. I was wondering when you'd go after the *Hornet* as soon as I heard how you escaped."

Captain Kitano just nodded, leaving Pipra to shake her head, and mutter, "Navy," in exasperation.

"My problem," Kris said once that was settled, "is that I'm wearing three hats at the moment: military commander, viceroy, and CEO of half our industrial wherewithal."

"And you called us three why?" Granny asked with a sly smile.

"Captain Kitano, I want you to take over the defense mission. You will dispatch two ships to spread surveillance buoys at all jumps within six jumps of Alwa. That won't leave you a lot of ships here until the four new frigates complete their shakedown process, so concentrate on them. Do you have any questions?"

Captain Kitano seemed a bit stunned by the load that had just been dumped on her but said nothing.

"Granny, can I trust you to function as Ray's royal viceroy for a month without starting a war between me and Ada?"

"Kris, my child, you wrong me greatly," Granny said through a grin. "Yes, I've been following what you and Ada have been up to. I should be able to maintain your momentum. And if we have any problems, I'll call the captain here, or Ms. Strongarm."

"You're dumping the industrial mess on me!" Pipra said. She greeted Kris's nod with a serious scowl. "I've hardly gotten used to having to juggle Nuu Enterprises and the other two companies that joined us, and now I have to handle the other three as well!"

"Lead," Kris said, "not handle. If you run into trouble, call on Granny."

Kris and Pipra both got a look at Granny's big grin. It had a lot of teeth showing. "Or, on second thought," Kris added, "you can threaten to bring Granny into it."

"Yes, that should work," Pipra finished, almost under her breath.

"I am foully slandered," Granny said, grinning.

"Some of us have been dirtside long enough to pick up stories of the early days of your colony," Pipra said.

"Lies, all lies," Granny said, smiling as she lied through teeth.

"A reputation is a great thing," Kris said, herself grinning. "Don't waste it. Put it to use. You can never tell when you'll need it to scare some kids into going to bed on time."

"I've had a few Sailors bring me up to date on you, kid," Granny said.

"And doubtless they traded you some good sea stories. Now, if you'll excuse me, I have to transfer my flag back to the *Wasp* and see if I can talk my security chief into coming with me."

That brought another round of canards which Kris strove not to participate in. While she was letting that wash over her, she had Nelly ask Penny if she'd like to be included in this trip. She did and asked if she could bring along Masao. Kris agreed.

An hour later, Abby had Kris packed and a half dozen Sailors lugging several hand trucks full of gear from the *Princess Royal* to the *Wasp*.

A corporal and two privates brought along all of Jack's gear.

Next morning, they were away from the pier at 0730.

36

They had already left a buoy at the jump into the system where the battle took place. Now they headed for the desperate jump they'd taken out of the system. They passed close to the still-tumbling wreck of the alien mother ship.

A thorough scan showed no new changes in the wreck. Maybe they'd scared the bastards off. Kris could only hope.

They dropped off a buoy on the other side of the jump. The vacuum there still glowed from the wreckage of so many alien ships and the little bit that was the *Fearless*. They followed the same course and acceleration to the next jump. At this speed, they could not leave a buoy. It would have to be covered by another ship.

They made the same long jump they had last time. This system had seen no fight, so they sped on, picking up speed, but at a slower acceleration. The old *Wasp*'s engines had started to show wear from heavy use.

The next jump brought them to the system where the limping *Intrepid* had fought its last fight, struggling to buy time for the *Wasp* and *Hornet* to make their escape. Once again, the scientific measurements showed a much more crowded and warmer vacuum.

The *Intrepid* had died hard.

This time, the new *Wasp* headed for the closest conventional jump. The *Hornet* had taken that one, letting the old *Wasp* slip away through the new fuzzy jump before the aliens had a chance to take notice. They had to guess a bit. The *Hornet* probably also had to slow down its acceleration. Still, they put on forty revolutions a minute and crossed their fingers.

The jump took them close, Captain Drago's low whistle said way too close, to a gas giant.

"There's a lot of vaporized ship out there," the sensor team reported. "Can't tell how much at this point, but there was a fight here."

"Nelly, could Commander Taussig have done a loop around the gas giant and come back at the aliens following him?"

"I'll have to back the system up a few months. It's impossible to say where this jump was then. They do wander. However, it does look like he could have used several of the moons as well as the gas giant itself to help him break. It might have added some fuel to his tanks as he did it. It would have been a lot harder on the *Hornet* than any of the cloud dancing we did."

"But his ship didn't have all the containers the old *Wasp* had," Captain Drago pointed out. "It would be easier for him than for us."

"Is there any ship in this system?" Kris asked Senior Chief Beni, ret.

"I show no active reactors. No squawkers are talking to me."

Kris let that walk around in her gut for a second. She didn't like it, but it might be what she would have to take home with her. Two of her corvettes had fought the aliens, and both had died. If a fight had taken place here, the odds were that it had cost the *Hornet*'s crew all they had. Jack maneuvered his egg over to hers, once more at Weapons on the *Wasp*, and rested a supporting hand on her shoulder.

She gave his hand a squeeze.

"If I were stuck out here in this corner of the universe, I'd choke my squawker," Jack said. "Is there any way to interrogate a squawker that's been turned off?"

"Our Identification, Friend or Foe has three levels," Captain Drago said. "On, off, and passive. What were the codes we were using on the old *Wasp*?"

Senior Chief Beni needed a moment for his computer to call up the old code and send it. The interrogatory went out at the speed of light as they broke at two gees toward the gas giant. Minutes went by. Ten. Twenty. Thirty.

"Are there any planets in the Goldilocks' zone?" Kris asked, trying to fill time as the clock went longer and longer.

"There are three," the chief reported. "One a bit close to the star. The other's a bit far out. There's one about in the middle, but it's on the other side of the sun at the moment."

"So it might need a long time to reply to our message," Jack said.

"Yes," the chief answered. "Hours. A day."

The time passed slowly as the *Wasp* decelerated, aiming to graze past one moon, then another as she swung around the gas giant. Time for a reply from the closer planets came and went.

"I've got something," the chief didn't quite shout, waking Kris as she dozed in her egg.

"What?" Kris demanded.

"It sounds like the reply code," Chief Beni said. "It's weak and a bit garbled, but it's got four of the right alphas and numbers."

"Captain Drago, will you please set a course for the other side of this sun?"

"Happily, Your Highness. Very happily."

With a sigh of relief and hope, they set a long, slowing course for a responder that had hardly responded at all.

37

"That's the *Hornet*," Captain Drago said, as they closed on their target.

"What's left of her," Kris agreed. Half the engines were shot away. The hull had been holed clear through in three, maybe four places. The ship now tumbled in space, derelict.

The docking bays were empty. The longboats were gone.

"It appears to have been evacuated," Kris said. "Comm, broadcast on the longboat frequencies that we're here."

That brought no reply. Ahead of them, the planet turned. They continued broadcasting as Captain Drago brought them into a parking orbit a hundred kilometers from the hulk. The planet remained silent, refusing to give up its secret.

"Sensors," Kris ordered, "get with the boffins and map that planet. Somewhere down there are four longboats and a gig. They can't have disappeared. Find them."

What they found was a planet that looked like a pit of hell. Or maybe what Earth itself looked like when giant dinosaurs roamed it. The huge landmass that rolled below them was covered with dark swamps and marshes. Huge creatures chased the smaller ones, and rarely did they evade becoming dinner.

"How could humans survive down there?" was a question Kris heard far too often as the mapping progressed.

"Even if the humans haven't, monsters don't eat longboats. Find me the boats, guys. Find me those longboats."

The search continued.

It was near the end of their sixth orbit, over nine hours after they began, that the morning beneath them coughed up an island. A volcanic central core rose almost to the clouds, surrounded by sandy beaches and reefs. There, drawn up on the water's edge of a lagoon protected by the reef, were the four missing longboats and a smaller gig.

The longboats were as dead as beached whales, their antimatter pods exhausted. Unfortunately, a study of the island revealed it as dead as the boats. No smoke rose from fires. No sign of human habitation showed on the optical scans.

"They couldn't have come this far and . . ." Kris ran out of words.

Captain Drago turned to Jack. "Colonel, prepare a Marine landing party. You drop next orbit. I would recommend fully armored space suits."

"Yeah," Jack agreed. "Don't drink the water and don't breathe the air. If that planet's a killer, we won't bring it back."

An hour later, Kris gave Jack a kiss. "Find them, if you can," she whispered, "but don't you go dying on me."

"Trust me. I'm good at not doing that. I've had a lot of practice around you."

Kris would have slugged him, but he was in full armor, and even a squid had to learn sooner or later not to punch people with hides as tough as Marines.

"And thank you for not coming," Jack whispered back.

"I'm learning to be a boring senior officer," Kris grumbled. "Don't get too senior, or I'll be telling you not to go fun places, either. It would serve you right, you know."

That got a chuckle out of Jack, and Gunny at his elbow, even as the NCO tapped the watch at his wrist. Their time together was gone.

Kris drifted back, and Jack shoved off for Longboat 1. He didn't look back, and she didn't expect him to.

Kris glided back to the bridge. All good stuff was going on elsewhere. Why wait for it to be processed and passed along to her station? There was a limit to how much she'd let herself be senior officered out of the fun.

As she went, she couldn't help but think about her and Jack. She'd often wondered how a woman could kiss her man and wave him off to where he might die. Now she found the answer. She did it because she had to. Jack was Jack, and he had a job to do and it was a job worth doing.

Meanwhile, Kris was Kris, and she had a job to do, as well. "Nelly, get ready to spawn some nanos. That wreck ahead of us came with two good reactors and four 24-inch pulse lasers. It may be a hunk of junk, but it's my hunk of junk, and I will not ignore anything that might help me and mine stay alive."

38

Jack had often wondered how a man could kiss his wife good-bye and head off to where he might get his head blown off. Now he knew. You went because you had a job to do. A job that someone had to do. It didn't mean he loved Kris any less. In fact, he was kind of glad to go, knowing that she would be staying behind, out of harm's way.

There wasn't a lot of time for introspection. He did have a job to do. He had Sal project an overhead picture of his target. It showed a big, lush, green island. At a glance, it could pass for a paradise.

So, what was wrong with this picture?

For one thing, there was no sign of humans. No huts, no smoke, no cleared area. The *Hornet*'s crew had been here for four or five months. Why was there no human footprint?

The good news was that the picture showed no evidence of the monsters they'd spotted on the mainland. There were a few instances of something large and nasty driving fish to jump out of the water, but those were all outside the reef. It looked like the reef was keeping the monsters at a distance. Jack wondered what the fishing was like.

All the time they'd studied the island, no human had gone down to toss in a line.

Jack did a quick check of his fire teams. Every other trigger puller had a grenade launcher attached to their M-6. If there were monsters, they were ready. All of the four Marine teams had a medic attached. There were extra medical supplies secured in the back of the shuttle. Every one of his ten fire teams was prepared to fight or save . . . very likely both at the same time.

Longboat 1 made an easy landing in the lagoon, then motored slowly for the beaching area. Jack and Gunny studied the long, wide, sandy beach. The noise of their sonic boom should have brought Sailors down to greet them.

The beach showed something like a turtle making its way back to the sea but nothing human. "This is past strange," Gunny muttered.

"Okay, Marines," Jack said, turning to his teams. "There may be monsters, so be ready. But for God's sake, let's not be too itchy on the trigger finger. We don't want to kill any good guys."

"Ooh-rah," greeted his order.

"Don't beach the longboat," Jack ordered. "If it gets nasty, I want you to be able to back out fast and get out of here," he told the bosuns flying the shuttle. "Open the forward hatch when it shows a meter of water."

The longboat was fifteen meters from the beach, rocking in gentle swells, when the pilot applied reverse thrusters to take way off the boat.

Gunny popped the hatch and ordered the first fire team out. Was it a coincidence that they were some of the tallest Marines in the crew? They splashed out and quickly waded ashore, rifles ready.

The turtle thing fifty meters down the beach ignored them and continued on its slow path to water. Gunny ordered out the second team, then the third. Jack went with the fourth.

Ashore, his Marines formed a perimeter, guns aimed at the trees for the most part though four were covering the lagoon behind them. In his helmet, Jack heard the lapping waves, the buzzing of small creatures, and an occasional grunt, snort, croak, or call.

Animals all. Nothing human in the mix.

"Sensors, talk to me."

The tech sergeant carrying the sensor pod strode across the sand, but even in space armor, Jack could see him shaking his head. "I've got biologicals all over the place, some whose heart function even matches some of our own critters. Of human cardiology, I got the Marines here on the beach; but other than that, nothing."

"Well, keep an eye out and give a holler the first time you see something."

"I will, Skipper, but there's something in the soil or plants that's cutting my range down next to nothing. You'll likely see something before I get a heartbeat."

Jack did not like it when his technology funked out, but with forty-three Marines keeping careful watch, he could at least search with the Mark I eyeball. Jack ordered the last two of his ten fire teams to break out the medical supplies and food and form a chain to pass them to the beach. With that done, he waved the shuttle out to midlagoon.

Jack checked out the beached shuttles with Gunny and five of the medics. They were stripped of anything that might help a struggling camp and now occupied by something like land crabs. "I wonder if you can eat those things," Gunny muttered on net.

"I'll ask Phil Taussig when I see him," Jack said.

The longboats revealed nothing more. No arrow pointing inland, no cryptic note. The longboats were just as silent as the island.

"There may be a trail over here," Sergeant Bruce announced on net.

"Show me," Jack said, heading for the sergeant.

"It's not much of a trail," Bruce added. "I can't tell if there are footprints or just animal tracks."

What Jack saw was just as ambiguous as reported. He studied the beach; a high tide or two had washed the sand clear of prints. The shuttles were tied to trees. A close look at their hulls showed where they'd been tossed around on the beach, scraped against the sand, and knocked against trees. Clearly, this planet had weather, and just as clearly, that weather was doing its best to remove any marks men had made.

"Let's follow the trail. Gunny, you secure the beach with five fire teams. I'll move inland with the other five."

"Aye, aye, Skipper," was solidly neutral. If Gunny thought an officer ought to leave rooting around in the jungle to enlisted swine, he wasn't prepared to take a solid position. Jack reconsidered his order for a second. What lay ahead was way past unknown. Officers got the big bucks to lead into those dark places where monsters might lurk. He'd made the right call.

Jack sent one fire team ahead of him, then followed with the other four behind him.

The Marines, professionals that they were, spread out, letting five paces stretch out between them. Eyes and guns roamed the jungle ahead and above them. Alternate Marines concentrated to the right and left of the path.

They moved through a jungle that quickly became deadly quiet.

"Snake," a Marine called on net, and the teams halted, taking a knee. Even through the faceplate, Jack could see the grin on a Marine's face as she held up a headless, long, round something. "It tried to bite my boot. Hardly dented the shine, sir," she said. The bayonet on her rifle dripped green goo.

The sand gave way to marshy ground; the heavy Marines sank ankle deep into mud that slithered with things that made wakes in the water. A kind of sea grass waved in the wind around them, waist high. There were side tracks through the stuff, game trails that would let something with big teeth charge them without warning.

Jack was taking a serious dislike to this place.

"I found something," the point Marine called. He held up a tattered piece of cloth, with foam still attached to it. "It looks like part of a longboat seat, sir."

Jack shook off his willies, and said, "Let's keep going."

They came to a pond. Sergeant Bruce cut off a long, tough plant, the local equivalent of bamboo, and tossed it high. It came down and planted itself maybe a quarter of a meter deep in the "lake."

"This could have been a nice meadow before the last storm," Bruce said.

Jack ordered the Marines to slog through it. At least out here, they had a better field of fire at anything trying to take a bite out of them. They shot two snakes that didn't get the word.

SONIC BOOM. RIFLE FIRE, Sergeant Bruce said to Jack on Nelly Net. BUT NO REACTION FROM THE *HORNET*'S CREW. THIS IS EITHER CRAZY OR BAD, SKIPPER.

Jack said nothing.

On the other side, the trail wound uphill into the volcanic heart of the island, and the jungle grew thicker. Jack was about to order his Marines to hunt around for another trail leading off the pond when Sergeant Bruce pointed uphill. "Isn't that a ration pack?"

"I think you might be right," Jack said, and led the way up the trail to its first twist. There, held down by a rock, was the foil wrapper for an egg omelet that was uniformly detested by boonie rats.

"Sensors, talk to me."

"Nothing new to report, sir. I've got even worse reception around this rock pile."

"Well, stay close. Something human passed this way."

"Aye, aye, Skipper."

They started up the trail. There were broken limbs and branches on the trees and bushes, but it was impossible to tell if it had been done by man, animal, or wind. They came to a fork in the trail. One path led farther up, the other down the slope. Jack pointed down.

Again, the trail was full of switchbacks. Under the thick canopy, the ground was covered with a mosslike purple stuff that was slimy and slippery. Marines paired up to help each other over rocks and fallen tree trunks.

"Maybe we should head back," Sergeant Bruce suggested. "Why would anyone lug their gear over this kind of ground?"

Jack might have agreed, but on net, another Marine chimed in. "My old man is a guide in the mountains of Arkana. You'll do a lot of stuff for good, clean water. That stuff we walked through looked stagnant. It would make you sick. I suspect these rocks have a spring in them somewhere."

Jack took the input under consideration and found it good. "We'll keep following this trail."

Jack saw him before sensors reported a human outside the Marine line of march.

He was a naked scarecrow of a man, heavily bearded and

making slow, stumbling progress with the help of a crocked pole. He was on the switchback below them.

"Corpsman, forward on the double!"

It still took Jack a long minute to cover the ground to the wreck of a human being. In that minute, the man gave up the effort and collapsed into the mud. Jack saw why when he arrived. Diarrhea. Fecal matter dripped down his leg into the mud.

"Medic, to me! We got a man down."

"Coming, sir."

"I knew you'd come. I kept telling the crew, Kris Longknife won't leave us out here."

The living skeleton in Jack's arms didn't look anything like the ship captain Jack had known, but the voice said this was Phil Taussig.

"What happened?" Jack asked as one corpsman arrived, followed quickly by another. They had trouble finding a vein, but it didn't keep them from quickly getting a liter of water going into one arm and a liter of glucose into the other.

"This planet is killing us," Phil managed to get out. "The stuff we were eating tore up our guts. You had to be horribly hungry to eat it. But when you're starved, and there's nothing else, what can you do?"

"We're here, and we've got meds and food at the beach. Where's the camp?"

"Down the trail. At the pool. The only drinkable water we could find."

Thank God for a young Marine's dad.

It was another thirty minutes to the camp. If Phil was bad, others were worse. Kris had been right to come as soon as she could. In another few days, they would have started dying in droves. Three had died already.

A call to the *Wasp* brought more medics down on the next orbit. Most of the boffins who knew anything about planets were back on Alwa, but a pair of astrophysicists volunteered to do their best as analytical chemists. After they ran their first set of tests, they leaned back and shook their heads.

"Aluminum. That and arsenic and a couple of other heavy metals. Every plant is poison. Slow poison, but poison nonetheless."

Phil choked on his bitter laugh. "We knew we couldn't fight the big monsters on the mainland. We had to find some place they weren't. They weren't here." He cackled again. "Now I know why."

"You survived until we got here," Jack said. "That's all that matters. You'd have never survived on the mainland. That's for sure."

"Maybe I should have tried the other planets," Phil said, his voice now reduced to a whisper. "But the *Hornet* was so beat-up. We killed the last three of those bastards chasing us, but they hit us good right back."

"They're dead. You're alive. We'll have you back on your feet in no time," Jack promised, hoping the docs could come up with a magic potion to get all the heavy metals out of Phil's and his crew's system.

All his calls back to the *Wasp* that day were directed at getting more Marines and medical personnel flowing to the planet below. He didn't ask for Kris, and she never came on the line. Jack wondered what she was doing with her day but didn't bother her. He had his hands full.

Still, he had to wonder, what was so important to keep Kris from giving Phil an immediate call. He hoped she wasn't getting herself—and them—in trouble again.

39

Kris Longknife breathed a sigh when the word came back from Jack that he'd found Phil. But she kept her eyes on the reports flowing back from the wreck of the *Hornet*.

Phil had fought her until she was fit for space no more. Kris thought the old *Wasp* was a wreck when they got her back to human space, but the *Hornet* was little more than a lump of metal with a bit of oxygen and pressure here and there.

If the reports coming up from engineering were right, however, both of the *Hornet*'s reactors were in decent shape. Not something you'd want to power up and ride home, but still worth saving.

The same was true of the forward 24-inch pulse lasers. They hadn't been hit although the power lines to two were shot away somewhere amidships. Still, with some refurbishment, they would shoot again.

The computers had been destroyed with thermite charges.

The problem was, of course, how to get what could be salvaged back to Alwa.

Kris called Captain Drago in. He called in a half dozen of his ship maintainers. Together, under Kris's unbending pressure, they put their heads together and began to solve Kris's problem.

"You want us to swallow two huge chunks of that hulk, then kind of trash compact the rest of the wreckage, and swallow it into the *Wasp* as well!" This incredulous three-part harmony showed a certain lack of commitment to meeting Kris's objectives. However, being a Longknife, Kris didn't allow that to slow her down. Patiently, she explained again that she needed all that wreckage back in orbit above Alwa. That was her first guess as to how to do it. "Do you have a better idea?"

"Yeah, forget the whole thing," the chief engineer grumbled.

"Our princess rarely does that," Drago said. "Now, how do we move that wreck?"

Later that day, the *Wasp* pulled in closer to the *Hornet*. Then she began to very carefully apply her new 20-inch lasers to slicing certain portions of the hulk off the rest. First, the engines were cut away, then the reactors and the delicate instruments that made them work were sliced off. While the pinnace rounded up those stray parts before they wandered off, the *Wasp* turned her attention to the bow and its pulse lasers. Once they were free of the rest, the *Wasp* began dicing the hull into more digestible chunks.

"I don't mind having the pinnace kind of engulf the reactors and lasers," Captain Drago muttered to Kris. "It's the idea of using part of my beautiful ship as a trash compactor to squish the rest of the *Hornet* into a nice compact box that worries me."

"If the Smart Metal of the *Wasp* protests too much," Kris said, trying to sound perfectly reasonable as she laid a charge on her flag captain that had never been ordered before, "we'll call it quits. We can start with the rocket engines. They're big and hollow. They ought to collapse easily."

The young lieutenant on defense looked pale as he programmed his hull material to spread out, then squeeze together . . . with huge rocket motors in between. The moaning of the motors . . . or the hull . . . or both, rang through the *Wasp*.

However, both reports from the ship's skin and eyeball assessments from Sailors on the outside said that the process went surprisingly smooth. The pinnace, with the lasers and reactors kind of lashed to one side, used the other side to nudge wreckage toward the *Wasp*.

Together, they made it happen.

When they were done and the *Wasp*'s pinnace was merging back in, there were a lot of bumps and bulges on the *Wasp*, enough to move her captain almost to tears.

"Almost to tears doesn't count," Kris said, scolding him good-naturedly.

"But my beautiful ship!"

"Will be beautiful once more as soon as we get this junk back to Alwa."

Captain Drago didn't look all that convinced.

Longboats were coming back as Kris finished her house-keeping chores, so she drifted down to the docking bay. She thought by now that she'd seen it all. Still, the shock of the starved Sailors had her kicking herself for not launching her search sooner. She thought of all the time she'd wasted while this poor crew was having their guts torn apart by poison, and wished some people, like Grampa Ray and Admiral Crossen-shield, could see what she saw.

Politicians who called the tunes should have to physically face the price good men and women paid for their shenani-gans. Kris swore if she ever found herself in their place, a risk all Longknifes ran, that she'd remember these faces when she was calling the shots.

Then Jack arrived, drifting along with a stretcher. He waved Kris toward him, and she shoved herself away from the bulkhead and floated in his direction.

"Kris," Jack said, "Phil Taussig wants to thank you, personally."

Kris looked down on a man whose face she couldn't recog-nize. It wasn't just the bush of hair and beard or the gaunt, sunken eyes. There was nothing here of the ready smile or the confident commander that she'd known. Kris wondered if that man could ever reinhabit this broken body.

"Thank you, Kris. I knew you'd come for us. I knew you wouldn't desert us. Thank you," Phil gushed, with tears run-ning down his face. The water and glucose bags above his head had 3 written on them in grease pencil. She suspected that the poor man could cry only because they'd pumped six liters of liquid into him.

"I came as soon as I could," Kris told him, taking his hand. "Now, you rest. We'll be heading back to Alwa as soon as we can."

"Alwa?"

"Yes. The planet we saved. It also has a human colony on it that we didn't know about when we fought off the invaders. I found my great-grandma Rita Longknife." She'd explain the full family dysfunction later.

"We saved the planet. They didn't wipe it out." Now Phil really was crying, though these were tears of joy. "Crew." Phil managed to raise his voice. "We saved the planet."

Around the landing bay, people strapped to stretchers muttered as much joy as their broken bodies could express.

"Then it was all worth it," Phil whispered as he sank into a stupor.

"How bad?" Kris asked in a whisper to Jack.

"We won't know for a while. We think it's all heavy metal poisoning, but there may be other things as well. They're creating an isolation sick ward just off the landing bay. As soon as we get them all moved in, we'll douse down the bay and our suits to kill anything we can. You do realize you may be contaminated?"

"Why didn't somebody hand me a moon suit?" Kris wasn't the only person in the landing bay protected by nothing more than the cotton in their shipsuit.

"I guess the message didn't get across. Sorry about that."

"So we set up quarantine for us, too," Kris grumbled.

"We'll see how long it takes," Jack said. Inside his faceplate, he didn't look any happier about having Kris on one side of quarantine and him on the other.

Fortunately, the docs did blood cultures and took samples of the mud on the Marines' boots and found nothing that looked dangerous to humans. The heavy-metal contamination seemed to be the only problem.

Twelve hours later, Kris was out of quarantine. Which was a good thing, since half an hour later, an alien ship jumped into the system.

40

Kris and Jack had hardly had time to finish a quick shower when the Klaxon went off. "Battle stations, battle stations. All hands to battle stations."

They hastily dressed. Abby must have taken up mind reading, because a set of Jack's khakis was laid out beside Kris's blue shipsuit. Done, they shot from Kris's day cabin onto the bridge.

"What's the situation?" Kris asked in her commodore voice.

"An alien ship just jumped in using a jump we haven't used," Captain Drago reported. "It's about six hours out, assuming it holds to their usual two gees and flips at midpoint."

"Have they spotted us?"

"We are not squawking, but our reactors are online, and our lasers are charged."

"Then we can assume they know we're here and will be coming to visit," Kris concluded.

"We could try to run for the other jump," the captain offered.

"Has the navigator plotted a course?" One showed up on the main screen.

"If they hold to their usual two to 2.5-gee acceleration, and we go at 3.5, we should just make it to the jump before they get in range," the navigator reported.

"Can we make 3.5 gees in our present condition?" Kris asked.

"Condition?" Jack echoed.

"The *Wasp* is pregnant with the *Hornet*," Kris said.

"I was wondering where the *Hornet* went and why the *Wasp* has all these bumps and lumps," Jack said.

"You didn't think I'd abandon two perfectly good reactors, did you?"

Captain Drago cleared his throat. "We can't make over 2.5 gees in our present state. We'll need to drop our load to show them our heels in a run."

Kris mulled that. "Has any other ship jumped in?"

"None so far, but remember, we're only getting our information from that jump point at the speed of light, so it's been a while."

"Captain Drago, will you please join me in my quarters," Kris said, and wheeling herself in microgravity, pushed off the closest station and launched herself for the door to her day quarters. Captain Drago did not look happy, but he followed her, Jack right behind him.

"You don't intend to fight, do you?" the captain demanded, as soon as Jack closed the door behind them.

"There is only one ship."

"Maybe. That could change any second."

"We have the 20-inch lasers. We should outrange them."

"We suspect that. We don't know for sure," Captain Drago shot back.

"We'll need to find out the answer to that sooner or later. Why not now?"

"My ship is loaded down with a wreck and my sick bay full of barely alive survivors. Do you really want a fight just now?"

"We've never had a one-on-one fight with one, not since the first fight. Admittedly, this is probably one of those four- or five-hundred-thousand-tonners the aliens are so fond of. Still, it's even odds. I'd like to take this one alive, or at least separate it from its reactors enough that it isn't blown to gas."

Captain Drago didn't fire back a response to that but settled down at Kris's staff table. "Know your enemy, huh?"

Kris nodded. "Have we had a better chance? They think they're coming in on a badly damaged hulk. Likely, they intend to board it for intelligence. Maybe they even think they can capture the crew."

"They're looking for one ship," Jack said, settling into the chair across from the captain. "They only found one."

"Yes, but we've got our lasers charged and our reactors online," the captain pointed out.

"So maybe they won't be all surprised," Kris agreed, "but if our 20-inch lasers *can* outrange them, we could do damage to their lasers while *we* run away and keep the range where we want it."

"Assuming they can't do more than two gees," Drago said. "Remember, the 20-inchers are our surprise. What kind of surprise do they have up their sleeves?"

"We can always dump the *Hornet* and run faster," Kris said. She'd hate to do that, but if needs must, she would.

"I'm disliking this idea of yours, Your Highness, a bit less than most," Captain Drago said slowly. "But I have a few sneaky tricks we can add to your pot."

For the next half hour they laid their plans. For the next half hour, no reports came into Kris's quarters of a second ship. As it began to look like they might, indeed, have their first ever even fight, a grin slowly spread on the captain's face.

"Yes, we might just have the souvenir Professor Labao would just love to field-strip. Your Highness, would you care to take Weapons again, just for old times' sake?"

"Why, I don't mind if I do," Kris said, sounding less like her commodore self and more like her old self.

Together, they headed back to the bridge.

41

The alien did have a few new tricks up its sleeve. A bit before the halfway point, it flipped ship and began to decelerate. The navigator plotted the course. It showed the alien warship coming to a dead stop in space a good five hundred thousand kilometers short of orbiting the planet.

"You can't park a ship there," Jack observed.

"I doubt they intend to," Captain Drago said, rubbing his chin. "However, with less energy on their ship, they can choose how they'll close with us. I doubt they intend to give us a shot at their vulnerable stern."

"Yes," Kris said. "They'll come at us headfirst, with lasers blasting. Does this change anything for you, Captain?"

"Not at all. I don't think our plan requires them to be as dumb as usual."

The *Wasp* continued its predictable path in orbit. They did drop off probes to keep an eye on the alien when they were on the other side of the planet, and relays to keep them in the loop. At a million klicks out, the alien began to adjust its deceleration.

"She's aiming to arrive just as we're coming around the planet," Captain Drago reported. "That will cause a problem. No way do I want to let them have a whole half orbit to shoot at us."

The plan Kris and the captain had hatched depended on their ducking behind the planet right after they got their first shots off. Being stuck in an orbit that kept them in the alien's crosshairs for an hour was not healthy for them.

As they vanished behind the planet for the second-to-last orbit before the battle started, the *Wasp* flipped, applied a retro burn, and dove toward the planet. As they did, they went to a modified Condition Zed, collapsing all the space not needed for battle and sending the Smart Metal™ off to the ship's sides to be honeycombed with near-frozen reaction mass.

The *Wasp* was going to war.

"Now, we'll see how he likes that surprise," Captain Drago said, a tight grin on his lips.

Forty minutes later, they were looping out *toward* the alien ship. It was still braking. Suddenly, it went to a full 2.5 gees deceleration that appreciably slowed its approach.

"You don't like that, do you fellow?" Kris said as she used optics to range the alien. "You thought all the moves were yours. Didn't expect us to make one, did you?" A plot on the main screen showed their orbit beginning to fall back some two hundred thousand miles short of the present predicted point of meeting the alien.

"Now," Captain Drago muttered, leaning forward in his command chair, "how will you take to us eliminating our final orbit? Will you charge us or choose to trail us. Your move, bastard."

The alien began to cut back on his deceleration, gradually dropping from 2.5 gees down to 1.5.

"He's going to come up on our rear," Kris said. Normally that would be a smart fighting move. They'd have first shot at the *Wasp*'s vulnerable jets and reactors.

Assuming the *Wasp* kept her rear pointed that way.

The *Wasp* reached the apogee of its orbit and began to fall back toward the planet, picking up speed as she went. The alien was still decelerating, but closing the distance on the *Wasp* that, having once applied thrust, seemed just as dead in space as it had before.

Of course, the alien's sensors must have told him the *Wasp*'s lasers were charged and ready. But with the *Wasp*'s reactors at minimum power, the alien might assume their intended victim had one shot left and could not reload.

What were they guessing? Were they guessing any better than Kris? In a few more minutes, whoever survived the coming battle would know who had guessed right.

Whoever guessed wrong would be dead.

The alien was coming up on 150,000 klicks, and closing. The *Wasp* was falling back faster and faster toward the planet. If no power was applied, she'd graze the atmosphere of the planet, 150 klicks up. Would the aliens follow them or go higher, cutting down on the time they could keep the *Wasp* in their sights?

Then, suddenly, the alien flipped ship and presented its bow, bristling with lasers.

Surprise, surprise. Well, Kris had her own surprise ready.

"Flip ship," Kris ordered as the alien crossed to within 120,000 klicks. Theory said the 20-inch lasers could do damage at that range and the alien lasers would still be out of range of the *Wasp*.

Kris fired Laser 1. It reached out, hit, and the alien ship became a blur.

"What the heck?" Captain Drago growled.

"Rock, sir," Senior Chief Beni, ret., reported from Sensors. "Our lasers are hitting pumice. Volcanic rock. They've coated their bow with blocks of rock, sir, for armor."

"Sneaky little bastards learned a lesson," Kris said, as she fired Lasers 2 and 3 while beginning to recharge 1. The target shed more dust but seemed otherwise unaffected by the hits.

Kris switched to Lasers 4 and 5 and added the other two empty lasers to her recharge list.

More dust.

Laser 6 stirred more dust, then suddenly there was a flare, and something blew up.

"Maybe they needed more armor than they put on," Kris said. "Flip ship again." The *Wasp* turned its vulnerable stern to the alien. But the *Wasp*'s stern had four stingers. Now Kris fired all four of them at once, carefully aiming them for different sections of the bulbous alien bow filling her sights.

These sparked explosions as alien lasers and rockets blew up.

As soon as the lasers were exhausted, Kris put them in line to recharge.

"Flip ship, begin retrofire on my mark," Captain Drago ordered. The burn would be short and carefully calculated. Instead of blazing past the planet below, the *Wasp* would risk the heat of the upper atmosphere, shooting through it at 110 klicks altitude.

It was going to get hot.

Behind them, the alien had again flipped ship and slammed on 2.5 gees deceleration, aiming to make orbit right behind the *Wasp*, where her lasers could overwhelm and destroy the human ship. But the huge alien ship dared not follow the *Wasp*, now tiny and tight, its outer hull cooled by its own reaction mass.

The alien reduced its deceleration and fell behind, disappearing below the horizon.

Kris watched as the lasers slowly reloaded. Second after slow second ticked by. Laser 1 showed fully charged after thirteen seconds. The other forward lasers took a full fifteen. This was the price of putting six 20-inch lasers on the bow of a ship whose power plant was designed for four 18-inchers. As the forward battery finished charging, the aft battery began to suck up the electricity. It was twenty-two seconds before all ten of the *Wasp*'s lasers showed red again.

For the moment, it didn't matter. The *Wasp* was diving down, hastened by gravity, slowed by friction. Exactly what its speed would be coming out of this orbit change was anybody's guess.

Where the alien would be was also a guess. How close would it follow? If it risked following them too close, what would the atmosphere do to his damaged bow? Questions piled up, but with ionized atmosphere blanketing the few sensors that the *Wasp* risked using, there were no answers in sight.

They blazed their way across the night of the planet below. Did the monsters look up and wonder at what the strange lights were in the sky? Would they care?

The outer hull of the *Wasp* heated up. Defense thickened the bow, changing the depth of the honeycombed armor from one to two, then three meters. The firing ports of the lasers were covered over.

Isn't this new and fancier Smart Metal fantastic?

They vented cool reaction mass from the bow. It boiled away but protected the surface beneath.

The *Wasp* shot out into deeper space, and the hull began to cool. Quickly, they deployed their sensors, visuals, radar, and lasers.

There was the alien, right behind them. Its bow glowed red. Flaming chunks of it fell away. The alien captain had risked the low pass.

Kris could only wonder what price his crew paid for his desperate effort, but it was paying off for her. The alien was closing fast on a hundred thousand klicks.

"Prepare to flip ship," Captain Drago ordered, ready for the *Wasp* to charge the alien.

But Kris was busy using the four aft lasers while she still had them aimed at the target. Short, split-second bursts speared at the already flaming ship, first here, then there. Explosion followed on explosion.

NELLY, ANALYZE THE ENEMY BOW. IS THERE ANYPLACE NOT BURNING? ANY LASER POD NOT HIT.

Nelly took the controls and applied the last two short bursts from each laser. Then she got out an even shorter burst. The reactors had already started to recharge them, and Nelly got every little bit available.

"If there's anything alive and shooting in that hell, I can't make it out," Kris's computer reported, as the lasers went silent and the reloading began.

The alien was staggered by the hits. Its acceleration out from the low pass faltered, coming not in a steady curve but with stutters and spurts. It was hurt.

"Flip ship," Captain Drago ordered. Still at 3.5 gees acceleration, the *Wasp* turned to charge the alien. With any luck, it was blind, its sensors burned out.

Not quite, nor was the damage as complete as Kris had wished. First one, then several lasers reached out from the ruined bow to try to catch the *Wasp*. Most failed, their fire control unable to track the charging human ship, which now went into one of Nelly's jinking patterns.

There were still enough lasers left in the mangled bow to crisscross the space the *Wasp* must pass through. Two connected. The *Wasp* rang with hits.

But the *Wasp* was committed to a course that crossed above the alien, pinning it between the planet below and the *Wasp*'s forward batteries. As they flashed by, Kris swung the bow of the *Wasp* to bear. Four lasers reached out to slice through the stern of the alien, separating its rockets obliquely from the ship it had powered. The engineering spaces with the reactors slid off, diving planetward, while they drove the rest of the alien ship into a spin as they left.

Kris had other targets to roast and took them under fire with the last two forward lasers. Two reactors showed along the central core of the ship. Those powered the forward batteries of lasers. If allowed to go critical, they'd blow the forward section to atoms.

Nelly had gotten the locations of those two reactors from Senior Chief Beni's sensors. Now, as Kris sliced the aft reactors off, Nelly took a stab at disabling the amidships reactors.

It might work. It might not. Kris had explained to her computer beforehand that no one had ever succeeded in disabling a reactor. They had no idea where the controls were or what would vent the plasma directly to space without taking the rest of the ship with it.

Nelly had seemed to understand that this was not something she could approach with any hope of precision. Still, the computer had accepted the assignment. Now playing staccato notes on the two last lasers like musical instruments, she poked blasts of coherent light at the area around the reactors for fractions of a second.

First, she jabbed at where the forward reactors' controls might be. Next, she slid her stabs aft, sending a few through the heart of the plasma. That might open up vents to either side for the superhot demons to flee through. Nelly aimed her final thrusts at the possible control spaces aft of the reactor.

Flaming plasma spewed from the sides of the alien ship, sending it spinning. Even in their death throes, amidship lasers tried to light up the *Wasp*. The wild gyrations of their ship made it impossible to aim, however, and their power quickly bled away.

The alien ship corkscrewed away from the planet, leaving Kris to breathe a sigh of relief. It was headed for a high apogee. They'd have time to correct its wild flight before it went crashing into the planet below.

The stern, with the four reactors, however, did dive into the atmosphere, glowing hot with entry burns before burying itself in a muddy plain and turning it into a blistering inferno.

Maybe the monsters below should have kept a better eye on the monsters above.

"Flipping ship," Captain Drago ordered, then applied deceleration to cancel out their own dive into heated death.

"Your Highness, I hope you're happy," Captain Drago muttered, "because I sincerely never want to do that again."

"Now that we've caught it," Jack said, from his high-gee station beside Kris, "what do we do with it?"

"Didn't you ever have a puppy follow you home, Jack? Now we entice it to follow us."

"Remind me to quit asking dumb questions around you."

"I don't think that's my duty as either your commodore or your wife."

"I'll have my computer remind me instead," Jack said with a good Irish sigh.

42

Fighting the alien ship was one thing. Salvaging it for study was another thing entirely.

As the *Wasp* closed on it, Kris saw a wildly spinning and twisting wreck. "No human could survive in that," Nelly judged, and Captain Drago was willing to accept that judgment even before their visuals showed every hatch opened to space.

"Do you think there are any survivors in airtight compartments?" Jack asked, clearly getting ready to lead a boarding party.

"I doubt it," Kris said. "There weren't many airtight bulkheads on the mother ship we examined."

"So it's not just Victory or Death," Captain Drago said, "but everything goes fine or death. I know you want to take that thing home to granny and the good professor, but I'm not taking this ship within fifty klicks of that out-of-control hulk."

"Nelly, we need to stabilize that mess," Kris said, then glanced at the course that appeared on the main screen. The hulk was in a wildly elliptical orbit with a high apogee, but its plunge back to the planet would be a close graze on the first orbit followed by a spectacular crash the second. "And we need to do it fast."

"Like in this orbit," the captain muttered. "I've had my ship's feathers singed once today. I will not risk it again."

Kris noted the possessiveness Captain Drago was showing toward the *Wasp*. There would be no more pushing him where *his* ship was concerned.

"I'll need all the longboats," Nelly said. "No crew; we'll control them from here."

Fast as only a computer can do, Nelly and her brood had the launches away and reconfiguring in flight. All eight of the *Wasp*'s auxiliary antimatter power plants were also drafted into the mission, rerigged to power reaction motors and sent on their way.

"Kris, I really love this new Smart Metal. It's like magic."

"We all do, Nelly."

All this time they had been doing their best to map the spinning, tumbling wreck. The damage control teams on the *Wasp* helped Nelly spot the alien ship's primary hull strength members where they'd been revealed by Kris's laser slices. Nelly and family plotted courses for the auxiliary rocket motors and had them dart in as their targets spun into view. Only one motor missed and got batted out fast, narrowly missing the *Wasp* and just barely avoiding a dive into the planet.

"Damn," Nelly said.

"Doing it right eleven out of twelve times at bat would put you in the record books for baseball," Jack pointed out.

"Yes, for a *human*," Nelly agreed.

Kris and Jack just shook their heads.

They were approaching apogee when the eleven rocket motors fired. First they took the spin off. Then, with the problem more manageable, they adjusted the rockets to suppress the tumbling. Faster than Kris would have expected, Nelly had the alien wreck lying docile in space.

And beginning its dive back to the planet's flaming embrace.

"There are twelve main hull longitudinal strength members poking out the aft end," Nelly reported. "Kris cut them off a bit ragged, but that may help us make a solid connection."

Kris was glad her computer found her work acceptable. Jack just grinned.

As the *Wasp* extended twelve girders of Smart Metal™ out

to connect with the target, Captain Drago brought the *Wasp* close alongside the battered stern of the alien. Soon, it loomed over them. He halted his approach five klicks out.

"I'm not going any closer until someone assures me that hulk is dead and no one has hung around to blow me up."

"There's not enough time for my Marines to get over there if you also want to get this mess nudged into a high orbit."

"Then have your marvelous Nelly send her minions over there for a quick look-see."

"Nanos on their way," Nelly replied as a swarm of them departed from the tips of the docking girders. "I'll replace them before you need to dock," she assured the humans.

For a long fifteen minutes, the nanos scoured the aft-most compartments of the hulk. All showed signs of explosive decompression as the departure of the engineering section opened the stern to space. There was no evidence of explosives or booby traps left behind.

There were lots of bodies. A horrible lot of them.

Even Jack gulped as the picture became clear. "I think we'll leave the examination of the hulk to nanos. I'm not sure I could get my Marines through that."

Kris agreed.

Captain Drago brought his *Wasp* in to mate with the alien wreck a good half hour before they were due to graze the atmosphere. By applying power in a slow, gently rising fashion, they secured the mating and got themselves edged into an orbit that never came closer than 150 klicks to the grasping planet below.

"That is one huge hood ornament," Captain Drago said finally with a major sigh. "I hope Your Highness wasn't expecting us to make more than one gee on our way back to Alwa."

"One gee was more than I dared hope for," Kris admitted.

They strengthened the docking with the hulk as they swung around the planet and headed back out to a second apogee. The *Wasp* began applying power to the jury-rigged docking collar as they approached their highest point and had them drawing free of the distant planet before they began another dive.

Around them, the hull of the *Wasp* groaned and moaned,

but nothing broke loose. "Quarters are going to be a bit tight. I'm going to keep the *Wasp* at something between Condition Baker and Charlie," Captain Drago announced to all hands, "but we're headed home."

In the privacy of her day quarters Kris wondered aloud to Jack, "You think Captain Drago would appreciate it if you moved in with me? Think of the space we'd save."

Jack gave her a good-night kiss and sent her on her way to her lonely night cabin.

But the question would soon come up again.

43

TWO days later, they were accelerating at one gee on approach to their jump out. There was no question of hitting it with the speed they'd come in with, nor was anyone willing to put twenty revolutions per minute on the jury-rigged wreck hanging on the *Wasp*'s nose.

The way home would be a different set of jumps from the way here.

Kris wasn't expecting Captain Drago when he came in and plopped down on her couch.

"Something on your mind?" Kris asked.

"Jack's been spending a lot of time here."

"Yes," Kris was quick to point out, "in my day quarters. He has his own night cabin a deck down and halfway around the ship."

"Yes, I know. You two have been scrupulous to give the ship's company a good example." The conversation hung there for a long time. Kris joined the captain, taking an overstuffed chair beside his couch. Jack took the chair opposite her.

"What's on your mind, Captain?" Kris finally said. She knew how to wait out a reluctant petitioner, but being Commodore was teaching her the bad habit of not wasting time.

"Cookie's moved in with Mother MacCreedy," Captain Drago finally spat out.

"Those two must be approaching eighty," Kris said.

The captain scowled. "Trust me, young lady, when you are old and gray, you will find the comfort of human companionship no less desirable."

"That wasn't what I meant," Kris said, then realized it was what she meant. "Well, they're both contractors, consenting adults, and old enough to know better. I don't see how it's a Navy problem."

So the captain told her. "In the last two days, with quarters shrunk, a lot of folks have chosen to merge their living space, and no doubt other things as well. I suspect the vast majority of my contractors and your boffins have set up abbreviated housekeeping."

"Still not my problem," Kris pointed out.

"You know that cute astrophysicist that made the diagnosis of heavy-metal poisoning? Well, at breakfast she suggested to the skipper of the Musashi Marine detachment that he move in with her."

"Now that's my problem," Jack said.

"It's not your only one," the captain said. "Abby and Sergeant Bruce are a couple."

"What about Cara?" Kris asked. She would have considered a teenager as good a chaperone as any seventy-year-old.

"Cara is spending most of her time with your younger women Marines," Captain Drago said. "They've even fitted her for a uniform of sorts and have found her a battle station with their central aid station. She's almost fourteen and getting quite handy."

"And leaving my maid free time on her hands to get in trouble."

"I think we can count on Abby to take care of herself," Jack put in.

"How far has this, ah, adjustment of quarters gone?" Kris asked.

"I really don't know," the captain said, raising his eyes to the overhead. Which meant he had a pretty good idea but officially was working hard not to notice.

"Ah," Nelly said. "I can get you an answer, ah, if you want it."

"Nelly, you're getting quite tactful," Kris said. "Captain, do we want it?"

"Before we decide that," Jack said, "can we first examine the situation we're in?"

"Such as?" Kris said.

"We've come close to being killed twice in the last month. Only one fight was at close to even odds. We're all the way across the galaxy from most of our next of kin. Or any kin at all. I'd also like to point out we don't have any shore establishment to speak of. It's not like we can reassign one-half of a couple, wed or otherwise, dirtside. And if we start shuffling crews because folks are seeking creature comforts, we'll be breaking up trained teams on the eve of battle, and we are *always* on the eve of some battle. Kris, Captain, this is one major problem, and it's not going to fit into any of the usual answers."

"And we do know that the other ships of the squadron were having issues with people using that app to open doors between quarters," Kris said, "and we chose to look the other way."

"I wonder what we'll be going back to," the captain said with a frown that had way too much grin in it.

"So, what I'm hearing is that we need a solution for the moment, here on the *Wasp*, but we better be ready to apply it throughout the squadron when we get back."

"And, we hope," Jack pointed out, "that the squadron will be reinforced."

"Jack, I love you, but I'm hating you at the moment," Kris replied.

"You're the commodore, viceroy, and CEO, dearest love."

Kris would have stuck her tongue out at Jack, but they weren't alone. She chose to let him have the last word and turned to Captain Drago.

"So you brought this monkey in. Are you just dumping it on my back, or do you have some idea for getting it off all of our backs?"

"I have discussed it with the *Wasp*'s senior chiefs, but I

didn't want you hearing it the first time when you go to dinner."

"Thank you for caring about my digestion," Kris said dryly.

"I intend to let my division heads and leading chiefs know that I'm willing to loosen the rules on Navy personnel since it's already come loose for all the contractors. We couldn't limit the Forward Lounge to just civilians, could we?"

"Good analogy," Jack said.

"I'll tell them this is just a *Wasp* practice and we'll see how things go when we get back to the squadron."

"Where this will land in my lap," Kris said.

"Yep."

"Tell me, Captain, is there a girl you have your eye on?" Kris asked.

"No," Captain Drago shot back bluntly. "I don't think there's anyone willing or able to break the splendid solitude of my command." He paused. "Though I might have trouble saying no to a few of the more mature women aboard. Let us pray that I am not led into temptation."

"One question," Kris said as the captain stood to go. "I'm assuming that your female contractor personnel have been issued the same birth-control implants that are required by the Navy for all females signing up." Kris had been issued her first set right after she was sworn in. Three years in, she'd been issued a second set. What with Jack around, she'd better make sure she got her new implants in a couple of months, when she passed her sixth year in the Navy.

"You don't think Admiral Crossenshield would forget a thing like that, do you? Strange, if I do say so after some thirty years of service, how we insist that our men and women not use certain gear God issued them, but we make real sure that nothing can come of it if they do."

"The right way, the wrong way, and the Navy way," Kris said for the millionth or more time since she'd raised her right hand and been sworn in.

With that, the captain left, leaving Kris and Jack alone.

"You know, this is going to cause trouble," Kris said.

"Men and women, being men and women, have caused trouble since time began," Jack pointed out.

"We'll have spats and breakups and love triangles," Kris said.

"Just like they do in the civilian world. Ever watched the movies?"

"I found those topics deadly dull."

"Somehow, I don't think there will be any dull in our future. Still, if things get too messed up for anyone, we can ship them off to another frigate, and we do have the station to keep staffed."

"The worst offenders can find themselves protecting the fisherfolk," Kris muttered.

"That's my girl, solving every problem before we come to it."

Which left Kris staring at Jack as he stared at her. The question hung in the air between them, thick enough to stab with a knife.

At the same moment, both shook their head. Maybe Nelly could have spotted who started shaking first, but Kris really didn't want to know who first came to the obvious conclusion and who took a split second longer.

"I'll keep my separate quarters," Jack said, "and I will sleep there."

"I think that's a good idea. At least until, and if, this question is dumped in my lap for the whole squadron."

For a moment longer, they stared at each other, tasting their decision and finding it good. Then Kris let herself slip on an impish grin. "But we can save water if we shower together."

"That sounds like a great idea," Jack said. "And I could use a shower about now."

As soon as he had shucked his uniform, it was clear he needed a shower. A cold one.

Kris was only too happy to provide an alternate solution to his problem.

44

The trip back held few other surprises. The *Wasp* and the wreck held together. Nelly found a route that almost landed them in Alwa. They dropped into a system with a working jump buoy just as Captain Drago called time to refuel. While they used the jump buoy to message Alwa that they would be home in a just a few days, they settled into orbit around a gas giant, and the *Wasp*'s pinnace did two refueling runs.

That made it possible for Captain Drago to accelerate at one gee until halfway to the jumps, then decelerate the rest of the way. They went through dead slow and on an even keel. Three days later, they nudged their way into Alwa system to find the *Princess Royal* and the *Constellation* waiting for them.

"Good Lord, *Wasp*," Captain Kitano said on screen. "What happened to you?"

"Look what followed me home," Kris said proudly.

"More like what you pushed home," Kitano replied.

"It does kind of look that way. Nelly, send to the professor. 'Have I got an alien artifact for you to study!'"

"It doesn't look in very good shape," Kitano said.

"Again, no survivors, but this time I sliced the reactors off so they couldn't blow themselves to dust. No one has been aboard the wreck, but our nanos report it's crammed with bodies. They popped the hatches at the last second and spaced themselves."

Kitano just shook her head. Then she seemed to change her thoughts. "Commodore, I hate to say it, but I'm very glad to see you back. Is it safe for me to come aboard the *Wasp*, or would you prefer to come to the *P Royal*?"

"The *Wasp* is quite safe. We've proved it through more jumps than I care to count. Come aboard, Captain. I would like a full report on what's happened. By the way, we saved the *Hornet*'s crew. All but three. We arrived in the nick of time."

"I'm glad to hear that, ma'am. I'll be with you in fifteen minutes."

"I'll have Captain Drago delay starting our acceleration until you're here."

Ten minutes later, as the *Princess Royal*'s gig docked solidly with the *Wasp*, Captain Drago put on one gee of acceleration, and the deck was once again down. A few minutes later, Captain Kitano joined Kris in her day quarters. Jack and Captain Drago came in a second later.

"What's our situation?" Kris asked, as the four of them settled onto the couch and stuffed chairs.

"We deployed the buoys, as you no doubt noticed. We've lost one, six jumps out from the one the aliens would have used if they made it past your fleet, Commodore."

"So they're out there and nibbling, but they're keeping their distance."

"It seems that way."

"And our defensive efforts?"

"We've dug bases a thousand meters down on all three moons. One is mainly ice, but we found something solid. We've got two launch tunnels dug on all three and are working on a third one for each. The Hellburners have gone live on all those satellites. The crews are mainly the Ostriches with a few Roosters, colonial and Navy thrown in. The second division of the squadron is online and has shaken down very well."

"Well done," Kris said.

"I'll leave the situation dirtside to Granny Rita, and the industrial situation to Pipra, but I think you'll find them all satisfactory or better. It's my handling of the Navy personnel that may be a problem, ma'am."

"That app that opens doors between quarters?" Kris said, to save the young woman from beating around the bush.

"Yes, ma'am. I thought that when we off-loaded most of the boffins, our problem would go with them, but no. Many that went dirtside to work on the food supply came back with attachments. Some local, but lots of Navy. Once some officers relaxed discipline, others followed. I tried jacking up the security on the Smart Metal and having only the chiefs be able to move metal. But we want people to do damage control, and the chiefs don't want to be answering calls for every little thing." Katano shrugged.

"Beside, some smart Sailor cracked the new code. If I keep increasing it, ma'am, I run the risk of getting close to the hull algorithm, and I don't want that. I've got morale problems with the Sailors, chiefs, and officers. We're trying to follow the regs, ma'am, but it's not working. Now, I don't know what to do. It's not like I can order half the couples ashore permanently. I'd be grounding twenty, thirty percent of our crews."

"They sent us the younger officers and enlisted personnel, the ones with no attachments," Kris supplied. "And now they're forming attachments under the threat that any day could well be their last."

"I can't tell you how many times I've heard that from my division heads and chiefs, ma'am."

"Has it caused trouble? Damaged unit cohesion?" Jack asked.

"That's what has surprised me," Captain Kitano said. "There have been a few blowups, but not all that many. Where things went sour, I usually get a request from one or the other for a reassignment. So far, they've been few enough for us to handle, and they've had no impact on our battle efficiency. I don't know how the folks back home would take to this, but here, just letting Sailors be boys and girls works best."

"We are here, and we do have an alien something nibbling at our perimeter, and everyone knows that any day they could be fighting for their lives," Kris concluded. "Am I missing something, or are all hands handling themselves to meet their needs and the needs of the mission?"

"I wouldn't want to tell the king that, but yes, ma'am, it does look that way."

"Let me handle my grampa," Kris said.

"You don't seem very surprised," Captain Kitano said.

"The *Wasp* has had the same pressures on its crew, and they've been in two fights to boot. Captain Drago here issued his own order violating Navy policy before we started home. I would have been surprised if you hadn't dropped this in my lap."

"What do you plan to do, Commodore?" Captain Kitano asked.

"When we dock, I'll call the captains and key staff together and hash it out. If we can come to a unanimous consensus, I'll go that way."

"I don't think you'll have too much of a problem," Kitano said.

"Kris," Nelly said, "there's a message coming in from the jump buoy at Jump Point Beta. Ships from the U.S. have jumped into a system three jumps out."

"Hmm," Kris said, "Do we get our own consensus or wait for the new kids to arrive?"

"I'm glad I don't have your job," three voices said in harmony.

Half an hour later, Kris transferred her flag from the *Wasp* to the *Princess Royal* and headed for Alwa at 2.5 gees. That gave her time to get a report from her vice viceroy.

Alwa was producing a lot more food . . . if you liked fish. The Alwans were bringing a lot of forest edibles to market and did like the electronic goods the moon base was starting to turn out. Also, that copper mountain was slowly dripping copper into the nonpolluting catch basins.

There was grumbling from some of the old elders, but not from the new not-quite-so-elders stepping forward. They were more in step with the average Alwan on the path and only too aware the new humans were the only thing standing between them and the biggest "eats everything" they had ever dreamed of.

Pipra reported to Kris in her day quarters on the *Princess Royal* as soon as she docked. Kris invited her to take a comfortable chair away from the table. "The fabricators are starting to produce parts for weapon-caliber lasers. The miners aren't interested in being in unarmed ships when the aliens show up." The asteroid mining was going as well as could be expected. "I could use more ships to bring rare earths and other metals down system." Pipra was sure her techs would be excited to get their hands on the *Hornet*'s reactors.

"So you found what you were looking for." Pipra seemed quite surprised.

"They were on an island and near death. We got there just in time. Now, how are we coming on making our own reactors and Smart Metal?"

"We're getting there. We've started a prototype reactor on the moon. Not much output yet, but it's not breaking down, either. We've put out some Smart Metal. They're using it for trucks dirtside, freeing up your metal to go back to the frigates. We're having much better luck with aluminum and steel. We're replacing the fishing fleet with them. Our main problem is getting enough rare earths to power things. We've got a solar-cell plant up, but without batteries, you can't keep the ship out after dark. Same for trucks."

"Keep on it, then. How are your personnel holding up to being on the front line of humanity's next fight with the alien bastards?"

"I figured that would come next," Pipra said, leaning back in her chair. "The three managers who tried to drink Canopus Station dry were cut off at the bar and sent dirtside. Two are working as farmhands. One disappeared into the forest. We've had a few suicides. Nothing above the average for folks in high-stress jobs. Since we started closing up the bars early, folks have been going home and finding their own comfort. Lots of marriages, handfastings, and civil unions for folks who don't want a preacher involved. Not a few of our folks are bedding down with your Sailors, ma'am. I hope that isn't a problem, Your Highness."

"That's my next meeting. Any of your folks want to ship on with the Navy if some of our folks wanted to try their hand at your trades?"

"Our skill sets are nowhere close, ma'am. We're a pretty select set of specialists here. Retraining your folks to our jobs and our folks to yours would not be an efficient use of resources at this critical time. All of us heard about that buoy six systems out that went silent. We're working twelve or more hours a day, six or seven days a week."

"Work hard. Play hard," Kris said.

"Yes, ma'am, and we treat them like adults. What they do on their own time, what they have of it, is their own business."

"My next meeting may see that applied to the fleet as well."

"Good. It's about time if you don't mind my saying so, that you uniform types treated grown-ups as grown-ups."

"You tend to your knitting and I'll tend to mine," Kris said, dismissing the future CEO before she decided to give Kris more advice she didn't need.

"Yes, ma'am," Pipra said, standing. "Glad to have you back. Looking forward to working with you. How soon do you think we have before the bastards attack?"

"If I knew that, I'd be a lot more relaxed than I am," Kris said as she ushered Pipra to the door.

That left her with exactly three minutes before her meeting with the frigate skippers. That was scheduled for the wardroom. XOs, chief engineers, and skippers of the Marine detachments had been invited as well as command senior chiefs and Gunnies. Kris was none too sure how far she'd go with this consensus process, but she wanted all her ducks in a row, where she could knock them down with one stone if she had to.

She got the "Atten-hut" and "As you were" over with as quickly as possible. Again, most of the audience were close to the coffee urns, so she took her stance beside it. She first announced that the crew of the *Hornet* had been found, starving and sick, but were on their way here. Those present cheered, only too aware that it could have been them, and they had a commander who would go the extra million light-years to find them.

That done, Kris glanced at Captain Kitano, half expecting her to report the issue that was to be the main topic of this meeting, but Kitano didn't respond to a glance. When Kris opened the floor up for any problems, the captains only eyed each other. Then Kris saw the reason.

Lieutenant Commander Sampson, former skipper of the

Constellation, had taken a seat at Kris's far right, half looking at her, half eyeing the other skippers. When their eyes met, Sampson locked on her, a cruel twist to her lips. Was she daring Kris and the other skippers to step across the line, to violate Navy regs?

Kris had no intention of letting a failed skipper dictate policy to a Longknife.

As she took a deep breath to start, the door opened, and Admiral Benson, ret., stepped inside. He quickly but quietly covered the distance to the chair next to Sampson and settled into it.

The failed skipper did not look very happy to have her new supervisor seated at her elbow.

Kris took another breath and began to lay the problem out in a methodical way. She explained that most of them had been chosen for this assignment so far from any other humans because of their lack of personal attachments. Few had left wives, husbands, or significant others on the other side of the galaxy. All hands needed to be able to make quick, emergency adjustments to Smart Metal™. That also made it easy to acquire attachments, and the lack of shore facilities made it hard, if not impossible, for commanders to respond to violations of regulations. That, and the total lack of any replacements to take the place of anyone detached for punishment put leadership in a lose-lose situation.

"So, what do we do?" Kris asked rhetorically.

"You don't violate Navy regs," Sampson snapped.

"Thank you, Lieutenant Commander, but I'd like to hear from officers actually facing this leadership challenge."

"They should face it, but they're not. They're all in violation of Navy regs," Sampson almost shouted, keeping the floor from any others.

Since she insisted on doing all the talking, Kris decided to give her the floor.

For a while.

"And how would you propose solving this leadership challenge, miss."

Sampson cringed at Kris's slap, addressed as one might a middy or boot ensign, but she charged ahead. "As I did with the *Constellation*. Open space barracks and bed checks."

"And we saw how well it worked for you," Captain Kitano shot back. "Most of your crew wanted off your ship."

"Only because your love boats were out there for them to transfer to," was her comeback.

"May I remind everyone that we're here to fight a pretty nasty set of aliens, not bicker like kids in the sandbox," Kris pointed out.

"But you're all behaving like kids," Sampson growled.

"More like teenagers," retired admiral, now yard supervisor Benson put in. "These young men and women have a tough job to do, a deadly fate looming in their future, and the need to work it out without the external discipline that usually goes with this job. It's not a good place to be."

Sampson glared at her supervisor, who ignored her and gave Kris a placid look.

Jack and four Marines marched through the door before Kris said another word. Jack glanced around, spotted Sampson, and marched for her. "As I understand it, you are not on the approved list for this meeting. Would you please come with me?"

"I'm a serving officer in the U.S. Navy. I can go where I wish."

"This meeting is for skippers and their key staff," Jack snapped. "You are not in any of those billets. Either come with me now, or I will have my Marines remove you to the brig."

Sputtering nasties under her breath that Kris was careful not to hear, Sampson went where Jack led. At the door, she whirled and pointed at the yard supervisor. "What's he doing here?"

"I invited him," Kris said. With that, Jack half ushered, half shoved the red-faced officer out of the room. The last Marine out closed the door.

Kris now turned to her officers. "Okay, let's talk. Now that you've lived with the app that lets doors show up where we'll never know, what problems have you identified, and what do you think we should do about them?"

Kris heard no surprises. The list of problems was what you'd expect to hear when men and women worked hard in close proximity. Admiral Benson was kind enough to point out that he was facing them at the shipyard where most of his personnel were civilian and living under looser rules.

Captain Kitano summed it up for all. "They're grown-ups. They're going to live or die because of what the Sailor or officer next to them does. They know it as well as we do. So, if they want to be treated as grown-ups, why shouldn't we let them?"

"There are reinforcements coming, only a few systems out," Sims of the *Constellation* said. "Shouldn't we wait for them to establish policy?"

"We've been living with this for a lot longer than they have," another skipper said. "Let's do it and let them adjust to us. The more that show up, the more likely we are to get people like Sampson."

"Besides, the commodore didn't wait to get any chops on her marriage request," someone in the back tossed in. It sounded like an old chief.

"Pipe down, or that Marine that frog-marched Sampson out of here may do you next," an XO snapped.

Kris frowned; was she losing control of the meeting?

Kitano stood up. "Enough of that. Commodore Longknife had a narrow window when she could do what she wanted, and it wasn't illegal. She grabbed it. I don't know about you, but I like her style. She's offering us a similar window. I say we take it."

The room seemed to mull that over for a few seconds, then sounds of agreement filled the wardroom.

"If we're going to suspend one set of Navy regs, we need to put something in its place," Kris said. "I hate to do this, but I need a committee. Two or three skippers. Two from each of the rest of you: XOs, engineering, Marines. Chiefs. This policy will be yours to manage. I want the command senior chief and Gunny from each frigate working on this."

"I think we need two from Weapons and two from Deck Division," Captain Kitano tossed in.

"Okay," Kris said. "I want names on my desk in an hour. I want a rough draft on my desk by 0800 tomorrow. If that means some folks miss a night's sleep, so be it."

Kris walked out while the skippers were volunteering either themselves or someone of their teams.

Jack was waiting for her outside.

"Sorry about not being there immediately. Nelly called, and I came running as fast as I could grab four stray Marines."

"Nelly, thanks for the initiative, and Jack, thanks for the help. Where is our failed skipper?"

"I had the Marines escort Sampson to the brig to cool off. Once we had her in the passageway, she blew up. She started shouting stuff that, if I'd heard it, might make me have to bring her up on charges for Unbecoming and Prejudicial."

"She did that to me last time we talked. Have a medical officer drop down to check her out in the brig. I have to wonder if something's wrong with her."

"Besides being just plain wrongheaded?"

"Yes."

Superintendent Benson slipped out of the meeting. "Sorry about that. Sampson got away from her desk when I wasn't looking. I'd heard you were back and figured you'd be trying to solve this matter. As soon as I spotted her missing, I came."

"Thanks for the support. Tell me, in your previous incarnation as an admiral, and considering that an admiral might be included in the reinforcements headed our way, how would you take to what is going on here and what I'm doing?"

Admiral Benson, ret., rolled his eyes at the overhead. "I'd probably have an epileptic fit, to tell you the truth. Sampson's problem is that she's old school, like I was. We don't handle some leadership challenges very well."

"But you've got a similar situation at the yard."

"Yes, but as I keep reminding myself, I'm a civilian, and so are those working for me. None of us have to get a laser on target the first time, every time. Don't get me wrong. I never faced any leadership challenge like you're up against, so I'm not going to tell you that you're wrong. It's just not something I would ever do."

He paused, then looked Kris hard in the eye. "That's likely one of the reasons why King Ray chose you for command here and not one of the more senior types around."

Which gave Kris pause. Had her Grampa Ray once more handpicked her for one of his worst messes?

"Thank you, sir," Kris said, "for your advice and guidance."

"It's worth every penny you paid for it. Now, where's my gal, and how much will it cost me to bail her out?"

"She's in the brig, Superintendent," Kris said, "but I'd really like to have a medical officer look her over before we turn her loose. I'd hate to discover six weeks from now that she had a brain tumor, and we didn't spot it after she acted up like that."

"A brain tumor would be easier to handle than her just being old-line," the former admiral said as he headed down to the brig.

"So, you got any more hand grenades to toss today, my lovely Viceroy and Sector Commander?" Jack asked.

"Nope, I can't think of a thing more to do. Oh, when's the *Wasp* due in with our prize? Have we arranged for it to dock?"

"I have arranged a dock for the *Wasp*," Nelly said. "I'm assuming we'll park the wreck in a trailing orbit fifty klicks behind the station."

"Another well done, Nelly. Gosh, Jack, what can we do with ourselves?"

"How about me take you to dinner on the station?" Jack suggested. "It's been a while since I had a date with my wife."

45

Dinner with Jack was beyond nice. They were ushered to a quiet corner and left alone for the evening. The meal was unrecognizable, but Kris enjoyed what the chef had done with meat, roots, and sprouts that had never seen Earth's sun. And there was a band.

They danced to tunes from the present to long before humanity ventured from its home. "You know, we don't have *our* song," Jack said.

"I'm sure we'll find one sooner or later," Kris assured him.

They returned to Kris's quarters and soon needed a shower. "You know, you have your quarters and I'm down a deck and around the other side, but I really don't think we've quite got the spirit of the policy correct," Jack whispered in Kris's ear as he scrubbed her back.

"We'll see what the policy is tomorrow," Kris said, and started on his front.

Still, before 2100, Jack was on his way to his quarters and Kris was back at her desk going through reports. One caused her pause. Professor Labao thought they had matched the star fields that always decorated the overhead of sacred places on the alien ships. If true, it was about three thousand light-years back the way Kris and the Fleet of Discovery had come.

Interesting.

Kris pondered what to do. Knowledge was power. Would a visit to the alien home world give them power? Would any ship dispatched on such a recon mission survive? Kris would have to balance the risk against the return.

If she did choose to send someone, who should it be?

It would be nice to give Sampson another ship and get her out of Kris's hair. The problem was, she was more likely to take off for home, whining all the way, rather than risk her neck to answer any questions.

Kris could think of at least one person who was good at asking and answering questions. The only question was, could she risk her?

Kris fell asleep at her desk, reviewing food production projections from both the colonial farms and Alwan.

Next morning, on her way to breakfast, Kris found a bleary-eyed XO with two senior chiefs at her side waiting outside the wardroom. "Here's our draft policy."

Kris flipped through it. "You left a place for me to sign?" she pointed out.

"Captain Kitano said we might as well do a full staff job. Whatever draft you sign will need a place to do it at, right?"

Kris thanked the chiefs for their effort and led the XO into the wardroom. She read the policy through, with Jack looking over her shoulder.

"You see a problem from the Marine side?" she asked him.

"Nope. I trust my Gunnies. Besides, if there is a problem, that's what mod 1 and mod 12 are for."

Kris signed it and handed it back to the XO. "See that this is published before noon today."

The young lieutenant was grinning from ear to ear. "Yes, ma'am," she said. "There is an upside to having a Longknife for a commander."

"Not many," Jack assured her, "but a few."

The exec saluted and headed off at a jog.

"Is that your first policy?" Jack asked.

"Maybe," Kris said around a bite of bran muffin. "Certainly my first to supplant a Navy reg. We'll have to wait to see how that goes."

"Yes, we will."

Kris was back at her desk in her day quarters when the screens on her walls came to life. "Commodore," Captain Kitano reported, "we've got activity at Jump Point Beta. Lots of it."

"Show me what you're getting."

Jack, who had been going over his Marine reports on the couch, stood up to join Kris in front of her screens.

"Ships are coming through. U.S. registry out of Wardhaven," Kitano reported. "*Renown, Repulse, Royal Sovereign, Resistance*, and *Resolute*. The chief thinks those are heavy frigates. They're followed by the *Supply* and *Ajax*. Auxiliaries, but none of them are in our recognition books, nor are their pennant numbers ones we have."

"Send my greetings. If we don't hear something friendly from them in two hours, we'll take the squadron to general quarters and sortie. Issue a preliminary order for a sortie."

"Aye, aye, Commodore."

Then another section of Kris's screen lit up. "Commodore Hawkings, here. I hope we didn't scare you, Admiral. Yep, it's admiral. The king sends his compliments and your official promotion to captain and frocks you up to rear admiral. You'll need the rank, I'm just the first division through the jump. Wait until you see what's behind me. Over to you."

KRIS, THERE IS A COMMANDER HAWKINGS IN OUR DATA-BASE. FACIAL RECOGNITION GIVES A NINETY-NINE-POINT-EIGHTY-NINE-PERCENT MATCH TO HIM. HE WAS ON THE FAST TRACK, AND IT LOOKS LIKE THEY MOVED HIM AHEAD OF A LOT OF SENIORS TO COME HERE.

LET'S HOPE HE'S AS GOOD AS THEY THINK HE IS. "Commodore Hawkings, good to see you. We've got plenty of seats by the fire. Come on down."

Kris knew there would be a long wait for any reply.

"More ships," Captain Kitano reported. "*Triumph, Swiftsure, Hotspur*, and *Spitfire*. All from the Helvetican Confederacy. They've got two ships following them, *North Star* and *Enchanter*. Heavy frigates and supply, too."

"Let's hope these *Triumph* and *Swiftsure* have more luck under my command than the last two," Kris muttered. Jack came to rest a supporting hand on her shoulder.

"Captain Kitano, are all these ships Smart Metal?" Kris asked on net.

"Sensors say they are. Why?"

"Because we're going to need more docks real soon. I hope some of the auxiliaries can be merged into Canopus Station, or it's going to get downright cozy here. Pass that along to Admiral Benson."

"Doing so, ma'am. Oh, and by the way, congratulations on your promotion, Admiral."

"Let's wait until we see the orders that come with it. I no longer trust my grampa, your king."

"Yes, ma'am," the captain said with equanimity. Apparently, she was getting used to Kris's attitude toward the large herd of elephants she descended from. If she kept up with Kris, she might find herself commodore of a frigate squadron since there was now an opening for a new boss for the eight frigates who had held down the fort for six weeks.

"More ships coming through," Kitano reported. On Kris's screen, more green dots popped into view. Names quickly appeared next to them. *Haruna*, *Chikuma*, *Atago*, and *Tone*. There was a pause, then more appeared. *Arasi*, *Hubuki*, *Amatukaze*, and *Arare*. Musashi was making a major contribution.

Again, Kris's screen came to life. "I am glad to greet you in a better space, Admiral Longknife," said now Commodore Miyoshi. "I see something huge and mangled approaching your station with a ship I don't recognize, but engines my sensor people say are Mitsubishi built. I hope you have left something for us to hunt."

"I'm very glad to see you again, too, Commodore, as well as the ships you've brought. And yes, the space around Alwa is still a target-rich environment. Glad to have you aboard." That message would also take a while to be received and responded to.

"Following those large frigates are four more ships. *Taigei*, *Soyo*, *Zingei*, and *Kagu Maru*. That last one is huge. As in Canopus size. They may be bringing their own space dock."

"I'll talk to Commodore Miyoshi about merging it with Canopus Station," Kris said. "Or they can do what they want; I'm just glad to have them."

"I heard there was a lot of fun going on," Penny said, joining Kris and Jack in Kris's day quarters.

"It looks like the cavalry just arrived," Jack said. "Hope it's enough."

"Ever the pessimist," Kris said.

"We need at least one in this shop," Penny said.

"Be nice to her," Jack said. "She's now a permanent captain and a frocked-up rear admiral."

"They're fattening the calf before the slaughter," Penny said wryly.

"The bastards will certainly know they've been in a fight this time," Kris said.

"When we were picking the bones of the last mother ship, I didn't notice that they hadn't been in a fight last time. Don't think we did either," Jack said.

"Quiet in the peanut gallery. More ships coming through," Kris said.

"U.S. from Lorna Do. *Warrior*, *Warspite*, *Nelson*, and *Churchill*. How very British of them," Katano said. "*Argus* and *Activity* are their supply ships. Good show."

"You think that's the last of the parade?" Jack asked.

"I hope not. What's that give us? Nine Wardhaven ships to start with plus five more. Eight Musashi, and four each from Lorna Do and Helvetica. Thirty to face two hundred or more, depending on how many mother ships hit us next time."

"Now who's the pessimist?" Jack asked.

"So we take turns. For the next five minutes, you be the optimist," Kris said.

"Hold it, there are more," Penny said. "Another U.S. ship, the *Lion*, from Savannah. That sounds familiar, but . . ."

"An industrial planet we helped train fast attacks for," Kris said. "Until someone tried to bomb me, and we got the boot."

"Right, I remember them. It was the second place we got bombed," Jack said.

"And the fourth place we got the bum's rush out of," Penny recalled. "That was before we ended up on Chance. Now those were good times."

"Good times," Kris said. "The only thing good about them was we didn't get suddenly dead."

"Yes, but we survived," Jack said. "And we went on to greater and more fun things, and now we can look back on them fondly. Just think. Five years from now, we'll be looking back on this and saying, 'Now those were the good times.'"

"Because we're in worse trouble than this?" Penny said. "God help us."

"Rest assured, He will," Jack said.

"She will," Penny shot back.

"Crew, crew, look at what Santa brought us. *Lion*, *Tiger*, *Jaguar*, and *Puma*."

"What, no skunk?"

"Trust me, Penny, if it would get me another 20-inch frigate, I'd make it my flag."

"Well, Savannah is adding a *Cougar*, *Cheetah*, *Lynx*, and *Leopard*," Jack said.

"Still no skunk." Penny sighed.

"No, but *Sirius*, *Regulus*, *Polaris*, *Castor*, and *Pollux* should help keep us supplied."

"Thirty-eight frigates and fifteen auxiliaries," Jack said. "Now tell me, how are we going to feed them all?"

"You were supposed to be the optimist," Kris pointed out.

"My time was up. I can go back to my default mode. An optimistic Marine is usually a dead one. You want me pessimistic. Pessimists are cautious and stay alive."

"Okay, my love, you may be a pessimist if it will keep you coming home to me," Kris said, and gave him a quick kiss.

Penny raised an eyebrow.

"Haven't you read my first policy memo, Penny?"

The new lieutenant commander shook her head.

"Fraternizing is now allowed, so long as it is not harassment. If he harasses me, I get to shove him off to another ship."

"But she only fraternizes with me," Jack put in.

"You're biting the bullet," Penny said.

"Will this change anything between you and Iizuka Masao?"

"I don't dare. The last time I loved a guy and married him, he got killed. I almost got killed, and Wardhaven nearly got pounded to dust. I'm unlucky at love for all those around me."

"More ships coming through," Captain Kitano announced on net.

"We're not done," Kris said, turning from her friend to the

screen. More blips appeared identified as *Altair*, *Algol*, *Andromeda*, and *Diphada* of the Star Line.

"They've only got two reactors," Senior Chief Beni, ret., announced on net. "I'm showing no lasers, but they're big. As an old chief, I'd bet they're transports. Big ones."

"What has Santa Claus sent this good little girl?" Kris asked with a grin.

"Are you a good *little* girl?" Penny shot back.

Kris gave Jack a sideways glance.

"Well, she's certainly a *good* girl," her loving husband supplied, right on cue.

Kris rewarded him with another quick peck before turning to Penny. "We'll find out what they are when they get here. Now, Penny, girlfriend to girlfriend, you can't really believe you're responsible for what happened at Wardhaven. Vicky Peterwald as much as told us that her old man was behind the whole attack."

"I know," Penny said. "In my head, I know. But somewhere between there and my heart, my gut, and lower down, I can't seem to get it."

The jump point had finished disgorging presents for Kris. She pointed Penny at the couch, and the two of them adjourned to the comfortable seats. Jack seemed to sense girl talk was on the schedule and excused himself for Marine business.

"Penny, how well is your head screwed on?" Kris asked. She'd planned to give Penny a job. A critically important and very dangerous job. However, if her friend was only holding on to herself by her fingernails, Kris might have to look elsewhere.

"Kris, I'm fine," Penny said, folding her hands into her lap. "Have you had any problems with my work?"

"None whatsoever," Kris said. "Are you up to commanding a ship?"

Penny made a face. "The last time I commanded a ship, I think I killed Hank Peterwald. Have you got another old boyfriend you want popped?"

"He was *never* a boyfriend, and *you* didn't kill him. Whoever sabotaged his survival pod did that. But actually, this time, I would most definitely not want you to get in a fight."

"You're ordering me to command a ship but not get in a fight? Strange words from a Longknife. What's my potential command, a garbage scow?"

"I'm not sure what your command is, at the moment, though I'm sure it will have the six 18-inch lasers we took off the *Wasp*. Three pointing forward, the others aft."

"So I've got just as much firepower running as chasing, huh?"

"Pretty much. Here's the situation. Professor Labao thinks he's narrowed the location of the alien home world to four or five stars. Assuming the stars we saw in several places on the overhead of the alien mother ship is actually a night sky of their home world. I need someone to go look, see, and run back home fast to report."

"You're not sending me with any Hellburners, are you?"

"No. And I mean no. Take a peek. If you see any ships, run. That will tell me as much as your seeing the planet. I have a hunch that these folks have all but abandoned their home world. However, if you start running into heavy traffic, that tells me to forget that hunch."

"I see," Penny said, thoughtfully. "I poke my nose under the tent but keep one eye on the exit the whole time." She paused for a moment to think. "I can be that timid."

"This really has to be a recon. One where I learn what you see. Heroes need not apply."

"I get the point, Kris. I'm your coward."

"I don't think any coward would take this mission. It takes a lot of guts to stick your head where the lion's mouth may be."

"What ship can you give me? The *Wasp*?"

"Sorry, I can't let a 20-inch laser out of orbit here, Penny. I was thinking of patching some of our 'spare' Smart Metal to the leftover *Hornet* reactors and six of the 18-inch lasers, but these new ships arriving may give me other options."

"As in respinning a Smart Metal transport into a scout ship?"

"Something like that."

"How do you think the crew will take to that?"

"Part of me says not well, but another part of me wonders why anyone would agree to come out here if they weren't overstocked on a spirit of adventure."

Penny smiled as she shook her head. "You expect a lot out of folks, Kris."

"And sometimes they give me more than I have any right to ask for. Like you, Penny. Will you take Iizuka Masao with you?"

"The man is waiting with more patience than I deserve for me to get my act together. Will he follow me into the lion's den? I'll have to ask him."

"You go ask him, and Nelly, make sure Mimzy gets a copy of my new fraternization policy."

"My kids already have it, Kris. It's you humans who haven't opened your mail."

"I'll read it. I'll read it," Penny said. "Now, don't you have some other fine person's life to ruin?"

"As a matter of fact, I do. Have a good one, Penny, you deserve it. And change your shoulder boards. A frigate skipper is a commander's billet."

Penny was already making for the door. "Thank you, Kris. Good-bye, Kris." Leaving Kris smiling . . . and wondering whose day a princess should mess with next.

Nelly settled it. She had the manifests from the Star Line ships.

46

Kris doubted she was messing with Granny Rita's day when she called her.

"Granny, you won't guess what just dropped into the system."

"You sound chipper, so it can't be aliens. Don't keep the old girl guessing. Life's too short to waste it on silly games."

"Yes, Grandmother," Kris drawled. "Your king and former husband seems to remember you fondly."

"What makes you say that?" was lathered in caution.

"Twenty-eight frigates and fifteen auxiliaries just jumped into your nice system."

"How are we going to feed them all?" Granny sighed.

"There are four, honest to God transports trailing them, and I just got the inventory of their cargo. They're loaded with farm implements, trucks, Smart Metal fishing boats. All kinds of goodies."

"How will we power them all?"

"Granny, you are a disgusting downer. Don't you credit Grampa Ray with the sense God promised a billy goat?"

"A goat, yes. Your grampa, not so much."

"They're also loaded with solar-power plants and individual cells. Grampa Ray has not sent you gear that will just sit there and frustrate you."

"Farm gear, transportation, boats, and power. Did you say anything to Ray?"

"Nope."

"He wasn't here long enough to see much of anything," his former wife mused.

"He did take off with twenty or so of your best young people," Kris pointed out.

"I figured the old bag of wind would be doing all the talking. Ray does have an ego."

"Apparently, he must have listened a bit, because those ships are full of stuff you need."

"You keep this up, and you're going to force me to reassess the old fool."

"He is a mystery, isn't he, Granny?"

"So how soon do we get all these wonderful presents?"

"The fleet came in by Jump Point Beta and are making a one-gee approach. Say sometime late today. Probably too late to do much until tomorrow."

"Do you have port facilities for all of them?"

"Not even close," Kris said.

"Well, have fun. Don't you hate being a grown-up?"

"Good-bye Granny."

Kris's next call was to Ada. There was no reason for her to hear the good news secondhand. The Chief of Ministries sent back a "Glory, alleluia" reply and said she'd get the colonials ready for the king's largesse.

That left Kris with the problem of conjuring a ship for Penny out of thin air. She decided the shipyard was the best place to look for a solution. Besides, if she did what she was thinking of doing, the yard would have a whole lot of new problems to solve.

Admiral Benson, ret., was in his office with a large window overlooking the shop floor beneath him. No surprise, he had already heard of the new arrivals. "It's nice to see the tip of the spear getting a bit sharper."

"Thirty-eight frigates to hold off a mother ship and her brood of a couple of hundred huge monsters. Odds leave something to be desired," Kris said.

"Yes, but they're three, four times better than they were yesterday."

"I have some problems I could use your help solving."

"How many and how bad?" the old Navy man said.

"First, rumor is I've been made an admiral. You didn't bring along any old shoulder boards, did you?"

He was grinning before she finished the sentence and reaching into a drawer of his desk. "I kept my first set of admiral shoulder boards around for good luck. May you wear them in good health," he said, tossing a pair of boards across the desk to Kris.

"Would you mind helping me put them on?" Kris asked.

"Shouldn't your husband do that?"

"If they're your lucky shoulder boards, I wouldn't want to do anything to jinx the luck."

He did the honor, then stood back and gave her a salute. He might be a civilian at the moment, but Gunny would thoroughly approve of his form.

"So, one problem down. What next?"

"All the auxiliaries are Smart Metal. What kind of warship do you think you could respin two or three of them into?"

"What do you have in mind? The asteroids are coming up with all kinds of rare and exotic materials, just what we need for making lasers of our own. The crew in my weapons lab can't wait to get their hands on the old *Hornet*'s lasers and start reworking them. Same for her reactors though I'm not sure I'd trust them out of my sight. What's the phrase, they been rid hard and put away wet."

"Yes, I suspected you'd say something like that. Yes, I want more support ships for the asteroid mines, but I need to spin out a frigate as well. Are the *Wasp*'s and *Intrepid*'s original 18-inchers gathering dust?"

"We put one of them in each of the Hellburner bases we set up on the moons. Assuming they get slagged real good by the bastards, we'll need to recut our launch tunnels to get the Hellfires out."

"That still leaves eight, or five. Have we dug bases to cover the Beta Jump Point?"

"Just starting, but those lasers aren't being wasted. I've got them mounted on my station, and we've trained Ostriches to man them. Those birds are smart and not afraid to be mean."

"Any chance they might sign up for ship duty?" Kris asked.

"What do you have in mind?"

Kris told him. His reaction was, at best, noncommittal. "I

don't know. Spin out a frigate to the *Wasp*'s design? I think we can do that. Find a crew? That might be a problem. You sure the merchant folks arriving planned to stay?"

"I haven't asked them," Kris admitted.

"Ever heard of shanghaiing?"

"Likely I've been guilty of that a few times in my life."

"Come to think about it, a lot of folks might want to hitch a ride back on those empty transports. Any idea how we keep from hemorrhaging our workforce?"

"By my count, there were twenty-eight frigates escorting those nineteen auxiliary and merchant ships. How many folks do you think would want to ride the convoy home with no escort?"

"You're a hard woman."

"I'm a Longknife. I've got a fight coming and thirty-eight warships to hold the line. Would you lose a few to an escort mission?"

The retired admiral didn't say anything for a long while. Finally, he muttered, "I guess I'd look at my orders."

"Mine are rather vague. Put up a fight. I don't have to win, I just have to make it look good enough that the bastards don't think they need to go looking for where we might be from. Me, I'd prefer to win. I get to stay alive if I win."

"We sure don't if we lose," Benson agreed.

"You just get ready to respin a lot of Smart Metal into what we need. Leave the personnel to me."

"Gladly."

The *Wasp* was on its final approach. It parked the wreck a good hundred klicks back, trailing the station. Good idea; there might well be more ships stuck swinging around each other if there wasn't anything to grow the station coming in. The *Wasp* also dumped the wreckage of the *Hornet* ten klicks back. Yard tugs were quickly picking though the pieces; the reactors were the first to be towed in for examination.

There were shuttles coming up from Alwa loaded with boffins wanting a first look at the alien technology. There were also docs who had been dirtside, researching the local biology or starting up the geriatrics clinic. Every medical type available had been recalled to help with Phil Taussig's survivors.

Kris was there when they wheeled Phil up from the *Wasp*'s pier.

"Good heavens, Kris, you've got quite a setup here. Oh, pardon me, Admiral." In bed, weak as he was, he tried to lie at attention. How many generations of Navy did he have stiffening his backbone?

"At ease, Commander. I'm just a jumped-up captain my grandfather, the king, frocked up to an admiral. And you'll be a full commander as quickly as Nelly can cut the paperwork. Listen, Phil, I've got a problem."

"Don't you Longknifes always?"

Kris quickly filled him in on what she'd found on Alwa. "Wow, so we weren't just fighting for a bunch of weird bird folks, huh?"

"Nope, my own granny and two shipfuls of survivors and their kids and grandkids."

"So, what's the situation now?"

"We've got a potential alien attack marshaling somewhere out there. They could hit us anytime. My problem is that I want to hang on to every asset I've got. My second problem is that if ever survivors deserved home leave, you and your crew do. If I send a ship back for you, I may have a whole lot of people hitching a ride along with you."

"I see," Phil said. His head sank deeper into the pillow. Was moving him tiring him out, or was it the heavy load she'd just dumped on him? Maybe she shouldn't have said anything. After all, if she got hit with a full-fledged mutiny, or if a couple of those frigates had orders already to escort the merchants back, this might all be for nothing.

If so, she would do whatever she had to do.

"We're here, Kris. That's all that matters. Do with us what you will," Phil said, then seemed to collapse into his gurney.

She left Phil as a flock of people in white coats began to gather around him. Kris found herself in a situation she was all too familiar with. It was that time before battle, when she'd done everything she could and now had to wait to see if it had been enough.

She hunted up Jack, and they had a quiet lunch. He listened as she recounted her morning, nodding support, asking a few questions that helped clarify her thoughts. Yes, she was prepared to countermand orders given back in human space.

What came here, stayed here.

Would she force the crew of the *Hornet* to sit out the coming attack in hospital beds? That stumped her. She needed ships. She needed crews. Certainly she owed the *Hornet*. She and the *Wasp*'s crew would likely have been stuck there with them if Phil hadn't gone one way and let her go the other.

"I think I'm starting to understand how Grampa Ray got to be such a bastard," Kris finally muttered.

Kris returned to her desk; reports were piling up. Professor Labao wanted to know if Kris was going to do anything about the possible alien home planet. If so, a lot of boffins that Kris would have credited with good sense wanted in on the mission. Ada had already started making plans to extend the colonial farmlands. Her question was where the labor would come from and did Kris think any of the newly pacified forestland could be made available to the colonials.

Ada hadn't yet contacted the Alwan elders about that hot potato. It looked like she wanted Kris to handle it.

The planetary survey was not quite done. They'd found some rare earths and other minerals needed for lasers and Smart Metal™, but they were not in places easy to get to. As far away as the asteroids were, it was likely that they could be exploited faster. There was something about biological research that seemed to offer hope of a spectacular breakthrough, but the report was very vague. Like everyone in human space, Kris had heard about potential world-changing science, only to find it vanish down the "no, not really" tubes with as little fanfare as possible.

Kris read on. About suppertime, Jack came to dig her out.

"I've got something special for you."

"Want to show it to me?" Kris purred.

"You have a one-track mind."

"I've had a very bad day."

The surprise was a new restaurant, The Burger Carnival. The proprietor had painted it up like an ancient traveling circus, complete with clowns and old Earth animals.

"Remind you of any place?" Jack said.

Kris wondered if she blushed, but apparently admirals were too shameless for such things. "The place where I decided to draft you," Kris admitted.

"I thought so," Jack said.

"Can you forgive me?" Kris asked.

"For starting us on the road to here? What's to forgive?"

They ordered hamburgers and fries. Cheese apparently was not available for love nor money. Jack led Kris to a table in the back of the restaurant, which was actually the front of the station. They had a spectacular view of Alwa as it revolved below them. Kris tried not to look for anything she'd read about in her reports.

I'm having dinner with my husband. Right!

"Do you know what's special about today?" Jack said, reaching across the table for her hands.

"Besides the cavalry arriving to either rescue us or go down in our defeat?"

"Forget the job," Jack growled. "Today is our second anniversary. It's been two months since we let Granny Rita talk us into taking the plunge. Do you regret it?"

"Never," Kris said, squeezing Jack's hand. "Two months. I totally forgot about it. I can hardly keep track of the time. How'd you do it?"

"I had Sal do it for me."

"Nelly, why didn't you tell me?"

"I didn't know it mattered to you. I know it's a very romantic thing for you humans. I just didn't know if it would include you, Kris."

"Yes, I'm human, and, yes, I'm romantic, at least for Jack, and Jack, why are you doing all the girl things and me doing all the stupid boy stuff?"

"You're the admiral," he said with a shrug.

Kris let out a sigh. "I don't like that, Jack."

"But you have to. That's what Longknifes do. They do what they have to do."

"Well, I want to do more. Stuff I want to do as well as what I have to do."

Dinner arrived, brought by a moonlighting Marine. The haircut gave him away. "Just what you ordered, Colonel, two burgers with all the trimmings and two orders of fries."

Kris took a breath, and was transported back in time. Then she frowned.

"Onions, tomatoes, real potatoes. How'd you do it, Jack?"

A quick glance around showed other diners making do with produce from the native Alwan fields.

"These are from your Granny Rita's garden. Don't look too closely at the meat, though. It's from the deep forest. But I promise, it's off one of the more delectable vegetarians, rather than a tough type that still thinks Marine might taste good."

Jack awarded a grin to their waiter. He blushed at his superior's attention.

"You amaze me, Jack. You remember our anniversary and do it enough ahead of time to talk my granny out of the fruits of her garden."

"Oh, I didn't talk her out of anything, it was pure horse-trading. My Marines will deliver a truckload of fish offal to her and all her neighbors' gardens. Nobody gets anything free from your granny."

"Which leads me wondering if she's all that different from Ray," Kris said, taking a bite.

"I will do my best to stay different enough to save you from the Longknife curse," Jack said as he began to enjoy his own dinner. They ate in quiet ease, content to bask in each other's company.

Maybe I can become a comfortable old married woman, Kris thought with as much hope as doubt.

They were almost done when their view window suddenly lost its view.

"What the . . . ?" Jack said, standing.

Kris was on her feet almost as fast. A huge cylinder slowly moved between them and the planet below. On its side was KAGU MARU in Standard and Kanji. There was also the Mitsubishi Heavy Space Industry logo. It was easily as big around as Canopus Station. Maybe longer. Once it was fully in view, it began to edge slowly into formation ahead of the station. When it covered the entire front, the thing began to take on spin, first slowly, then faster, until it was matching the rotation of Canopus Station.

Then it began to creep back.

"Somebody's awfully confident they aren't going to rupture a hull," Kris said.

That brought looks of terror from the other diners, and some abandoned their meals to head for the exit.

"Both stations are made of Smart Metal," Jack said in a

raised command voice. "If anything rips, they can have it fixed in seconds."

The exit slowed.

The hull rang as the two cylinders made contact. Canopus Station lurched backward, but hardly enough to make Kris sway on her feet. "Not bad," she said in admiration.

"Want to bet your buddy Katsu-san is at the bottom of this?"

"Good Lord, if he came out again, I just might have to send him back," Kris said.

"Then again, he might be very helpful in respinning ships."

"Now you're taking on my nasty role."

"Whatever," Jack said with a shrug. "Want to bet the fleet's in, and you need to see a lot of new officers? Let them see you?"

"Oh, yes. Nelly, send to all the ships, frigates, auxiliaries, and merchants. Officers' call in two hours. Captains and execs required. Marines, boffins, engineering and weapons and chiefs of the boat may also attend. The location is the *Wasp*'s Forward Lounge. Two-drink limit."

Kris had been approached by Mother MacCreedy as spokesperson for all the tapshops on station, requesting the two-drink limit. "It will stretch the supply. Besides, we've got a foul drink that the Alwans guzzle coming up. Two of them will put any old drunk under the table."

Kris had signed the order.

Kris did paperwork before the meeting. This time it was the good kind, a promotion list. Kitano went to full commander and was frocked up to commodore. She'd find out why later. All the frigate skippers got full commander. They'd have to do the paperwork to promote their XOs and division heads themselves. The *Wasp* presented Kris an interesting challenge. She solved it in the usual Longknife way.

"Nelly, activate Captain Drago's reserve commission, bring him out of retirement, and give him a captain's rank."

"Kris, I'm not sure I can jump a man from lieutenant to captain in one afternoon."

"Nelly, he dropped himself from rear admiral to lieutenant in less time. If you have to, ask him how he did it."

Of course, Nelly found a way. The magnificent Nelly did not ask mere mortals for help.

47

TWO hours later, the Forward Lounge was going strong. The crews of Kris's squadron had arrived first and occupied the tables closest to the bar. Apparently Musashi had been first to dock, probably on their own section of the station, and Commodore Miyoshi and his command teams were catching up with the Musashi Navy folks who had come out on the *Wasp*. Commodore Hawkings had set up shop for the newly arrived U.S. contingent against the far wall, and officers from Lorna Do, Savannah, and Wardhaven mixed freely. The Helveticans joined the Musashi Navy in the middle.

The four merchant skippers and their first mates had a table next to the door.

As Kris entered, she took all this in with a glance, even as someone shouted, "Atten-hut. Admiral on deck," and she got "As you were" out before most people could even start to get to their feet.

The merchantmen didn't even make an effort. They would be a challenge.

Kris marched to the table in the front Penny had reserved for them. Her shoulder boards showed commander's stripes. Jack stayed two steps behind Kris. Once at the front of the lounge, Kris turned and let her eyes rove over the young men and women before her. Silence quickly fell.

"Thank you for coming on such short notice," Kris said, and let chuckles roll around the room at the double meaning of her words.

"Commodore Hawkings, I haven't gotten a copy of your orders. Can you share them with us?"

The man pointed his wrist at the screen behind Kris and it came to life. "I am ordered to report to you, Admiral, and conform to your orders."

"Thank you," Kris said. *Will I for once have a chain of command that isn't a knot fit only for a kitten to play with?*

She turned to Commodore Bethea from Savannah. She stood to attention, and announced, "My orders are the same. We are U.S. Navy, and we follow you."

Apparently, Grampa Ray was getting more United in his societies than when Kris last passed though. Or maybe they'd just sent her the committed Federalists.

The captain from Lorna Do quickly rose to her feet. "Same here. We are at your command, Your Highness."

Kris would have preferred Admiral, but she'd answer to whatever got her a fighting fleet.

Now she turned to the hard one. "Commodore Miyoshi, it's so good to see you again."

"And very nice it is to see you in better circumstances," he said. He also pointed his wrist unit at the screen and his orders appeared. "I am to place myself and my command under your orders and serve honorably at your side, Admiral. You will note that my orders were endorsed by the Emperor himself. I know of no naval force that has ever sailed with that kind of an endorsement from the throne."

"I am honored," Kris said, giving the commodore a deep bow from the waist that he promptly returned.

Now it was the Helvetican captain's turn. "It looks to me like everyone's been drinking from the same beer mug. My orders are identical to yours, Commodore," he said, raising his wrist and letting the screen show basically the same orders, without the imperial chop.

That settled, Kris asked the obvious question. "How was your voyage out?"

The three commodores glanced around at each other, seemed to toss a coin among them, then Hawkings began. "Not bad. We took a separate route than the king took. We did pass through a system with something going on. Definitely a reactor, but it was planet-bound and nothing hailed or shot at us."

"Good. Your auxiliaries, will they be staying here?" Kris asked.

"The repair ships, certainly. Having two dockyards should be nice, but having your own repair ship that I command for my division is better. The supply ships? That's an interesting question. I have no orders there. Do any of you other folks have orders?"

That was met with a lot of head shaking. Commodore Miyoshi seemed to speak for all. "What are your orders, Admiral?"

"They're Smart Metal, and we've found a lot of uses for it," Kris said, vaguely, then turned to the table with the merchantmen in the rear. "What about you? You're from the Star Line."

They took stock among themselves, then an old salt stood. "We were told to unload and head back, immediately."

"You'll be going without an escort," Kris said.

That brought another look around among the skippers. "We can't sail without an escort," someone still seated said. "No insurance if we do."

"Aren't you going to give us an escort?" the standing salt asked.

"I need all the frigates here with me," Kris said.

"I told you they was going to get us good," came from someone.

"I think we ought to make a run for it," was someone's input.

"May I point out," Kris said, softly, "that Star Lines is a wholly owned subsidiary of Nuu Enterprises, and I'm the authorized CEO of said enterprises here on Alwa."

That was met by groans from the back and quite a few chuckles from the Navies.

"We been had."

"Yes, I think you have," Kris admitted. "Please continue offloading tomorrow. When you're done, I'd like you to dock your ships in the yard portion of the station. We're likely going to use you for ore carriers. We want to make our own lasers. We've found the ore and are mining it, but we need to ship it from the asteroid belt to the moon here." That was met with more groans.

"There is, however, one other possibility." Several heads came up. "I want to dispatch a ship on a dangerous recon mission. We'll arm the ship, but it's not intended that you will fight. Just take a peek and run back."

"Take a peek at what?"

"What we think may be the home planet of the aliens," Kris said. That brought on louder groans from the merchants and longer chuckles from the Navy types.

When quiet returned, a young woman stood. "I'm pushing the *Altair*, ma'am. Me and mine wouldn't mind talking a bit more about that scout mission, if you will."

Kris had to work real hard not to hear some of the comments from the other merchant types. "You can join me at my table for a drink after we finish here," Kris said.

The woman sat down and pulled her chair a bit away from the other merchant skippers.

"Now, for the fleet. We've got warning buoys six jumps out. One of the outer ones has gone silent. We haven't checked to see if it just broke or if it's been shot up. I don't intend to. The fleet that's here will stand by to fight when, not if, the aliens come at us again. For that fight, we need to reorganize."

Kris turned to her old squadron mates. "Commodore Kitano, you will command BatRon 1, with two divisions of four frigates each."

"Aye, aye, Admiral."

"Commodore Hawkings, you and the Lorna Do contingent will form BatRon 2, with two divisions."

"Yes, Admiral. Pardon me for asking, ma'am, but we were dispatched as a frigate squadron. Battle squadron?"

"You're packing 20-inch lasers, Commodore. Our ships may be frigates, but we're forming battle squadrons. Does that answer your question?"

"Certainly, Admiral."

"Commodore Bethea, Savannah will form BatRon 3."

"Glad to, Admiral Longknife."

"Commodore Miyoshi, you have BatRon 4."

"Honored to serve with you, Admiral."

"The Helvetican division will form independent Division 9. If we can knock together some lasers, you may have some of the auxiliaries up-gunned into fighting ships with you."

Several of the auxiliary skippers looked more than willing to follow that path.

"Captain Drago," Kris said, and the old sea dog stood, now in a full Navy captain's uniform. "The *Wasp* and the *Intrepid* will form independent Division 10. I'm aware of the handicap your slower reload rate places on you. You will continue to be my flag, and we will accommodate your ship's limitations."

"The *Wasp* is a very good ship, Admiral."

"I know very well that it is, Captain," Kris said, then turned back to the fleet in general. "Tomorrow, at 0900, the battle fleet will sortie for a speed run to the nearest gas giant. We will proceed through the asteroid belt and use them for target practice. No asteroids larger than one meter will be targeted. We don't want to spoil any miner's claim. We will launch pinnaces and refuel from the gas giant. Any questions?"

There were none.

"Then, all hands, as Viceroy of Alwa, let me thank you for coming to the aid of both the colonials and natives of this planet. Know that we are in for a fight, but that there is every prospect that we will be the victors in it. Now, enjoy your first night on Canopus Station, and yes, we have a policy restricting you to two drinks. Sorry, but the resources of the planet beneath us are being pushed to their limits to support us. I appreciate the agricultural gear you brought, but must point out that it may be several months before a new crop comes in."

Kris paused to see how this sank in. From the looks she got, their logistics problem was not a surprise. She'd have to check in with the commodores after the meeting to see just how well supplied they were. "Again, thank you, and please enjoy our hospitality."

The room broke out in talk. As Kris expected, the four commodores quickly gravitated to her table. All were young, clearly advanced ahead of their time. The war would show if they truly merited the honors. No surprise, their supply ships were loaded. All expected to be self-supporting for the next three months. That took a load off Kris.

It was newly promoted Commodore Kitano who caused Kris to cancel the next day's sortie. She asked if the other frigates had been modified to permit high-speed jinking? That brought blank stares. She and Captain Drago explained the need for dodging and the required mods they had made to their ships. Instead of drills, the next day would need to be devoted to bringing the new frigates up to Alwa fighting standards. Both Kitano and Drago promised to share expertise with the newcomers.

All the time this conversation was going on, Kris kept catching the skipper of the cargo ship *Altair* waiting close but not too close. Only after the commodores moved off to share schematics of changes and schedule visits by chief technicians, did the young skipper and the two women who worked for her settle down at Kris's table.

"An all-woman crew, Captain?" Kris asked.

"No, just most of the officers willing to serve with me," the woman skipper answered.

Kris introduced Penny to Jade O'dell. "Penny is my intelligence officer and will be nominally in command of the frigate *Endeavor*."

"You already have a ship?"

"No, but when your ship is respun, it will be a frigate with six 18-inch lasers."

"Nobody said anything about fighting," her engineering officer said.

"Three guns will point aft and three forward. With the bastards we're dealing with, you don't want to just have running as your only option though I'd prefer it."

"Okay. I got engineering, but I don't have anyone trained with guns," O'dell said.

"The Canopus Station manager wanted to have some protection. He mounted the smaller lasers from the *Wasp* and hired Alwans to fire them. I plan to borrow both."

"Reprogramming my ship into a warship," O'dell mused. "Mounting guns manned by aliens. Any more surprises?"

"The boffins are standing in line to go with you. Half the scientists want to get a look at the alien world. They all figure they can extract the real meaning of the place."

"So we'll have a mob of eggheads," the first mate said.

"No," Penny said. "You will have only as many as I and Professor Labao say go. Fifty, a hundred at most."

"Passengers," the chief engineer said, and made it sound like a dirty word.

"Many have sailed with me," Kris said, "and I can vouch

that they are housebroken. If they don't behave themselves, Penny here will activate their reserve commission and make them toe the mark in uniform."

"And us?" the captain asked.

"Penny and I are used to having a contractor commanding our ship, the *Wasp*. Penny will make the call where you go and when you run. Any problem with that?"

"How many years you been with this Longknife?" the engineer asked.

"Over five, and I'm still alive and kicking," Penny said.

"Sounds good enough. We'll get a chance to do something important. See the galaxy. Have a story to tell and shame those prissy boys. Win all around," O'dell said.

Kris watched them go. On lesser things great victories had turned.

Then she turned to her next problem. Making sure that the other merchant skippers didn't try to make a run for it with their cargo still aboard.

"Not a problem, Kris," Nelly said. "I checked. Their tanks are as bone dry as you can get. One jump. Not a bit more. Oh, and their ships have two reactors and aren't programmed to spin off a pinnace. I checked."

"So, they have to stay. Good planning on someone's part." Which left her wondering whose. Just how twisted was Grampa Ray's mind? Or had he just delegated that to someone like Commodore Hawkings?

She glanced around and spotted Jack talking to several other Marines. Their eyes met, and Jack quickly finished up what he'd been doing.

"You ready to head home?" he asked as he joined her.

"All meetinged out."

"Hope you saved something. I moved my gear into your quarters and let Drago have my space back."

"There has to be some advantage to being all the way across the galaxy from people who make silly regs."

"I'll set up a Marine command center tomorrow. Could I borrow one of your screens?"

"Half of what I have is yours."

"One screen will do. I'll do my Marine work there."

"But you're sleeping beside me?"

48

Without the sortie, Kris was stuck with administrative work the next day. The prospects seemed less onerous after waking up beside Jack and showering and dressing together before dropping down to the wardroom for breakfast.

Granny Rita didn't let Kris finish her bran muffin and juice . . . of an unidentified variety . . . before she had Nelly get her a list of what each ship had and started arguing over what priority to land them.

She didn't like it when she heard that the *Altair* would unload first. She was still grumbling as Kris explained why. Longknifes, even former Longknifes, could be a real pain.

Kris oversaw getting the flow of material dirtside started, then touched base with Admiral Benson, ret. He was already pulling his hair out. "Have you any idea how much energy it takes to get Smart Metal flowing?" Kris admitted she didn't. He told her.

"Have you asked the folks on the Musashi half of the station if you can have one of their huge reactors?" Kris asked.

"Will you ask them? I don't want to seem too needy and, you know."

Kris knew very well how it was with businessmen. She put on her CEO of local Nuu Enterprises hat and had tea with a kind old gentleman, Hiroshi, the manager of the Mitsubishi yard. It turned out that he expected to surrender three of his many reactors. He was just waiting for someone to tell him where to send them.

Kris connected him with Superintendent Benson, and they were soon best of friends, since Benson only coveted one of those reactors.

Kris's next stop was Pipra. She now had a very spartan office next to the Thai restaurant. Wasn't Smart Metal™ nice. "That was one hard-assed twist you took to drafting those ships and their crew," was her greeting for Kris.

"I need them. At least one of those ships is going to be a frigate and go scout the alien home world."

"Still, you might have offered them a bonus for staying on."

Kris paused to consider that. "Good point. I keep forgetting that money is a motivator for your sector of the economy."

"Don't make it sound dirty; it's getting you lasers."

"How's that coming?"

"We've started shipping the parts for a couple of them up to the station."

"You'll get most of the ships when they're unloaded."

"It will help. How long do you think we have?"

"I don't know," Kris said. Then Nelly cut in.

"Kris, they want you back at the command center."

"Why?"

"Another jump buoy just got popped."

"I'll be right there. Get the commodores headed that way as well."

"Ask a stupid question," Pipra said, "get the answer you don't want to hear."

"Please keep this under your hat," Kris said. "At least until I get back to you with something more definite than we lost a buoy. I don't even know which one."

"I'll keep quiet until lunch. Having the latest news gives me points. You must know that."

What Kris knew was that Father did his best to keep news away from the news.

She headed for the *Wasp* and found herself walking briskly beside Commodore Miyoshi. "Is this it?" he asked.

"We've got six layers of buoys. This could be a fifth one out or another of the farthest ones."

"Or they could have done a big jump like we did."

"It's hard to get a base ship moving very fast. Would you want to risk twenty, thirty billion people on a bad jump?"

"I know what I'd do," Commodore Miyoshi said. "I don't know what they'd do. What's a bad jump for folks that are born and live their whole lives in space?"

"Good point, but they're after us. Jumping all to hell and gone won't do us any damage. Let's quit guessing and see what's happening."

They crossed the brow to the *Wasp* just as the other commodores arrived. It was a silent group that entered Kris's day quarters. Jack was there, as was Penny. Captain Drago entered from the bridge as they came in from the passageway.

Kris's screens lit up. "We've lost another buoy," said Drago. "It's one of the outer ones."

"That's good," Commodore Miyoshi said.

"Maybe not so good," Kris said. "Nelly, am I right? Does that system lead to the Beta Jump Point?"

"Yes, Kris."

"Nelly, get me Pipra."

"On the line, Kris."

"Pipra, I'm glad you're not out gossiping about what you heard. Tell me, how are things coming at digging in a Hell-burner base on the gas giant's moons near Beta Jump Point?"

"I thought the aliens were coming in the Alpha Jump again."

"Looks like they are keeping their options open. We need to get a base near Beta."

"We haven't started."

"We need to start right now."

"That's going to slow down the mining and transportation for more lasers."

"Can't be helped. Lasers aren't going to dent a mother ship. Get the drilling operation moving to Beta. Change the unloading priorities. Push the *Altair*, but concentrate on one of the others as much as you can. Ignore the other two. Once you get the second unloaded, respin it into two transports and get them out to the mines for ore. Then we can do the third and fourth."

"Granny Rita is not going to be happy. She wanted specific stuff out of all four of them in her own order."

"Leave Granny to me. Whether or not we survive the next attack depends on this."

"Understood, Longknife. There goes my lunch. Now you've fixed it so I won't have a chance to gossip about all my inside tidbits."

"You can tell everyone whose day you have to ruin by changing their priorities all about how you learned it from rubbing elbows with that damn Longknife."

"You took the words right out of my mouth. Pipra out."

"That young woman is downright insubordinate," Hawkings said.

"She's a civilian. They don't have to be subordinate. And whether or not we win the next battle depends as much on what those civilians do as what we war fighters do. Get used to it." Kris paused a moment to let that sink in, then went on.

"Captain Drago, run though the situation with these warning buoys for the new members of our command staff."

"Nelly, could you please call up the system where we just lost our buoy?" the captain said.

Nelly did. It showed a worthless system with three jumps. Two led into it. One led inward toward Alwa. "The buoy we lost was this one." One of the outer jumps lit up. "Immediately upon its falling silent, the buoy at the inbound jump slipped out of the system and started the report coming in."

"Could it tell how strong the force entering the system was," Commodore Miyoshi asked, "or how many reactors jumped in?"

"Our jump buoys have been modified," Penny put in. "Yes, they identify reactors, so even if they aren't shot up, we know they've been visited."

"The bastards, however," Kris said, "always shoot. Shoot and never talk."

"Would it help if you knew how many reactors had jumped in the system?" Nelly asked.

"Definitely," Kris said, as the commodores nodded.

"I can do a software mod and add that capability to the buoys. It might take a few days for the upload to reach the outer buoys."

"Is there a downside to the change?"

"None that I can project, Kris."

"Then get started immediately. Nelly, change the screen to show all the systems we've put buoys in." Nelly did. "We lost sensors in these two systems. So now we have two buoys waiting at the next jump. We only need one. Nelly, after you get the updated software to these two outer buoys, order one of them to duck back into the silenced system, do a reactor count for thirty minutes, then come back."

"Good," Jack said. "We'll know if those systems are now bases or were just hit-and-run raids."

"Do you think they're playing with us?" Commodore Hawkings asked.

"I would be very surprised if the bastards even allowed their children to play," Kris said. "No, I think they are feeling around our perimeter. They lost a mother ship and a whole lot of her little monsters. Now they've lost a few more. We would recon a target more thoroughly that gave us a bloody nose. Especially if this is the first bloody nose we'd had in a long time. They are feeling us out."

"Do they have to come through all six layers of our buoys?" Commodore Miyoshi asked.

"No," Nelly said. "There are several of the systems four out that they could jump into directly. That is why I recommended as thick a warning perimeter as we could make."

The commodores seemed startled that Kris's computer would answer them direct. All but Miyoshi, who only smiled at the others' surprise.

"Exactly," Kris agreed. "Ladies and gentlemen, thank you for coming. Now, I suggest we all get back to work. The bastards are out there. I'm not surprised they are threatening us. They won't be here today. Let's get ready for them when they do come."

The commodores left with hurried steps.

Throughout the station, people walked faster, looked more intent. The enemy wasn't something just seen in media reports. It was blasting human gear out of space scant jumps from them. Things needed doing that might just save lives, your own life. Time was blood.

The *Altair* finished unloading and was moved into the yard for reconstruction.

Granny Rita complained she had containers dirtside that needed to be on the moon. There were plenty of lighters going down, so that meant plenty to get stuff back up. Still, cargo masters were warned to be more careful.

The team of diggers who had just finished arming three moons around one gas giant took off at two gees for the other one a third of the way across the system. No one complained about the weight.

Even before the *Algol* was unloaded, it gave up a reactor to the *Endeavor*. That scout would still be underpowered compared to the *Wasp*, but that was the best Kris could do for Penny. Once unloaded, the *Algol* would take on two huge reactors from the former *Kagu Maru* and ship them to the factories on the moon. That would free up several ship-size reactors to power potential armed merchant cruisers.

The engines from the old *Hornet* could not be recertified for space. They also headed for the moon to release more power plants for ships.

A suggestion came from one of the loadmasters that the three cargo ships just park their containers in orbit a few klicks from the station. Then they could start splitting the cargo ships into smaller ore carriers and get them headed for the asteroid belt.

Kris slapped her forehead and agreed to the change. That likely meant more containers routed wrong, but there was nothing critical for the moon in the shipment, and the asteroid ore was desperately needed for the laser-building program. The change was made smoothly.

The ordered chaos lasted all day as decisions were made and their application identified problems. Those were examined by not only the command staff but the people doing the work and better ideas often came up. Kris was amazed at how fast the decision cycle could whirl through that process, but her people were good.

They knew their lives were on the line.

Jack took Kris to dinner. This time it was Kiet's Thai Food, and the stir-fry was distinctively local. Even the spices had been replaced with things available dirtside. "Some of my customers are telling me I should change the sign to KIET'S ALWAN FOOD, but a couple of Alwans have dropped by," Kiet himself explained to Kris as he seated them. "Both the Roosters and the Ostriches turned up their noses at my best."

"No accounting for taste," Jack said, and ordered from the

menu for Kris. "One of my officers suggested this. I think I can trust her taste."

As it turned out, they very much could. The food served them had the echo of ancient Earth behind it, but it clearly was something new. It delighted Kris's taste buds.

"This is the first time humanity and another species have come together without trying to kill each other," Kris muttered when the meal was done. "We've got to save these people."

"That's what you're doing your level best to do," Jack said.

The meal was wonderful, romantic, and relaxing, even if they were interrupted twice. Jack took Kris back to their quarters and insisted on taking his time to fill the evening with slow lovemaking. Kris smiled and relaxed into his arms, knowing full well they'd be interrupted before Jack got too far along.

Surprise! Kris's expected calls never came. Next morning, Jack admitted to having bribed Nelly to hold all calls. How he bribed a computer he didn't say, but Kris's call-back list didn't turn up anything during breakfast that hadn't been solved without her.

"Who says you Longknifes are indispensable?" Jack said with a knowing grin.

The fleet sortied at exactly 0900. Division 10 with the *Wasp* and *Intrepid* dropped back to a trailing orbit while Div 9's four frigates pulled away to form up forward of the station. That smartly done, the four battle squadrons began to spin off the station smoothly. Each BatRon was to form on the station at ninety-degree intervals—north, east, south, and west of the station's long axes. Each rotation, a ship would spin off at each major point of the compass and head out to join its squadron flag. Eight rotations, and the eight ships of each squadron were in line.

Kris looked upon what she had ordered and found it good. "Deorbiting Burn 3 on my mark," she sent. It had been years since battle fleets had formed up. And those fleets had been ponderous, ice-encrusted monsters that lumbered along in formation, hardly budging in their course, confident in their powerful lasers and thick ice armor.

Kris had never gone to war in such a line, and she had no intention of doing so now. She was a product of the fast attack boats: nimble, quick, thin-skinned but heavily armed, and deadly. That was how she intended to fight this new enemy. In a battle formation, but with each ship free to do its own dance with death, dodging and thrusting while laying on heavy laser fire at the longest range possible.

It had worked for her before. She intended to make it work now.

Nelly had come up with a series of fleet orders. Kris had reviewed them with Jack the night before and found them probably workable. Nelly had issued the fleet its new order books with graphics to show her dozen jinks patterns.

Now they would find out if it worked. Today, all ships were at triple intervals. If this didn't work as well as it should, hopefully they wouldn't dent any of their Smart Metal™.

The deorbiting burn worked as planned. They dropped no lower than Kris wanted, then blasted off for the closest gas giant. Along the way, Kris had the fleet form a line ahead of her.

"Yes, Jack, I'm keeping my flag at the rear of the line," she told her security chief.

"Fine, Admiral. I really don't see any reason for you to be at the head of it. Do you?"

Kris didn't offer an answer, but then ordered the fleet to Condition Charlie and upped acceleration to two gees. Not an engine sputtered. This was going better than she'd expected.

Then again, they'd spent a day getting ready for this and weren't making any of the mistakes Kris's first squadron had in *their* first drill.

Kris crossed her fingers and ordered the fleet into a line abreast to the left. Ponderous battle lines had done this in years gone by, with the lead ship making a hard left turn and then having all the ships follow, making their turn at the same point in space. Then, when all the ships were in a column going left, or whatever degree had been ordered, they would all turn ninety degrees again and be in the desired column abreast.

Kris very much doubted the bastards would give them time for all those twists and turns.

Her fleet did it differently. The lead ship held its course and acceleration. The other ships altered course a few degrees in the desired direction and added a fraction of a gee to their speed. The entire line *swung* wide into the line Kris wanted. Once in position, the ships altered course and acceleration back to the fleet's course, and there they were. All thirty-four of them with their six 20-inch lasers pointed at whatever they were headed toward.

"About-turn on my mark," Kris ordered. She paused for acknowledgments from the squadron leaders to come in. They waited until all of their division flags reported that each ship had The Word.

This takes way too long!

Kris drew up a revised plan for her fighting instructions, where every ship would send its acknowledgment straight to her board. She'd implement that before they finished today's exercises, but for now she was doing it the old Navy way.

"Execute about-turn," she said, and the fleet did it at two gees. There were some interesting burbles in the drill. Some ships flipped up, others down. One ship swung to the right. Kris smiled. An old-line admiral would probably throw a fit, but she wanted her ships to be unpredictable.

"Well done, fleet. I liked the uncertainty in your maneuver. We never help the enemy by being predictable."

How many of you commodores are biting your nails at that?

They went through the order book, with Nelly sounding more and more proud of herself. There were no surprises though Kris decided that she'd never have her ships at less than double interval when hard maneuvering was expected. Ships needed their room.

They were in two lines abreast, one atop the other, doing 3.75 gees and following Nelly's jinks pattern 6, the toughest, when they approached the asteroid belt. Kris had altered the course to keep them clear of the big ones that had mining operations going full tilt. Still, she restricted her target practice to rocks of less than half a meter in size. There were plenty of targets, and few of them survived long enough to need a second shot.

Kris had wondered how good her personnel were. A cursory review of their files showed them young, fit, and all volunteers. Their officers were young, too, promoted ahead of their classmates. Often twice. The records had given Kris pause. Now she saw she had no reason to doubt them.

They drilled like grizzled vets. When they faced a wall of hostile fire, would it be another matter?

They made orbit around the gas giant, and each ship deployed a pinnace to refuel it. Again, Kris had the ships convert to Condition Able with extra fuel tankage. They loaded almost four times their maximum reaction mass and headed back to Alwa, looking like a maternity ward waiting to happen. Kris held the acceleration down to 1.5 gees and no jinks. Still, they went through different maneuvering drills and swept another section of the asteroid belt free of small targets.

They were back by 0900 the next day.

Docking didn't go as smoothly as the departure. Several ships missed their hook to the station and had to wait for a second revolution to catch the pier. Still, when the *Wasp* came in last, the fleet landing had taken less than twice as long as it would have if done perfectly.

Kris called for her commodores and independent division heads to report.

"Well done. I know the book I gave you just hours before we sortied was different from any you ever would have expected."

"I know Longknifes," Commodore Miyoshi said, "and I expected strange, but you managed to surprise me."

"With any luck, we'll surprise the enemy. Have you reviewed thoroughly the reports of my last two fights?"

"Yes," Hawkings said. "They've added some kind of stone armor, at least to their bows, but the 20-inch laser seems to have the range on them."

"Exactly," Kris said. "Our maneuvers are designed to take advantage of the longer range. We can expect to fight running away from them, so flipping ship will be a regular and reoccurring maneuver. Did jinking at 3.5 gees cause any crew casualties?"

Commodore Bethea from Savannah shook her head. "They told us you preferred young crews. I thought it was just because of your youth. Now I see why."

"I've tried those jinks patterns with fortysomething officers and CPOs with disastrous results," Kris said, and found herself wondering how Cookie, Mother MacCreedy, and some of the older boffins managed. None had ever complained. Likely it was a secret the old farts were keeping to themselves. Kris wondered if the day would ever come when she'd need to beg admission to their secret society.

"Kris, the *Endeavor* is about to seal locks," Nelly reported.

"If we have nothing else, I'd like to see that ship off. Maybe it will find some answers about the people who insist we kill them or they will kill us."

No one had any further business, so Kris fast-walked the short distance to where the *Endeavor* was tied up. Kris requested permission to come aboard from an Ostrich who seemed very serious about being the OOD. She quickly passed through familiar territory. The *Endeavor* was a replica of the earlier *Wasp* before the recent changes.

"Admiral on deck," surprised Kris as much as it did the bridge crew.

"As you were," still left a bridge watch of civilians, borrowed Navy, and Alwans of both varieties a bit flustered. Before anyone could speak, Kris said, "I'm just here to say good luck and Godspeed. I want you to come home with information."

"We'll do you proud," Captain O'dell said.

"And we'll come home, with as much to report as we timid souls can find," Penny added.

"Fair winds," Kris said, and excused herself.

As she walked back, the *Endeavor* was already backing out. Was that quick visit a waste of her time? Kris shook her head. A fighting team is a lot more than metal and circuitry. It was human heart and blood. Had Grampa Ray forgotten that, or was it just harder to spot under all the scar tissue? Jack was waiting as she returned to the *Wasp*.

"You give them a good send-off?"

"The best a Longknife can do."

"Then they are well sent."

"So why are you here?"

"We've got a report from one of our probes, and it's ugly."

Kris started to jog for the *Wasp*, then slowed. Admirals don't jog. Not in public. Not when people around the A deck of the station are watching and looking worried. Kris walked briskly beside Jack, smiling, and even managed a laugh. Let the watchers wonder about the joke her security chief had told her.

She arrived in her command center only a few seconds later than a jog would have gotten her there. "What do we have?" she asked Captain Drago.

"A series of reports, of sorts, from our probes at Datum 2, the one that leads to the Beta Jump. We sent a probe through, and it reported several thousand reactors. More than it could specifically count."

"That's a mother ship and brood," Kris said.

"Likely," Drago agreed. "It pulled back and sent the report as expected. Then we sent the other through with orders to stay an hour and report back. It never did."

"So they either don't like us peeking at them, or they're coming," Jack said.

"Anything from the next system in?" Kris asked.

"Nothing, but remember we're dealing with a lot of speed-of-light lag time."

"How can I forget?" Kris muttered. "Thank you, Captain. Now, if you don't mind, I have reports to catch up on. Running the fleet around on my string is fun, but I've got these two other hats, and I've got to wear them."

Captain Drago withdrew.

"You know, Kris, you need a chief of staff," Jack said.

"You applying for the job?"

"Nope. I got to drop down and do Marine stuff. The Alwans are now making hunting rifles and smokeless ammo. They've got a lot more power and range. They're working night and day to arm the colonials and as many Alwans as want to fight. It's surprising how many do. The hold of the elders is slipping away as the aliens get closer."

"So what are you doing?"

"Ada has drawn up an evacuation plan. If the aliens get through you, we don't intend to give them any big targets. And when they come dirtside, we'll be waiting for them. My Marines are training the locals to hit something from four hundred meters."

"Until they steal your air and water, or gas you, you'll put up quite a fight."

"Who knows, maybe you won't be as dead as you could be. Maybe you can come charging back with a fleet to blast them out of orbit and save us poor settlers' hides."

"Happy thoughts. I thought you Marines were pessimists."

"We just have to save our optimism for the right time."

"Like when your back is against the wall, huh?"

"I'll miss you while I'm dirtside."

"I'll miss you, too. And yes, I'll try to stay safe and stay human."

Jack gave her a kiss, then went on his way. She waited until the scent of him was pulled away by the air circulation, then dove into her reports. Good, the first 20-inch laser was up and holding a charge. It even worked when test fired.

While she was gone, the two last Star Line cargo ships had been respun into four smaller vessels and sent off to the asteroid belt. Big ships were nice, but when you needed them in four different places, smaller was better.

The miners had arrived at the second gas giant and were already digging into two moons. The third was a problem. It had a water ocean beneath a kilometer of ice. They were hunting for an island, but so far had found none. They doubted they would.

That gas giant might only have two battle moons.

So, of course, Beta Jump *would* be the one the raiders looked to use.

Kris sent a "well done" to all concerned with each project. It was nice to let them know the boss was watching and happy.

Kris went to sleep that night wishing Jack were in bed to distract her. She could not stop her mind from whirling from one project to another. She found herself staring at the overhead at 0200. She fell asleep only to find herself being chased by Vicky Peterwald and a dozen ugly bug-eyed monsters. Vicky insisted Kris dress for a ball. The monsters didn't say anything but had huge teeth. Kris wasn't about to let them get close.

At 0730 the next morning, Kris was awakened by a knock at her door. The aliens had made their move.

49

"The aliens have jumped from Hot Datum 2 to a system only three jumps out," Captain Drago reported to Kris in her day cabin. She was still in her sleep shorts and tank top.

"How'd they go from five jumps out to only three?" Kris demanded.

"It was always possible," Nelly answered. "We covered all the jump points in a system, but some of the jumps take you farther than others, even if you stay at half a gee and no spin. This was one of the long ones, and why I said we had to cover six jumps."

"Thank you, Nelly. Are there any more surprise double jumps that I don't know?"

"No, Kris. There were a few jumps outside the six that went to four. To get to the closer systems, you have to be in one we're monitoring."

"Okay, they've jumped closer, faster. What do the probes show?" Kris said, moving on.

"They blasted the buoy when they came through the jump. The reporter buoy across the system immediately jumped in to let us know we had a hot datum. The receiving buoy then dropped back into the invaded system. It's likely filling up with lots and lots of reactors."

"How soon before they can jump to the next system?"

"Assuming the mother ship doesn't go above one gee, we've got four days plus before they get here. If the baby monsters put on two gees, we've got less than two days."

"So we wait and see," Kris said, and went to shower and dress.

She took the reports that had kept her awake most of the night to breakfast with her and was asking for updates even as she ate. Pipra must have gotten even less sleep because she had them flowing back to Kris before she finished eating. The diggers were working on both Hellburner bases. Still no luck with the third. The lasers were doing well. All the Smart Metal™ from dirtside was back. Did Kris want to return it to the frigates it had been borrowed from or spin out more ships using the new lasers?

Kris thought long and hard on that question but had no one to talk it over with. Jack was dirtside, and Penny was flossing some lion's teeth. This issue didn't seem appropriate to Abby's pay grade. She was pretty sure Captain Drago would vote for getting his armor back.

When she dropped by the bridge to ask him, Drago surprised her by thinking long and hard. "Yes, I'd like the armor back, but that will take yard time, and it would be nice to have more targets to confuse the aliens' aim. Hard choice. How will you crew these new warships?"

"Good question. Bring back the Navy folks dirtside. Throw in some Alwans. See if anyone in the yard or station wants to ship out for the fight. There are merchant crews on the ships we're likely to spin into frigates."

Drago grinned. "You think they'll be any more enthusiastic than they were when you shanghaied them into staying here?"

"I kind of thought with the aliens this close, they'd see the benefit of fighting."

"Or running."

Kris had gotten used to thinking in heroic mode. Should she offer her civilians a chance to go home, like she had the Fleet of Discovery? She shook her head. Unescorted, any transport was likely to end up boarded and dead. It could also give away too much information.

No, Kris would have to figure out a way to keep those

unwilling to fight somewhere out of harm's way, or at least not in her line of fire.

"I take it that you'd like your armor back? If I can get any effective fighting out of these jumped-up merchant hulls, I should consider it a bonus."

"Untrained. Inexperienced. No practice either as a ship's company or in formation. They strike me as more a hazard to navigation than as a fighting force."

"Thanks for your advice. I'll talk to the yard about rotating BatRon 1 and Div 10 frigates through the yard."

"You do that and make it happen soonest. The hairs on the back of my neck are standing at attention."

Kris really didn't want to do what she had to do next. Shipyard artificers were a limited skill set. Still, in a few days, she'd be desperate for war fighters. Kris found Admiral Benson, ret., in his office, with his feet up on his desk, watching the analysis of the latest laser test firings. He seemed happy.

"Admiral, have I got a deal for you."

The old Navy man put his feet down, leaned forward, and scowled. "My wife warned me when I took this job that you'd be saying that to me one day."

"We've got all the Smart Metal back from dirtside. I need it pumped back into the frigates. Can you do it in the yard, or should we try to do it pierside?"

"It will go faster in the yard, what with the new reactor Mitsubishi loaned me. Bring the ships in tomorrow, and we can probably do all nine in one day."

"Good, that brings me to my second offer. Do you want to spend the next fight here, a sitting duck, or would you like the plates of a fighting ship under your feet?"

He eyed her. "The answer is obvious, but, no doubt, the devil is in the details."

"So true. Here's the situation. We've recovered almost all the Smart Metal from the moon base. Can you believe some of it was replaced with stone?"

"The aliens are using stone for armor. What's wrong with simple?"

"Well, we've got Smart Metal and reactors enough to spin out two frigates. When you add the ore carriers and mining ships, I think we could patch together another four."

"Assuming the bastards give us time."

"Yes. If we have the time, how many lasers can you produce?"

"I've got a dozen ready now and we're doing four a day. We could go to eight if we got the materials."

"Which are on the ore carriers we want to convert."

"What about crews?" the retired admiral said, his face slipping into something sly and not at all ready to buy a pig in a poke.

"That is a problem. How many of your yard personnel are old Navy and don't like being sitting ducks? How many Ostriches have you trained to fire the lasers? How many of the merchant crews will volunteer?"

"And are they any good? I'd trust a Rooster before I'd trust some merchies."

"Down, Admiral. We're all in this boat together, and we sink or swim together."

"So I've heard. I haven't heard it from any of them." He paused, then said, "What do you propose to do with this bunch of untrained amateurs? I can't picture Drago wanting them in a line with his *Wasp*."

"He's already suggested I not do that."

"Smart man."

"How about you commanding the auxiliary squadron?"

The old Navy man said nothing, just pushed back in his chair, gaining distance from Kris. "That's what my wife warned me about. An offer of a fighting command in a hopeless situation. Damn you, Temptress!"

"It has been a long peace, hasn't it?" Kris said. She knew she was talking to a highly trained and experienced leader of men who'd spent his entire career training for one thing that never happened. He had probably dreamed all his life of a fight in the worst way. And now Kris was offering him a chance to wade into a fight, but in the worst possible way.

He took a deep breath. "How long do I have to decide?"

"The longer you take, the less time you have to make it happen."

"I hate your logic," he said, as he tapped his wrist unit. "Send out Standard Memo A to all hands. Tell them they have two hours to volunteer or they get to wave good-bye to us war-riors from the pier."

"You already had the memo written!"

"The day after my wife warned me this would happen. She knew me better than I did myself. Smart woman. Promised she'd never speak to me again if I got myself killed."

"I'm going to have Mitsubishi start spinning out the first two frigates, what with you up-armoring BatRon 1."

"You tell Admiral Hiroshi that he can't have more than one of those ships for his volunteers. And we all have to contribute crews to the other four."

"The yard superintendent there is old Navy, too?"

"Who else do you think would volunteer for this kind of duty? The Emperor said there was a good chance of a hopeless fight with no survivors, and Hiroshi was out the gate a run-ning. Just like me. Don't worry, Admiral, Your Highness, Viceroy. You'll have your ships."

"BatRon 5," Kris said. "In reserve, behind the line, and I'll go easy on you old-timers when it comes to jinking."

"You young brat. Remember, you're getting older every day. Someday, you'll be as old as I am if you're smart enough to live that long."

"No one is taking bets that I will," Kris said as she headed for the door.

By the time she closed it, Benson was already talking to Hiroshi.

That evening, Kris got a surprise she didn't want.

50

Kris was halfway through her supper when Captain Drago hurried in and took the empty chair next to her. "We've lost the probe in Hot Datum 3's system."

It took Kris a moment to switch gears. "Weren't we supposed to keep that until tomorrow morning, even if they headed for it at two gees?"

"Yes, Kris," Nelly said. "My calculations say they must have had a ship cross the system at 3.5 gees."

"They either squished the dickens out of the crew of one of their monster ships, or they have knocked together some speedsters," Drago said.

"Just a second," Kris said, glancing down at where Nelly rode below her collarbone. "How come you're telling me this, and not Nelly?"

"I told Nelly I wanted to tell you," Captain Drago said.

"And I concluded," Nelly said, "that no harm would come from this being delivered a bit slow. Having a human do it might help you."

"I guess I thank you, both. Don't do it when time matters."

"I won't," both said at once. Maybe Nelly was a bit faster.

"Have they made the next jump?" Kris asked.

"No. I think they will wait until the mother ship is ready to go through with them."

"Why?" both Nelly and Kris asked.

"We're waiting for them here because you have the Hellburners up your sleeve. They don't know that. They don't know that you won't cut behind them and hit their mother ship when the fleet is rushing off to meet us. No, if the mother ship has most of their people, they will protect it. Somewhere, there's a report from the boffins on the wreck you brought in. When they sorted out the bodies, we found a six-to-four ratio of men to women. About like our warships. Want to bet the mother ship has more women and children?"

"No bet, Captain. You want to organize an attack from their rear?"

"No. Not unless they actually do move faster than the mother ship can. I think after the way you smashed up the last one, these folks are taking very good care of mother."

Kris thought for a long minute. "Nelly, design me some low-tech probes that can do a good job of tracking them. That can get me a real count on the number of reactors; maybe lasers, too. Drago, alert the *Intrepid* that she'll be sortieing at once to drop those probes off in the systems in the aliens' direct path."

"They'll be tiptoeing right up to a jump the aliens could be on the other side of," the captain pointed out.

"It's a risk we have to take. Tell her to run if she sees anything. No fighting allowed until the rest of us can get a piece of the action."

"You're telling a lot of folks to get close but not touch."

"Trust me, when the time comes, I'll switch gears without a thought."

The captain left to give the orders. Nelly went quiet for a while, then said, "I've got the shipyard knocking out six probes. They're large and clunky with optics, radar, and a crude atom laser to count alien noses. An old type computer with plenty of storage. They'll be ready in two hours. Kris, could the *Intrepid* be up-armored before she leaves?"

"Ask Superintendent Benson if he can do it before they finish the probes?"

"He says no. They aren't ready to begin uploading the Smart Metal. They'd need two more hours."

"I'm not willing to trust we'll have those two extra hours. Tell the skipper to have the *Intrepid* ready to go in two hours and to put the spurs to it—3.5 gees or more all the way."

"I passed along your order, Kris. Doesn't it bother you to send them out to face the enemy with less than they should have?"

That was not a question Kris had expected from Nelly, but then, she'd never expected Captain Drago to persuade Nelly to hold her tongue so he could talk first. More surprises.

"Yes, Nelly, it bothers me, but the *Wasp* fought its last battle with thin armor, and we had the wreckage of the *Hornet* aboard. In situations like this, risk is just a part of the job."

"You have a dangerous job, Kris. But then, you usually have a dangerous job. I'm just now realizing how dangerous it is. I guess I'll have to get used to it."

"Sorry, Nelly. Next time we're back on Wardhaven, would you like me to give you to one of my nieces? One of them should be getting school-tall soon."

"No, Kris. I'm your computer, and you're my person. I see the difference between me and my children growing every day as they relate to their own human. Your niece might be safer to be around, but I'd be so bored singing nursery rhymes like we once did."

Kris did a walk-around after dinner. More material had arrived from the moon fabricators. Eight 20-inch lasers were laid out and under construction on the shop floor at one yard. Kris dropped in on all four of her commodores. Each was happy to see her but busy. Apparently more gear had come loose during yesterday's training cruise than had been passed up the chain of command. The repair ships and ship personnel were busy.

In the Mitsubishi yard, two frigates were already spinning themselves into shape. It had taken months to build the *Wasp*. Admittedly, here they had the reactors, lasers, and merchant ships to form the seed around. Still, the speed at which they took shape amazed Kris.

One ship already had her name visible. *Temptress*, no doubt, would be Benson's flag.

Kris crossed the brow of the *Intrepid* a good fifteen minutes before it was scheduled to depart. She found the young captain busy on the bridge and managed to suppress their immediate reaction before they started it.

"I want to wish you good luck and Godspeed," she told the bridge crew. "I know this mission is risky, but we need to know what we're facing. Is this one alien mother ship or two? How many escort ships do they have? Go quickly, avoid a fight, deploy your probes, and get back here fast. If your orders don't fit your situation, please be guided by the principle of calculated risk. We need the probes out there, but we need you here when the fight starts."

"You can count on us, Admiral," the captain assured her. Kris shook her hand, then left. Again, she'd done all she could do to emphasize her orders. *Do the job and run.*

Before long, she would have to issue different orders, but for the moment, running for home was what she wanted. No heroics for now. Tomorrow, Kris would somehow have to figure out a way for each of her ships to kill seven or eight of the aliens'.

That assumed there were only two hundred coming. The corvette *Fearless* had killed her seven or eight, but at the cost of her life. Kris didn't want to trade one of her ships for eight of the aliens'. That wouldn't guarantee that Jack and Granny Rita would not be pounded by the survivors. No, Kris had to repel the aliens with as much of her fleet intact as possible.

How would she do that?

Kris returned to the *Wasp.* There were no new surprises. The aliens were still in Hot Datum 3, doing whatever they wanted to do, with Kris none the wiser.

Kris went to bed with visions of ships sweeping through space. Her fleet would flee, as long as it could, to keep the range open for the 20-inch guns.

Assuming the aliens didn't have a surprise of their own in the gun category.

But Kris could only run so far before she had her back to Alwa.

Kris brought Nelly into her thoughts, and the two of them studied the battles that Grampa Ray and Granny Rita had fought against the Iteeche. Kris examined them and found them wanting. The frigates really did mean a new way of fighting. They reached back farther into the appalling history of human slaughter. In the bloody twentieth century, Kris began to find bits and pieces that seemed to fit into her puzzle.

She finally fell asleep to dream of aircraft climbing and diving as freely as her frigates in a three-dimensional battlefield.

51

TWO days later, Kris was on the pier, impatiently waiting for the *Intrepid* to lock down and unseal her quarterdeck. As soon as she did, Kris was aboard and headed for the bridge. Someone from the quarterdeck must have been on their toes this time. The captain called "Atten-hut" even before Kris entered the bridge. For the first time in her life, Kris let them stay at attention.

"I thought I ordered you not to get in a fight."

"We didn't, Admiral. The lasers never fired." The captain was trying to avoid smiling, but it was clear she was proud of herself and her crew.

Kris knew exactly how it felt. She'd done that often enough when she was a junior officer and hung a senior officer on his own petard. Kris didn't like being that senior.

"You came very close to having to unload a few rounds. I've seen the reports. Their fast squadron was closing in on you."

"We left an hour before they got there, Admiral. You told me to be guided by calculated risk. We detached the first probe at the farthest jump, and it came up dead. I launched the next two and sent them through while we retrieved the first probe and fixed it. Then one of the probes returned and gave us a picture of what was happening on the other side. Yes, there were three ships headed for us at 3.5 gees, but they were hours away. So we hung there, switching probes through the jump point and getting a better and better picture of what was on the other side."

"Yes," Kris said. "You got very good intel. You deserve a very well done."

"Thank you, ma'am." Now the proud smile did slip out. "We left an hour before they were in range of the probe. They did enter the system, but when they saw us an hour ahead of them, they went back, after blowing up our probes. Ma'am, I was an hour ahead of them, and if I'd had to, I could have gone to four gees."

"And showed them what we have," Kris pointed out.

"Yes, ma'am, but if they had gotten there any sooner, they would have showed me what *they* had. Our cursory review of the intel says the big monsters are stuck at two gees and the mother ship is holding at around .75 gees. The new fast ones can't beat 3.5. From the look of smaller ships spread out behind the three that reached our jump, I'd say they built a lot of fast ships, but most of them can't hold 3.5 gees."

Kris's analysis of the report agreed with hers. "Thank you, Captain. I'm glad to see you back. Now, the yard is waiting to reinforce your armor. Next time out, I'm sure you'll need it."

"Yes, ma'am," sounded way too eager for the coming fight.

Two days later, Kris was at the Mitsubishi yard to christen ships: the *Temptress* and the *Kikukei*, which someone said meant *Lucky Chrysanthemum*. If so, Admiral Benson's *Temptress* had started something of a competition for the most outrageous name. The next two ships spinning at Mitsubishi were the *Proud Unicorn* and the *Lucky Leprechaun*. The two forming at the Canopus yard would be the *Fairy Princess*, with hints Kris should use it for her flag, and the *Mischievous Pixie*.

While Kris had her reservations about approving the names, they seemed to be working. Crews were lined up for all six ships, and they might go to space with more than they needed.

Kris said a few encouraging words, then stood by as two

lovely young women from each of the yards broke a bottle of water over each ship's bows.

"Lovely girl, isn't she?" Admiral Benson said as the girl emptied the water on the *Temptress*.

"Very lovely," Kris agreed, hoping her new policy hadn't started April to December hookups.

"My granddaughter," the retired admiral said.

"Your wife let her come?" Kris said, raising an eyebrow to back up the question.

"My granddaughter signed up on her own. I spotted her name on the crew list and ordered her ashore. She hid out until we sailed. That little pixie has a heart of oak and a whim of iron."

"Will she be fighting with you on the *Temptress*?"

"I've tried to persuade her she should join the Marines dirtside. How much luck do you think I've had?"

The young woman caught sight of her grandfather. She gave him a sassy wave.

"About as much luck as my great-grandfather had keeping me safe," Kris said.

"Oh, the younger generation. Thank God they aren't as bad as my generation was."

And with that Kris returned to work.

The aliens were in the last system out. Their speedy scouts had blown away the probes at the last jump, but not before the probes had gotten solid intel. Kris knew exactly what she faced.

One mother ship, of the gigantic variety. Of the four- or five-hundred-tonners, there were 257 in two flavors. Most shared the same power plants as the three raiders Kris had fought around the dead mother ship and the *Hornet*'s refuge. Forty-five had different reactors, of the kind Kris had fought with the first alien horde. Apparently, the survivors had transferred their allegiance to this swarm.

And swarm they were. Kris had poured over the reports, studying the way the smaller monsters huddled around the slow-moving mother ship or came to roost on it. Of squadrons or divisions, she could spot nothing. The ships seemed to ebb and flow around the central ship like a hive of bees.

Would they fight that way?

Kris arranged for one last probe to be deployed at the jump point. This tiny spy alternately deployed two different periscopes through the jump, getting a visual and a sensor fix on the advancing death. Together, they told Kris she had a good seventy-two hours before the mother ship would be ready to come through the jump.

The twenty-four smaller but high-speed ships that lurked around the jump failed to detect the periscopes. Kris hoped they stayed as blind while she readied her deployment for battle.

Kris had finally come up with an idea for how to get a Hellburner on that third, watery moon. Kris's research in the twentieth century had given her the hint. They'd quickly spun out a submarine from the last of the Smart Metal™ and shipped it off. They drilled a hole through the kilometer-thick ice to launch it. The aliens could scorch a lot of ice and not get close to the sub deep in the ocean below. They would have to retrieve the sub as soon as the battle was over; it had only a week's worth of oxygen.

If the fleet died in battle, the sub crew would die a long, slow, and cold death.

All through the system, operations were closing down. The last loads of ore and their miners had ridden in on the carriers that were now being converted to fighting ships. The moon fabricators were processing their final stock and shipping most personnel to Alwa, where they'd at least have air to breathe and a fighting chance. A handful of volunteers would keep the reactors going. In the event of the fleet's defeat, they'd make sure the reactors lost containment. The aliens would find little to examine in their victory.

When the fleet sortied, Canopus Station would not be totally abandoned. The fleet's auxiliaries, the repair and replenishment ships, were still tied up to their piers. Their reactors produced enough plasma to blow them to gas. The last of the 18-inch lasers were being mounted on the station. Several teams of trained Ostriches had refused to withdraw and were demanding the chance to fight. Other than the Alwans and a volunteer reactor watch, the last humans would depart for Alwa in a matter of hours to hide away. There to await the victory or a long, bitter war of wits against overwhelming force.

If Kris's fleet couldn't keep the aliens out of Alwa's orbit, the station and the attached auxiliaries would also blow themselves to atoms. There was one last shuttle still attached. The crew on final reactor watch could use it to try for Alwa.

They might make it if they were lucky.

Very lucky.

Kris's next reinforcements weren't due for at least a month, probably two. Those would be cruel days on Alwa if Kris's fleet couldn't stop the aliens.

Kris went down her to-do list and found very little left. Nelly interrupted. "Kris, there's a call from Jack."

"Hi, love. Have you found a nice south sea island to sit out the war on?" she asked.

"Any south sea island here would be surrounded by 'eats everythings' and no fun to be on. How are you doing, Kris?"

"I'm about done. We're closing up shop and sending you everyone but the reactor operators and a few die-hard laser gunners."

"I know. We're putting folks to work digging shelters in the deep woods or anyplace else we think they won't flatten. There are a lot of colonials and elders who don't want to abandon their homes. Despite my best effort, the bombardment may get a few people."

"You can only advise folk. This is a democracy, I think."

Jack paused to think long and hard before he asked, "Do you want me back?"

"Of course I do, but you've got your job, and I've got mine. Isn't that the way it goes?"

"How are you making do? Your entire team is scattered to the winds."

"Lord, do I miss a good argument with you or Penny or lots of folks," Kris said, seeing ghosts around herself.

"When this is over, we've got to take a hard look at setting you up a staff," Jack said.

"*When* this is done," Kris repeated. Emphasizing the "when." No "if."

"Have you come up with a battle plan?"

"I've got an idea that should take advantage of all we've got," she said.

"I know it's a good one, honey, trust your gut. It's taken good care of you so far."

"Thanks, love. You take care. I'll see you in a little bit."

"I'm looking forward to that. I've reserved our cabin on the beach for us once this is over."

"I'll take you up on that promise. As I see it, I deserve a monthlong honeymoon, and only one day's been used up."

Jack chuckled. "I like a girl who keeps count."

Maybe Jack ended the call with a kiss. Kris knew she did.

She looked around the station. The silence echoed. Somewhere, Ostriches shouted in their own language as they rigged the last laser. They'd be sitting ducks if the fleet lost, but at least they would not be shot in the rear with their head in the sand. Kris found she was beginning to like those crazy folks. Maybe she should have one on her staff.

She boarded the *Wasp*. This time out, it would be the last to leave the station. The battle squadrons were already launched and forming up. It was time to go.

Kris crossed the brow and turned to salute the flag painted on the aft bulkhead, then saluted the OOD. "Permission to come aboard," she said.

"Permission granted."

Somewhere, the 1MC announced, "Alwa Defense Commander arriving."

Immediately, the order came down. "Seal hatches. Single up the lines. Prepare to stand out."

Kris headed for her command center. The final battle. No. *This* battle had just begun.

52

Kris sat in her egg. With the *Wasp* at Condition Zed, she commanded from a much-reduced and very solitary flag bridge. The screens around her showed her fleet array a hundred thousand klicks from the Beta Jump Point.

If this was going to be a running gunfight, she intended to give herself a lot of running room.

At the moment, Commodore Kitano, newly frocked up, had her BatRon 1 drifting in microgravity with their forward batteries aimed at the jump. Kitano commanded the seven big Wardhaven frigates that had been here the longest: *Princess Royal*, *Constitution*, *Constellation*, *Congress*, *Royal*, *Bulwark*, and *Hornet*, reinforced with the newly arrived *Resistance*.

Each of the other three squadrons were deployed in a line by divisions to form a loose box around the jump. Commodore Hawkings's BatRon 2 was high with the new Wardhaven ships, *Renown*, *Repulse*, *Royal Sovereign*, and *Resolute* brigaded with the contribution from Lorna Do, *Warrior*, *Warspite*, *Nelson*, and *Churchill*. Commodore Miyoshi's BatRon 3 held the low position with *Haruna*, *Chikuma*, *Atago*, *Tone*, *Arasi*, *Hubuki*, *Amatukaze*, and *Arare*. Commodore Bethea's BatRon 4 with the big cats from Savannah prowled off to the left.

These last three squadrons were not in battle mode but had extended a pole from one ship to another so that four pairs of ships swung around each other, giving the crew some benefits of down for now.

Twenty thousand klicks behind the four battle squadrons, the Ninth Division with the Helveticans' *Triumph*, *Swiftsure*, *Hotspur*, and *Spitfire* held position beside Captain Drago's own tiny Tenth Division of Kris's flagship *Wasp* and the *Intrepid*. All swung at anchor.

Thirty thousand klicks farther back, Commodore Benson's reserve squadron of merchant cruisers swung in three pairs as best they could. Unbalanced, each pair did its own crazy little jig. What could you expect from the likes of unicorns, pixies, and leprechauns, Kris heard Navy types grumble.

All the crews: Navy hands, retreads, or volunteers of human or Alwan persuasion now waited for battle in their high-gee stations. Every hour, one of the forward BatRons would break out into a fighting line, and the other would go into anchor mode.

A second board showed Kris that all the ships were green: reactors online, lasers charged, armor and structure undamaged. No doubt, that would change soon enough.

However, the fleet had been waiting for hours for the aliens to make their move, and the bad guys had declined to do much of anything. The periscope into the next system showed the alien mother ship parked ten thousand klicks out from the jump. Her monster brood ebbed and flowed around her. The speedsters were up next to the jump, but they, too, seemed to be waiting for the auspicious moment.

Kris was as prepared for battle as she'd ever be. She waited, wondering if under another star, some alien honcho was sacrificing a goat and studying its entrails. She wished he'd hurry up. Waiting was boring.

At that moment, one of the speedy ships nudged through the jump and began to flip for a hasty return.

One laser from each of BatRon 1's ships shot out, and the smaller ship vanished in a ball of gas. Apparently, the small guys hadn't gotten the rock armor.

Half a minute later, a second and a third ship shot out of the jump, accelerating at 3.5 gees. Each was taken under fire by

BatRon 1. As the rest of the squadrons deployed for the coming fight, BatRon 1 held the line.

Then there was a long pause. Apparently, another goat was needed for sacrifice. Kris waited for what the aliens might come up with next.

What came through next was tiny but moving fast. Kris thought atomics even as four recharged lasers from Katano's BatRon 1 tore into it. Whatever it was, it vaporized before it did anything.

"That had plutonium in it," reported Professor Labao on net. "They're using nasty stuff."

"BatRon 5, reverse course a hundred thousand klicks and return to alert." If atomics were going to be flying around, Kris wanted those folks well back.

"Aye, aye, Admiral," Commodore Benson replied and began the hard job of shepherding his enthusiastic, if undrilled, charges back. Their line was ragged as they came out of their anchorage, but they did move quickly to obey.

Three more fast movers shot through the jump, accelerating as they came, but dying nevertheless. Kris wondered how long their boss would keep this up. He had less than twenty of the small type left.

This time, three bombs shot out of the jump. The gunners of BatRon 1 were on a hair trigger. Their lasers got all three again before any of them self-immolated.

"Isn't there supposed to be something about fratricidal destruction of other atomics when one goes off?" Kris asked Nelly.

"It's in the literature I was able to find. Maybe they don't know about it?"

"Or maybe they'd be happy if any of them got us, but we've caught them before they could arm and explode," Captain Drago said. "They must have some safeties on them to keep them from exploding on the other side of the jump."

This time three huge monster ships popped though the jump. Kris had been expecting them. Three had led the way into the system the last time Kris had fought a mother ship and her brood. Three battle squadrons took them under fire. Sixteen lasers slashed into each one as they appeared. The stone armor bled to dust as a second volley speared the alien ships.

They exploded, as reactors suffered damage, and containment failed.

Kris frowned. Boss man on the mother ship must be getting tired of sending ships and none reporting back. What would a frustrated alien killer do? By now, he must know that Kris was holding the bridge. What was her weakness?

"BatDiv 9, hold in place," Kris ordered. "BatRons 1 through 4, reverse course. One-quarter-gee acceleration. BatDiv 10, reverse course and join the squadrons when they pass. Prepare for atomic attack."

Kris's board lit up with acknowledgments as ships immediately responded to her order. In this battle, there was no time for a preliminary order to be followed later by an execute. Kris had rewritten the book. In an hour, she would know if her book was better than the old one.

As the squadrons fell back to 120,000 klicks from the jump, the *Wasp* and *Intrepid* flipped ship and joined the withdrawal. Throughout the fleet, any sensor that didn't have to be out was retracted and covered with armor.

Three small objects shot through the jump and immediately separated into four smaller ones that spun away on wild courses. The four Helvetica frigates took out eight immediately. Their fire controls switched to the remainders as quickly as computers could. Three more vanished. One took a hit, but still blew.

"Low-order detonation," Professor Labao reported. "Less than a megaton." He used the ancient form of measurement, one that Kris had no frame of reference for. "Our regular hardening for space's radiation should handle this pulse."

That answered Kris's question before she asked it.

Kris's screens showed the status of her entire fleet. BatDiv 9's ships switched from green to red as two reported damage to their sensors.

"BatDiv 9, reverse course, one-gee acceleration. All others cease deceleration. Reverse ship." The fleet went to zero gee but momentum continued to move it away from the jump, rear first, forward batteries aimed at the jump.

The last holders of the bridge decamped and moved to join the rest. Kris ordered a small deceleration burn to park her fleet 140,000 klicks from the jump. Their 20-inch lasers were still in range. They waited for what came next.

All too soon, it came. The jump began spitting out monster ships every second. BatDiv 9's rear batteries took out the first one. "Squadrons, engage by Plan A," Kris ordered.

The eight ships of BatRon 1 engaged the next ship out, firing half their forward lasers. The second ship through the jump exploded.

But there were more. The battle squadrons engaged in order the third, fourth, and fifth targets. Alien ships came through the jump, and alien ships died. It was BatRon 1's turn again, but the wreckage and roiling gases from the earlier ships were making the lasers less effective.

"Let them get out five hundred klicks," Kris ordered, and the squadrons held their fire for a fraction of a second before laying on again. Still, there were ships through now that hadn't been fired upon. For every ship they blew, one slipped through and raced off at two gees acceleration.

On the orders of their own commodores, the squadrons flipped to bring their aft batteries to bear. More monster ships died—some in spectacular explosions, some from a series of internal blows that tore them apart. Alien ships fired back, but their lasers dissipated before they could reach Kris's fleet.

Yes, alien ships died, but Kris's ships were shooting themselves dry. They needed more time to recharge. As Kris's screens showed her ships firing their last pair of ready lasers, she gave her next order.

"Deploy chaff. Set course to two-ten by fifteen." That would aim the fleet sunward and toward the nearest gas giant. "Accelerate at one gee. Deploy mines on my mark."

Kris waited ten seconds for the fleet to begin its move away from the laid chaff before giving the mark. As the mines silently slid from the frigates, canisters of ball bearings, metal cubes, and simple rocks left behind became active and blasted toward the alien ships. Some chaff canisters held bits of magnesium and white phosphorus with delayed timers to mix them with oxygen and set them to burning bright and hot. Behind the fleet, space began to sparkle, as the chaff masked where the mines waited patiently.

Almost thirty alien ships were dead, but they had forced the jump for their master. Kris had made them pay a cruel price, but it was a price someone had paid willingly.

More ships came through the jump every second. Kris would not have risked ships at that short an interval, but the aliens commander did. He paid with a couple of collisions that Kris spotted. Maybe more that she didn't.

While her fleet spent fifteen precious seconds recharging, fifteen ships came through, spread out, and went to two gees acceleration.

They formed a circle, then slowed their acceleration while later arrivals filled in the center. "A fighting dish," Kris observed. She'd considered that but dropped it for the advantage that articulated squadrons and divisions gave her. These guys had been doing this a whole lot longer than humans had. Was it nearly instinctive to them?

Lasers recharged; still, Kris continued to back off. The dish came on as more ships came through the jump and formed up in more circles.

The lead alien formation approached the waiting mines, their lasers sweeping the space ahead of them. A few mines took hits, but not many. The mines were actually high-acceleration missiles with passive sensors. Once the sensors found reactors of an unknown origin near them, they waited until the aliens passed them by. Then the missiles took off at nine-gee acceleration, aiming their antimatter warheads for the vulnerable engines.

More lasers came alive as a few ships recognized the attack, but the missiles were close and coming in fast on an erratic course Nelly herself had designed. Explosions began to mark the fighting dish. Ships lost balanced power and shot off in wild course changes. Others began to eat themselves as reactors failed and plasma ripped through the ship. There were two more collisions.

The fighting dish shattered.

"Reverse course," Kris ordered. "One-gee acceleration, if you please."

Her fleet flipped and charged, jinking as it closed the distance to the flailing enemy. The aliens were too busy with damage control, or they'd lost their sensors. Only a few fired at Kris's fleet or tried to dodge.

Kris's squadrons mopped up the residue of the dish.

"Fifty-seven down," Nelly reported.

Kris had no time to celebrate. Four more fighting dishes had formed up and were now headed her way at two gees.

"Pop more chaff," Kris ordered, then reversed course at one gee. The oncoming alien dishes began to sweep the space in front of them with their huge battery of lasers. Kris didn't try another mine drop, but she had plenty of chaff. So she did what she could to keep them working their lasers where she wanted them. Forward.

"Professor, Chief, let me know if their weapons begin to heat up." Human lasers lost some of their efficiency and power when the system overheated. Physics was the same galaxy-wide. Kris wanted the aliens worn down before they reached the gas giant.

The alien fighting dishes were now arrayed in a box much like Kris's squadrons but covering more space. Kris's flanks, right, left, up, and down, were covered. Kris could retreat, but if she turned to fight, she invited the aliens to swarm around her flanks and into her rear.

It was not a good picture on the screens of Kris's lonely flag bridge.

Another set of four dishes formed up. Thirty ships to a dish, four dishes to a square, made for 120 ships. Two squares should account for all the enemy she'd identified and then some. Either the last square was short a few ships or Kris's intel hadn't counted them all.

Either way, the mother ship should be coming through soon.

Finally, it did.

The monster fighting ships were huge, at four or five hundred thousand tons. The mother ship dwarfed them. This one was the size of a moon. Unless Kris was wrong, it was cut from the same mold as the one she'd disposed of before.

Well, if you have a successful design, why mess with it?

While the first square of dishes continued to close on Kris at two gees, the second held back, forming a shield around the mother ship. The smaller, faster ships darted around mother, using their few lasers to vaporize anything that came even close to her.

Yep, they'd gotten the word about how Kris blew away their sister. Kris hadn't expected to use the same trick twice.

The only question was, would they spot the new trick any faster?

The lead box of dishes was 150,000 klicks away and closing. Kris let them get to 120,000 before she went to two gees. She ordered the hooligan squadron into the line well to the left of BatRon 1. With BatRon 1 now facing the enemy's center, Kris edged the rest of her squadrons a bit to the right.

Then the aliens pulled their first surprise.

53

"The lead alien square of dishes has jumped to 2.5-gee acceleration, Kris," Nelly said.

They aren't supposed to do that! No doubt, a lot of aliens are feeling the pain.

"Squadrons, fifteen degrees right, engage the closest dish," Kris ordered, as the aliens came within range. The fifteen-degree angle protected their vulnerable engines. BatRons 1 through 4 engaged the enemy's far-right dish. But the enemy was coming on fast, switching their fire from motes of dust to Kris's ships. At extreme range for their lasers, damage was light, but there was plenty of it.

On Kris's board, ships' armor switched from green to yellow as they began to stream steam and take hits.

But the aliens were well within range of Kris's 20-inch guns. Her ships lit up the aliens; twenty-six ships engaged thirty aliens.

In a minute, the dish was an expanding ball of gas.

But to finish off the aliens, Kris's ships had to flip to use their forward battery. That put the enemy way too close. "Accelerate away at 2.75 gees," Kris ordered. "Pop chaff. Launch a missile volley."

One dish was gone, but the top and bottom dishes had

angled over, getting the range. The far dish was hammering Commodore Benson's hooligans of BatRon 5. The cheery volunteers gave as good as they got, but Benson had to order them to run for it ahead of Kris's orders.

The fleet accelerated away from the aliens, who settled back to two gees.

Kris's board was red. *Constitution*, *Tiger*, *Hotspur*, and *Spitfire* reported damage to their engines. Kris ordered them to three gees to form up as a reserve. All obeyed except *Hotspur*, who couldn't manage even the fleet's 2.75.

Four alien ships accelerated away from the rest and leapt out to engage the trailing *Hotspur*. They shot it out, with the other three ships from of the Helvetican Ninth Div trying to support their sister. Two more alien ships died, but so did *Hotspur*.

The three other ships, what Kris labeled CripDiv 1, for crippled division, pulled ahead.

Each side paused to lick its wounds.

The aliens reorganized themselves. The three remaining dishes re-formed in a triangle.

Kris reorganized, too. Despite showing yellow for damage, *Triumph* and *Swiftsure* moved up from BatDiv 9 to replace *Constitution* and *Tiger* in BatRons 1 and 2. *Spitfire* swung around to join Captain Drago's BatDiv 10, pretty much eliminating not only one division but half of Kris's reserves.

Kris did get to smile at one thing. Their pressure on the aliens' right had driven the mother ship to the left. Her course was edging closer to the gas giant.

Good!

The aliens had a problem. They could not handle the edge Kris's long-range 20-inch lasers gave her.

The fight drew away from the jump point, but three ships still hovered there. That puzzled Kris. "Chief, talk to me about those three aliens holding back."

"I've been meaning to mention those, ma'am. Their reactor configuration is different from the ones fighting us. One has ten smaller reactors. One has eight. Even the one with six is different. I think its reactors are more powerful than the ones we're fighting."

"Opinion, Captain Drago?" Kris asked.

"Military observers from other countries. It's an old tradition."

"So our next visitors are watching how we handle this bunch for future reference."

"I hate to say so, but it looks that way."

"Oh, God," Kris kind of prayed. "We haven't figured out how to handle this bunch, and someone is setting us up for the next match."

"That's what happens when you're the champ."

"And if we aren't the champ, we're dead," Kris muttered. "Thank you, Captain."

"Anytime, Admiral. How long are we going to hang out here, catching our breath?"

"They're on the course I want. Let's see what they do next."

The aliens chased. Kris fled, now at a sedate 1.75 gees. Once, she ordered an attack at long range on the lower dish, but they quickly killed their acceleration, inviting Kris to close on them while the other two dishes advanced above her.

She declined.

"Smart move. You're learning," Kris mused. *"You're advancing, which you want to do. I'm falling back, which I don't want to do."*

Kris adjusted her course to take her close to the gas giant and between two Hellburner command stations, then made a feint at the higher dish. When it flinched back, she swung toward the middle one.

They all fell back and ended up pretty much in line again.

Kris's fleet kept littering their retreat with chaff. Soon, Professor Labao reported the aliens' lasers were heating up, and they were cutting back on sweeping their path. Kris dropped off a half dozen mines along with more chaff.

Three mines caught ships.

The aliens went back to blasting everything in front of them.

Kris smiled as they developed the habit she wanted.

The dish opposite the hooligan of BatRon 5 suddenly went to 2.5 acceleration, closing the distance between them in a leap. Commodore Benson saw his danger and upped the acceleration, too, but his ships had suffered more damage than they knew. The *Proud Unicorn*'s motors sputtered, and one blew away into space. The *Lucky Leprechaun* was no luckier. They failed to pull away. Kris ordered BatRons 1, 2, and 3 to swing inward, threatening the attacking dish's flank.

Still, the aliens came on. The other two dishes now were back up to two gees and edging closer. Kris ordered missiles fired at them and had Drago move BatDiv 10 in to support BatRon 4's efforts to meet those two.

On her left flank, the hooligans fought their battle with one dish, aided by the arrival of most of the fleet. The *Unicorn* and *Leprechaun* struggled to keep up, then flipped and fired full bow batteries at their tormentors. That cost the aliens two ships, but it cost the two volunteers seconds of precious acceleration. The aliens came on.

Now the dish's flank burned under the fire of three battle squadrons. Ship after ship blew or stumbled out of formation, internal explosions erupting into space. Still, what was left of the dish locked its teeth onto its two unlucky victims and a third, the *Kikukei*, was proving no luckier than the *Leprechaun*.

Commodore Miyashi's ships concentrated on supporting the *Kikukei*, and that may have saved her. Still, both the *Unicorn* and the *Leprechaun* fell farther behind, bleeding steam and armor from hits even as they fired ever-decreasing salvos. At close range, they both managed a missile salvo that took their closest enemies with them as their final moment came.

Suddenly, the fight was over as quickly as it had begun. Two more of Kris's ships were gone, but an alien dish was gone with them. The *Kikukei* managed to put on enough gees to crawl ahead and join CripDiv 1.

With BatRon 5 reduced to three ships, Kris offered Commodore Benson the chance to take all his ships out of the line and join the cripples in reserve.

"We've just begun to fight, Admiral," was his reply. On Kris's board, many of her ships were showing some red for damaged. However, as the quiet between storms stretched out, *Temptress*'s, *Fairy Princess*'s, and *Pixie*'s hardworking damage control parties brought them back into yellow.

The alien commander also seemed to need time to reassess the situation. The two remaining dishes, both battered, slowed their advance to half a gee. The rear four dishes and mother ship closed on them at one gee.

The clan was gathering, and their swords were sharp.

Kris had started with forty-four ships. She'd lost three and held four damaged ships in reserve. The tip of her spear, the four battle squadrons still had eight ships each, but she had little to play with otherwise. The remnants of BatRon 5 weren't even a full division, and she wasn't supposed to send her flagship charging into the line.

Across space, some 180 monsters formed a hexagon. Possibly worse, eighteen speedy small boys were doing a fast run, dropping well below the lowest dish to get behind Kris. So far, those little boys hadn't shown a lot of firepower, but if they got across Kris's line of flight and started tossing atomics at her, things could get messy.

"*Constitution*, *Tiger*, and *Spitfire*, you up for a high-speed run and some shooting?" Kris asked. In theory, their boards showed green again, but Kris didn't trust she was getting the real word. She left the *Kikukei* out. It showed only two lasers online.

"We're ready now," the skipper of the *Constitution* said for all.

"You see their little boys. We can't have them behind us. Proceed independently and stop them."

Three big war wagons went to 2.75 gees and headed down, jinking all the way.

Kris could only watch that battle out of the corner of her eye. The hexagon of dishes were again trying to engulf her tiny battle array. First, the top dish would edge its speed up, closing the distance a bit, then one of the side dishes would make the threat.

Kris chose to feint toward one, shoot a few long-range salvos, never from more than one division of a squadron, then up her own speed to match the creeper. She picked off a ship here, another ship there, and she kept them at bay. But if they kept this up, there would still be a whole lot of them when they made orbit above Alwa.

This was no way to win the war.

The battle of Kris's cripples and the aliens' fast movers evolved into a swirling fight as the aliens spread out and charged in. Kris could respect their courage and their tactics; she'd developed similar tactics herself for the fast attack boats.

"Their jinking patterns are primitive and predicable," Nelly sniffed.

Kris's frigates met them, and with longer-range guns and

the ability to maneuver almost as wildly as they did, the battle was joined.

The fast movers died one by one.

But the lower dish didn't ignore the life-and-death fight so near. Suddenly they were doing 2.65 gees and closing on the frigates. Kris shouted a warning and ordered Commodore Miyoshi to take his BatRon 3, the low squadron, down to help. The lower corners of the hexagon put on speed, and Kris had to take her entire fleet down to cover the Musashi squadron's top.

Suddenly, the entire alien formation was pushing itself to higher acceleration.

"Withdraw fighting," Kris ordered. "Fleet, go to three gees."

Among the battle squadrons, ships fired full salvos from their bow lasers, then flipped and began to fall back at three gees. The *Constitution* flipped, but as it accelerated, several engines failed, sending it into a wild twist. Smart Metal™ could be repaired, but it took time for armor to flow back and form new engines. The *Constitution* didn't have time. She was pinned by more lasers that fried away her armor and let later hits slash deep into the hull. Like the enemy ships had done so many times before, the *Constitution* began to blow herself apart.

The reactors lost containment, and the ship was a hot mass of expanding gas.

The *Tiger* suffered the same fate.

Only the *Spitfire* managed to put on three gees and escape the ambush.

Worse, the *Atago* had taken hits in the effort to save the independent frigates. It stayed in formation but showed bright red on Kris's board in too many departments.

Kris gave up the idea of re-forming a CripDiv. She had nothing in reserve to replace damaged ships in the line, and it looked like soon, the entire fleet would be showing damage.

Still, she'd gained what she intended. Her rear was safe, and one of the aliens' six dishes was showing thin. She dropped more chaff and a few mines.

The aliens kept burning lasers to sweep the space ahead of them.

And, finally, Kris was approaching the gas giant. Her hopes for victory would be decided in the next few hours.

54

Orbiting the gas giant were thousands of large canisters of rocks, pebbles, and dust. Their controls were crude and their solid-rocket motors cruder still. However, when Kris ordered the cans to launch themselves toward the incoming aliens, only three failed to start. Two more didn't blow their dumb cargo into an expanding cloud in the path of the raiders.

Kris edged her squadrons toward a path through the rubble, then spiked it with chaff and several dozen mines. The fleet's track wasn't free of rocks, but the 5-inch secondaries handled them well, leaving the main battery to load, wait . . . and cool.

The aliens found themselves in a hailstorm of crud. Their main batteries fired just as fast as they could recharge. "They're really heating up," Professor Labao reported. "Heating up and getting weaker. More dispersion and less power per shot."

Kris smiled as three mines that had been missed came to life and climbed up the engines of the closest monsters.

If possible, the aliens got even more frantic as they shot the rubble from their path.

But they didn't ignore the larger problems. Two dozen ships

broke away from the six dishes and set course for the eight moons orbiting the gas giant. Three worked over each of the moons thoroughly. Anything on their surface was vaporized.

Out of the corner of her eye, Kris watched the moons being sanitized. She concentrated on the main fleet as it was battered by rocks. Their stone bow armor glowed red with the kiss of dust hitting them at several thousand kilometers an hour. Here and there, a laser blew as something more substantial got through.

Kris led the aliens through the rocky system, making a few sallies in to shoot up a ship here or there, but the aliens seemed too busy with their own stony torment to do anything to Kris. That was what Kris wanted, an enemy fixated on the problems coming at them and too much on the ropes to waste time at what was behind them.

The mother ship was not exempt from the rocks. Plenty got through the dishes ahead of her, and others had been launched from different directions. The mother ship's lasers criss-crossed the space ahead of her, heated up, and fixated on what lay ahead.

The mother ship had passed close to the icy moon with the ocean beneath its thick ice cap. The acolytes had burned the ice, but likely only singed the top. Now the sub cut a hole through its protection using one of the old *Hornet*'s salvaged 24-inch pulse lasers and launched three Hellburners.

The Hellburners didn't shoot hell-for-leather for the mother ship; Kris and Nelly had planned for a much more indirect approach. The missiles set the tiny chunks of superheavy neutron star on a course that would pass close by the mother ship but not hit it.

To a fire-control computer, the flying bit of flotsam was just another bit of rubble. A chunk that didn't threaten the mother ship and could be ignored while other, more dangerous pebbles got the attention of the overheated lasers.

So the ignored Hellburners drifted through space behind the mother ship.

And suddenly came to life and slammed into a high-acceleration attack. Their specially designed engines sent them roaring toward the aliens' vulnerable stern, with all its huge engines.

The attack started and finished in hardly more time than it took to blink, but Kris wasn't blinking. She caught the moment when three missiles came to life.

The aliens weren't totally mesmerized by the threat to their front. One laser winged a Hellburner as it made its killing dive. Damaged, its engines sent it off course, but it passed close enough to the mother ship to blow itself up and stove in five hundred square kilometers of laser-battery-covered hide. Possibly one of the other two was hit, but it was already committed to its final crash. Both smashed into the stern engines.

Suddenly, the gigantic alien traveling moon had no stern. Not just the engineering space, but a huge section forward of it was gone. The immense ship twisted on its long axis. Kris could only imagine how that must be hurtling people about. Secondary explosions showed along the hull, as things that were never intended to be tumbled about took exception and went to pieces.

Kris found it easy to pray that she'd never experience what she was putting those aliens through.

"Stand by, fleet," Kris sent, "the aliens are likely to be even more irrational for the next couple of minutes."

Kris was right.

One of the dishes broke away from the others and put on three gees, charging Kris's fleet. One ship blew up, and another suddenly lost all way, but the rest hurtled on. Kris had her squadrons do a quick turn away, then speared the attackers with their rear batteries. Lasers cut through ships already stressed way beyond their specs. Alien ships collapsed upon themselves in rolling explosions. The other dishes watched as their sisters threw themselves on their enemy and achieved nothing.

Somewhere, some sense of proportion must have survived. Four dishes formed a square to hold Kris at bay while the other one, what was left of the lower dish, went to the aid of the stricken mother ship.

Six more Hellburners were already launched at the alien. Five were spotted and shot out of space, with their huge explosions wasted on nothing but rock dust. The sixth made it into a formation of a half dozen monsters, busy trying to figure out how to approach the twisting mother ship. The Hellburner blew one up, hurled its wreckage against two more, and sent them hurtling into the mother ship.

Still, the aliens struggled to succor their mother ship, leaving Kris to wonder if there was someone or something they held so sacred that they had to save it.

Kris had other problems. From the looks of it, some fifty of the ships she had just fought were refugees from the ship she'd fought earlier. Did she want to fight all these ships again, after they joined up with the three watchers?

Not really.

The odds were now down to just 120 of them to 38 of hers. They were the best she'd had all day. She measured the situation and found she liked it.

Quickly, she ordered three BatRons to hit the saucer at the left-hand corner of the square. BatRon 1 and the survivors of BatRon 5 with Kris's flag division would hold off the rest.

The aliens must have been distracted. Half the dish vanished under her frigates' fire before the survivors broke ranks and fled. But not all were running. The right-hand dish launched itself at Kris's flank. Her two battered squadrons held the line long enough for Kris to bring the rest around to reinforce them. The second dish crumbled as half or more of its ships vanished into balls of glowing gas.

Now the other two dishes broke and ran.

Kris ordered her commodores to pursue, but cautiously.

"Damaged ships will fall out of line," she ordered, which left a dozen frigates forming up slowly in her rear. Kris didn't mind that; she needed ships to give the final *coup de grace* to alien ships that were damaged themselves and unable to keep up with their fleeing comrades.

The aliens were in a bad way. To flee, they had to show Kris's ships their vulnerable engines, and they fled at a slower acceleration than Kris's fleet pursued. Twice, fleeing alien ships turned and tried to charge Kris's reduced battle squadrons. Twice, Kris had the fleet dance back out of the aliens' desperate grasp.

The *Atago* approached three hulks spinning in space and prepared to give them the *coup de grace*. One came to life and shot toward her. The *Atago* and the alien died in one ball of gas.

Kris ordered her cleanup ships to be more careful. She doubted that order was necessary.

A dozen ships around the dying mother ship held station too long and were destroyed in Kris's sweep.

None offered to surrender. None in final distress deployed lifeboats.

Kris was sickened by the slaughter, but she did not order her ships to break off. It was several hours later before the final ship, running for the jump point at 3.25 gees, crumbled under the fire of the *Haruna*. That was fitting, because Commodore Miyoshi's BatRon 3 had led the pursuit.

"Now we are avenged," he reported to Kris when the final ship was disposed of. "*Banzai!* May their brave spirits now rest in peace."

Kris thanked him, but when the remnant of his squadron came to a halt before the jump point with only four ships still with him, he asked Kris if he should continue the pursuit. Kris didn't have to think long on his question. She ordered him to stay in system.

"We don't know what they've got waiting for us and we've just shown them how to hold one side of a jump point."

Commodore Miyoshi did not question the order.

Indeed, Kris could hardly count on half of her ships being in any kind of fighting shape.

The jump brought a question to Kris. "Nelly, did you notice when the three alien observers ducked out?"

"They took their leave shortly after the mother ship was hit, and the general rout began, Kris. I can't tell if they'd seen enough or whether they wanted to get a good head start on us pursuing them."

Kris took a second look at her options of charging through that jump point; she carefully checked her board. Not one ship was undamaged. Even the *Wasp* had been lased hard during the long battle.

"Nelly, if I ordered a pursuit at 3.5 gees, could I catch them before they jumped out of the next system?"

"The next system has four jumps. It's very unlikely you could catch all of them, assuming even a 2.5-gee flight, before they jumped out of that system. You know very well how hard a stern chase like that can be."

As a survivor of one, Kris did. The idea of ordering her ships to stick their noses in that noose when the pursued aliens could be waiting for them with atomics gave her the shivers. "This battle is over," she pronounced, and found it good.

She gave the order to the commodores to bring their ships back to the station at whatever acceleration they thought they could maintain. *The cost of a battle is not tallied until the last ship made port.*

"Jack, I think we won," she reported. "But I need your help. Some of our ships are dead in space. Could you get the crews of the repair ships to the head of the line for the trip to Canopus Station? We need them out here, helping our worst-hit ships limp back."

When she got his reply of, "Thank God and the Navy. Help is on the way, hon," longboats were already lifting from Alwa.

Help didn't arrive soon enough. The *Warrior* of Lorna Do suffered an internal fire they couldn't control. It reached the reactors. They succeeded in abandoning ship before it blew.

Kris had started the battle with forty-four ships. Seven had paid the ultimate price to save Alwa.

This time.

"Kris, a ship just jumped into the system," Nelly said. Before Kris could hit the panic button, her computer added, "Its signature matches the *Endeavor*. I think Penny's back."

A message from Kris's friend arrived hours later. "Kris, just a quick report. We found the alien home world! I think. More interestingly, we found a world just one jump from it that was attacked with atomics and rocks until it's nothing but a blackened jumble. Hardly anything alive right down to bacteria and viruses. Someone seriously wailed on that planet.

"The home planet shows some serious hits from space, too. But it still has people. Primitive hunter-gatherers, not even farming. Our probes got DNA off several. They match the aliens we're fighting, but no likely mixing for over a hundred thousand years.

"Oh, and get this, one of the badly damaged areas, little more than a glassy plain, has a pyramid right in the middle of it. We didn't land. Your orders, remember. But I'd sure like to see what someone built in the middle of a dead zone. I've got a lot more. Seems like you've been busy. See you back at Alwa."

Kris sent Penny a "See you at Alwa" response.

That would wait. Other things couldn't. There were wounded. Not many. With Smart Metal™, damage was either controlled or catastrophic. No, a memorial service would have to be near the top of Kris's to-do list.

Kris tallied her losses and wondered what more might be added to them before the last ship struggled back to Canopus Station.

"And, Kris," Nelly said, "you promised yourself and Jack some more of that honeymoon time, too. Don't forget that. I doubt he will."

Kris looked at what she had done and could only mutter, "I hope not. I sincerely hope not."

•

About the Author

Mike Shepherd grew up Navy. It taught him early about change and the chain of command. He's worked as a bartender and cabdriver, personnel advisor and labor negotiator. Now retired from building databases about the endangered critters of the Pacific Northwest, he's looking forward to some fun reading and writing.

Mike lives in Vancouver, Washington, with his wife, Ellen, and close to his daughter and grandchildren. He enjoys reading, writing, dreaming, watching grandchildren for story ideas, and upgrading his computer—all are never-ending.

He's hard at work on books coming from Ace in 2014: *Kris Longknife: Tenacious* (10/14), *Vicky Peterwald: Target* (6/14), and *To Do or Die* (2/14), which tells of Ray Longknife and Trouble's trials and tribulations while peacemaking after the Unity War and just before the Iteeche War started.

You can learn more about Mike and all his books at his website www.mikeshepherd.org, e-mail him at Mike_Shepherd@comcast.net, or follow Kris Longknife on Facebook.

From National Bestselling Author
MIKE SHEPHERD

. . .

The Kris Longknife Series

MUTINEER
DESERTER
DEFIANT
RESOLUTE
AUDACIOUS
INTREPID
UNDAUNTED
REDOUBTABLE
DARING
FURIOUS
DEFENDER

. . .

Praise for the Kris Longknife novels

"A whopping good read . . . Fast-paced, exciting, nicely detailed, with some innovative touches."

—Elizabeth Moon, *New York Times* bestselling author of *Limits of Power*

mikeshepherd.org
penguin.com

M905AS0613